Relative interest

Relative Interest

Anita Bunkley

Dafina
Books

KENSINGTON BOOKS
http://www.kensingtonbooks.com

DAFINA BOOKS are published by

Kensington Publishing Corp.
850 Third Avenue
New York, NY 10022

Special book excerpts or customized printings can also be created to fit specific needs. For details, write or phone the office of the Kensington Special Sales Manager: Kensington Publishing Corp., 850 Third Avenue, New York, NY 10022, Attn. Special Sales Department. Phone: 1-800-221-2647.

Dafina Books and the Dafina logo Reg. U.S. Pat. & TM Off.

ISBN 0-7582-0079-X

Printed in the United States of America

With much love to my daughters, Angela and Ramona

CHAPTER 1

Exhaust fumes drifted through the open windows of the well-traveled minivan as it idled at the side of the single-lane road, making room for three men on mud-splattered motor scooters to squeeze by. One by one, the men waved their thanks, then sped off into the predawn darkness, swallowed by the profusion of palm trees, jungle brush, and broad-leaved vines that still glistened from the rainstorm that had raged through the village overnight.

Kira Forester turned around in her seat and watched the few lights that had come on in the village begin to fade as the aging transport vehicle in which she was riding wheezed and groaned its way back onto the slick muddy road to resume its journey to the coast. The shrill voice of a macaw perched somewhere in the dark, lush landscape sounded out, creating in Kira a sharp sense of regret, though tinged with relief, at leaving. After two and a half months of bouncing over rough terrain, inching through narrow mountain passes, and fording the numerous shallow streams that laced the rugged landscape of western Africa, Kira's ten-week assignment was over and she was heading home.

For Kira, this first overseas assignment had been long, difficult, and exhausting, yet she had managed to do her job. She had found the children who labored in small, dark factories, bent over looms, sewing machines, and cutting boards instead of sitting at desks with schoolbooks and writing pads in their hands. She had documented their plight, and had listened with concern to the local officials who bragged that the children of their villages were happy to work for pennies a day in the factories and armed camps where men in fatigues carried heavy assault rifles to protect their remote manufacturing compounds. The officials firmly believed that the meager wages the children earned making clothing and soft goods for export made their lives so much better.

With the photographs, sketches, audio, and videotapes that Kira was taking home, she would create a collage to testify to the exploitive conditions here that were contributing to the rapid decline of the American textile industry.

Back in Charlotte, North Carolina, her work as a columnist for the *Business & Professional Recorder (BPR)* usually revolved around power breakfasts in downtown restaurants, trade shows, luncheon meetings in executive suites, and interviews with businessmen and women at national conferences in luxury hotels. But this special assignment for *World Societies Today*, the parent publication of *BPR*, had taken Kira far away from everything familiar. Documenting the impact of cheap labor on the declining American textile industry had consumed her, making her unconcerned about anything other than locating her sources, getting the story, and protecting as much skin as possible from the ever-present swarms of biting, flying insects.

Kira shoved a stray lock of crinkly auburn hair beneath her canvas bushman's hat and attempted to smooth the wrinkles from her damp khaki shirt. The early rise, in order to make it to the helicopter that would get her to Malabo by daybreak, had meant loading the van during the height of the rainstorm, and the relentless downpour had soaked her thoroughly, forcing her to travel in a soggy shirt, sludge-splashed jeans, and heavy lace-up hiking boots that were encased in clumps of mud. During the night, the rain had pounded the roof of her hut like an angry hammer, drumming above her head until she had gotten up at three A.M. and double-checked her gear. She felt satisfied that she had been able to get the photos and documentation that Julie Ays, her editor at *World Societies Today*, wanted. Kira hoped she would be pleased.

Kira's damp shirt clung to her back and her chest, and she shook it out as she thought about how far she had strayed from the perfectly groomed, stylishly dressed journalist she used to be. Back in the States Kira spent close to two hundred dollars a month just to maintain her tightly waved, shoulder-length hair that now framed her honey-tan face in a riot of burnished curls, a tangled mess that she barely bothered to comb anymore. Her working wardrobe prior to this assignment had consisted of conservatively tailored dresses and pantsuits, imported leather pumps matched with equally expensive handbags, silk blouses, and real gold jewelry to validate her professional image. Appearances had been extremely important back home, but now she peeked at her reflection in the rearview mirror and flinched: neither a makeup sponge nor powdered blush had touched her bare, sunburned face since the day she left North Carolina ten weeks ago.

The driver of the minivan began to push the aging vehicle harder, trying to make up for the time they had lost while waiting for the storm to ease. Kira hoped he'd manage to get her to the airstrip before another storm swept the area and delayed her flight home. Despite the overpowering choke of carbon monoxide and the wash of humid air that flooded into the van, Kira turned her face toward the open window and drew in a deep breath, praying that the helicopter Amid had chartered to take her from Bata to Malabo was waiting for her on the other side of the jungle. If she missed that connection, her carefully arranged itinerary from Bata to Malabo, to Madrid, and on to New York would be ruined, and she might be stuck in Equatorial Guinea for at least three more days.

Closing her eyes, Kira let her mind go blank, hoping she might be able to relax and trust Amid to do his job, but her attempt to ease her anxiety was quickly interrupted when the tires of the van began to grind over roadbed that was clearly drier and much rougher than the terrain they had been driving on. Kira jerked alert, leaned forward, and squinted into the bug-splattered windshield.

"What's going on, Amid?" she asked her driver. Two men dressed in green military-style fatigues, with rifles resting on their shoulders, were standing in the middle of the road watching the van approach.

"We will soon find out," Amid replied, slowing to a crawl but not stopping as he assessed the men who were waving their arms in an attempt to make him halt.

"What do you think they want, Amid?" Kira pressed, apprehensive about the stern expressions on the men's faces. So far, she had not encountered any serious problems during her time in Africa, but she was well aware of the tension that existed between the Fang and the Bubi clans—militant, marginalized groups that opposed the government and thought nothing of provoking foreigners like her. She did not want to get involved in any unpleasant situation now that she was so close to leaving.

Ignoring Kira's question, just as he continued to ignore the men's orders to stop, Amid Nabir, who had been Kira's driver for the past ten weeks, shifted into low gear and proceeded. He glanced back at his American passenger, his ebony profile sharpened by the reflection of the van's headlights that bounced off the greenish-black vegetation banking the road.

"Sit back from the window, Miss Kira, and fasten your seat belt," he politely ordered. "We are very near the landing strip. It's just on the other side of the village up ahead, but it seems we are not welcome." He reached over and slightly raised the tip of his rifle so that it rested on the dashboard, in clear view of the approaching guards. "When they come to the window, do not speak to them. I will handle this."

Kira frowned in concern, but reminded herself that Amid knew the countryside, the politics, and the dangers better than she did. This was his country. He knew how to handle situations like this, and she had faith that he would protect her.

Edging into the center of the backseat, she scooted away from the open window and snapped the two frayed safety straps into place just as one of the armed men outside began banging against the hood of the van, yelling for Amid to stop. Kira swallowed dryly, tensed her hands into fists, and then tuned her ear to the conversation, glad that she had studied enough Spanish, the language of Equatorial Guinea, to understand what the men were saying.

Finally, Amid pressed on the brakes and brought the van to a jerky stop, remaining rigid at the steering wheel as if primed to take off at any moment. He stared, expressionless, through the windshield, waiting until the armed man caught up with the now-halted van.

Where did they come from? Kira silently asked herself. The road had been completely deserted only a few moments ago, and now suddenly these men had appeared. She trained her eyes along the beams of light coming from the van, nervous to have been stopped in such an isolated section of the road. There was nothing around but blackness, humid vegetation, and the shrieks of the wildlife coming from the jungle.

"We'll soon see who they are and what they want," Amid calmly replied, as if reading her thoughts.

Kira sucked in a long, slow breath, determined to stay calm.

"*Su destinación?*" one man demanded as he arrived outside Amid's open window.

"*Bata. Un helicóptero me espera al otro lado de Pangi,*" Amid stated, telling the man that he needed to cut through the village ahead in order to get to the landing area.

"*No es posible,*" the armed man answered, going on to tell Amid that the road ahead had been turned into a lake and the area was nothing more than a swamp. The overnight rains had flooded the entire countryside and most likely washed out the hard, flat surface that served as a landing strip, he explained.

Kira glanced ahead. Yes, the rains had left their mark, but the area did not look as flooded as the guard was implying. She saw a few twisted roots and tree limbs jutting out of a pool of black water that partially covered the road, but the flooding appeared to be very shallow. A few clumps of soggy brush floating in water were not a serious enough reason to turn back.

"Thank you for the warning, but I think I can get through," Amid countered in Spanish. "I have an American passenger who must get to Bata. Very important."

"No. No way to get through," the man flatly declared, pushing his sweat-stained beret higher on his domed forehead. He clucked his tongue, then leaned into the driver's side window of the van, straining to see Kira, who eased back in her seat, but boldly held his gaze.

"Are you the American reporter who has been in the area taking photos and asking questions?" he asked.

Kira shook her head, acting as if she did not understand, glad to follow Amid's orders to be quiet.

"Why are you in this area?" he tersely pressed, eyeing Kira suspiciously.

Again, Kira shook her head, lifting both shoulders in a gesture of ignorance. The guard grunted his disgust, then turned back to Amid, scowling.

"Who is she?" he wanted to know.

Amid raised a hand, palm up, as he answered, "Simply a tourist. She got separated from her group and now I must get her to the helicopter at Bata by dawn for a flight to Malabo."

The guard scratched his beard, licked his full, dark lips, then frowned. "You must go back. You can use the lower coast route from Mbini to get to Bata, but you cannot go through Pangi. Much too dangerous. Much water there." He suddenly stepped away from the van and went to stand in the headlights, blocking the road as the man with him began motioning for Amid to back up and leave.

"Oh no," Kira groaned, dreading the prospect of any delay that might make her miss her flight. "Do we have to?"

"So it seems," Amid dully informed her.

"If we are not there by dawn, the pilot will not wait, and I'll have to make other arrangements."

"I know, Miss Kira," Amid replied as he carefully watched the dark road in his rearview mirror. "I know."

"Is there another way to get to Bata, without going through Pangi? How far back is the coastal route?" Kira tossed her questions rapid-fire at Amid, who said nothing, his face lined with frustration.

"Don't worry," he assured her. "I know this area like the cracks in the mud bricks of my house. But this man clearly does not think I do. There is a back road that will take us directly into Pangi, then on to the airstrip at Bata, but we will lose some time." He paused, waiting for Kira's response.

"How much time?" was all Kira wanted to know.

"The detour will add at least thirty miles to the journey," Amid replied.

"Fine. Let's go," Kira said, determined to keep going.

"It's not an easy route, but it will get us where we need to be on time," Amid went on. "The road circles to the east and meets up with this very road we are on, then keeps on straight to Bata."

"Great," Kira said, settling into her seat as Amid made a sharp right turn and swung onto another dark road. She was willing to go wherever Amid suggested if it would get her to the helicopter on time.

Amid stopped the van, pushed open his door, swung down into the muddy road, and went to inspect the stretch of road ahead. After getting back into the driver's seat, he nodded at Kira, then continued on.

Kira calculated that if Amid was right, she'd be out of Africa and in Madrid within six hours, then on to New York to meet with Julie

Ays, and finally home to Charlotte. She hoped time was on her side.

Within half an hour, the slowing of the van stirred Kira. Placing her hands on her blue jeans-clad knees, she scooted forward and looked over Amid's shoulder, heartened to see bright lights ahead.

"Where are we?" she asked.

"Approaching Pangi," Amid replied.

"Good. How much farther to Bata?" she asked, concerned about the faint lightening of the sky. The helicopter was set to depart Bata at first light, and Kira could tell that dawn was fast approaching.

"Nearly there," he answered, in the casual way he calculated distance.

Kira blinked and sat back, knowing better than to press for more than Amid was willing to tell her. Instinctively, she picked up her camera as the van approached the brightly lit village and centered herself in the open window at her side, planning to squeeze off a few last shots of the country she doubted she'd ever visit again.

The brightly lit low, tin-roofed structures that lined one side of the road struck Kira as highly unusual. In rural areas like this one, electricity was generally conserved, and no work began before daylight. Kira pressed her camera to her eye as the van pulled up to the first building, and when she saw the young girls inside bent over rows of old-fashioned sewing machines, guarded by the two men they had seen on the road, she began clicking away.

Another sweatshop, Kira realized, understanding why the men who had stopped them had not wanted her in their village. The van slipped past one building, then another, and inside each one Kira saw the same scene—long wooden tables piled high with fabric; ten or twelve girls who looked to be no older than nine or ten years old, sitting in front of old-fashioned sewing machines, stitching away; rifle-toting guards standing nearby.

Very quickly one of the guards inside a shanty noticed the arrival of the van. Kira tensed when he raced outside, gun lifted high above his head.

"*Alto!*" The angry guard ordered, looking directly at Kira. "*No fotos. No fotos aqui!*"

Instantly, three more guards fled into the street, their rifles drawn as they ran toward the van. Most of the girls quickly abandoned their workstations and crowded into the doorways of the shanties to see what was going on.

"Alto!" The guards shouted almost in unison, aiming their guns at the intruders. Several shots rang out, but none hit the van.

"Let's get out of here!" Kira yelled at Amid, who had braced his own rifle in the passenger side window and was preparing to fire back.

"Please. Don't shoot at them! Let's just go!" she shouted, terrified.

But Amid pulled the trigger anyway, then grinned, one eye on the road, the other on the guards who were screaming at him to stop.

"Put your camera away!" Amid yelled at Kira. "Get down! Stay down!" Then he tossed his rifle aside and jammed down hard on the gas pedal, rocking Kira back from the window, forcing her camera from her hands. She hurried to pick it up, refocused, and centered a final shot on the furious guards, who were scrambling to get into their Jeeps, shaking their fists in outrage.

As Amid plunged back into the jungle, Kira quickly stuck her camera into its bag and squeezed down on the floor, her head between her knees, where she remained until the van lurched to a stop.

After inching up off the floor, she looked around and was relieved to see the dark shape of a helicopter sitting in a wide, flat clearing, its blades whirling, as if about to depart without her. The sky was now streaked with the first blush of sunrise, and the checkpoint guards were setting up their barriers, preparing for their day.

Amid jumped out, ran around to the passenger side of his van, and rolled back the sliding door. "Hurry," he told her, yanking her arm, pushing her toward the landing strip. "Hurry. The men from Pangi are not far behind."

Clutching her backpack, her camera gear, and the small valise that held her research, Kira raced toward the checkpoint, her passport in her hand. The security guards nodded when she explained that she was the passenger scheduled to depart on the helicopter poised to take off. They stamped her departure ticket, pointed to the helicopter, and watched as Kira hurried on board. Inside, she greeted the pilot with a curt but friendly nod, then threw herself into a seat and buckled the seat belt just as the pilot revved the engine and prepared to take off.

Trembling, Kira pressed her face to the glass enclosure and searched the gray-lit road, engulfed by a sudden sense of apprehension, emptiness, and regret. She watched Amid vanish into the jungle, a trail of exhaust fumes curling up behind him, then fell back into her seat and gripped the armrests, thankful to be alive, safe, and on her way home.

Pressing her spine into the hard seat-back, she let out a long, slow breath, wishing she had had time to tell Amid good-bye and thank him for saving her life.

CHAPTER 2

"So, going without makeup, pantyhose, and nail polish for ten weeks didn't do much harm, after all," Julie Ays said with a laugh, the smooth brown skin at the corners of her eyes easing into tiny folds. Touching her slim gold pen to her magenta lips, she continued to assess Kira, who was standing on the other side of the room, studying the congested Manhattan traffic far below. "I'm glad you returned, and in good shape, girlfriend, because I have to admit I was worried. You never were the outdoorsy type, you know?"

"Absolutely not. You're right," Kira conceded as she turned to face Julie. "In fact, I was pretty worried myself, but after a few days, I discovered that it was a relief not to have to deal with how I looked. My appearance was the last thing on my mind. Plus, I kept telling myself that I was saving a bunch of money on hair styling and dry cleaning, not to mention how good it felt to be free of the uptight rat race in Charlotte."

"Well, you'll soon be back in it, and I understand your new boss is eager for your return. He called yesterday to make sure you were on your way home."

Kira's reply was a playful groan of irritation. "Great. Just what I need . . . a long-distance supervisor."

Julie lowered her chin to peek at Kira over the top of her half-glasses, poised to clarify the situation. "Bruce Davison does have a reputation as a clock-watcher, a real stickler for effective time management. When he worked here at headquarters, no one in his department came in late during the entire two years he was the manager. I'm sure they were happy to see him move on to your operation."

"It will be interesting to see how he makes out at *BPR*. In Charlotte, we're pretty laid back." Walking to Julie's desk, Kira changed the subject, tilting her head toward the spread of glossy photographs covering Julie's desk. "Well, what do you think?"

"These are great, Kira," said Julie, picking up one of the photos. She thoughtfully studied the faces of a group of children standing outside a factory in a remote African village. They were grinning at the camera; some were waving. "Glad you were able to send back this early film. As soon as I developed it, I knew you were on the right track. Exactly what I was looking for . . . and such fabulous detail. I'm very impressed."

The remark pleased Kira, who knew that Julie Ays had a reputation in the magazine publishing industry as a hard-edged professional who rarely praised anyone's work unless it was close to exceptional.

Julie put down the photo and absently stroked the diamond-shaped medallion hanging from a gold chain around her neck, her carefully manicured nails making a clicking sound as she caressed it. "Those kids can't be more than seven or eight years old. And look at those eyes. Really touching."

"I know," Kira murmured. "It is hard to understand—unless you've been there. Those kids are not sad. In fact, they brag about having real jobs and are proud of what they're doing. They'd rather earn a few pennies a day than go to school and learn how to read and write. It was very touching to hear them boast about how much money they were making."

Kira's mind turned back to the day that she took that photo, remembering how excited the children had been to pose for an American photographer. During the entire ten weeks that Kira had been in Africa, she had kept Julie's exacting standards uppermost in her mind, striving to capture images that would please herself and her editor. Kira could hardly believe that she had been halfway around the world only a few days ago and was now sitting in the New York headquarters of one of the most prestigious international magazines in the world.

" 'Touching' is the perfect word," Julie repeated, shifting the photos around to study each one.

Kira sat down in a sleek gray suede-and-chrome chair opposite her editor, a thoughtful expression on her face. "Julie, child labor exists all over the world, and hopefully documentaries like mine will help spread awareness of the problem, but it will take a lot of policing by major players in the textile industry to get to those who are behind it. It was an amazing, eye-opening trip, Julie. And frightening, too, at the end."

A wrinkle on Julie's forehead indicated her concern over what Kira had told her earlier. "Have you spoken to Amid? Do you know if he got away from those guards who shot at you in Pangi?"

Kira shook her head. "No. I tried calling from Madrid, and again when I arrived in New York yesterday. No answer."

"Well, I can't say I'm surprised. He's a well-known guide, in great demand, and is probably already out in the field with a new client."

"We were definitely not welcome in that village," Kira said.

"Well, in that part of the world, things are complicated—politically, economically, emotionally. I'm just glad you got out, and with some great stuff that I can't wait to see in print. I'm eager to see the rest of it." She began to gather up the photos. "Are you sure this is the kind of reporting you want to do, Kira? It can be gritty, and a lot more risky than covering North Carolina furniture and trade shows, you know?"

"I know, and, yes, I'm sure," Kira replied with conviction. "This assignment was a challenge, but it was absolutely fascinating. The people I met seemed, on the surface at least, to be honest and hard-working, but I was aware that some resented the fact that I was poking around in their villages." Kira picked up the photo Julie had referred to earlier and scrutinized the faces of the children. "Look at their huge brown eyes staring straight at me. Amid gave them some kind of hard candy that they loved, and then they gathered around, eager for me to take their pictures. I doubt they understood why I had come or what I wanted. I remember that village so clearly. The people were poor, their huts devoid of everything we Americans think is necessary to be happy." Kira shook her head, remembering. "It's amazing what you can do without, when you have to."

Julie placed her arms on her desk and entwined her scarlet-tipped fingers, twisting her emerald ring as she spoke. "When I first suggested you for this assignment, Henderson was not so sure you were the right one to take it on, though he knew you were doing a good job at *BPR* in Charlotte and had grown up in North

Carolina. Turner York was the one who convinced him that you knew the industry inside and out because your parents had worked in textile processing while you were growing up. York and I had to work hard to convince my boss to take a chance on you, but you haven't let us down. Fabulous work, Kira. This is going to score big points. Maybe finally get you out of Charlotte."

"And I *do* thank you, Julie," Kira said, smiling. "And Turner York, too. I wish he hadn't retired. I'm going to miss him back in Charlotte. He was a great man to work for. He understood how important this assignment was to me: a dream come true, as well as a chance to boost my profile within the company and my credibility as a journalist."

"And your bank account, too, I believe?" Julie grinned.

"True," Kira agreed. "Can't deny that. My auto insurance increased twenty percent when I bought my new PT Cruiser, and I didn't have but a week to enjoy it before I left for Africa. Can't wait to get home and get behind the wheel. But you know I didn't take this assignment for the money alone. As you said, this story was a natural fit, and one I wanted to do."

Julie nodded. "I remember you telling me about your parents and how hard they worked, stitching sheets and pillowcases at Urtex to pay for your college education. I knew your personal experiences would bring authenticity to the issue, and Henderson had read many of your columns and knew your style. He must have thought it good enough to take this on. Thank God Turner York agreed to let you go."

"Right. He was a gem. Too bad he's gone."

"Henderson is gonna love this stuff, Kira," Julie said, lifting a hand in a high-five gesture. "Hey, girl, you did me proud."

"Americans need to know that the domestic textile business is rapidly dissolving. I remember back when I was growing up that a job at the mill after high school graduation was a given."

"Not now," Julie replied.

"That's for sure. Urtex is gone. Shubert Mills just laid off twenty-five hundred employees. Watch: Roytown will be next. Really devastating to the communities that depended on those mills for survival."

"I know," Julie agreed, sighing. "And your investigation is going to shed a lot of light on why this is happening." She tilted her head to one side, assessing her client and friend. "You're so talented, Kira. Henderson knows you are exactly what we need." She picked up an oversized pad that was filled with pen-and-ink sketches of birds, flowers, foliage, and landscapes that Kira had done during the trip, and flipped through the pages, scrutinizing the jungle flowers, straw huts, and natives in crowded markets. "Fantastic. I didn't realize how well you could draw."

"Never thought my doodling meant much." Kira shrugged. "Just something I do to relax."

"Well, I plan to use some of these to illustrate your story . . . add texture to the piece," Julie went on, studying the drawings. "This is the kind of material that will move your career right along, so don't unpack too soon. I have a feeling that once I get this over to Henderson, he is going to offer you a job. What do you think about moving to New York?"

Those words brought a huge smile to Kira's face. After college she had been thrilled to accept a job as a proofreader at *BPR*, and had stayed with the company long enough to move into a position where she now had her own byline on her business column for the paper. But all along her eye had been on a job with the parent company in New York, and now, after fifteen years, maybe it was about to happen. It was long past time for a change.

"Me move to New York? No problem. I'll be waiting for the call," Kira joked, yet her tone was dead-on serious. "A full-time position at a publication like *World Societies Today?* What more could a small-town reporter like me ask for?"

"I'd love to see it happen," Julie stated. "But this place is a lot different from *BPR*. Working for *World* is no picnic. You gotta really put in the hours and put up with the stress that comes with writing for an international market. You have to be self-motivated and hungry to survive up here."

"I'm hungry," Kira assured Julie. "And after this short foray into the *World* environment, returning to North Carolina to cover shareholders' meetings and trade expos will be like drinking cheap wine after being exposed to fine imported champagne."

Julie chuckled. "Kira, I'll do what I can to help you get on here at *World*, but you know I don't make hiring decisions." She paused, then added, "But we could use some new blood and a little more color around here, if you know what I mean. We have no female African-American writers or photographers on staff right now, so your timing might be just right."

"Sounds encouraging," Kira said, easing to the edge of her chair as she checked her watch. "But now I've got to get going. My leave of absence at *BPR* officially ends tomorrow, and I can't afford to let my desk be taken over by some fresh-faced college kid because I didn't show up. Things at the office were shaky when I left—new management, and all. Now I've got this assignment to finish up for you while trying to get back into the swing of things at home, so I'm gonna be swamped."

"I wish you didn't have to leave so soon," Julie complained. "I had hoped we might go shopping or at least have lunch at B. Smith's. You don't get to the Big Apple very often, and I wanted to show you a little more of my city."

Kira snapped shut the folder holding her sketches. "Next time. I promise. I've got to get back. Besides, I need some sunshine. I saw on the Weather Channel this morning that it's pushing seventy in Charlotte today. This dreary New York weather is wearing on me. It's March already; when does the weather change up here?"

"Could be better next week . . . but, then, it might not really warm up until April, either. We don't worry too much about it," Julie replied, shuffling the glossy photos into a neat stack that she placed in a folder and set aside. "I'll get copies of the production schedule and the photos that still need to be developed off to you ASAP. I'll FedEx them, okay?"

"Fine," Kira said, slipping her sketchbook into her oversized carry-on bag.

"What time's your flight?"

Kira checked her watch. "Two o'clock."

"Darn. I wish you could stay for lunch. There's this new guy at the magazine you ought to meet. He's—"

"No, thanks," Kira cut Julie off. "I am definitely not in the market for meeting anyone right now."

"Are you still involved with the Latin lover you told me about?" Julie asked.

Kira shook her head, eyes narrowed. "Absolutely not."

"Well, good. The guy might have been drop-dead gorgeous, but from what you told me, he sounded a tad immature and pretty self-involved."

"Yeah. Brandon was all that, and more," Kira murmured softly. "But, sadly, I didn't have enough sense to avoid involvement with my personal trainer. It was fun. Really pretty seductive to be romanced by a handsome hunk while pumping iron and walking the track. He was cute, but he was high-maintenance and high-stress. I hate to think of running into him when I return to the gym."

Julie waved her hand, as if brushing away an annoying fly. "Huh!" she grunted. "Focus on your workout and ignore him. He was a player, and you don't have time for his kind of games anymore. But don't be too fast to say no to meeting someone new. What are you? Thirty-five? Thirty-six?"

"Thirty-seven."

"Right, one year younger than I am."

"And I am happily unattached and it suits me fine."

"Well, just because you had a rough patch, don't write all men off, Kira. You're sharp, attractive, got a lot going on. What's wrong with adding a good man to the mix?"

"Julie, you're starting to sound more like my mother, God rest her soul, than my editor."

"I'm your friend, too, not just your editor, Kira, and I truly think you and this guy I want you to meet would hit it off. He's witty, Ivy League smart, has a great personality, and is stable. If I were single, I'd be interested."

"So, he's got everything you think I need in a man?" Kira laughed.

"Could be."

"But this is New York. I live in North Carolina, remember?"

"Well, who knows how long that's going to last? You'll be back, I feel it. And next time you're here, promise . . . we'll have lunch."

"Okay. Next time. I promise. Right now, I'd better get going. It's spring break for a lot of schools, and you know what that means at the airport." Kira slipped on her black leather jacket, pulled her shades over her eyes, fluffed her freshly washed hair, and then glanced over quickly at Julie. "Oh, my mail. You have it?"

"Right," Julie replied, getting up to go over to a file cabinet. She opened it and pulled out a thick manila envelope. "It's all here, though I took the liberty of tossing obvious junk mail."

"Thanks, and I appreciate you letting me forward it to you while I was away. I'll read it on the way to the airport."

Julie watched as Kira stuck the packet into the side pocket of her bag. "I'll speak to Henderson and feel him out on bringing you on board, but don't expect an answer too soon. He'll take his time making a decision, I'm sure. I'll give you a buzz next week."

"Appreciate it," Kira said, giving Julie a quick hug before leaving.

In the taxi on her way to JFK, Kira sorted her mail, separating business correspondence from personal letters and invitations.

Luckily, there were few bills, since she had prepaid her rent, credit-card charges, and utility bills before leaving. While prioritizing her on-plane reading material, she came across an official-looking letter from the North Carolina Department of Health and Human Services (DHHS). Hesitantly, Kira slid her fingernail under the flap, praying the letter did not contain bad news. She had not received a letter from DHHS in years, and the blue logo on the envelope brought on a rush of unsettling memories.

The first thing she noticed after opening the letter was the date: January 14, 2000, only a few days after she had left Charlotte for New York, on her way Africa. Apprehensively, Kira began to read.

Dear Miss Forester:

This is to inform you that your niece, Vicky Jordan, is no longer residing in foster care with Mrs. Alvia Elderton, of Wilmington, N.C. Mrs. Elderton passed away on January 12, 2000, and due to her untimely death, Vicky has been placed with Mr. and Mrs. Ralph Roper of Monroeville, N.C., pending adoption. Prior notice of adoption hearings must be given to all persons required by law to give consent to the adoption. According to our files, your consent is not required, but this notice is sent to you as a courtesy since you are Vicky Jordan's only blood relative. Our records contain your request that information regarding any changes in your niece's status in her foster placement be forwarded to you. If you have any questions please contact Evan Conley of Sheltering Hearts Placement Agency in Stallings, N.C., at 704-555-9080.

Sincerely,
Jean Carter, Director of Children's Services
North Carolina Division of Social Services

Kira stared at the piece of paper, her eyes tracing over the sentences again and again until the words turned into a blurry black line. Alvia Elderton was dead? Vicky was living with a couple in Monroeville who planned to adopt her? A coil of panic began to form inside Kira. How in the world had her niece's situation changed so quickly? This was not supposed to have happened. Slumping down, she rested her head against the seat and closed her eyes, allowing this unexpected turn of events to sink in, knowing she had to get home as quickly as possible and find out what she needed to do to set things back in order.

As the taxi wound its way toward the airport, Kira let her mind go back more than six years to the day when Miranda Forester, Kira's only sister, had called to tell her that she was pregnant and that her live-in boyfriend, the father of the unborn child, had left her. Miranda had been depressed, angry, and drinking heavily, rambling about having to go on public assistance in order to raise the child. Kira had quickly driven two hundred miles from Charlotte to Wilmington to visit Miranda, offering to take her in and help her get on her feet—but only if Miranda stopped drinking. Kira loved Miranda, but when Miranda began drinking heavily Kira no longer knew her, nor could she reach her. After Vicky was born, Miranda became very resentful of Kira's career and independence. Every telephone conversation eventually deteriorated into an argument in which Miranda would try to convince Kira that she was doing just fine, though Kira knew she wasn't. She'd complain about how broke she was and how awful things were, then turn around and brag about how much money she had won playing cards the night before. But whenever Kira tried to intervene in her sister's self-destructive lifestyle, it only caused more problems. Kira remembered the one time she had called the state social services office because she suspected Miranda had been drinking heavily for days. When they investigated, they found her sober, the house clean, and Vicky well fed and happy. No abuse or reason to take action. Miranda was furious with her sister for calling the authorities on her, and told Kira to leave her alone. Her rejection was difficult for Kira to accept, but she stayed away, tired of arguing, stressing out over Miranda's situation, and trying to deal with her. But two years later, Kira received bad news: Miranda had died of alcohol poisoning, and her daughter, Vicky, who had become a ward of the state, was in the protective custody of Children's Services.

Devastated, Kira had returned home to Wilmington to bury her sister in the Wilmington Rosewood Cemetery, next to their parents, but had not stepped forward to accept legal responsibility for Vicky, convinced that she should not take on the job of raising a two-year-old child while launching her career as a journalist. Kira knew she needed the freedom and space of an unencumbered lifestyle in order to continue her pursuit of a career as an international journalist. Convinced that it would be in Vicky's best interests to remain at the comfortable beachfront home of Alvia Elderton, the attentive foster mother who was caring for Vicky and four other foster children, Kira had left, promising to return and visit Vicky on a regular basis.

But time had passed. Kira became consumed with her singles lifestyle, her career, and her drive to succeed, allowing the situation with Vicky to simply drift.

Now, Kira forced herself to calm down. As soon as she got home, she'd call this man, Evan Conley, at Sheltering Hearts, and find out what was going on. She wanted details about what had happened to Mrs. Elderton, and information about the couple who planned on adopting her niece. The idea of Vicky being formally adopted had never seriously crossed Kira's mind, and the prospect was suddenly confusing. With Monroeville only forty-five minutes away from Charlotte, she might finally be able to spend quality time with Vicky and become a real part of her only niece's life. Could this adoption be the best solution to her and Vicky's situation? Kira wondered as the taxi inched through traffic.

CHAPTER 3

Kira shrugged on her jacket and began gathering her things when the security gates of her apartment complex swung back to let the taxi in. The driver turned onto the street leading to her apartment, and for the first time since arriving back in the States, Kira began to feel the toll of her journey. All she wanted to do was get inside her apartment, drop her suitcases in the entry, fall into bed, and sleep for twelve hours straight, but she knew that would be the wrong thing to do. If she planned to be worth a darn at the office tomorrow she was going to have to force herself to stay awake, even though a bad case of jet lag was definitely coming on.

During the flight from Equatorial Guinea to Madrid she had been tense and preoccupied, still worried about Amid. Had he made it safely out of the jungle? Had the angry guards who chased them out of Pangi followed him, questioned him, punished him for bringing the American photographer into their village? During the long trip from Madrid to New York, she had watched every movie, read every available magazine, eaten every snack and meal offered by the flight attendants, and worried over whether or not she had captured what Julie expected her to bring back. And while traveling from New York to Charlotte, Kira had not even tried to sleep, an impossible task whenever she was on a plane, a train, or even in a car. She envied people who could drop off immediately after takeoff, miss the entire flight, and then awaken precisely upon arrival at their destination. She just had to tough it out.

She sighed in relief to see that her new car, shrouded in its protective canvas cover, was still parked in her designated spot where she had left it. Everything appeared to be in order. When the driver stopped in front of her redbrick, two-story building, Kira checked the meter, rummaged in her purse, then took out a twenty-dollar bill and paid the fare, glad to be home.

Kira entered her apartment, grateful she lived on the first floor, shoved her bags inside, shut the door, and leaned against it, assessing her surroundings with a new perspective. For ten weeks she had slept on cots in tents, in hard beds in hostels, in the simply furnished homes of natives in their villages, and several times on the ground in a sleeping bag under the stars. What a contrast to what greeted her now.

She proudly surveyed the soothing, monochromatic interior of her apartment, fighting the urge to head straight for the bedroom and lie down. Decorated in various shades of cream and beige, the neutral background created a showcase for her extensive collection of ethnic pottery and art. She tossed her jacket on the arm of her cream-colored sofa, then unzipped the smallest of her bags to take out one of a set of three African masks she had bought in the marketplace at Cameroon. Holding it high, she decided that the trio would look great on the wall above the antique, golden oak rolltop desk that she had rescued from the loading dock of the local Salvation Army ten years ago. It had needed no refinishing and was her favorite piece of furniture: sturdy, beautiful, and extremely useful.

With a sigh, Kira set down the mask, went to the desk, rolled back the top, and placed her keys in the center cubbyhole, knowing she was going to spend a great deal of time there working on her assignment for *World Societies Today*. The work that lay ahead—the writing, editing, and finalization of her story—would mean long hours after a full day's work at the paper, but Kira was mentally prepared for the task. She thought about Julie's promise to talk to Henderson, the managing editor of *World*, about a job, intrigued by the prospect of moving to New York. At last, after years of hard work, planning, and focused preparation, a position with the parent company was within her reach, and Kira knew that the research, tapes, notes, and photos that she had crammed into her luggage were her ticket to the next stage in her career.

Kira rubbed the back of her neck, trying to ease some of the stiffness that had built up during the flight from New York to Charlotte. She was looking forward to a long, hot shower and several cups of strong coffee before she even thought about unpacking, which she dreaded. Moving toward the kitchen, she noticed that the sunlight coming through the vertical blinds covering her patio door was creating bold yellow stripes on her beige Mexican tile, warming the room, which seemed stale and smelled of emptiness. She looked around. Everything was exactly as she had left it, except for a sheen of dust on the green marble kitchen countertops—and the change in the red poinsettia that she had not had the heart to toss into the trash before leaving. It was now a mass of withered, yellow leaves, and a scattering of its brittle petals had settled on the green-veined marble. Kira swept the leaves into one hand, picked up the dead plant and tossed it into the trash can in the laundry room, then opened the sliding glass door to her fenced patio and stepped out. The sight that greeted her was disheartening. The wilted, weathered potted plants around the enclosure begged for attention, and many, Kira knew, would have to be replaced.

"Later," she murmured, leaving the door slightly open to allow fresh air into the apartment as she went to pick up the cordless phone. She punched in the speed-dial number to *BPR*, anxious to check in with her coworker Sharon Reed, to let her know that she was back, and get a quick heads-up on what was going on.

While waiting for the call to go through, Kira opened her refrigerator, inspected its contents, wrinkling her nose at the bottled water, ketchup, mustard, and two jars of pickles on her near-empty shelves. She took out a small bottle of water, twisted off the cap, and took a quick swig before the operator came on.

"Sharon Reed, please," Kira told the switchboard operator, not recognizing the woman's voice, thinking Carol, the regular receptionist, must be out. As soon as Sharon came on the line Kira's face broke into a smile, her travel fatigue temporarily forgotten. "Hey, girl. I'm home."

"Kira!" Sharon replied in a surprised but welcoming tone. "I was just talking to Theo about you this morning. We were wondering if you were back yet."

"Just got in. Haven't even unpacked," Kira said, taking another quick swallow of water. "But I had to find out what was happening over there. New manager's in place, I assume?"

"You assume right," Sharon shot back. "Hold on. I'm not at my desk. Let me get to my phone." After a few seconds she returned, speaking in a voice that was lower and much less exuberant. "Well . . . things are a whole lot different around here, that's about all I can say, Kira."

"Yeah? What's that mean. Different? How?"

"This new leader of ours is something else. It's hard to describe him. He's preoccupied with running a tight ship. With shaping us up, I guess. And I'm not talking about organizing the place or cleaning out old files. Nothing as simple as that. I'm talking staff cuts, supply cuts, pay cuts, longer workdays. Lunch is now half an hour, and, believe me, he knows who is five minutes over or under. You name it, Bruce Davison's got a line on it, and probably cutting it back. Now, are you sure you want to come back?"

"Damn," Kira countered. At the last staff meeting before she had taken off on her leave of absence, the staff had been informed of an upcoming change in management. The news that Kira's boss, Turner York, was retiring had saddened her because York had been the one to hire her, train her, and support her desire to move up in the company. The prospect of returning to her office and not finding Turner York sitting at his cluttered desk, telephone pressed to his ear, was upsetting, not only because he would be missed, but also because Kira knew that her boss and mentor had been forced out of the company due to his advancing age, though no one would ever admit it. The thought of having to adjust to a new manager was not one she wanted to think about. "So, what's he like, personality-wise?" she asked her coworker.

"Uptight," Sharon said flatly. "From Boston. Got that East Coast accent that is, frankly, difficult for southerners to understand. Never stays in his office like old Turner used to do. This man is everywhere, in everybody's face. Can't escape him, so don't even try." Sharon lowered her voice to a near whisper and went on. "Tough as a piece of rawhide, though," she declared. "And his wife is just like him—thin, bony, pale, and pushy. Her name is Marilyn. Came in a few times. Always looks around, as if she wants to re-arrange the furniture, barely speaks to anyone, and then goes into Davison's office and shuts the door. They have a boy at North Carolina State and a married daughter who lives in Pennsylvania. You know, I don't think his marriage is in great shape because he lives at the paper, stays here until the wee hours of the night, and rarely returns his wife's phone calls."

Kira laughed at her coworker's in-depth description, knowing that Sharon, the medical and health reporter for the paper, was probably right on. The two women worked with their desks facing one another in shared space in the open newsroom and had be-come good friends early on, sharing lunch hours, problems, and from time to time weekend outings to art fairs, flea markets, and museums.

Sharon Reed was a forty-four-year-old happily divorced single mother of a ten-year-old daughter named Rachel. Outspoken and devoted to her job, Sharon was a veteran at *BPR,* having worked at the paper longer than anyone currently on staff. A devout Irish Catholic with flaming red hair and pale skin that was liberally sprinkled with freckles, Sharon lived by the motto that was printed on a poster tacked to the side of her computer: TEAMWORK PLUS HARD WORK EQUALS GOOD WORK. Kira enjoyed Sharon's sharp wit, brutal honesty, and her low-key approach to surviving in the hectic, fast-paced environment at *BPR,* where everyone counted on Sharon Reed to keep a level head when the work got crazy and stress levels rose. She was well known as the person who could get the 411 on anybody. All news, gossip, and in-house secrets got to Sharon first, and a conversation with her, whose reporter's knack for digging up dirt was finely tuned, was never a waste of time.

"So he's nosy, driven, tough, and ignores his wife, huh?" Kira jokingly summarized. "Tell me . . . how tough? What's really happening over there?"

Sharon cleared her throat, then started right in, ticking off a litany of casualties. "First to go was Samantha."

"Samantha Marsh?"

"Yep, and I've been assigned to edit her column on farm markets and pig prices as well as do my regular work."

"That's a drag."

"Tell me about it, girl." Sharon sighed. "Then Carol got the ax. Davison said she didn't sound professional enough on the phone."

"I noticed it wasn't Carol who answered."

"Right. And he knew that Carol was struggling, going to night school, and raising three kids, one of whom is disabled. And her husband is a laid-off trucker. We took up a collection in the newsroom when she left. Gave her a two-hundred-dollar gift certificate to Target so she can get some of the things she and the kids really need. A sad situation, really sad."

"That's terrible," Kira said, remembering how badly Carol had needed her job and how hard she had worked at it.

"And the meetings!" Sharon continued. "Editorial every morning at eight A.M. sharp. Support staff in the afternoons. That's not so bad, but it's the way he talks to us—as if we aren't veterans at this. He can go on forever, just to make a point that nobody cares about. A real drag. So you better not miss the one tomorrow, let alone be late. Get here early in the A.M. if you plan to get a cup of coffee to take with you to the meeting."

"Sounds crazy," Kira replied.

"Exactly," Sharon agreed. "Rafael Cortez, over in accounting, resigned yesterday. Going to Bank of America. Big increase in pay."

"Good for him."

"Exactly," Sharon agreed. "Oh, and get this: no one leaves the building before Davison reviews final copy and signs off on it, even if you have to hang around for hours until he gets to you. Yesterday Joe got tired of waiting, went home to eat dinner with his wife, planning to return, of course, but he got a blistering phone call at home from Davison ordering him back to work immediately. Needless to say, morale around here is below zip."

"Whew. Glad I checked in before I showed up and got hit with all of this in the morning," Kira replied, genuinely surprised that things were so different. Her former boss, Turner York, had been an easygoing man, chatty and long-winded—the kind of boss who preferred to stand back and give his staff room to do their jobs rather than ride them in a controlling way. He had been professional and exacting, yet friendly, and his confidence in Kira's skill as a photographer and reporter, coupled with her loyalty to *BPR*, had convinced him to grant her the leave of absence to do the story for *World.* York had known how eager Kira was to acquire the kind of experience that would help her talent grow, and he had personally hammered out the details of her contract so that it would be beneficial to everyone involved. Having been managing editor at *BPR* for twenty-eight years, York had a wealth of knowledge and had been a good friend to Kira since she had started there fifteen years ago.

"Well," Kira said, "I've checked my mail, and there wasn't a letter informing me that I no longer have a job, so I'll be back tomorrow. I know there's a lot to catch up on."

"Sure is. Your desk is stacked sky-high, awaiting your return, my dear. You are going to be a busy, busy lady for some time, I promise." A buzz on Sharon's line interrupted the conversation. "Hold on a minute." She clicked off, then came right back. "Gotta go, Kira. Been waiting for this callback all day. Why don't you call me later? Fill me in on your adventure. There won't be time for much chitchat in the office."

"Wish I could, Sharon, but I haven't even unpacked. I'm exhausted, and I've got a few important calls to get out of the way. Tomorrow maybe we can go for Chinese after work?"

"You got it," Sharon tossed back, then added, "Get a good night's sleep, Kira. You are going to need all of your strength in the morning."

Laughing, Kira clicked off, drained the last of the water from the plastic bottle, then tossed it into the trash. After opening the mini-blinds in the kitchen to let more light into the apartment, she put on a pot of coffee, then went into the hallway, where she had dropped her purse with her luggage and retrieved the letter from the North Carolina Department of Health and Human Services. Rereading the notice as she made her way to her desk, she sensed her joy at returning home begin to fade. The new manager sounded awful. Carol and Samantha had been fired! And now she had to deal with this disturbing situation with her niece, along with a bad case of jet lag that was about to send her crashing into bed.

Kira unzipped her soft leather ankle boots and kicked them off, then tucked her sock-clad feet under her hips, resting her head on the back of the chair, forcing herself to relax. She had to gather her thoughts before picking up the phone; she had to be certain about what she was going to say. First of all, she wanted information about Vicky's current situation. Was her niece happy? Who were the people who wanted to adopt her? And how had Alvia Elderton, Vicky's former foster mother, died? And, finally, would Sheltering Hearts help Kira initiate a reunion with Vicky?

So much had happened so fast. Kira had to slow things down, get professional guidance and a better understanding of what to expect. What could, or ought, she do to make sure Vicky was happy?

The letter of pending adoption had startled Kira, initiating a sense of urgency that also brought back feelings of guilt, though she hated to admit it. She should have been a better aunt to Vicky. She should have tried harder to create opportunities for the two of them to establish some kind of a bond. Vicky was now six years old, no longer the frightened little toddler she remembered, and as Kira's only living blood relative, the child deserved to know that her mother's sister existed.

Kira stared across the room at her impressive collection of alabaster, clay, and porcelain figurines of Aztec, Navajo, Mayan, and Inca Indian chiefs, which she had assembled on a low table near her fireplace. Several of the statuettes were one-of-a-kind pieces created by native craftsmen, worth hundreds of dollars and quite rare. She scrutinized her light beige carpet, the elegant, clean lines of her cream-colored chaise lounge (her favorite place to sit and read), and the pale cream silk that covered the walls of her dining area. The two tall crystal vases sitting on top of the end tables flanking the sofa were empty now, but tomorrow she'd make her usual run to the Flower Cart and pick out a variety of long-stemmed blooms to put in them, bringing her home back to life. She took pride in the soothing, fashionable environment she had created, and she loved the way it suited her lifestyle.

Would having a six-year-old child around the house require putting her treasures away? Kira wondered, assessing her carefully coordinated decor. If Vicky came often to visit, Kira would have to be more conscious about her niece's needs and would be obligated to consider her interests. She had no coloring books, Barbie dolls, paints, or Disney videos to entertain a child. How would a close relationship with Vicky change things?

Quickly, Kira punched in the phone number to Sheltering Hearts, determined to get on with settling this aspect of her personal life that she had kept on hold too long.

The woman who answered asked for Kira's name, then told her to hold for a moment—Mr. Conley was finishing up a call, but he'd be right with her. He came on the line almost immediately.

"Miss Forester?" Evan Conley prompted, then paused.

"Yes," Kira answered, going on to tell him about the letter she had received.

"Fine, fine. Yes. I'm handling your niece's adoption, and I am aware, from her foster-placement file, that you are interested in knowing what happens to her. Thank you for calling. Input and support from blood relatives in adoption cases are always important and valued. I'd like to visit with you about Vicky."

"Yes," Kira started. "I have a lot of questions—"

"And I'll be happy to answer them," he interjected. "When can you come in?"

In the split second that followed, the immediacy of her niece's situation finally hit Kira, forcing her to acknowledge that she had been very unprepared to deal with the matter. But what had she expected? To settle things over the phone? Of course she'd have to go to Mr. Conley's office, sit down for a face-to-face, and get the information she needed to take the next step, whatever it might be. Giving herself a mental shake, she muttered, "When can you see me?"

"Well, the sooner, the better, Miss Forester. Your niece's placement is moving right along, and we don't expect any problems. Let's see. Today is Tuesday. I could squeeze you in tomorrow morning. About eight-thirty? I'm afraid I have to leave for a conference in Winston-Salem at noon tomorrow, and I'll be out of my office until next Monday. Can you possibly come tomorrow?"

"Tomorrow? At eight-thirty?" Kira repeated, her thoughts flashing back to Sharon's assessment of the situation at the office. She had to show up, meet her new boss, and get back into the groove of her regular workday. "I'm not sure," she said hesitantly.

"I wish you could make it. I'd like to meet with you personally. You see, Sheltering Hearts is a small, private adoption agency, and I only have two full-time caseworkers on staff. Though one of my staff could meet with you, I'd prefer to be the one to talk to you."

"I understand. Where exactly are you located?" Kira asked.

"We're in Stallings, a half mile south of Four-Eighty-Five. Take the Guilfred exit."

"Yes, I know where that is. Well, I'll have to speak to my boss and see if I can get away from the office," Kira drew out her words, silently worried. From her office to Stallings was at least a thirty-minute drive one way, if traffic was moving. That would mean an hour of drive time, plus an hour at least for the meeting. She doubted Davison was going to go for that. "Mr. Conley, I really don't think I can make it tomorrow. You see, I've been out of my office for quite a while. I just returned from Africa and have a ton of work facing me right now."

"Oh? Africa? Really? Vacation?" Evan asked.

"No, work. I'm a journalist. I work for the *Business & Professional Recorder* in Charlotte. I was on a special assignment."

"I see. Sounds like intriguing work."

"It can be," Kira agreed, biting her lip, thinking. Did she dare ask Bruce Davison for time off on her first day back? According to Sharon, their new boss was not a man who cut his employees much slack, and job security at *BPR* could no longer be taken for granted. Kira might be putting her job in jeopardy if she asked for even an extra hour tacked onto her lunch break, especially on short notice. However, she also knew that she couldn't push the situation with Vicky onto the back burner forever. For the past four years she'd refused to prioritize her relationship with her niece, convinced that Vicky was fine where she was and nothing needed to be done. But things had changed. Kira had to get involved, and she had to start right away.

"On second thought, I'll be there, Mr. Conley," Kira decided, praying Bruce Davison would understand.

CHAPTER 4

At seven the next morning, Kira strode into the lobby of the building that housed the offices of the *Business & Professional Recorder*. It was an older structure with lots of gray marble, shiny brass, and gleaming dark woodwork throughout its interior, creating a pleasant sense of history and old-fashioned style. It had been built in the early fifties specifically to house the offices of insurance agents, CPAs, attorneys, and small investment firms. The lobby was never crowded. Now, Kira's heels made a hollow clicking sound on the highly polished marble floor as she crossed toward the security guard who was standing near the elevators.

Kira flashed her employee ID at the guard, giving him a friendly nod, but her pleasant greeting faded when he gave her a stern look and said, "Hold on," in a very official tone. Then he extended his arm in her path, clearly blocking her from going any farther.

Surprised at his rude maneuver, she glared at him, waiting to see what he wanted.

"I need to see another photo ID," he ordered.

"Oh?" She had never needed anything but her *BPR* ID card before, but she took a closer look at the guard and then complied with his request, realizing that he was not the regular one who used to be at the entry. The former guard had known her on sight, and had flirted outrageously, not only with Kira but also with most of the female employees who passed by. He had been a jovial, gray-haired man with a great sense of humor.

"No problem," Kira told the guard in a courteous voice, searching her purse for her wallet.

"You a new employee?" the guard asked. "I haven't seen you around before."

"No," Kira replied, deciding he needed no additional information. "I'm not new, but you must be." She handed him her driver's license. "I've been working here for fifteen years. When did you start?"

"Two weeks ago, Miss . . ." he glanced at her ID again, "Forester." He let his eyes roam over her, then handed back her license. "Thank you. I won't need to see it again. I'm sure I'll remember you."

"Good," Kira said, snatching her card, which she stuck into her wallet. Turning on her heel, she rushed to catch the nearest open elevator, feeling the guard's eyes on her back. "Sure have been a lot of changes around here," she muttered as she made it inside just before the doors slid closed.

Glad to be alone, she checked herself in the mirror, relieved to see her usual corporate image staring back. Her tightly crimped hair had been tamed with moisturizer and it was soft and shiny once more. The sprinkling of freckles across her nose, acquired under the African sun, had been erased with honey-beige foundation that matched her complexion perfectly. The last vestiges of travel fatigue, dark circles and puffiness under her eyes, had also disappeared overnight. Her favorite navy blue suit gave her the crisp, efficient image that she liked, and she was glad she had decided to wear it today. In fact, when she had slipped it on this morning, she had been pleasantly surprised at how nicely it fit across her hips—a lot less snug than the last time she had worn it.

"A benefit of jungle life," she told herself, remembering all of the walking, hiking, and climbing she had done while in Africa, not to mention the drastic changes she'd had to make in her diet. Munching on chips and candy bars in the afternoon was a distant memory, and she was determined to keep it that way.

"Back to the gym tomorrow, though," she muttered, giving her jacket a tug as she admired the hammered copper earrings she had purchased in the lively, crowded outdoor market in Cameroon, an early stop on her trip. "Just the right touch," she told herself, pleased with the way the exotic jewelry accented and softened her corporate image.

The only female African-American reporter on staff at *BPR*, Kira enjoyed blending touches of her ethnicity with her stylish, tailored suits, and her passion for exotic costume jewelry, especially earrings, was well known. Whenever she traveled, or simply shopped, she remained on the lookout for one-of-a kind handcrafted pieces to add to her jewelry box. The more colorful the better, and she especially sought out pieces created in a variety of medias that were unusual and eye-catching. She had leather disks studded with semiprecious stones; wooden squares carved with delicate designs; copper, brass, and silver wires twisted into shapes of animals and flowers. She had brought back a pair of earrings made of yellow stone beads for Sharon.

The elevator reached the fourth floor, and the doors slid open. As Kira made her way to the main entrance of *BPR*, she suddenly became nervous. Did she dare ask for time off on her first day back? Taking a deep breath, she nodded, knowing that she had no choice. This matter had to be taken care of today.

After her telephone conversation with Evan Conley, Kira had showered, shampooed her hair, unpacked her bags, and thrown a load of laundry into the washing machine—anything to keep from lying down on her bed. But when she sat down on her chaise longue to watch the six o'clock news, she had dropped off to sleep shortly after the newscast began. At two A.M. she awakened to the sound of laughter coming from an old black-and-white movie on television, and then groped her way into the bedroom, where she crashed again, forgetting to set her alarm. Thank God, she had awakened on her own early enough to get up, dress, and grab a cup of coffee before heading out into drive-time traffic.

During her twenty-minute drive to the office she had rehearsed a variety of ways to broach the subject of taking a few hours off, dreading the encounter but knowing she had no choice but to ask. If Turner York had still been in charge, she would have had no hesitation about telling him why she had to leave. But she did not know Bruce Davison, or how much of her personal life she ought to reveal to him.

Instead of going directly to her workstation in the newsroom, where other early-arriving staffers were getting started on their day, she went to the partially open door marked MANAGEMENT and paused, inhaling a long, deep breath. It was the same office that her former boss had used, where she had spent many hours talking about ideas for a story, getting advice, requesting input on a problem she needed to solve. The realization that her mentor and friend was not on the other side of the door hit home, and Kira began to panic.

She remained outside Bruce Davison's office, gathering her courage as she peered through the crack, observing the profile of the slim white man with closely cut gray hair. Round, wire-rimmed glasses were perched midway down his nose, which was buried in the folds of a newspaper. He was wearing a white shirt with a red and blue striped tie, and a frown of concentration had pulled the skin taut over his narrow forehead.

Kira tapped lightly on the door as she eased it more fully open. Davison's head jerked up. He scrutinized Kira for a moment, then quickly folded his newspaper and set it aside.

"Mr. Davison?" Kira said, remaining in the doorway.

"Yes?" he replied in a vague way, clearly questioning who she was. He tilted his head to one side, waiting for her to go on.

"I'm Kira Forester." She gave him a weak half-smile, feeling awkward that he did not even know who she was. When he remained silent, she knew she had to prompt him. "Back from Africa? The *World Societies Today* special assignment?"

He immediately stood up. "Oh yes! Yes, Kira. Glad you are back. Great to finally meet you. Come in. Sit down over here at the table. Please." His greeting was effusive, yet jerky, and Kira sensed a strain in his smile, as if he was going to a great deal of effort to make her feel welcome.

Kira crossed the room and took a seat at the round conference table in a corner, immediately taking notice of the rearrangement of the furniture. Davison had removed the odd but interesting *BPR* memorabilia that Turner York had showcased on his walls and on shelves that had lined every available surface. Gone were the celebrity photos, framed yellowed newspaper clippings, and the official letters *BPR* had received from politicians, charities, and prominent businesspeople whose careers had often been boosted by feature stories in *BPR*. The piles of magazines and books that had been stacked everywhere were gone, too, as well as the glass showcases housing trophies and awards won by staff members over the years.

Now the office seemed tidy, uncluttered, and cold, with only a few stacks of folders, neatly bound with fat rubber bands, sitting on top of a lateral file cabinet. Davison's desk looked entirely too organized for the manager of a newspaper, and Kira noticed that his IN tray was empty. The only other items on his desk besides the folded newspaper were a yellow legal pad and three silver pens lined up next to the telephone. As her eyes quickly scanned the desk, Kira realized she had never seen the beautiful solid walnut surface of it before. Turner's work had kept it buried the entire time he had been managing editor.

Davison pulled up a chair across from Kira, leaned back, and rested his folded arms on his chest. "Welcome back, Kira. How did everything go?"

"Very well," Kira replied, going on to fill her boss in on the major aspects of the trip, focusing on her successful documentation of several child-labor camps in the area. "I stopped in New York on the way back—met with Julie Ays, who is working with me to get the finished copy and photos in to *World*."

"Hmm," Davison murmured. "What's your deadline?"

"April fifteenth."

"Hmm, less than a month," Davison commented in an offhand manner that implied a lack of concern over this particular story.

"Tight, but enough time to get it done, I think," Kira confidently replied. "I sent film and copy back while I was on assignment, so Julie got a start on the layout. We went over some of the material while I was in New York, so I have a pretty good idea how she wants it to come together."

"And when is the piece scheduled to run?"

"It will be in *World's* July issue."

"And after that I understand we have serial rights."

"Yes," Kira agreed. "That's right. Mr. York held fast on that when he was negotiating my contract."

Davison cleared his throat, eased forward, unfolded his arms, and put his elbows on the table. "Well, to be honest—and you will learn this about me soon enough, Kira: I don't mince words—if I had been managing editor when this assignment came up, I never would have allowed a member of my staff to take a leave of absence unless *BPR* got first rights of publication. *World Societies Today* may be our parent company, but they don't have a say in how I run my day-to-day operation. My staff's first allegiance ought to be to *BPR*."

Kira tensed, but decided not to say anything until she got a handle on where Davison was headed. Clearly his opinion of *World* was not as high as hers.

"Everyone who reads the *Business & Professional Recorder,* as well as anyone who is even peripherally involved in the American textile industry, knows that cheap overseas labor is the biggest threat to the survival of the industry. The story belongs with us—we cover state news—and should not be coming out of New York."

After considering his remark for a moment, Kira spoke up. "But *World* is an international publication, and the problem has worldwide implications."

"That may be true, Kira, but the greatest impact can be felt right here in North Carolina."

"True," she admitted. "However, my angle will be to take a look at the bigger picture, not simply an industry that is close to my hometown. My assignment was to put a human face on the threat that the American textile industry faces, to analyze the interconnections between the way we do things and vastly different operations, demonstrating how complicated the issue is. The situation *is* complicated, and Americans need to see the poverty in the African villages, the desperation in the faces of the underage workers, the circumstances that make it profitable for them but hard on us. We can't ignore the human drama that revolves around this delicate economic balance. The problem is fraught with political overtones, and it is not easy to analyze. You see, I grew up in the textile industry. My parents worked in the mills. I worked in a factory to put myself through Wake Forest University, so I fully understand the anger and disappointment that Americans are feeling, but I also better understand why and how this decline occurred."

Davison, who had fixed Kira with a stony look while she was talking, lifted one shoulder in a dismissive gesture. "But you didn't have to travel halfway around the world to find that out. Your time and talent could have been put to much better use here. Since you've missed all of our staff meetings, let me fill you in on what is going on. First, you should know that the circulation figures for *BPR* are dismal. Down fifteen percent over last year—twenty-seven percent from three years ago. We're facing an uphill battle due to the deluge of business news available on the Internet, CNN, and other satellite all-news channels, dailies like the *Charlotte Observer* and *USA Today*, as well as the *Wall Street Journal*, et cetera. *BPR* must distinguish itself, become a publication that provides news that is not already floating around out there."

"I understand what you mean," Kira agreed, beginning to feel slightly deflated and dismissed. This was not the welcome back that she had envisioned, nor the reception she would have received from Turner York, who would have been bubbling with enthusiasm, about not only the story she was working on, but the fact that one of *his* reporters had been chosen by the parent company to cover it. York had recognized the value of having such credentials attributed to one of his staff and had unselfishly supported Kira's trip.

"I don't mean to sound as if your investigation and the angle of your story have no value, Kira," Davison went on. "They do. And *BPR* will carry your piece, as agreed. But from now on, I want my staff to focus less on people and concentrate on business. The textile-driven economy has taken a hit in our state, but there are many businesses that are gaining ground. We need to showcase them. Give credit to those that are moving in, hiring people, and filling the gaps left behind when the mills closed down. I want facts, statistics, charts, profiles of business models, and less coverage of the personal fluff that does little more than evoke emotion. I want to give our readers factual information that they can use to increase their wages, boost their earning potential, and better understand the workings of the economy and how it affects them. Understand?"

"Exactly," Kira answered, struggling to keep disappointment from her voice. "Sure. Less emotion, more facts."

"That's it, precisely." Davison got up from the table, went to the file cabinet, and slipped the rubber band off of a stack of folders. After rifling through them, he pulled one out and returned to the table. "Our staff is a lot leaner now. Those who are here have to do double duty. I want you to do fewer human-interest stories and cover more issues related to the economic marketplace, and . . . you will also take over the education beat from Robert Morrat, who is no longer with us."

"Robert resigned?" Kira asked.

"Yes. Yesterday was his last day with us," Davison said curtly, then handed the folder to Kira. "Two years ago, the Mecklenburg County School Board voted to turn three of its high schools over to private industry and let businessmen run them. The board wanted to determine if private industry could do a better job managing the schools than the local board, and to determine if the businessmen used tax dollars more wisely. The results of the study are to be announced at a press conference at ten-thirty this morning. I want you over there. Get the numbers, the facts, the proof. Don't bring back a lot of weepy reaction from the taxpayers, the teachers, or any parents. Stick to what can be proven with the results of the study, okay?"

Slowly, Kira nodded, leafing through the folder, unable to concentrate on the statistical charts, color-coded graphs, dense memos, and numerical projections that it contained. No way could she cover a press conference at the school board at ten-thirty and keep her appointment at Sheltering Hearts, that was clear. "This sounds very . . . interesting," she finally managed, holding her emotions in check as she closed the folder and centered it between herself and Davison. She met his intense look with a level one of her own, preparing to tell him what was uppermost on her mind. Boldly, she plunged ahead.

"Mr. Davison," she began.

"Call me Bruce, please."

"Fine. Bruce. There's something I'd like to discuss with you."

"Shoot," he tossed back, pushing his glasses higher on his nose.

"I have a very important personal matter to take care of . . . a situation with a family member that occurred while I was away, and I need a few hours this morning."

"A few hours? Today?"

"Yes. I was thinking that perhaps Theo could cover the school board press conference today, then I could take it from there? I think this is a great subject for a series of stories, maybe select one school run by the county, the other run like a business. Compare—"

Shaking his head, Davison lifted a hand, interrupting Kira. He squinted at her, examining her face as if she were some kind of strange object that had dropped into his office from outer space. "Impossible. Have you forgotten that you've been out of the office for ten weeks? And that, according to your contract, today is the date of your return to work?"

"I do, and I hate to ask, but this is important. My niece, my only—"

"I don't need the details," he stopped her. "The answer is no. You cannot have a few hours off today, or any day in the near future. You agreed to incorporate this year's sick and vacation days in your leave of absence, so you have no more days off until next year." He stood up, clearly ending the discussion. "I suggest you get to your workstation and get on with your day. The last time I saw your desk it was stacked pretty high."

Swallowing hard, Kira fought the impulse to make a remark that she might regret, and after picking up the folder, shouldered her purse and headed to the door.

"Kira?" Davison stopped her.

She turned and looked at him. "Yes?"

"I understand Mr. York let you take *BPR*'s Nikon camera with you on assignment?"

"He did."

"Make sure you return it to the equipment room today."

"I will," she coldly replied, relieved that she had stashed it in the trunk of her car this morning.

On her way to her desk, Kira burned with humiliation and disappointment, though she was not sorry she had spoken up. Now she knew exactly where she stood with Davison and what to expect from him. Obviously, he cared only about the paper and expected her to keep her personal life out of his way. She'd have to make the best of it, and push on.

I'll call Evan Conley and reschedule, she decided, convincing herself that it was probably a good idea, anyway. Maybe she needed more time to think about the ramifications of getting involved in Vicky's life. Maybe she had reacted too quickly to the news of Vicky's upcoming adoption. Perhaps meeting Vicky and her prospective adoptive parents would not be such a good idea. And what if her niece, or the Ropers, wanted nothing to do with her? Kira wasn't naive enough to believe that everything would go smoothly. The situation was very complicated, and she might be better off moving into it more slowly.

She tossed the school board folder on top of the pile of papers covering her desk, pulled out her chair, and sat down, swiveling to glance across the room at a small knot of employees who were standing near the copy machine, talking in low tones. Sharon was there, along with Joe Chomsky, the sports and celebrity reporter who had once played college football for North Carolina State, and Theo Sorrel, whose beat included state and local politics. All three, along with Turner York, had been enthusiastically encouraging to Kira when she received the news that she had been selected to cover the African segment of the textile story for *World Societies Today*.

"Hey, Kira," Joe called out, unzipping his red and gray windbreaker as he headed her way. "Welcome back."

Though it took a good deal of effort, Kira managed a bright

smile, truly glad to be back among her coworkers again. Her trip to Africa had been her first time outside the United States, not counting a long weekend jaunt to Jamaica with Brandon, the loser she had thought she loved. That trip had been a disaster. Brandon had ruined the romantic interlude with his constant flirting with girls on the beach and incessant desire to party. The dreadful experience had taught Kira a lot about herself and had defined her expectations of future travel. Visiting historical sites, eating strange foods, and meeting new people meant more to her than sitting by a swimming pool sipping wine coolers and catching the sun's rays.

Her trip to Africa had been an eye-opening experience, providing Kira with valuable knowledge and memories that would stay with her forever. But while making her way through the lush jungles and remote villages of Equatorial Guinea, it had been impossible not to yearn for familiar faces, the foods she loved, and those everyday routines that went with being an American, and she was very glad to be back with her coworkers despite the change in circumstances.

"You look great, Kira."

"Thanks, Joe," Kira said, smiling.

"When'd you get back?" Theo asked, heading toward her desk.

"Yesterday afternoon," she told him, nodding conspiratorially at Sharon, who had followed Joe and Theo toward her workstation. The three reporters crowded around Kira, obviously wanting to hear about her trip. Kira pushed her unsettling encounter with Bruce Davison to the back of her mind and launched into a quick overview of her experiences, answering their questions with vivid descriptions of the people, the geography, the work, and of course, the blazing send-off she had received when her driver cut through Pangi.

"Lucky you made it out alive," Joe commented. "You think they shot at you because you photographed those girls in those sheds?"

"Sure," Kira replied. "What else? Child labor is common in many countries, and the locals don't want photographs of what is going on splashed over the pages of American newspapers and magazines."

"Where are the photos?" Theo asked. "I'd like to see them."

"In New York, being developed at *World*. They'll e-mail copies to me in a day or two. Then you can see what I'm talking about."

"Sounds like you had a fantastic experience," Theo remarked. "I'm jealous. Maybe I need to call your friend Julie and see if she can get me one of those exotic assignments. Anything to get out of here."

Arching a brow, Kira slid her eyes over the faces of each of her coworkers, stopping when she got to Sharon. So, Theo was ready to bolt, too. "I've heard all about it," she remarked, having noticed that the usual cheer in Theo's voice was gone. He sounded flat.

"And now you're back to the real deal," Sharon joked, breaking the moment as she wagged a finger. "The fun stuff is over. This is reality, here."

"Reality?" Theo questioned, adjusting his rectangle-shaped glasses. "Honey, this place can't be reality, can it?"

Sharon chuckled, then nodded slowly, as if considering how to phrase her response. "For a while, maybe it is. But I can't promise anyone how long it's gonna be my reality."

Kira's head snapped up, and she focused on Sharon, sensing that something was going on that she didn't know about. "What's that mean, Sharon? You going somewhere?"

"It's that job at *The Sentinel*, isn't it?" Joe prompted.

"Please," Sharon tossed back.

"*The Sentinel?* In Orlando?" Kira pressed. "Sharon, you're taking a job in Florida?"

"Not yet, but I'm working on it." Sharon slipped into the chair at her computer, swiveled to face Kira, then sighed. "Can't say more right now, but I promise to keep all of you posted." Then she jerked her head to the side. "Watch out. We are under observation."

A few seconds later, Davison crossed the newsroom and headed to one of the copiers, but his eyes never left the group gathered around Kira's desk.

"Better get busy, guys," Sharon hissed. "Here comes Super Boss."

Theo and Joe frowned, nodded, and hurried toward their own workstations, leaving Sharon and Kira alone.

"You seriously thinking about leaving *BPR*?" Kira asked, hating to think about losing her best friend at the paper.

"Yep."

"But, Sharon," Kira started. "Why? You've been here . . . what? Nineteen years?"

"That's right."

"And you're so well-connected in the business community. You *are* the face of *BPR* on the local scene. Do you really want to start over in some strange town?"

"Kira, I started at *BPR* as a mailroom clerk right after I graduated from high school, worked my way up to executive secretary to the manager, then to my own column. Yes, I might be well-connected, and I can't complain about my salary, but I need some respect."

The silver pen in Sharon's hand reflected the overhead lights as she doodled on her calendar. "I've got to get out of here before I really blow it. Bruce is impossible to work for. If I get an offer from any paper that will cover my moving expenses, my house note, my car note, my MasterCard bill, I'm gone. It's too stressful around here, and I'm too old to deal with this man who seems determined to run everybody off. Right now, I am concentrating on doing my job and finding a way out of here."

"I understand," Kira replied, picking up a stack of mail. She began sorting through it, noticing that the temp who had worked her desk had already opened many of the envelopes while she was away. "Sharon, I hate to think of you leaving." She tossed an outdated invitation to the grand opening of the new offices of the Mecklenburg County Chamber of Commerce into the wastebasket, then reached into her purse and took out a small red box. Leaning over, she placed it in front of Sharon. "A little something for you from Africa," she said.

Startled, Sharon looked up. Then, grinning, she removed the lid from the small square box. "How beautiful!" She held one of the dangling earrings to the side of her face and tilted her head to one side. "Neat. Kira, thanks. I will really enjoy wearing these."

"Glad you like them," Kira said. Turning serious, she added, "You can't jump ship now, Sharon."

Sharon put the earrings back inside the box and closed it. "That's not what I want to do, but things change. I've enjoyed working here, and the thought of starting over, adjusting to new people, a new city, a new boss, makes me crazy, but I don't look forward to coming in to work anymore." Sharon pulled a stack of papers from her IN box and began looking them over. "You met Davison, didn't you?"

"Yeah, first thing this morning."

"And . . . ?" Sharon queried.

"And he's definitely not Turner York."

"You can say that again."

"But I guess he has the paper's best interests at heart. Circulation is down; competition is up. He wants us to survive. I can understand that."

"He won't survive by cutting personnel and expecting us to do the same quality of work with less staff. I don't like his management style. He needs respect and cooperation from his staff if he expects things to change for the better, and he has neither right now. Look around. You've been gone, but you'll find out soon enough. Our workloads have doubled; our paychecks have not. The time we have to spend at our desks has increased, but his respect for us has not. And it's not just me, Kira. Joe, Theo, everyone is skittish. This place is about to self-destruct."

"Maybe Bruce needs more time," Kira replied, surprised that she was defending the man who had coldly dismissed her this morning. "He's been here . . . what? Six or seven weeks? Once he gets to know us better, and we get to know him, maybe—"

"Ha!" Sharon laughed. "Get to know us? Did he ask you one personal question this morning? Did you get the impression that he cares what goes on outside these walls? I'm telling you . . . Last week Rachel got sick and the school nurse called me at ten-thirty in the morning to come pick her up. Her temperature was a hundred and four. Bruce told me I couldn't leave until after a staff meeting he was calling for two o'clock."

"What'd you do?"

"Called my sister, Ellen. Thank God she works nights and could go get Rachel and take her to the doctor. I don't have a husband to pick up the slack, and I need my job. You know York would have *made* me go home, and told me to stay there until Rachel was better."

Kira opened her mouth, then closed it, not sure what she could say. She gave Sharon an understanding nod of sympathy. "I know."

"Did Bruce ask you any personal questions? Did he act as if he wanted to get to know you? Do you think he cares about what matters to you personally?" Sharon went on.

"Not really," Kira admitted, seeing where Sharon was coming from.

"All right, then. You figure it out," Sharon said, just as the phone on her desk began to ring, interrupting their conversation. She took the call, launching into a discussion about the upswing in wholesale prices for wheat.

Grimacing, Kira returned to sorting her mail, but then she stopped and looked around the newsroom, silently counting the empty chairs as she assessed the stacks of folders on everyone's desk. The lighthearted banter that used to fill the newsroom was gone, replaced by a tense silence that seemed unnatural and unhealthy. The only voices in the office were those of the reporters on the television monitors that were anchored high above their desks in two corners of the newsroom. As Kira listened to the local weatherman give his predictions for the day, she felt her worries rise to the surface.

Sharon is right, Kira thought. *It's time to go. And if Julie's predictions are on target, I might soon be working in New York.*

CHAPTER 5

Evan Conley pushed the button to project the final slide of his presentation onto the big screen, sending a photograph of a Caucasian couple beaming with pride and surrounded by four children to the front of the darkened room. The children in the slide, who appeared to range in age from toddler to teenager, were of Asian, Hispanic, and African-American heritage and were wearing grins as broad their parents'.

"Every child deserves the warmth, security, and unconditional love of a permanent family," Evan said, continuing with his presentation, pausing long enough for his words to connect with the images, a technique he had learned from past presentations to create the emotional ending to his recruitment pitch.

"Since 1985 the foster-care population in the United States has increased by an average of five percent a year," he stated, "creating a generation of legal orphans with few prospects for legal adoption. As foster-care caseworkers, you are on the front lines of this battle, and you provide an important link to the support needed to move children off foster-care rolls and into adoptive placements."

One of the women in the audience raised her hand, and Evan quickly acknowledged her. "But so many of the children in my agency are older, or of ethnic backgrounds that make them extremely hard to place."

"That is true," Evan agreed. "To solve this dilemma we must be creative, open-minded, and strive to recruit families who are not only qualified to adopt but who are also willing to accept the challenges that come with special-needs children. At Sheltering Hearts, we strive to create 'forever families.' As I am sure you know, nothing is quite as difficult for all parties involved than to have a prospective adoption fall through. During my presentation this afternoon I have shown you examples of many racial and ethnic combinations that can come together to make up a family. When men and women who are willing to love and care for a child regardless of race or ethnicity step forward, we move quickly to support them. Nothing is more frustrating than to lose a placement because of slow-moving, bureaucratic red tape. Sheltering Hearts specializes in finding adoptive families for older children, siblings, Asian, Hispanic, and African-American children. We also place those with physical and/or emotional conditions that often require professional services."

"That can be a turnoff because of the expense," one of the conference attendees interjected.

"Yes," Evan replied. "But we go to great lengths to find resources to assist with those costs." He punched the button and moved to another slide of the same family. "Here we have Mr. and Mrs. Thomas Rizola of Ashville and their four adopted children at their beach house. Mr. Rizola is an Italian immigrant who came to the United States when he was nine years old. He's a Duke University graduate who has been successful with his own landscaping business for seventeen years. His wife is a dental hygienist. When they decided to adopt, they came to Sheltering Hearts, ready to accept any child who truly needed them, and over the next five years, they found three more. The Rizolas opened their hearts and their home to children who might never have been placed because of their ages and ethnicity. These children had been shuffled through the foster-care system for years. At Sheltering Hearts, kids like the Rizola children are the ones we are dedicated to placing in quality adoptive situations. So I hope you will consider turning to us, to let us help you with those children under your care who are in desperate need of placement."

Evan paused, allowing his message to sink in, before pressing the button to end his slide program. When he turned up the lights, the one hundred and twenty conference attendees began to applaud.

"Thank you for the opportunity to tell you about Sheltering Hearts," he said, handing the handheld microphone back to the conference chairwoman, a petite brunette in a black suit, swathed in a striking black-and-white print scarf.

"Thank you, Mr. Conley. As chair of the North Carolina Association of Foster Care Reviewers, I want to thank you for coming out and for being a part of our conference." The woman moved to the center of the room and stuck the microphone into the holder on the podium. "Congratulations on the wonderful work you are doing. I am sure you will hear from many us very soon."

"I hope so," Evan replied as he began gathering his things while the chairwoman launched into her wrap-up announcements to end the conference.

Evan was anxious to leave and get on the road. He was the kind of person who tried to squeeze twelve hours of work into a ten-hour day. His position as owner and director of Sheltering Hearts Placement Agency kept his appointment book full, his telephone ringing, and his evenings crammed with speaking engagements where he publicized his critical need for adoptive parents for his special-needs children. As one of only five private placement agencies with a contract with the state of North Carolina, he devoted himself to designing innovative strategies to place his kids. Sheltering Hearts was a small agency with a solid reputation as one that did an excellent job of placing African-American children, and Evan Conley managed his staff of four in a friendly yet professional manner. He was not afraid to allow his compassionate nature to shine and was known in the industry as an understanding and fair man—but also as an impatient man, one who never wasted time.

He removed his slides from the projector and placed them, along with his packet of conference materials, into his briefcase and snapped it shut. Slipping out through the door at the back of the room, he made his way down the hallway, across the hotel lobby, and outside to his car, thinking that the conference had been much better attended than he had expected. He attended many such conferences throughout the state, making contacts with members of associations who could work with him to recruit prospective adoptive parents. The forums also provided Evan an opportunity to put a personal face on Sheltering Hearts.

When not attending conferences, he visited with social workers, educators, people in law enforcement, lawyers, judges, foster-care reviewers, and even blood relatives of the children's families—anyone who might help him move a child from foster care into a permanent home. He visited remote parts of North Carolina as well as urban centers, exploring sources for families that were often overlooked by other adoption agencies, anxious for them to know who

Sheltering Hearts and Evan Conley were and what they stood for in the community.

After pulling out of the parking lot, Evan headed toward the Interstate, his mind turning to the beginnings of Sheltering Hearts. Opening an adoption agency for special-needs children seven years ago had been a huge step for him, but a natural one for the then thirty-seven-year-old divorcé whose masters degree in social work and thirteen years of experience in the area of child welfare had prepared him for such a commitment.

Sheltering Hearts was understaffed, housed in a four-room suite in an older building that was only one-quarter occupied. But it was his. He had purchased the entire building at auction seven years ago for a price far below market value, and he had worked hard to meet the state of North Carolina's requirements to keep his agency solvent, productive, and in compliance with the ever-growing number of state, local, and federal regulations that affected the field of adoption.

Evan lived for his work, and nearly lived at the office, since his nondescript second-floor studio apartment was only one block from his office building, making it easy for him to move quickly between home and work. Unconsciously, he often blended both places so easily that he hardly bothered to differentiate between the two. He considered his simply furnished bachelor apartment a necessity—a place to sleep, dress, and occasionally watch TV. He ate the majority of his meals at the nearby Luby's cafeteria and didn't even own a set of pots and pans. His work was all-consuming. He traveled all over the state and spent long hours on the road, recruiting families, educating the public, and learning about new regulations—tasks that were necessary and neverending. He was extremely proud to be counted among the handful of black men in the nation who owned a private adoption agency.

An adoptee himself, Evan knew that bonds of love and kinship could develop between a parent and child for life even without a blood relationship. He was told at a young age that he had been adopted but had never attempted to find out who his birth parents were. Evan saw no need to dig into the part of his life that was behind him, thinking his adoptive parents were, perhaps, better than his natural parents might have been. They were loving, supportive, and fair. And he still consulted his dad whenever he had a problem that seemed impossible to solve.

While he was growing up in the midsize city of Burlington,

North Carolina, his adoptive parents had helped him plan for his future. Evan's six-foot-two height, coupled with a natural sense of balance and dexterity, had turned him into a most valued player on the high school basketball team. His strong, square jaw, deep brown complexion, and easygoing temperament had also made him the object of affection for many of his female classmates. As a young man, he had thrived on such attention and loved being in the spotlight. During his high school years, he had dreamed of becoming a professional basketball player, hoping to live in the flashy world of idolized athletes and have all the women he wanted. But a serious knee injury in his senior year dashed those plans, putting a career as a professional athlete beyond his reach.

Evan's father, a level-headed elementary school principal who had guided Evan toward a career in education, encouraged him to become a coach. Taking his father's advice, Evan entered college to pursue a degree in education. While there, he had volunteered to work as a baseball referee for a Special Olympics competition for handicapped children living in foster care. He had been impressed by the positive attitudes of the kids and their ability to excel in competitive sports despite their physical disadvantages. Soon after, he decided to dedicate himself to social services instead of education. With a masters in social services, he eventually entered the field of adoption, focusing on children with special needs.

Beginning as a special-needs casework supervisor for the North Carolina Department of Health and Human Services, he developed a reputation as a caring, fair-minded supervisor dedicated to his job. While working there, he met Linda Felton, the woman he eventually would marry, but divorce ten years later. Now Evan's biggest regret was that his marriage had not worked out and that his ex-wife had decided to leave North Carolina, taking his then two-year-old daughter, Lora, with her to California.

As Evan headed back to Stallings, he thought about the work facing him.

I'll go into the office tomorrow and get started on the phone calls, he thought. He had found that Saturdays were very good days to take care of phone calls, as many people were at home and less distracted than during the week. He glanced at his speedometer when a highway patrol car zoomed past, then let out a sigh of relief. He had a tendency to speed, especially when he was out on the highway and preoccupied in thought, as he was today.

At the beginning of the year he and his staff had set a goal of placing every one of the twenty-seven children who were pending adoption with Sheltering Hearts. So far six had been adopted into permanent homes, and he was certain that due to his extensive recruitment efforts he was making progress. The in-depth screenings and investigations he conducted, coupled with the counseling sessions he personally sat in on with each prospective adoptive parent, gave his placements a better chance of surviving.

His thoughts drifted to the Vicky Jordan case, his next priority. So far everything looked good. The case was moving along very smoothly, and he was extremely pleased with the background report his caseworker had given him on Mr. and Mrs. Roper. There could not be a better match. Vicky was a very lucky little girl.

Uneasy with the dark clouds that were hanging low in the sky, Evan checked his rearview mirror, then sped up, hoping he could beat the rain and make good time. He wanted to get in a few hours' work on Vicky Jordan's case in preparation for his Monday-evening meeting with the girl's aunt. Her cancellation on Wednesday had disappointed him, and he hoped she was not going to back off again. According to Vicky's case file, Kira Forester had not seen her niece for four years, and he wondered if her sudden interest in Vicky was genuine, or fueled by curiosity.

Blood relatives can cause more problems than progress, he mused, flipping his turn signal to make a right turn. He crossed the intersection and headed onto the exit ramp toward Stallings. *When a long-absent relative shows up and starts poking into things, they can sabotage a perfectly good adoption.* Well, he'd find out soon enough what Kira Forester wanted. The woman couldn't possibly care very much about her deceased sister's child or she would have gotten involved before now.

The crowd at the Power Plus Gym on Independence Boulevard was sparse, just as Kira had expected it to be on a Saturday night at seven o'clock. Other people might be doing more exciting things than lifting weights, cycling, and running the track, but Kira wasn't, and it suited her just fine. Resuming her workout routine after nearly a three-month absence was absolutely necessary, even if it meant starting on a Saturday night. With piles of paperwork on her desk at work and the stress of keeping up with her regular assignments, she was putting in some very long days and late evenings since returning to BPR. The grueling schedule left little time to squeeze in a trip to the gym.

Kira nodded to an elderly man who was slowly and cautiously moving along the indoor track, then sidestepped two eager jocks who were hurrying toward the free-weight room. She strode to the row of stationary bicycles at the front of the gym, and after tossing her towel onto the seat of her usual bike, sat down next to a plump sister with a red scarf tied around her head who was huffing and puffing as she sweated down the minutes.

"Hey," the girl greeted Kira with a smile, wiping perspiration from her forehead with a red towel that matched her red-print bandana.

"Hey," Kira replied, getting settled on her bike, recognizing the other as a regular.

"Decided to skip the pizza with double cheese and get my butt over here tonight," the girl said with a laugh as she pumped her thick legs up and down.

"I know what you mean." Kira chuckled, offering a knowing grin before glancing around the room at a variety of weight machines neatly arranged along two walls. Then she mentally chastised herself for looking for Brandon.

Of course he wouldn't be here, she thought, having learned from experience that Saturday nights meant party time to Brandon, who was the ultimate party boy. Impulsive, unpredictable, and intriguing, he had a great body, a seductive smile, and flirtatious manner that Kira had found irresistible. But he had been young—four years younger than Kira—with a little too much of that bad-boy personality for her liking.

The night before she had been scheduled to leave for Africa, after six months of dating Brandon, she had broken off with him, worn down by his hectic, disorganized lifestyle and his constant need to be in touch with his mind-boggling number of friends.

Brandon Melzona had entered her life when she hired him to be her personal trainer to help her get in shape after neglecting her body too long. He had been the perfect gentleman during her initial interview with him, but as soon as the contract was signed he had begun to come on to her. During their first workout session he made his move, touching her suggestively on her neck. As the sessions progressed, so did his flattery until he had eased himself deeply into her emotions. While spotting her on the free weights and tracking her time on the Lifecycle he had been lighthearted and joking, fun to be around. Kira quickly fell under his spell, seduced by his smoothly delivered lines.

They began to go out on dates, and that was when the party-animal side of Brandon Melzona began to emerge, and though Kira was disappointed to discover how shallow and self-absorbed he was, it was difficult to shut him completely out of her life. She did have feelings for him, though deep down she knew she would be better off if she found a way to end the relationship.

When Brandon was not working at the gym, he had his cell phone pressed to his ear, busy arranging some party or tracking someone down. He loved to go out and be seen, but when they did stay in, as Kira sometimes preferred, all he wanted to do was either watch sports programs on ESPN or music videos on VH1. Kira had limited interest in both.

Kira knew she did not want Brandon as a permanent fixture in her life, and the assignment in Africa had been the perfect excuse to extricate herself from the relationship and move on, though she had to admit that she was going to miss the attention, the flattery, and the awesome sex they had shared in their brief, intense affair.

Now Kira took a deep breath, pulled back her shoulders, and prepared to get mentally focused on her workout, deliberately setting the program intensity on her bike at one level higher than usual. She began to pedal fast, pumping her feet up and down, stretching out her legs as she concentrated on her breathing. Pushing deeper into the ride, she found her rhythm and began working with the music playing in the background. The resistance against her legs and the burning sensation that began to creep into her calves stripped away the sense of sluggishness that had been with her all week. It felt great to submerge herself in mindless physical activity in an environment where no one bothered her and she could be in control.

CNN was playing on the television suspended above the row of bikes. Kira tried to follow the fast-moving captions streaming along the bottom of the screen but soon gave up and simply stared at the anchorwoman's lips, letting her thoughts drift as she pedaled.

An emptiness tinged with resentment had been nagging at Kira for days, and she knew it had to do with her job. Sharon had called it right on Kira's first day back: nothing at BPR was the same as it had been before she left. The atmosphere in the newsroom was tense, fueled by constant grumbling from employees who felt overworked, underpaid, and underappreciated. The undercurrent of dissatisfaction was getting to Kira, too, and she had never felt this overwhelmed and disorganized in her life. When she left the office yesterday evening, her desk had been covered with unreturned telephone messages, incomplete stories, interrupted research—a rarity for her. And she was uneasy with the fact that she had not set up several key interviews for next week and still had not completed the Internet search for statistics on the education piece Davison had dumped on her on Tuesday. But she had completed her regular column, "Business Week Watch," on time, even though Davison had brutally edited it before giving his okay.

Her work on the story for *World Societies Today* had stalled because Kira's ten- and twelve-hour days at BPR left her too exhausted to even think about working on it after she got home. Julie had not yet called to see how things were going, but Kira knew she'd hear from her editor very soon.

Panic was beginning to creep in—what Kira needed was support, not criticism, from her boss. Bruce was a man who dominated conversations and micromanaged his staff, treating them like amateurs instead of the experienced professionals they were. The sense of pride she had felt in being associated with the *Business & Professional Recorder* was fading fast, but, unlike Sharon, Kira did not want to quit. Not yet. She was going to stick it out until Henderson called and offered her a job, or until July, when *World* was scheduled to run her piece. Hopefully, the credibility she would garner from having an article published in that prestigious international publication would greatly increase her value on the job market.

CHAPTER 6

It was nine-fifteen when Kira stepped out of the shower. Pulling a fluffy white towel from the bar above the tub, she dried off, then slipped into her comfy peach-colored terry-cloth sweat suit. She cleared a film of steam from the bathroom mirror and examined her still-flushed face, thinking that she looked one hundred percent better than when she had entered the gym that evening. The exacting workout had been precisely what she'd needed to reenergize, refocus, and get rid of that edgy exhaustion that had been pulling her down all week. Now she felt pumped up, rejuvenated, and ready to tackle the folders of photos and papers and research waiting for her on her rolltop desk.

Kira went into the kitchen, pulled out the filter basket on her coffeemaker, dumped in a scoop of coffee, and filled the pot with water, preparing for a long night of writing. She hoped to complete a decent chunk of her article for *World*. After turning on the coffeemaker, she grabbed an overripe banana from the bowl of fruit on the counter, pulled back the peel, and was about to take a bite when the telephone rang. Kira glanced at the clock, her thoughts immediately going to Brandon, who had loved to call her on the spur of the moment and expect her to jump into some clothes and meet him at the club where he was partying away his Saturday night.

No more, she told herself, placing the uneaten banana on the counter. She gave her hair a final rubbing with the towel, then tossed it over the back of the chair and picked up the phone, deliberately adopting a breathless voice to sound as if she had been caught in the middle of doing something important.

"Hello?"

"Kira Forester, please."

Frowning, Kira hesitated, thinking it must be a telemarketer intruding on her Saturday evening. "Who's calling?" she wanted to know before going any further. Clearly this was not Brandon.

"Evan Conley of Sheltering Hearts."

"Oh," Kira replied, relaxing as she eased onto a barstool at her green marble counter. "Yes, Mr. Conley, this is Kira Forester."

"Good. I hope I didn't call at a bad time?"

"No, not at all. What can I do for you?"

"I wanted to confirm our six-thirty appointment on Monday evening."

"Certainly. I'll be there," Kira replied, thinking it odd that Mr. Conley would make such a routine business call on a Saturday night. "I'm looking forward to talking with you about my niece."

"Fine," Evan said. "I hesitated to call tonight, but I'm at the office now, and I've been reviewing your niece's case. Just to be sure everything is in order. The home study on the prospective adopting couple is underway, and the case is moving along. However, I would certainly like to visit with you before the adoption petition is placed before the judge."

"Can you tell me more about the process?" Kira asked, thinking things were moving much faster than she had expected.

"Certainly. When you come in, I'll be happy to explain everything in detail. Family court judges like to have a complete picture of the case, including information about blood relatives who might be supportive of the adoption."

"I see," Kira murmured, considering the implications of his comment. "So your visit with me becomes a part of Vicky's case file, I assume?"

"Yes indeed," Evan said. "You are in favor of the adoption, aren't you?"

Kira's reply came without hesitation. "Oh yes. I want Vicky to have a permanent home, and I'd love to know more about the family who is adopting her."

"Of course. Your interest in your niece's future could play a vital part in how well she adjusts to her new family. The court will be pleased to know that you are in the picture."

The importance of Evan's words settled over Kira, increasing her curiosity about the process. "Will I have to appear in court? Speak to the judge?" she asked.

"Well," Evan went on, "it depends. She may want to interview you—to get an understanding of how you may be able to help Vicky adapt to her adoptive parents. I think it's always good when all parties involved are willing to cooperate to make the placement work."

"Fine," Kira replied. "Let me know what I need to do. All I want is for Vicky to be happy."

"And so do I," Evan replied. "That's the mission of Sheltering Hearts. I'll see you on Monday, then. Six-thirty."

"Right," Kira said, hanging up the phone.

Sitting quietly, she could not help but let her thoughts turn back to the circumstances surrounding her niece's entry into the foster-care system four years ago. The memories were disturbing.

After high school graduation, Kira had left Wilmington to attend Wake Forest University in Winston-Salem, leaving her younger sister, Miranda, behind in Wilmington. During Kira's senior year, both of her parents died unexpectedly of cancer within two months of each other. The loss was devastating for both Kira and Miranda, but the two sisters grieved in very different ways. Kira returned to school and buried herself in studying for her exams, knowing her parents would have wanted her to finish her education. Miranda turned to alcohol and the arms of strange men to chase away her blues, spending much of her time in seedy motels and roadhouses along the seashore, vocally resentful of Kira for going on about the business of living by getting her education and moving on. When Kira graduated from college, Miranda didn't even bother to attend the ceremony, and after that, the sisters drifted apart.

Kira had headed to Charlotte to begin her career as a journalist while Miranda worked as little as possible and partied as much as she could, dancing and drinking her life away.

When Kira learned that her sister was unwed and pregnant, she had begged Miranda to come to Charlotte to live with her. But Miranda would have no part of Kira and was determined to raise her child alone. Kira backed off, stayed out of her sister's business, and decided that there was little she could do to make Miranda change her reckless ways.

Now Kira could still hear the voice on the phone informing her that her sister was dead. A social worker with Children's Services of North Carolina had called Kira in Charlotte to tell her in a brief, official conversation that Miranda Forester had died of alcohol poisoning and that her two-year-old daughter was in protective custody. Did Kira know where the child's father was? Sadly, Kira had not been able to give the social worker much information because she had never met Andrew Jordan, the man her sister had been living with during the time Vicky was conceived. All Kira knew about Andrew was that he had been a musician who traveled with a band that played gigs in small nightclubs and roadhouses along the Atlantic coast. But Kira did have a photo of Andrew, which Miranda had sent to her, and from that she was able to describe him to the social worker: Andrew Jordan was tall and slender with a light tan complexion, an intense, smoldering expression, and a wild mane of dark brown hair that touched his shoulders. In the photo he was smoking a cigarette and holding a can of beer, proudly showing off the guitar-shaped tattoo that covered the better part of his right forearm. That was all she had been able to tell the woman, who had asked Kira if she were willing to come to Wilmington to take responsibility for her sister's two-year-old child.

Kira caught a plane the next day, flew to Wilmington, and arranged for Miranda to be buried next to her parents in Wilmington's Rosewood Cemetery. Then she went to visit Vicky at the foster home where Children's Services had placed her, and been pleasantly surprised. Kira had expected to find a miserable, devastated child who would race into her arms, crying for her mother, desperately needing comfort. Instead she found a happily smiling toddler who was busy playing with her foster siblings and a foster mother who was warm, attentive, and had obviously already formed a loving bond with her newest charge.

Kira had immediately sensed that Vicky was content, and as she watched the child, who had inherited Miranda's beautiful brown eyes and her father's complexion, she held back from interfering. Perhaps Vicky was happier with this family than she had been while living in a trailer park with her alcoholic mother. Perhaps the child needed to be around other children, have playmates her own age. Perhaps this was the stable situation Vicky needed—with a full-time mother figure who could give her the attention Miranda never had.

After consulting with the caseworker in charge of Vicky's case, as well as the foster mother, Alvia Elderton, Kira decided to back off, at least temporarily, and leave Vicky where she was. Why yank the child out of what seemed to be a positive, beneficial situation and create more chaos and trauma in her young life? Besides, Kira had admitted, she was not prepared to accept full responsibility for a toddler. Not at that time; maybe later. So she had hugged Vicky hard, kissed her fat little cheeks, and left Wilmington, crying all the way back to Charlotte. Sadly, she never made another trip back to visit Vicky, and the next four years quickly slipped past.

Now Kira fought back tears as she got up and went into her bedroom, where she opened her closet door and reached up to the top shelf to retrieve an oversized brown envelope that contained the only items she had managed to salvage from Miranda's trailer. It still infuriated Kira to think about how savagely vandalized her sister's humble home had been by the time she arrived to pack her belongings. Kira treasured the few mementos that the vandals had left behind.

She emptied the contents of the envelope onto her blue and white patchwork quilt, then sat down and picked up the photo of Andrew. She studied it closely before setting it aside. Next she examined a Polaroid snapshot of Miranda sitting on the sofa in her trailer, holding her newborn daughter, Vicky.

She looks frightened and lonely, Kira thought, realizing that her sister had most likely gone through labor and delivery alone, with no one nearby to reassure her, to tell her that they loved her, or cared what happened to her or the baby.

"Oh, Miranda," Kira whispered. "Why did you shut me out?"

Next, Kira picked up a small, square black-and-white photo of Miranda and Kira standing waist-deep in the surf at Wilmington Beach, taken when they had been eight and ten years old, respectively. Kira traced her index finger over the photo, studying Miranda's childish image, trying to understand when and how Miranda's life had taken such a self-destructive turn. They had been happy that day at the beach, tumbling in the surf, burying each other in the sand, chasing the waves that crashed against the shore while their parents had watched from their blanket in the shade. Memories of that happy time flooded back in a vivid rush, bringing tears to Kira's eyes, filling her soul with regret.

Why hadn't she pressed Miranda harder to get help before her world spun out of control? Why hadn't she insisted that Miranda come to Charlotte to live with her until the child was born? What more could Kira have done to save her only sister?

Setting the photos aside, she picked up a pair of pearl drop earrings set in real gold and a Timex watch with a badly scratched crystal. The watch no longer kept time, and the band had been twisted in two places, making it useless, but the pearl-and-gold earrings were exquisite. Kira went to her dresser mirror and slipped the large pearls into her ears, then turned her head from side to side and let the earrings swing back and forth. Their rich luster caught the light from her bedside lamp, making Kira wonder how Miranda had acquired such valuable jewels. Had Andrew Jordan given them to her? Had she bought them for herself, simply because they were pretty? Or had she won them in one of her legendary week-long poker games that she used to brag about to Kira? For whatever reason, the vandals had overlooked the stunning jewels, and Kira was grateful that she had been able to save something of value to pass on to Miranda's daughter one day.

It's too late to save Miranda, Kira thought, *but I will do everything in my power to see that Vicky has a happier life, and I will not let her down.*

CHAPTER 7

The lobby of the three-story brown brick building that housed Sheltering Hearts' offices was eerily dim and quiet—so quiet that Kira could hear the cars and trucks outside barreling down nearby I-485 despite the whir of an air-conditioning unit that was struggling to improve the stuffy atmosphere. She glanced around, surprised at the neglected interior: slats in several of the miniblinds covering the bank of windows at the front of the lobby were missing, the dark gray tiled floor looked as if it could use a good polishing, and the obviously neglected potted ferns and palms placed throughout the area were screaming for attention. What kind of an agency was Sheltering Hearts? she wondered uneasily, pulling off her lightweight jacket, which she tossed over one arm. Opening her purse, she removed the letter she had received from Children's Services, checked the address again, then went to the building directory and scanned the short list of occupants. Sheltering Hearts was on the second floor.

Kira started toward the elevator, then changed her mind and headed to the staircase at the far side of the lobby; one flight of stairs would be easy enough to climb. On her way up, she felt the wooden stair railing shake when she grasped it, and her footsteps on the concrete steps echoed throughout the building.

Real low-rent operation, she thought, appraising the deserted-looking space. There were no people in the corridors, no voices coming from behind closed doors, no clacking of copy machines or telephones ringing. Disturbed, Kira wondered if this adoption agency was legitimate and if Evan Conley might be involved in some kind of child-for-sale ring, and she chastised herself for not taking the time to check him and his agency out. As a reporter, she seldom entered any interview situation without first doing her homework so she could be as informed as possible and able to ask the right questions. What in the world had she been thinking of, treating this important situation in such a cavalier manner?

Arriving on the second floor, she scanned the dark hallway until she found a door with the name SHELTERING HEARTS imprinted on a nameplate in bold block letters. Giving her slim gray skirt a tug, she took a deep breath, turned the doorknob, and stepped inside.

The change in atmosphere was startling. The reception area was tastefully decorated in shades of blue and green with framed color photographs of children of all ages and ethnicity arranged attractively on the walls. Fresh flowers filled a round white pottery vase on the reception desk, and trailing ivy spilled off a table near the watercooler. Two sage green faux-suede love seats faced each other over a low glass coffee table that held a bowl of peppermints and an assortment of magazines. Immediately, Kira's concerns faded, and her faith in her instinct to trust Mr. Conley was restored.

The chair behind the reception desk was empty. Kira waited for a few minutes, expecting the secretary to show up. When no one arrived, she ventured into the hallway and peeked into the nearest office. It was empty. Deciding not to go deeper into the suite, she returned to the reception area, sat down on the love seat facing the hallway, and began idly leafing through a well-read issue of *Parenting Today*.

Minutes passed. No one arrived, and Kira, who hated waiting, began to silently fume. She had worked like crazy all day in order to clear her desk and get out of the office by six, and still had to return for a few more hours this evening after her meeting with Mr. Conley.

If he wants to speak to me, he'd better show up pretty darn soon, she thought, tossing the magazine back on the table, tempted to get up and leave.

A full seven more minutes passed before she heard footsteps coming from the rear of the suite, then a man holding a pair of gold-rimmed glasses and a folder in one hand appeared in the doorway. She stood quickly, poised to convey her displeasure at having been left waiting.

"Can I help you?" the man asked.

"Yes, I have a six-thirty appointment with Mr. Evan Conley," she told him, quickly sizing up the man she assumed to be a case-worker.

He was African American, tall, and slim, yet the width of his shoulders gave him the appearance of a man who was solid and muscular. His dark blue suit fit him perfectly, complemented by a white shirt and a blue and red tie. He had neatly trimmed dark hair, a thin moustache, and brown eyes that bored intensely at her from beneath thick, arched brows. The resolute set to his square jaw sent a message of self-confidence, but there was a hint of indecision on his lips that softened his otherwise stern impression.

The man put on the glasses he had been holding, gave Kira a closer look, then took them off again. "Oh? You're Miss Forester?"

"Yes," Kira replied, wondering why he sounded so surprised. "I'm here to discuss Vicky Jordan, my niece."

"Yes, yes. I'm Evan Conley. Glad to meet you." He grinned warmly as he extended his hand, which Kira grasped and shook.

"Sorry to keep you waiting," he said. "Please forgive me and come on back to my office."

"Sure," Kira replied, exhaling slowly as she moved beside Evan. He was certainly a surprise, she thought, following him down the corridor. As she moved up beside him, she shifted her eyes to get a peek at his left hand, then raised her eyebrows when she saw that he was not wearing a ring.

"Been waiting long?" Evan asked.

"No, not really," Kira heard herself say, chastising herself for having stereotyped Conley. She had expected Evan Conley to be a middle-aged, average-looking white man in a polyester suit with the beginnings of a spare tire at his waistline, not this intriguing brother with a strong resemblance to Morris Chestnut.

"My receptionist left early today," Evan explained. "Had to take her son to the orthodontist, leaving me to cover the front. Got caught up on the phone," he said, tapping the folder in his hand. "A pretty complicated placement."

"I understand," Kira replied, preceding him into his office when he stepped back to let her enter first.

Evan circled to his desk while Kira sat down and appreciatively scanned the muted seascape prints and nautical paintings on the pale blue walls. Directly behind his sleek teakwood desk were several framed university degrees, certificates, and awards that Kira could not read but felt certain were legitimate. An impressive model of an eighteenth-century sailing ship mounted on a stainless-steel stand sat on a low credenza beneath the draped windows. The office exuded a sense of class and respectability that put her mind at ease and banished her earlier thoughts about Sheltering Hearts' credibility.

Kira crossed her legs, keenly aware of Evan's quick glance at them, folded her hands in her lap, and tilted her body slightly forward, staring straight into Evan Conley's dark brown eyes. His interest was quite obvious, and she didn't mind it. He was attractive in a subtly self-assured way that Kira found intriguing.

Evan made a small coughing sound, gave her a smile of welcome that showcased his white, even teeth, and reached for a red folder that was on top of a short stack of books. He opened the file and took out a few pages, gave them a quick once-over, then looked up and refocused on Kira. "I'm very glad you came in, and I'm certain the Ropers will be delighted to learn of your interest in Vicky."

"I hope so," Kira said.

"I encourage adoptive parents and supportive blood relatives to do everything possible to create a nurturing environment for the children, who benefit greatly from being around adults who they know care about them. Stabilizes the family unit." Pausing, he touched his pen to his lips. "I understand you are Vicky Jordan's mother's sister, correct?"

"Yes. Her only sister."

"No other relatives alive?"

"No, our parents died years ago, right before I finished school."

Evan nodded, then stated, as if the answer was obvious, "No idea where Vicky's father is."

"None. And I am pretty sure Miranda didn't know where he was when Vicky was born, either."

"The appropriate steps have been taken by the court to terminate Andrew Jordan's parental rights, so it seems that you are the only blood tie to Vicky's natural family." He nodded at the sheet of paper in his hand. "I've read this report several times, Miss Forester, and I'm familiar with Vicky's background. Have you ever had any contact or involvement with the child's natural father?"

"None," Kira stated, an edge of exasperation in her reply. "I never met him. Miranda told me about him . . . sent me a photo. He was a musician from someplace on the East Coast, I believe. But as far as I know, he ducked out of the picture and disappeared long before Vicky was born. I have to admit that I was surprised to learn that Miranda put the man's name on Vicky's birth certificate." Kira shrugged, at a loss to explain.

"It happens," said Evan. "Another question," he continued.

"Sure."

"It's about the interview that the Children's Services caseworker in Wilmington conducted with you shortly after Miranda Forester's death. I find it interesting that other than this interview there is no mention of you in Vicky Jordan's file."

Tensing, Kira uncrossed her legs and leaned back from Evan's desk, feeling the amicable mood between them suddenly shift. "That's correct," she admitted. "I have not been in touch with my niece or the custodial authorities since my sister died."

"Why not?" he asked in a low voice that was urgent, yet tinged with concern. "Weren't you curious about how your niece was doing with her foster family?"

Irritated at being put on the spot, Kira let the question linger between them for a few seconds, determined not to speak too quickly and come off as too self-protective or resentful. She had expected him to ask about her whereabouts for the past four years, but the answer was not easy for her to put into words.

Determined to be as forthright and honest as possible, she launched into the background of her estrangement from her sister, telling Evan of her numerous attempts to help Miranda, both during her pregnancy and after Vicky was born. Speaking in a calm, controlled voice, Kira went on to present a clear picture of the strained dynamics between her and her sister and justify her absence from Miranda's life.

"I don't know. Maybe if I had lived closer, I could have changed the eventual outcome. I wish I had been able to save Miranda from herself, but I wasn't. The next thing I knew, she was dead," Kira concluded.

"But your niece?" Evan prompted. "Did you ever think that Vicky might have needed for you to intervene?"

The question was one that had flickered through Kira's mind many times, leaving her frustrated and sad. "I did the best that I could at the time. The authorities promised to keep Miranda's case file open and check on her regularly. Whether they did or not, I don't know. But time passed, Mr. Conley," she added, a little too sharply. "I had a life of my own to live, a career that was demanding, and I was trying to establish myself in Charlotte. You can't believe that I was so insensitive as to—"

"Miss Forester," Evan interrupted, holding her gaze with steady, level perception. "The last thing I want is to make you uncomfortable. I'm simply trying to get a better feel for the family dynamics at the time Vicky was placed in foster care."

The anxiety building inside Kira began to ease as she took in Evan's expression. He appeared to be genuinely concerned, even sorry for upsetting her, and although he hadn't moved, Kira felt as if he were reaching out to touch her on the shoulder in a gesture of empathy.

"Please relax," Evan told her. "I'm not judging you, but it is important to establish what kind of relationship you've had with your niece. Vicky has been placed with a wonderful couple who wants to adopt her, and I hope you will be able to support them. As the custodial party, Sheltering Hearts is entrusted with ensuring Vicky's welfare, so I must feel confident that her introduction to you will be beneficial."

"Certainly," Kira acknowledged, allowing her tensed shoulders to relax. "The first time I visited Vicky at the home of her foster family, I knew right away that she was safe and in a place filled with love. At that moment, I was worried that my intervention might create more trauma and do more harm than good if I removed her from an environment that was stable and safe. She seemed, perhaps for the first time in her young life, happy. So I decided to back off. Vicky didn't know me. She was only two years old. I was a complete stranger to her. I could tell that she was content with her new foster mother and siblings. She was in Wilmington, I was in Charlotte, five hundred miles away. I left the situation alone."

"Understandable," Evan agreed, looking at Kira with new respect. "I think you did what any young woman in a similar situation might have done at the time. You are a journalist, you said?"

"Yes, I work for the *Business & Professional Recorder*. I travel a lot, stay pretty busy, and right now I have my sights set on a job with our parent company in New York. Not much time to do anything but work."

"I see," Evan responded; then, in a smooth rush of words, "Tell me a little more about yourself, Miss Forester. Do you mind?"

"Not at all," Kira said, clearing her throat, trying to calculate what he might want to know and how much she ought to reveal. It was clear from the way he was studying her that his interest went beyond the case-file data on his desk.

"I was born and grew up in Wilmington, left there to go to college in Winston-Salem on a scholarship at Wake Forest, where I got my undergraduate degree in journalism. Then I moved to Charlotte to work as a researcher for the *Observer*. A few months later, I joined the *Business & Professional Recorder*, where I have been ever since. I write a column called 'Business Week Watch'—deals with statewide business news. Maybe you've read it?"

"'Yes, in fact I think I have," Evan replied in an appreciative tone.

"I have my own apartment. I'm healthy, and single," she quickly slipped in, noticing the slight lift of one of Evan's eyebrows when she said those last two words. "And I am an extremely inquisitive and hardworking person." She laughed, shrugging. "Might say I lead a pretty ordinary life."

"Traveling to places like Africa doesn't sound very ordinary to me," Evan countered playfully. "You told me when I called that you had just returned? How often do you go out of the country?"

Kira chuckled, shaking her head. "Not often at all. That was a special situation," she conceded. "Not that I wouldn't jump at the chance to do it again. If I get on with our parent company in New York, I might travel on a more regular basis."

"So, do you want to leave Charlotte?" Evan clarified, zeroing in on her comment.

"If the right opportunity comes along, yes. I think most journalists would move to . . . wherever, if it meant advancing their careers. Working for *World Societies Today* would be a major coup. And I might make it, as a result of this recent assignment in Africa."

"I see," Evan replied, allowing his voice to trail off. He rubbed his thumb and index finger together, pondering her response. "You seem to be the kind of person who goes after what she wants, so I'm sure you'll get to New York, if you want to go there badly enough."

"That's exactly my attitude, too," Kira agreed, beginning to feel less like the target of an inquisition. She had been so worried about how the meeting would go, but Evan Conley had put her at ease.

He was really a very nice guy. It had been a long time since she had met a brother who was as polite, professional, and as easy to talk to as he was.

Evan put Kira's interview with CPS back into Vicky's folder, closed it, and replaced it on top of the stack on his desk. Folding his hands together, he settled back. "Now that Vicky will be living in Monroeville, you will be much closer to her, won't you?"

"Exactly. Less than an hour away."

"Is this new physical proximity your motivation to meet your niece?" Evan asked, sounding much more formal and official than he had a moment ago.

Kira opened her mouth to answer, then paused, hoping her favorable impression of Evan Conley had been on the mark and he'd had not been softening her up for an attack. "Not at all," Kira countered firmly.

"Suppose you get the job in New York. Or the couple that adopts Vicky decides to move after you have become a part of their extended family. What would you do? Would you disappear from Vicky's life again?"

Though aware of the point he was trying to drive home, Kira's nostrils flared as she gave him a hard look, then shook her head. "Never. No matter where she goes or where I live, I plan to stay in touch. Her being closer is convenient, now, but if I reconnect with my niece, it will not be a temporary relationship, I assure you."

"That's good." Evan closed his fingers into fists, then pressed them together on his desk, pondering her response. "Miss Forester, few things in life are permanent, except family. And as you have experienced, even families quickly change . . . for the better or for the worse. They can increase in size when people marry and have children or disintegrate into shambles through death or divorce. The mission of Sheltering Hearts is to place our children in permanent homes and do everything possible to provide the stability they deserve. Change is frightening for children, even under the best of circumstances, so you need to be certain that you are going to remain in the picture if you enter Vicky's life. Do you understand?"

His tone was stern, leaving the silence that followed ringing with implication. Suddenly the room was smothering hot, and Kira could feel the weight of the responsibility to which he had alluded pressing down on her. But she knew Evan Conley was right. She had never made a serious commitment to Vicky in the past, and now she wanted to make up for her neglect. Vicky had been a toddler when Miranda died, a vulnerable child in need of a mother, and that overwhelming sense of urgency had terrified Kira.

"Yes, I understand," she told Evan. "Once I believed that my presence or absence in Vicky's life would not make much difference. But now I know better. I understand, completely, what you mean."

"Fine," Evan murmured, tilting back his chair. His chin lifted. "If you had the ability to create the perfect scenario of your relationship with your niece, what would it look like?"

His question lightened the mood, making Kira feel less nervous. She nodded, thought for a moment, then launched into a description.

"I'd like to tell Vicky about her mother, the good things about Miranda, not the perfect sister, but a beautiful young woman with perhaps too much lust for life. I'd tell Vicky about her grandparents, show her family photos, tell her stories, answer questions . . . try to be a good aunt. She ought to know that her mother's sister is alive, cares about her, and will be there for her. I'd like Mr. and Mrs. Roper to get to know me, include me in Vicky's life, and make me a part of their family. You see, I have no blood relatives except Vicky, and it would be nice if the Ropers felt comfortable inviting me to Vicky's birthday parties, holiday gatherings . . . allow me to take her shopping, or for a weekend now and then. Things like that. I think experiences like those would be important for her, and for me, as she is growing up."

"Have you ever considered legally adopting Vicky?" Evan bluntly asked.

Kira bit her lip, frowning, aware that circumstances beyond her control had finally forced her to confront the question she had squeezed into a corner of her mind four years ago. As much as she wished she could say "yes," for the sake of sounding honorable and noble, she knew she couldn't.

"No," Kira stated clearly, relieved to verbalize her difficult decision. "I have never considered adopting Vicky or becoming her legal guardian."

Evan eased his tilted his chair back down, leaned over, and leveled his eyes with Kira's. "Why not?"

Placing a hand to the side of her face, she paused, trying to put her reply into the proper words. Over the years, she had alternately wished she had taken Vicky home with her the moment she had learned of Miranda's death, and at other times congratulated herself for not complicating her life by trying to raise a child as a single parent. The issue had been a persistent source of guilt—until now, when the opportunity had come for Kira to establish a genuine relationship with her niece, and that was all she wanted.

"Why not?" Kira repeated. "Because I live in a small apartment, work long hours at the office and at home. I'm single, without any family support, and, to be completely honest, I don't think I would be able to give a six-year-old child the kind of attention she deserves. Not on a day-to-day basis. What Vicky needs is a real family, and I am glad she is going to have one."

"That's an honest answer," Evan replied. "Thank you. That makes things perfectly clear. The prospective adoptive parents for your niece have devoted their love, time, and money to this placement. I expect that the adoption will proceed without a hitch."

"I'm glad," Kira replied, then added, "I'd love to meet the Ropers, and see Vicky, if that is possible."

"I think that can be arranged. I'll call Joe Hickman, the Ropers' attorney, and see what we can do."

"Mr. Conley. This is a good family, isn't it? Vicky will be happy, won't she?"

Evan's features brightened, and he quickly responded, "Couldn't be a better fit."

"Tell me about the Ropers. What are they like?"

Evan compressed his lips, tightening his square jaw. "They are a wonderful, stable couple. Ralph in his early forties. Helen, Mrs. Roper, is in her mid-thirties. Ralph is a successful businessman, well respected in the city of Monroeville. In fact, I understand he recently announced his candidacy for mayor."

"Oh yes, " Kira murmured, recalling a news item in the *Charlotte Observer* that an African American was running for mayor of Monroeville, a history-making situation for the small town of thirteen thousand that lay just beyond the edge of Charlotte's suburban sprawl. Yes, Vicky would have a life filled with advantages and experiences that Kira would not have been able to provide. "And Mrs. Roper?" Kira promoted. "What's she like?"

"She is quiet and soft-spoken, a distinct contrast to her husband, who is expansive and quite the talker, as most politicians are. Helen is more reserved, but very involved with several charities, especially International Relief Now, IRN, a nonprofit that provides assistance to recently arrived refugees. She is a very caring, sensitive woman, I believe."

"Do they have other children?"

"No, Helen can't have children . . . some longstanding medical condition. But she has opened her home on numerous occasions to refugee children in transit for IRN, usually housing them for a few days until their sponsors can make arrangements for transportation to their final destinations. She and her husband contacted Sheltering Hearts when they finally decided to adopt because they wanted an older child, not an infant."

"Is that unusual?" Kira asked.

"No, not at all. Many couples, especially busy, professional ones, opt to skip the late-night feedings and diaper changes that bringing an infant into the home requires. We specialize in placing older children, as well as those with special needs."

"Special needs? Such as?" Kira prompted.

"Handicapped children, siblings, racially mixed, and African-American children."

"I see," Kira murmured. "The ones that are hardest to place."

"Precisely."

The fact that she was dealing with an agency that had taken Vicky's racial heritage into consideration pleased Kira, who firmly believed that growing up with people who looked like you was important. "So what's next?" she asked, glancing at her watch, thinking she ought to cancel her plans to go back to the office. It was already seven-twenty, and traffic on the freeway back into town was going to be horrendous. Maybe she'd just go in early tomorrow morning.

"What's next? Well, I'll call you after I speak to the Ropers' attorney—let you know about meeting with the Ropers and Vicky. I'm sure they'll be pleased to know that Vicky has an aunt who is interested in her future."

"I hope so," Kira replied, gathering her purse, ready to leave. "I'm so glad I came and met with you. This really makes me feel better, knowing that Vicky is in good hands. I'm excited for her. She deserves this, and I promise I'll do all I can to help her adjust."

"That's a good way to look at it, Miss Forester."

Kira extended her hand, expecting Evan Conley to take it, shake it, and bid her good-bye, but instead of doing so, he sat forward, a serious expression bringing his eyebrows very close together. She hesitated, somewhat concerned by this unexpected change in his demeanor.

"Is there something else?" she asked, wondering if he was

thinking about asking her a personal question, like what she was doing for dinner or if she was in a relationship. Either question would have been welcome. Since ending her disastrous affair with Brandon, Kira had not been on a date in months, and her options were definitely open. Evan Conley might be worth getting to know better, she thought, anticipating his request for a less professional meeting.

"Yes. There is something I must tell you before you leave," Evan began, in a softer, more personal voice. He shifted uneasily in his chair, cleared his throat, and blinked. "I hope this doesn't offend you, or make any difference in how you now feel about everything we've discussed here tonight."

"Don't worry," Kira replied, suppressing her impulse to smile. He looked downright nervous, like a little boy about to confess that he was the one who left the bicycle in the driveway. "You won't offend me, I'm sure," she added, pausing at the edge of her seat, her purse strap over her shoulder. She looked expectantly at Evan, anticipating his request to see her again.

"I think you ought to know," he started slowly, then rushed on, "that the Ropers are white."

"What?"

"The couple that is adopting your niece is Caucasian."

"White?" Kira shot back, squinting at Evan in disbelief. "White?" Sinking back on her spine, she stared at him, hoping she hadn't heard him right.

CHAPTER 8

"What are you talking about?" Kira demanded, unable to comprehend what Evan had just said. "Didn't you just say that Roper is running for mayor of Monroeville? I read about him . . . something in the news about that. Isn't he black?"

"You're thinking of his opponent, Frank Thompson, who is African American. Ralph Roper is white, and so is his wife." Evan made a tent with his fingers, then tapped them lightly against the folder on his desk. "And they are an extremely nice couple who love Vicky very much."

"'Hold up," Kira said, dropping her purse on the floor with a thump. She lifted one hand, palm toward Evan as she struggled to regain her composure. "I thought you told me that your agency specializes in placing African-American children."

"We do. But not necessarily with black parents."

"Why didn't you tell me about this earlier?"

"Because the Ropers' race is not what you came here to talk about, and it is not the most important issue."

"Not important? Since when?" Kira could not believe how casually this man was treating what she considered an issue of paramount importance. No way was she going to let him ram this bit of news down her throat. He had some explaining to do.

Evan grimaced, clearly uneasy with Kira's reaction. "I concede that race is a factor that must be seriously considered in a transracial adoption, but it is not *the* most important issue. There are other conditions that could make a longer lasting impact on a child's welfare than the race of the parents. I've been involved in many transracial adoptions, and spent many hours with the Ropers. I've spoken to their caseworker, and I believe that race will not be a negative factor here. Vicky should have a successful adoption."

"But race sure as hell is important," Kira shot back, scooting right up to the edge of Evan's desk, as if preparing for a confrontation. This man had been plying her with platitudes, making her feel so damn comfortable, acting all understanding and sympathetic . . . while buttering her up so he could lay this on her! *Well, not so fast,* she thought, clearing her mind of her wild thoughts of the possibility of a personal relationship with him.

"I want a better explanation than that," she demanded. "Do you really expect me to believe that Vicky would be happy with a white mother and father after having lived her life with a black natural mother, then a black foster mother? One of the reasons I felt comfortable leaving Vicky with Mrs. Elderton after Miranda's death was because the woman reminded me of my mother. Vicky related to her. Mrs. Elderton had the same pretty brown skin that Miranda had. Her short, wavy hair was peppered with gray, and she reminded me of my own grandmother. She looked like my family . . . you know? Vicky seemed to fit with her."

A scowl of frustration came to Evan's features, but he inclined his head in understanding.

Kira kept on talking. "I'm sorry, Mr. Conley. I know you have a very difficult job to do, but in my heart I truly believe that black kids need to be raised by black people."

Now Evan got up, went to stand near the bookshelf behind his desk, and studied the model ship on the stainless-steel stand. He ran a finger along one of the stiff parchment sails, silent for a moment. He glanced back at Kira, unasked questions in his eyes. "I'm very surprised, Miss Forester."

The abrupt way he spoke to Kira made her shrink back into her seat. She clamped her mouth shut, waiting to hear what he had to say for himself, determined not to back down.

"I'm shocked and disappointed. Being an educated, professional person, and a journalist, too . . . I thought you would be more open-minded about this."

"I'm not close-minded," Kira snapped. "I'm shocked!" Kira spat the words, shaken by this unexpected twist in her niece's adoption. "It never crossed my mind that the Ropers were not black. You deliberately withheld that important bit of information until after you had pumped me . . . found out all you wanted to know about me and how I felt about Vicky being adopted. Pretty underhanded, Mr. Conley. You're disappointed? Give me a break!"

"I'm sorry you see it that way, Miss Forester. Sheltering Hearts is a federally assisted placement agency, and as such, we cannot deny the opportunity to any person who wants to be an adoptive parent solely based on their race, color, or national origin. You should know that."

"I do," Kira grudgingly admitted. "And I know that cross-cultural and transracial adoptions happen all the time. Maybe they are successful, too. But this is different. This is personal."

"Yes, it is. And believe me, we do everything possible to place our children in homes with parents of compatible backgrounds, including race, but there are not enough black families willing to adopt black children . . . or enough Hispanic or Asian parents to match everyone up. It's a very delicate and complicated process, Miss Forester. I recruit and screen the best possible candidates, conduct thorough home studies, in-depth evaluations of motive for adoption, including the ability to meet the child's emotional needs. The Ropers' petition for adoption is moving through proper channels, and unless something turns up to make me rethink this placement, Vicky will be their daughter very soon."

"How soon?" Kira asked.

Evan went to his desk and reached again for Vicky's case file. He removed a stapled set of papers and checked several pages. "She's been living with the Ropers since January twenty-eighth; their formal petition has been filed; my consent for the adoption has been approved by the judge—"

"Your consent?" Kira interjected.

"Yes, Sheltering Hearts is the agency legally empowered with custody of Vicky, and as such has the right to place her. Any child who has been in a foster-care situation for at least fifteen months can be made eligible for adoption once all issues related to terminating parental rights are resolved, as they have been in Vicky's case. It looks like the home study is nearly complete, too."

"And what's in the home study?" Kira suddenly wanted to know every single detail about what was going on, as well as what to expect. Maybe the Ropers were a wonderful family, but this news was hard to swallow.

"A home study is an in-depth investigation to determine the appropriateness of the adopting parents, and is required before an adoption can occur. It covers many areas: the personal and family background of the applicants and significant people in their lives, the stability of the marriage, the domestic environment, physical and mental health, education, financial status, employment history. And, of course, criminal-background clearances. When all of that is complete, we know quite a bit about the applicants, and from all indications, the Ropers will have no problems. They are more than qualified to adopt."

"But why a black child? Why Vicky?" Kira demanded.

"As I mentioned earlier, they came to me and specifically asked for information on adopting an older child. Not a black child or a white child. Once they met Vicky, everything clicked, and Mrs. Roper instantly bonded with your niece. So we moved forward."

"Ha," Kira grunted. This news had hit Kira like a sharp slap in the face, and it was not going to be easy to get over the shock. She wasn't stupid. She knew transracial adoptions could succeed, and she wanted to be fair . . . but Evan Conley should have prepared her for this news when he telephoned her at home Saturday night.

"I have to believe that the Ropers are honest, decent people and that they love Vicky enough to adopt her," she told Evan. "I have nothing against them. I don't even know them, but I know I'm uncomfortable with the way you handled this—holding back such crucial information until after you were satisfied that I would support the adoption. Not very honest of you." She slid her palms along the flat surface of his desk, trembling with concern. "Are you sure you can't find a black family willing to adopt Vicky?" Kira pressed. "There must be someone, somewhere. I'd adopt her if I could, but—"

"But you don't want that kind of responsibility," Evan finished, glaring pointedly at Kira.

"I didn't know . . . but now . . ."

Evan lifted a hand to stop her from going on. "It's clear that you are not willing, or interested, in raising a child at this time, Miss Forester, and therefore I would never consider you a suitable candidate to adopt, even if you stepped forward now. Adoption is forever. A huge commitment. Not one I would recommend to anyone who is not absolutely certain they can go the distance."

Kira stood up and angrily attempted to smooth the wrinkles from the front of her skirt, matching Evan's cold, piercing stare with one of her own. "Yes, I did say those things, but that was before I knew what was going on. Maybe I need to rethink my position."

"It's a little late," Evan sarcastically tossed back, clearly irritated. "Adopting a child is not like buying a new car. You can't take it back when it begins to rattle and squeak and get on your nerves. You can't trade it in when you get tired of it. A child is forever. Forever. And from what you have told me this evening, you are not interested in forever, Miss Forester. You say you love your job, but you seem to be looking for a new one. You love Charlotte? Why do you want to move to New York? Do you even know what the word stability means?"

Kira opened her mouth to shout a nasty reply, then pressed her lips into a firm line, jerked on her jacket, and crushed the straps of her purse in a fist. Evan Conley was obviously going to do as he pleased no matter what she said. Inhaling, she struggled to get perspective on the situation. She had to think things through, focus on what was best for Vicky, get her emotions out of the way.

"Yes," she managed tersely, teeth clenched. "I know exactly what stability means, but this is Vicky's life we're talking about, isn't it? Not mine. How dare you use personal information you pumped from me—under less than honest circumstances, I must say—to your advantage? I am as stable as this rock," she snapped, picking up a rock crystal paperweight on Evan's desk, then slamming it down with a hard, loud thump. "I resent your implying otherwise." Pulling back her shoulders, she raked Evan with a frigid glance, then frowned when he calmly stood and offered her his hand.

"You're right. I apologize. I had no right to say those things, and I'm sorry for my outburst. I should have been more up-front with you about the racial aspects of this placement."

Kira wanted to turn her back on him and leave him standing there with his hand in the air but checked the impulse to be rude, realizing that would solve nothing. "Yes, you should have," she threw back, suspiciously eyeing his outstretched hand. Though she was furious with Evan Conley, she also knew that he had done the best he could for Vicky. He had looked out for her best interests and had found the child a permanent home. If Kira had been around, she would have been consulted. Maybe she had no one to blame but herself for this mess.

"I accept your apology," she told Evan, shaking his hand

quickly, then walking to the door. Her spine was stiff, her shoulders drawn back, and though her legs were weak with indignation she forced herself to walk with dignity to the door, where she turned, swallowed dryly, then added, "Thank you for your time, Mr. Conley. I feel a bit overwhelmed. Let me put this news into perspective before I meet the Ropers."

"Good idea," Evan agreed. "Let me know when you're ready."

"Of course," Kira said in a less strained tone. "I'll call you in a day or two."

Evan rubbed the back of his neck as he stood at his office window and gazed down into the parking lot, which was well lit, though empty except for a shiny black PT Cruiser parked next to his well-traveled burgundy Dodge van. When Kira emerged from the building, he focused on her, watching as her slim, shadowy figure hurried toward the black car and got in. She pulled off right away, disappearing down the feeder road that would take her onto I-485 and back to Charlotte. He let out a whoosh of air, wishing the meeting had ended on a better note.

Kira Forester was an attractive, smart young woman who interested him very much. Too bad he couldn't get to know her on a more personal basis, he thought, knowing it was impossible. She was upset with him, as he had expected her to be, but that was too bad. He had to tell her the truth. Evan placed one hand to his lips, thinking. If Kira Forester had approached him in January, immediately after Alvia Elderton's death, expressing a desire to adopt Vicky Jordan, he would have considered her a viable option to the Ropers. He would have worked with Kira to quell her reservations, provided her the support and counseling she would need to be a good parent, done everything possible to help her reconnect with her niece, either as a legal guardian or a single adoptive parent. Evan struggled to place children with family members if at all possible, and often turned to grandparents, cousins, aunts, and uncles as first choices. But Kira Forester had not been around, so he had done what he had to do, and the Ropers desperately wanted the child.

Evan watched new shadows fill in the space where Kira's car had been, saddened by the way the meeting had turned out. He could never have abandoned his niece, or any blood-related child, as she had done. Not willingly, at least, he knew. His stomach tightened with regret as his thoughts swung to his daughter, Lora, who was thousands of miles away. In spite of their separation, he thought about her at least once a day, wishing he could see her, put his arms around her, and reassure her of his unconditional love. But he couldn't, so he made up for his absence with telephone calls, letters, gifts, and the limited visitation granted by the court.

Lora knows who I am, where I am, and that I'll always love her. That's what matters, he assured himself, moving from the window to sit down behind his desk. *Kira Forester may be upset, but she is not going to prevent this adoption from going through. The Ropers are qualified, and Vicky Jordan needs a family more than a relationship with an aunt who is so confused she doesn't even know what she wants.*

Evan checked his Rolodex, then began stabbing the phone keypad as he punched in the direct number to Ralph Roper's attorney's office.

"What I know now changes everything," Kira told Julie over the phone the next evening. "No way am I going to allow Miranda's child to be adopted by a white couple. No way."

"I understand how you feel, Kira, but what options do you have?" Julie asked. "You say you don't want to adopt your niece, and I don't think you should. You have to think about the long-term commitment—your career is really taking off. And if there is not a qualified black family standing by to step in and replace the one Mr. Conley recruited, let it alone. Henderson is seriously thinking of making you an offer. Do you really want to get involved in this adoption mess right now? Might be better to step back and not make waves."

Kira groaned. "I know, I know. Julie . . . this is terrible timing." She paced her kitchen floor as she spoke, frustrated by the tangle of emotions that had been with her since yesterday evening. At work today she had not been able to concentrate, her mind stuck on Vicky 's pending adoption, and every time her phone rang, she had snatched it up, hoping it might be Evan with news that he'd found a black family, that the Ropers had backed out, or that something had turned up in the home study to put the adoption on hold. But by the end of the day she'd realized the futility of such thoughts and decided to focus on what mattered: Vicky's happiness, not the race of her new family.

"What is wrong with me, Julie?" Kira lamented, unable to keep her thoughts from returning to the shock she had felt on learning that the Ropers were not black. "Shouldn't I feel relieved?"

Easing on to the barstool at her counter, she tried to clear her mind of the frustrating situation.

"Yes, you should. So get over it, and focus on finishing the story. Henderson is not going to like it if you miss your deadline. He's very impressed with your work."

"Really?" Kira replied, anxious for all of the details.

"He's over the moon," Julie said. "He's had a week to go over your photographs and the outline for the story, and he's been nodding his head ever since. Whenever your name comes up, he nods. And he didn't discount my not so subtle observation that we need some more color up in here."

Kira laughed. "Girl, you said that to him?"

"Sure did. Hey, he knows I never hold back and I'll tell him the truth. That's one of the reasons he listened to me when I recommended you for the African assignment in the first place. Values my opinion and my good taste."

"Girl, you need to quit," Kira chuckled, admiring her friend's ability to zero in on exactly what she wanted to say, make her point, and not worry about what anyone thought. For as long as Kira had known Julie, she'd never known her to bite her tongue when it came to telling it like it was.

"However," Julie continued, "Henderson most likely will not make a firm offer until after your piece runs in July and he gets feedback on it. And when he does call, don't act too anxious to come on board. Give him just enough positive reaction to let him know you will seriously consider his offer, then stall long enough to make him come up with some details on moving expenses, relocation per diem, and all the perks you can get. Okay?"

"No problem . . . if the conversation ever happens."

"Hey," Julie broke in. "What's with this negative attitude? It's coming. Trust me. You deserve it, too."

Sliding a finger over the edge of her counter, Kira struggled to summon up a positive comeback. "Julie, your assessment of the situation is right on—exactly what I need to help me with all this confusion. This adoption thing is heavy. Not what I want to deal with right now."

Julie's groan clearly expressed her desire for Kira to put this situation behind her, or at least into perspective. "Fine. It's not what you expected. But at the same time, it might be exactly right—for both you and Vicky," she said. "Kira, I've known you a long time, and though I didn't know Miranda, from what you have told me Miranda seemed like a real firecracker. Probably never should have had a child in the first place. But she did, and you need to remember that *her* child is not automatically *your* responsibility. This may not be what you want to hear, but I think you made the right decision leaving Vicky in foster care in Wilmington so you could get on with your life. Maybe you need to keep your distance now, too. Let this situation work its way out like it's supposed to. Let the professionals take care of it. This man Evan Conley, does he act like he knows what he's doing? Do you trust him?"

"Yes," Kira admitted.

"All right. Let him handle it. After all, he is in the business of adoption and you aren't. Vicky may have a better life with this white couple than she'd have with you."

The line was silent for a long moment as Kira filtered Julie's words through the cloud of indecision that had filled her mind all day.

"That's easy for you to say, Julie. You aren't as close to this as I am. You can't feel it."

"Feel what?" Julie shot back. "Love for a child you don't even know?"

Closing her eyes, Kira squeezed hard, forcing out a tear. "No, not love, Julie, " she murmured. "Responsibility. And, yes—guilt. I'd feel so damn guilty if I let this happen. I know I would."

"Why? Why can't you step back and be objective?" Julie asked.

Kira bit down hard on her bottom lip, then replied, "Because we're talking about my sister's flesh and blood. As long as Vicky was in foster care, I think a part of me thought that maybe someday, you know, when I found Mr. Right and got married and settled down, I'd bring her into my life . . . maybe not adopt her, but have legal custody. I think the finality of this adoption is what has me so rattled. It's so . . . permanent."

"But who are you to say what will or won't work? And what if you persuaded Conley to recruit a black couple to take Vicky, then they turned out to be awful parents? Color doesn't guarantee anything. Children need to feel loved and secure. Not much else matters after that. I think you're overreacting, Kira. Get a grip."

"I'm trying," Kira lamely admitted.

"Doesn't sound that way to me. So, when are you going to talk to Vicky? Meet the prospective adoptive parents? Maybe that will make you feel better."

"I have to call Conley when I'm ready. It's been a hell of a day, worrying about this."

"Well, do you actually want to stop the adoption from going through?" Julie pressed. "Be honest, Kira. Is that what you want?"

Thinking, Kira paused. Then she said, "Honestly, I don't know. I don't have any reason to interfere."

"Exactly! So go meet the people. Find out if Vicky is happy. The child might not even be the kind of kid you'd want to have around. She might be a real problem, you know? And the Ropers. Who are they? Get off your butt and find out. Duh . . . Kira, you're a reporter, remember? You get paid to get to the real deal. You're smart. Get the answers you need to settle this once and for all."

Julie's right, Kira thought. *The only way I can get control of my emotions and do what is best for Vicky is to be informed, and it is up to me to make the first move.*

After promising to call Julie in a few days to let her know how things were going, Kira hung up, then she logged on to her computer, went to her favorite search engine, and punched in the name Ralph Roper, hoping he might have a site to promote his mayoral candidacy.

As she tapped the keys on her keyboard, the weight of frustration and indecision that had plagued her all day finally began to lift, and after a few minutes Kira was actually looking forward to learning all she could about Mr. and Mrs. Ralph Roper.

After surfing through Web sites dedicated to a deceased English saint, a pro tennis player, an overseas missionary organization, and a Ralph Roper of Los Angeles who was a professional dog trainer, she tried the Web site of the city of Monroeville, North Carolina, and quickly found the Ralph Roper she was looking for.

Nodding as she read through the listing of the city's businesses, community leaders, and statistics, she came to the conclusion that Evan Conley had been right on the mark when he'd described Ralph Roper as wealthy and successful. His company, Roper Fiber Technology, was one of the major employers in Monroeville, with branches in four other states and three foreign countries. The company was a leader in fiber-lubricant technology, specializing in the research, manufacture, and production of fiber-processing solutions for both natural and synthetic textiles. His Web page contained information about, and photos of, the company's headquarters in Monroeville, a five-story concrete and glass structure with wraparound windows on either side that was nestled among tall pines on a hill overlooking the city.

There was a photo of Ralph Roper, the owner, and a paragraph about his recent declaration for the mayoral candidacy. His campaign slogan was "Make Monroeville Marketable," and he touted his hometown as the ideal city for new businesses to consider for relocation due to its low taxes, available land, excellent schools, and friendly citizens. His cheery expression and the way his lips turned up at the corners made Kira immediately think of the pitchman who advertised used cars on Channel 28. Clearly middle-aged, he wore his sandy brown hair in a blunt, almost military cut, with a short shock of it standing straight up near his forehead, making him look as if he had just come in from outside on a windy day. Roper exuded the kind of friendly appeal that made for good politics and would motivate people to shake his hand, write him a check, trust him with their city, and their children's future. He had the bearing of a man who was confident, ambitious, and shrewd.

Kira stared at the image, trying to imagine him at the dinner table with Vicky, at a ball game, taking her to school, but had a hard time summoning up a scenario that pleased her. She pressed the PRINT button to copy the information from the Web page, taking note of the address of Roper Fiber Technology. She would start there, where her press credentials ought to come in handy, she thought, waiting for the pages to slip out of the printer.

CHAPTER 9

"Where're you going?" Sharon hissed over the mouthpiece of her phone, one hand covering it as she reached for a pencil from the green and white mug on her desk. She scribbled some words on her yellow legal pad as she simultaneously listened to her caller and waited for Kira's reply.

"I've got to get over to Monroeville," Kira told Sharon, hurriedly stuffing her spiral notepad, two pens, a small tape recorder, and her cell phone into her roomy brown leather purse that doubled as her attaché case today. "I just got a heads-up on a noon meeting at the Union County Consolidated School District that I want to attend." She grabbed her tan trench coat off the coatrack near her workstation and began putting it on while she talked. "You know, the big business versus local school board management piece that Davison assigned to me. I'm hoping to get some input from a smaller school board. See what they think about doing a similar study."

Sharon balanced the phone between her neck and her shoulder while writing, eyeing Kira with caution. "Bruce told you to go? Now? You'll miss the afternoon staff meeting."

With a nonchalant shrug, Kira started away from her desk, not wanting to do any more explaining. Of *course* Bruce didn't know she was leaving, and she wanted to get out of the newsroom before he came snooping around. "Don't worry. I'll be back by two."

"Please hold on," Sharon finally asked the person she had been talking to, then turned her full attention on Kira. "What's that mean? He doesn't know, does he?"

Kira put a finger to her lips and frowned. "I'll be back. Gotta go."

"You were late for the last meeting, and you know you're on his list. Better not push it, Kira."

"Okay, okay," Kira assured her coworker. "I'm not going to stay for the entire meeting, just long enough to interview a few members of the board, get their take on this business management angle for my next column."

"Hmm . . . why do you act as if there is something else going on? Come on, Kira, I see it in your face."

"Nothing is going on, Sharon," Kira replied, not about to let on to her coworker that the trip to Monroeville had nothing to do with her assignment.

"You can't possibly make it to Monroeville and back by two," Sharon warned, rolling her eyes at the clock above her desk. "Bruce said everybody—writers and support staff—have to be here for this one. No exceptions."

"I know, I know," Kira called over her shoulder as she hurried toward the door, giving Sharon a wave, and the belt to her trench coat a final tug. Last week she had arrived fifteen minutes late to the editorial staff meeting, and Davison had called her into his office afterward to give her a verbal warning: If she was late again, he was going to place a written reprimand into her personnel file. *What a prick,* she thought, remembering. "See you in a bit. Cover for me for a few minutes if you have to. Please?"

"Whatever," Sharon called out, returning to her telephone conversation.

On her way to the parking lot at the corner of Tryon and East 2nd, Kira bit down on her bottom lip, walking as fast as she could without breaking into a run, hoping the parking attendant had not double-parked her car, as he was known to do on busy days. She could not afford to lose even the few minutes necessary for him to move cars around so she could get out. It was eleven thirty-five. She had two and a half hours in which to make the thirty-five-minute drive to Monroeville, sit in on part of the meeting, then shoot back to town.

A week had passed since her conversation with Julie, and Kira was making progress with her independent research on the Ropers. When she called Evan Conley to set up a meeting with Vicky's prospective adoptive parents, he had told her that Ralph Roper was out of town but as soon as he returned, Evan would arrange it. So she had continued to surf the Web, read the *Monroeville Mirror*, and make discreet inquiries of businessmen who knew Ralph Roper. Now she was headed to Monroeville, not to attend a school board meeting as she had told Sharon, but to get an up-close and personal look at the man who wanted to be Vicky Jordan's father.

When Kira had checked the Monroeville Chamber of Commerce Web site this morning she'd discovered that the day's schedule of events included a Meet the Candidates session at noon where Ralph Roper and the two other candidates for mayor would discuss their platforms and answer questions. She was glad to see he was back in town and immediately decided to attend, even if it meant rushing over, staying a few minutes, then rushing back for the staff meeting. However, she wouldn't introduce herself to Roper today; she would wait for Evan to do that. She merely wanted to observe him, see how he interacted with the other candidates and the citizens, hear his voice and watch his eyes, things she knew would tell her a lot about the man.

Kira stepped into the intersection when the traffic light turned green, then hurried across 2nd Street and turned left, relieved to see her black PT Cruiser was still parked where she had left it that morning, next to the driveway leading out into the street. She increased her pace, got into her car, and made a quick departure.

After a ten-minute crawl through a snarl in downtown traffic, she was soon headed southeast on US-74 toward Monroeville, a city of approximately 12,000 people with a growing business center, a low tax base, and many residents who drove into Charlotte to work every day. Monroeville was home to several midsize manufacturing companies and textile mills, along with numerous mom-and-pop retail and service establishments. Quite a few residents worked for the Union County Consolidated School District or were connected in some way to the longstanding industry of cotton and tobacco farming in the area.

As Kira drove along, she began to relax, enjoying the sense of liberation that came from escaping the city in the middle of the day. Fields of greening tobacco, corn, cotton, and wheat stretched out on either side of the road, and the tiny pink and blue flowers of wild alyssum had begun to form their delicate blankets of color along the sides of the highway.

Kira loved the North Carolina countryside in spring. It was lush and green and familiar. The gentle folds of the hills rising in the distance, the bushy-topped spiky pines, the stately hickory and oak trees that made shadowy glens among the forests brought a sense of calm. The sight was refreshing after weeks in the dense jungles and dusty villages of Western Africa, and it felt good to be surrounded once again by the sights and smells of childhood.

Both of Kira's parents had been born and raised in North Carolina and were buried in its rich red clay. She had made many trips over highways like this one over the years, chasing stories and working on assignments that took her all over the state. The serenity of the North Carolina landscape soothed her, and she took in a deep breath to banish the sudden rush of melancholy that threatened to take hold. Yet, as much as she loved the vibrant green hills and peaceful surroundings of the Carolinas, she would trade them in a heartbeat for the concrete sidewalks and glass skyscrapers of New York City if she were offered a job with *World Societies Today.*

At twelve-fifteen, Kira arrived at the Union County Consolidated School District Administration Building in Monroeville and entered the meeting room, where the program was already in session. She took a seat next to another reporter who was busy taking notes, sat back in her metal folding chair, crossed her legs, and looked around, taking time to catch her breath. The room was a simply furnished space with walls made of white concrete block. Indoor-outdoor carpeting covered the floor; a huge American flag hung on a pole next to an upright piano in front of neatly spaced rows of folding chairs. There was a podium and a long-skirted table at the front where two men and a woman were sitting, waiting to be introduced.

About sixty or so people had turned out, a racially mixed audience of housewives, professionals, businessmen and -women in suits and ties, others in overalls and jeans. A woman in a plum-colored suit who was standing at the podium rapped her gavel and ended her financial report, then closed her notebook and smiled at the audience, eyebrows raised high on her heavily powdered forehead.

"And now to the part of today's meeting that I know you all are waiting for: a chance to meet our three candidates for mayor, the position vacated by Herbert Young when he suddenly passed away." The woman adopted a somber expression. "We'll all miss Herbert, who contributed so much to Monroeville, and I am happy that we have three excellent candidates who are willing to step in to continue his work. As you know, the election is on May ninth, less than two months away, and our candidates want you to know who they are and what goals they have set for our city's growth." She threw a smug smile at the three people seated at the skirted table on her right. "Each of these citizens thinks Monroeville is the best place to live in North Carolina. So, now is your chance to hear what they have to say and to ask questions. In the interests of time, since I know many of you are on your lunch hours, each candidate will have ten minutes to talk about issues of concern, then will take three follow-up questions. Afterwards, for those of you who can stick around, we'll have coffee and cookies. Stay as long as you want, mix and mingle with the candidates and get to know them so you can decide who can best lead our city."

The first candidate to speak was Mattie Moore, a mature white woman with a long, narrow face, blue-gray hair, and a stern, almost disapproving expression. She had been on the city council when the former mayor died and was temporarily filling the vacant office until the special election. A retired educator and school board member with twenty years' experience in the classrooms of Monroeville, Mattie Moore immediately launched into a long-winded, frittering speech that wandered from topic to topic with little focus or substance, using five more than her allotted ten minutes.

Kira stifled a yawn, finding it difficult to pay attention. She fidgeted with her pen and nervously checked her watch as the minutes passed. If the next candidate followed Mattie's example, she'd never be able to stick it out long enough to hear what Roper had to say and make it back to work before two o'clock.

Polite, unenthusiastic applause broke the silence at the conclusion of Mattie Moore's speech, then a man in the audience raised his hand and asked for Moore's opinion on the harsh fines being imposed on residents whose loose pets had been picked up and treated as strays, even though they wore identification tags.

"I think it's justified," Mattie tersely replied. "If people can't control their pets, they deserve to pay the price. Stray dogs and cats are a danger and a health hazard to all residents of Monroeville, and the heavy fines are an appropriate way to raise money to build up the city treasury."

The man who had asked the question scratched his bearded jaw, pressed his lips into a firm line, and frowned, obviously not pleased with Mattie's opinion, but he thanked the candidate anyway and sat down.

Next to speak was Frank Thompson, an African-American man dressed in a blue pinstripe suit with hair that had just begun to gray at the temples. During his introduction, he stared at the audience, his nut-brown face composed in a serious mask, a hint of defiance in his calculating eyes, which swept the room as he quietly assessed the attendees, as if trying to discern who was for him and who was not.

The chairwoman stated that Frank Thompson was the owner of the local John Deere tractor dealership, and the first black candidate to run for any public office in Monroeville. Applause broke out after that remark. A third-generation son of Monroeville, he was a member of the Missionary Baptist Church and had been an active participant in civic projects his entire adult life.

Thompson took the podium and began to speak, starting with a short statement of his love for Monroeville. Kira was mesmerized by his sonorous tone, which contrasted sharply with Mattie Moore's high-pitched rambling voice. Thompson's manner of speech, astute bearing, and somber facial expression commanded immediate attention, and all eyes focused on him as he made his case for improving the economic and personal quality of life for all residents, and especially for those on the north side of the city.

"The north side has been underrepresented on the city council for as long as I have lived in Monroeville, and that is all fifty-two years of my life," he stated. "As mayor, I would make it a priority to revitalize that area because it's past time for some real change in the way our tax dollars are allocated. Streets in the north side need repair, the schools are in desperate need of renovation, as well as updated classroom equipment. There are inadequate sewage and drainage pipes for the number of homes that have been built in the area over the years. Every year the houses on Wind Run Creek flood something terrible, and every year the city promises to do something to alleviate the problem, but nothing ever happens. The city must pay attention to these matters. If I am elected mayor, I will allocate funds to take care of the people on the north side, who have been patient far too long. I live in the area, and I have experienced these problems firsthand."

Another burst of applause erupted, loud and encouraging, with several people in the audience calling out, "Amen!"

Kira nodded her agreement, recalling the potholes, shabby residences, and unattractive stretches of run-down property she had passed on the north side of Monroeville on her arrival into town.

She could remember when that stretch right off the highway had been a thriving center for shopping and eating, with clusters of restaurants and specialty stores that had been patronized by people who thought nothing of driving over from Charlotte for an afternoon of shopping. In the past, whenever she had passed through Monroeville going to or from an assignment, she had loved to go to the now-defunct Rib Shack and pick up barbeque and biscuits. Today, she had sadly noticed that the windows of the barbeque stand were boarded over, and the weeds were waist-high in front of the square brick building.

Frank continued: "In addition to our streets, schools, and parks, I'd like to see the city provide Perkins Roy with some kind of tax break or an incentive to help him renovate Flagg Valley Mill. It is in great need of modernization, and there must be funds available somewhere to help him upgrade. That mill has played a significant role in the development of the city's economy, as well as its history. It ought to be listed on the National Register of Historic Places. It's a shame how that place has gone down."

This last comment piqued Kira's interest, and she wondered what was so special about the old mill, which had once been one of the major employers of blacks in the area.

A woman with a toddler on her lap raised her hand and was recognized by the chairwoman.

"What about Inspiration Park?" the woman asked Frank. "It's awful—full of broken bottles, and the seats to the swings have been missing or broken for more than two years. I live right across the street, but I can't take my son over there to play. But the children, mostly white—who live in the south side of Monroeville—have Placid Park, a beautiful place with nature trails and a creek. A good place to go and spend the day. It's not right that the city has let Inspiration Park go down so bad."

Frank Thompson gripped both sides of the podium and stared directly at the woman. "You are absolutely right. If I am elected mayor, I promise you, Inspiration Park will be renovated and brought up to standards. There is no reason, other than willful neglect, for that park to be in such bad shape."

"You got my vote," the woman replied, giving Thompson a thumbs-up.

After she was seated, Thompson entertained two more questions from the audience, then thanked the people for coming out and returned to his place at the candidates' table.

Finally, the chairwoman introduced the man on her far right, Ralph Roper, spending a full five minutes praising him by reciting a litany of awards, accomplishments, and accolades he had received over the years. From what Kira had read about him, Roper seemed to be a progressive, innovative man whose family had been involved in the North Carolina textile industry for three generations. Kira noticed that Roper looked exactly like the photo on his Web page, and she quickly jotted down some of the new information she was getting from the chairwoman. As Roper approached the podium, Kira removed her tape recorder from her bag, pressed the red RECORD button, and turned her attention on him, anxious to capture every word he said.

Roper immediately downplayed his qualifications to sit in the governing seat of his city, telling the audience that he felt it was his duty to do what he could to keep Monroeville moving forward. Kira found herself paying more attention to his body language, hand gestures, and manner of speech than his platform, which first dealt with the end of term limitations for elected officials, then a one-half percent increase in local property taxes, and finally, an announcement that brought gasps from the audience.

"In reference to Frank Thompson's condemnation of the conditions at Flagg Valley Mill, I must agree with my opponent. However, the mill is too old and dangerous to renovate and is the source of grave pollution."

"Yes, that's true," Frank Thompson spoke up.

Roper nodded in his opponent's direction. "That is why I bought it . . . and at five-thirty this evening, the mill will cease operations. I plan to use the mill as a temporary warehouse for a few weeks, then tear it down and build a new state-of-the-art fiber-processing plant in its place."

The gasp of surprise that came from the audience erupted in unison, almost as if it had been rehearsed. Kira's head swiveled around when she heard a frantic voice cry out, "You bought Flagg Valley Mill? You're gonna tear it down?" She picked up her tape recorder and held it toward the African-American man who had shot to his feet, sputtering in shock and indignation. An incredulous frown wrinkled his brown forehead, and his mouth was fully open.

"Yes, Mr. Ivers," Ralph Roper replied in a clipped tone, as if he resented having to defend his latest business decision. "I closed the deal yesterday."

The whispers coming from the people in the audience increased in volume as they commented among themselves about this surprising turn of events, and when the undertone grew so loud that it was impossible to hear anything except the loud buzz of curious muttering, the chairwoman banged her gavel and called for order.

Roper coughed into his fist, straightened his tie, licked his lips, and regained his composure, preparing to press on as if the outburst had not occurred. "Now, I know this is a surprise to everyone, but hold on and let me explain. I've known the owner, Perkins Roy, for thirty years and I know how hard it has been for him to keep that mill going, but he just couldn't bring himself to close it down. However, production figures since last spring indicated that the profits had dwindled to less than sixty percent of the year before, and he's laid off close to two hundred folks already. Perkins is seventy-one years old, and he simply can't manage that mill any longer."

"But why tear it down?" Frank Thompson called out, not bothering to raise his hand or wait to be recognized. "It was the largest black-owned company in the county at one time. History was made at that mill. Why do you have to tear it down?"

"From a business perspective, it is not financially feasible to renovate the building," Roper replied. "Though I plan to demolish it, I will build an attractive modern facility on the land, a plant that will provide jobs, a decent place to work, with better conditions. It will also be an enticement to new residents to move to Monroeville, and if new people come in, commercial and economic opportunities will follow. But if we do nothing, we'll continue to experience a rapid decline in the population of our city."

Frank Thompson's head snapped up at Roper's last remark. He pointed a long finger at his opponent. "That mill has too much historical value for you to simply tear it down. I want you to know, Ralph Roper, that I will fight you on this!"

"Yes," an elderly African-American man in the audience agreed, tapping his cane noisily on the floor. "There are lots of dangerous and dilapidated buildings in Monroeville. Some in worse shape than Flagg Valley Mill. What are you going to do, Roper? Buy up the town? Get rid of everything that isn't shiny and new?"

Ralph Roper gave a short, hard laugh. "Don't get hysterical, now. You're blowing this all out of proportion."

"Oh no we're not," Frank jumped in. "You expect us to believe that once you tear down that mill you'll build anything in its place?

What you should have done was to help Perkins Roy hold on to his company, not snap it up because he was in a financial bind. How can you talk about tearing down the legacy of Jeremy Flagg and destroying a company built with six generations of sweat, bloodshed, and tears? I will never stand by and let you do this—at least not without a fight."

An appreciative round of applause erupted at this remark, and Kira quickly noticed that most of the people who were clapping were African-American while the whites in the audience sat quietly and watched.

"Please, please," the chairwoman interrupted. "We did not come here this afternoon to debate Mr. Roper's recent business decision, though I agree it will have a dramatic impact on the city. However, in the interests of time, we'll take one more question, then we must break for refreshments. You can continue your discussions individually."

Frank Thompson jerked around, almost turning his back to Roper as he vigorously shook his head in dismay.

Another black audience member raised her hand and was recognized by the chairwoman. "Mr. Roper. You can't go in with a bulldozer and simply level that mill just because it's old," she reprimanded him. "I agree with Mr. Thompson. The place means a lot to many of us. It never was just a place to work."

"But progress cannot be stopped," Roper countered, determined to make his point. "I promise to do everything in my power, if I am elected mayor, to create job opportunities for the residents of Monroeville, and tearing down a dilapidated building that is not productive makes sense." Again, his words were met with the same split reaction, and the tension in the room was palpable. "I want to 'Make Monroeville Marketable,'" Roper said, quoting his campaign slogan as he gestured at his audience. "I want to work for all of the people. This is not a racial issue. I will work to eliminate anything in this city that blocks progress."

The marked split between applause and groans of despair was manifest once more.

"Any other questions?" Roper asked, as if the chairwoman had not already stated that there would only be one more question allowed.

Frank Thompson boldly raised his hand, then stood. "Yes, I have one for you, Mr. Roper." He turned to face his opponent, smoldering rage on his face.

"I'm sure you do, Frank," Roper replied, a testy edge in his voice.

Kira perked up, eyes wide, interested in this obviously antagonistic exchange between the two men. She was curious about their personal history.

"To a point, I must agree with what you've said about Flagg Valley Mill," Thompson admitted. "You and I both want to see physical improvements to the buildings and the environment of Monroeville, I grant you that. And the mill may be past its prime, but once it closes at five-thirty today, what are the people who worked there going to do? Where will they get jobs? Ninety percent of the population on the north side is black, and I'd wager a good portion of the adults work for Perkins. Many are unskilled—can't do anything other than mill work. That's what they've done all their lives. Where will they find jobs when Flagg Valley shuts down?"

Roper's defensive posture softened, and he leveled a knowing look at Thompson, then clasped his hands together and leaned against the podium, folding his body across it. However, instead of directing his remarks at Frank, he zeroed in on the people in the audience, who were staring at him, waiting for his answer. "I will retain a small number of employees to work on the loading docks and process paperwork related to my temporary warehouse activities. Then I will personally assist anyone who needs help finding work." His voice was strong, his optimistic attitude unfazed.

The elderly black woman who had spoken earlier raised her hand again. "Mr. Roper," she asked, "how long will it take to build your new fiber-processing plant?"

Ralph nodded. "Fair question. At least eighteen months to two years to get it fully up and running."

"That's a long time, Mr. Roper. Could be two and a half years before there's jobs over there. What are working folks going to do in the meantime?" she pressed. "My husband's been at Flagg Valley for seventeen years. Conditions over there might not be the best, but we need that paycheck, Mr. Roper."

"I understand your concerns. I'll try to hire as many as are qualified to work at Roper Fiber Technology. I applied for a grant to start a training program to create a pool of skilled technicians who will be ready to move right into my new facility when it is ready. A man like your husband would be welcome in my program. His experience counts for a lot. Perhaps others can locate employment elsewhere or find financial assistance to go back to school and re-train for other types of work."

The woman nodded, then sat down.

Frank Thompson waved an arm, anxious to speak once more. "There's timber on that land that is pretty valuable, too. You compensate Perkins Roy for that?"

The chairwoman waved her manila folder at Ralph, signaling the end of the questions, but he lifted his hand and motioned for her to give him one more minute. Giving Frank a deadpan expression, he answered the question. "My compensation to Roy is a private matter, Frank. Go and ask him if he thinks he got a fair deal." Dismissing Frank, he turned his attention back to the audience. "There was a time when the population of Monroeville was close to thirty thousand; now it's less than fifteen. Growth cannot happen in Monroeville unless we provide room for growth, and right now that prime piece of real estate is tied up with a run-down, under-producing mill that ought to be demolished. I offered Mr. Roy a fair price, and he accepted."

Frank grunted, "Like you did for Justin Chatworth when you got his farmland to build that new place of yours on the south end? Snapped it up for little or nothing." Frank rolled his eyes to the ceiling, shaking his head.

Ralph lifted his shoulders in resignation, palms up. "He was happy with the price I paid, plus I relocated his workers—hired three of them as supervisors on my cotton farm up in Montgomery County."

The woman with the baby in her arms made a huffing sound, her eyes hard and cold on Roper.

Frank Thompson nodded slowly, as if grudgingly giving Roper his due, then added, "I agree that the community will have to make sacrifices in the name of progress, but we need to hold on to some sense of history. The landmarks that made Monroeville what it is today ought to be preserved."

Intrigued by the lopsided exchange between the two men, Kira watched Frank Thompson closely, keeping her eye on him until she managed to get his attention. She nodded at him, silently calculating that he might be precisely the contact she needed in order to learn more about Ralph Roper.

Frank acknowledged Kira's unspoken support with a slight inclination of his head, then turned his attention to the chairwoman, who had rushed to the podium during the last exchange and was now making a motion to close the gathering, glancing at the clock on the wall behind the piano. She tapped the podium with her gavel and broke into the flurry of conversation that had erupted after the candidates' last heated exchange. "I'm sorry, Ralph, but your time is absolutely up. We must close now." She quickly looked away from him to the audience, then said in a flustered tone, "I do want to thank everyone for coming out. Stick around, continue to talk to our candidates, and don't forget to speak with your vote."

The meeting broke up in a burst of conversation that sounded like the cries of children released for an overdue recess. Knots of citizens formed, eager to discuss what they had witnessed, and Kira tried to catch snatches of their conversations as she made her way toward Frank Thompson. Something very important had just happened, and she was more curious than ever to find out what it was about the community's history that would cause such a divisive reaction along racial lines. Was Roper simply talking a good game, espousing progress and fair play, with no plan to come through in the end? Would he actually build a new plant, or just harvest and sell the timber on the property, then let the land lay fallow?

The people milling around were talking in agitated voices as they drank coffee and munched on cookies, clustered in small groups of three or four, divided by race for the most part. Kira was tempted to go over to Roper, introduce herself, and ask him why, exactly, he wanted to adopt her niece, but knew it was neither the time nor place to make her presence known. However, after witnessing the obvious racial division among the citizens of Monroeville she was more confused than ever about Roper's motive to adopt Vicky. Did he hope that adopting a black child would improve his image in the black community? Enhance his odds at winning the election? Or make him appear to be a tolerant, open-minded citizen?

Okay, she silently told herself, trying to think her way past the unsettling mixture of concern and apprehension that suddenly overcame her. *You've seen Ralph Roper's public face, the one he uses to win votes and maintain his reputation, but is this really who he is? Is there another side to him that only those who know him well are aware of?* There were many unanswered questions and much ground for her to cover before she would feel certain that Vicky was going to be happy living with him.

Frank Thompson was busy shaking hands with several women who had come over to congratulate him on his decision to enter the mayoral race. Kira stood at the fringes of the conversation and listened to their remarks, struck by their vehement opposition to Roper and their unflinching support of Frank. When the ladies moved on, Kira stepped up and greeted their candidate.

"Hello," she started. "Congratulations on your decision to run for mayor."

"Thank you," Frank replied.

"I'd like to introduce myself. I'm Kira Forester, from the *Business & Professional Recorder* in Charlotte."

"From Charlotte, huh?" Frank's nut-brown face lost its seriousness when he grinned, and his eyes became alert with curiosity. "You mean our small-town election is of interest to you big-city reporters?"

Smiling, Kira nodded. "It certainly is. You're not that far down the road, you know?"

Frank laughed and extended his hand. "Glad to meet you. Welcome to Monroeville."

Kira shook his hand. "I write a weekly column for *BPR* called 'Business Week Watch.' I'm very interested in what just happened here. You seem passionate about preserving Flagg Valley Mill."

"I am indeed."

"I'd like to hear more about it . . . as well as any alternatives you might propose to solve the problem. In your opinion, the mill ought to be on the National Register of Historic Places?"

"Absolutely. If more people knew the history of that place, we might be able to block Roper's plan to demolish it."

"Are you willing to be interviewed?"

"I'd be more than happy to talk with you," Frank quickly agreed, assessing Kira with calculating eyes. "As you heard, my opponent's idea of progress is to tear everything down and start over. That's the easy way, you know? That mill provided jobs for many, many people over the years, people who could not get work anyplace else. Perkins Roy is one of the most respected black men in the county, and for years he's struggled to keep what I call the heart and soul of the black community alive. It's been the source of income for a whole lot of people, and they will need help now that it's about to be shut down."

"Mr. Roper seems to have a plan to help those who lose their jobs," Kira interjected.

"Well, Roper may have money, power, and good-old-boy connections, but I have the majority of the citizens' confidence. You see, for the first time in its history, the majority of Monroeville's population is not white. We're a small town, and this recent shift in demographics has drastically affected things around here. In the last ten or so years residential patterns have changed, with a hefty percentage of our population moving to Charlotte or Greensboro so they can find better jobs and housing. But those who have remained here, or want to move here, deserve better. It's time for the city to put a stop to this population drain and help Monroeville hold on to its citizens. This used to be a beautiful place to live and raise children."

"I'm sure it was, Mr. Thompson. I'm very interested in the outcome of this election." She handed him her business card. "Do you think we could talk this week?"

"Certainly," Frank replied, looking down at Kira's card. "I'll check my calendar and give you a call."

"Great. I'll be waiting to hear from you."

By one-thirty Kira was back on the road, headed to Charlotte, smugly pleased about having been able to see Ralph Roper in action without him knowing who she was. Now he was no longer a static image in her mind, no longer a vague threat that she could not bring into focus. He was real—a man who was plainspoken, focused, and determined to have his way, and who was facing an equally determined opponent.

When she arrived at the tall iron gates that protected the entrance to Flagg Valley Mill, Kira slowed down and stared at the deserted-looking place. Her parents had worked at the weaving looms in a similar outdated, drafty old mill in Brunswick County while she was growing up. They had been able to pay the mortgage, put food on the table, and help Kira stay in college despite working conditions that had been terrible, pay that had been too low, and hours that had been much too long. But what else could they have done? And what would have become of them if suddenly some politician had decided to buy the place and shut it down, leaving people hanging?

Flagg Valley Mill was a compound of several yellow-brick buildings connected by a series of tall brick towers that rose high above the uneven rooflines. The turrets had fancy concrete moldings around their tops, creating wide ledges that protruded from the base of each deeply set window. The walls of all of the buildings were pockmarked with old-fashioned, multipaned openings that were dark and smudged with dirt. The chain-link fence that surrounded the mill had lost so many of its support posts that it was sagging to the ground. A scattering of cars were parked on the cracked asphalt lot. Kira noticed three shiny white vans with the name Roper Fiber Technology painted on their sides sitting beside the guardhouse, which was empty. The scene reminded Kira of a ghost town, long abandoned and neglected.

Certainly not an inviting place to work, she thought, pulling over to the side of the road to jot down a few descriptive phrases in her notepad. She restarted her car and drove off, watching as the mill faded in her rearview mirror.

CHAPTER 10

Kira pulled into the parking space at Powerhouse Gym at seven fifty-nine, exhausted after a long, tiring day. She had made it back to the office in time for the staff meeting, which had lasted close to two hours, and had stayed late to finish up her work on the school board versus business piece for Bruce. At the meeting, her boss had held court as usual, detailing the latest numbers on circulation and advertising, both of which were down. He had announced the merger of two support-staff positions due to the resignation of a pool secretary and an administrative assistant, and stated that the news department budget was frozen and a six-month salary freeze was going into effect immediately. These announcements did little to boost the already low morale in the office, and everyone had left the meeting with words of concern and disappointment locked in their throats.

Kira hoped a long session on the stationary bike might clear her mind of the jumble of worries that crowded it, but before grabbing her bag and going inside the gym, she decided to check her messages at home. Hopefully, Evan Conley had called by now with a date for her to meet the Ropers. While still in her car, she punched in the number to her voice mail and listened to the only message: from Julie, asking Kira to call her at home tonight. Thinking Julie might have an update on Henderson's thoughts about bringing her on board, Kira immediately called Julie back.

"Julie," Kira began as soon as her editor answered. "Got your message. I'm at the gym. What's up?"

"Hi, Kira. Glad you could get back to me so quickly. We're moving right along on the layout for your story. The first draft was exactly what I—and Henderson—hoped for. I overnighted the edited copy to you yesterday, so look for it when you get home. Okay?"

"That'll work," Kira replied, pleased that the piece was in its final stages. "Today is Tuesday . . . . I can get it back to you by Friday. How's that?"

"Fine. Also, I sent along a packet of photos I'd like you to caption for me. Take a look at them and add any descriptive details we can use, then shoot them back with the manuscript. Okay?"

"Sure. As soon as I get home I'll get on it."

"Hate to press you like this, Kira, but we've decided to include more of your photos than we had originally planned. They really add to the story."

"No problem," Kira replied, barely able to contain her joy at the realization that her photography skills measured up to *World's* standards. Though she didn't want to put Julie on the spot, before hanging up, she had to ask, "Any progress to report on a possible opening up there?"

"Not really. Henderson's been out of the office for a few days. But, as I said, be patient. I know he's thinking about making you an offer."

"Okay, okay, just wondering," Kira said. "Our staff meeting this afternoon was less than encouraging, and I guess I'm feeling a bit nervous about my future here with *BPR*."

"I know what you mean. I heard about the budget freeze and the consolidation of positions out there. *BPR's* declining circulation is a huge problem. I hope Davison can turn it around."

"Me too," Kira replied, declining to go into the lack of support the staff was getting from their new boss, or the low morale that was dragging everybody down. It would take a miracle for Bruce to bring the paper back to its heyday, when circulation was very close to that of the daily paper.

"And what's happening with your niece?" Julie asked. "Have you met the adoptive family yet? Spoken to Vicky?"

"No, on both counts," Kira said, "though I did have an opportunity to sit in on a meeting where Ralph Roper was one of the speakers. I didn't introduce myself, but I was able to see him in action." She quickly filled Julie in on what had transpired at the meeting in Monroeville.

"So Roper doesn't know who you are? Or why you were there?"

"No, I didn't talk to him, but I spoke to his opponent. A black guy named Frank Thompson—the first African-American candidate for any political office in Monroeville. I have a hunch that Thompson knows quite a bit about Ralph Roper and could be very helpful, so I'm going to meet with him. I do want to do a story on the mill, but I also want to see what I can find out."

"Be careful, Kira. Small-town politics can be uglier than big-city elections sometimes. Don't underestimate how dirty they can play, and please don't spill your guts to Thompson just because he's black. Proceed with caution. Okay?"

"Don't worry," Kira said. "I know how to handle politicians."

"I'm sure you do," Julie admitted. "But don't get caught up in their drama."

The *Tonight Show* was on TV when Kira finally sat down at her desk and opened the thick padded envelope containing the edited manuscript and the photos that Julie had sent. Looking through the pictures she had taken in Pangi, she began to relive the wild chase through the jungle, the fear that had gripped her when the shooting had started, the puzzlement that had stayed with her for days after the encounter. She was relieved to know that Amid had escaped because she had finally gotten through to the driving service that Amid owned, and had been told that he was off in the interior someplace, driving another client.

She checked a photo of one of the brightly lit shacks more closely, studying the faces of two of the girls who had jumped up to see what was going on in the street. One young dark-skinned girl was peeking out of the doorway with fright-filled eyes. Another, who had dashed out onto the porch of the shanty, was cowering against a tall stack of crates, one hand pressed to her mouth as she gaped in shock at the scene unfolding before her.

Kira could still recall how the damp night air had smelled and how it had whooshed past her face when Amid sped off. She could hear the shots dinging the side of the van, the sound of Amid's stern voice ordering her down on the floor. She pushed her damp crinkly hair off her neck and massaged the muscles at the top of her shoulders, carefully assessing the photo, trying to decide how to caption it, her eyes traveling over the gun-toting guards, the frightened girls, the stacks of crates beneath the overhang of the porch. She analyzed the images, sensing the terror that had gripped the girls. She pressed her eyes closed, remembering, wishing she knew more about what had been going on in that isolated village halfway around the world.

* * *

Ralph Roper opened the brass-studded lid of the heavy ebony box, took out a cigar, and twirled it between his thumb and fore-finger, thinking about his day. Leaning back in his rich brown, tufted leather desk chair, he sank into its luxurious embrace, feet propped atop his desk. It had been the kind of day he loved: active, challenging, and lucrative.

After the Meet the Candidates session at the school board, he had gone over to the meeting of Church United Men to accept a three-thousand-dollar donation to his campaign, then visited with the women of the Red Rose Society, who were going to walk the streets and knock on doors to distribute his campaign literature. At six o'clock he had joined a group of politicians and businessmen to help cut the blue ribbon at the opening of the new Value Market Mall on US-74, the giant retail enterprise in which he had wisely invested a great deal of money. The two-hundred-acre shopping complex, on what had once been a vacant, trash-filled piece of land, was now the busiest, most profitable intersection between Charlotte and Monroeville. Ralph's share in the venture was going to greatly increase his personal wealth, while the property taxes would bolster Monroeville's treasury.

He lit his cigar, blew smoke through lips formed into a circle, and thought about his appearance at the Meet the Candidates session that morning. It had been the perfect venue for his disclosure of the fate of Flagg Valley Mill, and Frank Thompson's reaction had not surprised him. Frank was a predictable kind of guy, one who talked a lot but never acted on his threats—that was one reason why Ralph did not consider him much of a threat.

Ralph sighed, actually relieved that he and Frank had butted heads in public, providing the citizens an opportunity to see how edgy and negative Frank could be. No one wanted a hotheaded rabble-rouser for mayor, and Ralph was glad he had conducted the deal on Flagg Valley in secret, revealing his acquisition when it was far too late for Frank or anyone else to do a thing about it. Soon enough, the residents who had sided with Frank today would see things from Ralph's point of view, especially after he hired some of them to work in his factory.

Ralph spat out a piece of tobacco. Frank Thompson's campaign was a joke. Nothing more than an annoyance. In Ralph's opinion, Thompson was a little man with a big mouth who had no life, and he ought not go around poking his nose into business that was not his.

He might be good at firing people up and creating division, Ralph thought, *but that won't win an election. I can give the people jobs, training, and access to funds to go to school or learn a trade. Thompson can only give them rhetoric and outrage. I know what the people of Monroeville need, whether they want to admit it or not.*

Ralph exhaled another stream of smoke into the half-light of his massive study, watching as the gray-white wisps drifted toward the breakfront on the opposite wall. It was filled with thick green and brown leather-bound books, silver- and gilt-framed family photos, crystal plaques on gleaming wooden stands, certificates of recognition, and a cluster of silver hunting cups he'd won when he was a teenager. Roper looked around his sanctuary, the only place in his six-thousand-square-foot home that his wife, Helen, did not enter. Only he, and Betsy, the maid who came in twice a week to clean, ever ventured into this room. Eyes half closed against the cloud of cigar smoke pooling in the corner where he sat at his antique burled-wood desk, he glanced at the richly patterned Oriental rug he had bought in Hong Kong six years ago, which was butted up to the natural-stone fireplace. Above it hung the mounted twelve-point antlers from the first deer he had ever shot, flanked by a set of Civil War dueling pistols that had belonged to his great-grandfather. The burgundy drapes at the ceiling-high windows framing the massive fireplace fell in soft folds to the thick, ruddy carpet where low African stools had been pulled up to the hearth.

On the wall opposite the fireplace, along with a variety of small photographs of the factories, mills, and research labs that Ralph owned around the world, hung a framed pen-and-ink sketch of the old log house that Roper's great-grandfather had built one hundred twenty years ago. Now, the log cabin was nothing more than a shell of rotting timber, but Ralph owned the old homestead and had plans to restore it one day to re-create the farm exactly as it had been when his grandfather had lived there as a boy.

Ralph Roper could have made his home in a town house in London, a sprawling ranch in Guatemala, or a high rise in Tokyo, but he chose to live in North Carolina, close to his roots. The son of a hardworking cotton farmer, he'd been blessed with good luck, good sense, and a good wife, and he could not imagine living anyplace other than Monroeville, where he could walk down the street and everybody knew him, and where he could walk the land that had been in his family for six generations. Ralph had traveled to every major city in the world and stayed in the best hotels and villas, sometimes for extended periods of time, yet nothing meant more to him or made him happier than when he returned home and drove up the pine-shaded road leading to his front door. Often, after having been away for just a few days, he would find himself wandering from room to room, drinking in the familiar sense of place and peace that came only when he was back in Monroeville, where he belonged.

Ralph closed his eyes in contentment, stealing a rare moment from his hectic schedule to reflect on all that he had been able to accomplish while creating this perfect life. He had parlayed his inheritance—a tiny cotton farm and his father's mildly successful textile mill—into a worldwide consortium of textile processing and manufacturing facilities that was making him a fortune. It had been a journey fraught with financial risk, cutthroat politics, and more than a few devastating setbacks when economic and natural disasters had threatened his overseas facilities. But he had persevered, and managed to build a financial empire that secured his place as a successful, powerful businessman.

Becoming mayor of Monroeville might seem like small-time action for a man of his stature in the international business arena, but to Ralph it was a natural next step. He loved the strategic plotting that was involved in winning at anything—business, sports, romance, or politics—and he thrived on the tense energy that went into outwitting an opponent, whether at the ballot box or in the boardroom. And once this race for mayor was behind him he planned to keep his promise to Helen and slow down long enough to get on with finalizing the adoption of their soon-to-be daughter, Vicky.

His thoughts went to Vicky, the little girl who was tucked into the white canopy bed upstairs. She was a sweet child, well-mannered, soft-spoken, and cute as a button. It had been Helen's idea to visit Sheltering Hearts after reading about Vicky in a magazine story about the agency that specialized in hard-to-place children. They had been on a waiting list for a white child for nearly a year with another agency when Helen broached the subject of adopting Vicky Jordan. At first Ralph had been uneasy. He was not a racist, but he had been born and raised in the South, where traditionally the races stayed to their own. Helen was a southerner, too, but her views on interracial matters were much more open and accepting than his. Over the years, Helen's work with International Relief Now had brought Ralph into contact with orphaned children from

China, Korea, Africa, India, and South and Central America, opening his eyes to the similarities among the children, making their differences less important. The children stayed in his home for short periods of time, and Ralph soon began to welcome them, knowing how important they were to Helen. Hosting the children had not been difficult. All they wanted to do was swim in his pool, ride his horses, watch the big-screen TV, or play video games in the media room he had built upstairs especially for the young people. He was a busy man who worked long hours, traveled extensively, and often secluded himself in his office at home for days at a time, barely able to spend time with Helen, let alone the children she invited in. Raising Vicky was going to be up to Helen, though he'd try to be as involved as he could.

At first Ralph had been worried that adopting an African-American child might be a huge mistake in a small town like Monroeville, where racial lines were still clearly evident in many aspects of the community. But his hesitation had devastated Helen, sending her into a downward spiral of depression and isolation that frightened Ralph. He loved Helen more than he'd ever loved anyone. He knew that everything he had accumulated—land, money, position, and power—would mean nothing if she were not at his side. Fearing he might lose her completely, Ralph had relented, convinced that adopting Vicky was the best way to keep his wife happy, healthy, and in love with him. He loved Helen too much to deny her anything she wanted, and he had seen miraculous changes in her since Vicky had come to live with them. Lately, Helen was a totally different person than she had been in years. She was laughing again, working in her art studio once more, and had even driven to Cedar Grove twice to visit her sister, Ruth, from whom she had been estranged for years. Ralph sighed in contentment. Helen was finally emerging from the lengthening bouts of depression and insecurity brought on by three miscarriages in less than five years. Taking steps to adopt Vicky Jordan had initiated more positive change than he had anticipated, and his love for Helen swelled in his chest. Now that Vicky was here, Helen had told him, she had exactly what she wanted most—a child who would remain permanently in her life.

The delicate fragrance of pink sweetheart roses came to Helen as soon as she opened the door. Easing it forward another few inches, she peeked inside and spotted the basket of flowers that perfumed the bedroom, though it was nearly hidden by the pile of stuffed animals and dolls that Vicky had heaped onto her dresser. The pink and white interior glowed with a rosy hue from the night-light in the wall beside Vicky's bed, casting its pale light over the plush pink carpet to create a path leading to the adjoining mauve-tiled bathroom.

Helen settled her gaze on the tiny form beneath the coverlet on the white canopy bed, her heart quickening with love as she looked at her. Vicky was lying on her back, fast asleep, her tiny mouth dropped slightly open as she drew in even breaths. Her dark curls, free from the elasticized ribbons that usually held them away from her face, tumbled around her round cheeks, giving her the appearance of a tousle-headed angel.

Vicky was a beautiful child, with skin the color of tea laced with milk, huge brown, thickly lashed eyes, and a quick intelligence. And for a child who had spent most of her young life in foster care, Vicky was unusually even-tempered and emotionally balanced. Helen counted herself lucky to have found her.

Mentally reviewing the busy day they had shared, Helen sighed. The day had started with Helen driving Vicky to school, followed by an afternoon shopping trip to buy new clothes and shoes, and then on to Vicky's first piano lesson with Mrs. Marsh. The child had taken to the instrument with a zeal that impressed her teacher and delighted Helen, who was an accomplished pianist herself. A current of excitement coursed through Helen as she thought about the wonderful years that lay ahead, of the joy she was going to receive from being a mother to Vicky. She had waited a long time for this, and now that Vicky was actually under her roof, in her possession, Helen trembled in relief. For so many years she had dreamed of having a daughter to teach and guide and love. The disappointment and resulting emptiness of losing three children before they had even formed completely in her womb had nearly driven her out of her mind. *Thank God for Ralph,* Helen thought, aware that her husband's love for her was the only reason she had Vicky now. He never refused her anything she wanted and had never wavered in his love for her through the devastating disappointments and resulting depressions that had followed each of her miscarriages. He did not even complain about the fact that he would never have a natural son to carry on his family name and continue the Roper legacy.

It had taken less than a month for Evan Conley to arrange for her and Ralph to file the papers. Vicky was six years old, bright, healthy, and had no unresolved issues of custody to cloud her qualifications for adoption. With a shake of her head, Helen pulled the door closed and started down the hallway to her bedroom, a light smile on her lips. She felt better than she had in years.

At thirty-five, Helen Roper still wore a size six dress, as she had before marrying Ralph nine years ago. She did not have to dye her tawny, light brown hair, which was still as silky and thick as when she had been much younger, and she had never had plastic surgery—as many of her friends had done—to erase the tiny crow's feet at the corners of her radiant brown eyes. Having Vicky in her life made her feel vibrant, young, and useful, and had finally brought her the sense of peace and closure that she had been unable to achieve with any of the children she had host-mothered for IRN. She would never need to play host mother again, because at last she had the child she had been searching for: the child she planned to love and spoil and raise and guide. And that meant more to Helen than anyone could ever imagine.

CHAPTER 11

The noise level inside Amy's Smokehouse Grill was at its peak when Kira arrived at the popular eatery on State Street. The busy restaurant, always jam-packed at noon, was a convenient lunch spot for office workers in downtown Charlotte who wanted great food at a great price and had no problem waiting as long as an hour for a table, especially on Fridays. Only two blocks from *BPR*, Amy's had been Kira's first choice for her meeting with Frank Thompson, and she was relieved that he had been willing to drive into Charlotte to meet her there.

Kira had deliberately arrived half an hour early in order to snag a quiet table toward the back where they would be able to talk without screaming at each other. She also planned to review the packet of material she had brought along. Her article for *World* was finally finished, but she wanted to go over it one last time before sending it off to Julie, an impossible task to complete at the office. Lately, Bruce had begun striding through the newsroom, moving from desk to desk, casually examining his staff, as if trying to catch someone working on anything other than a scheduled assignment. The unrest among Kira's coworkers was steadily rising, and she had begun to think seriously that it might be time for her to leave. However, she was not about to give Bruce Davison the satisfaction of knowing he had run her off.

I'm sticking it out as long as I can, she silently vowed as she followed the waitress to a booth toward the rear of the restaurant. *An offer from* World Societies Today *will come through. It has to.*

After being seated, Kira ordered an iced tea, then opened the package containing the manuscript and the packet of photos that

Julie had sent, anxious to give the material one last review before sending it off to New York. Her plan was to get it to the Federal Express drop box before two o'clock today so it would arrive tomorrow, though she had promised to get it to Julie by this morning. The week had flown by in a blur of meetings and interviews and long hours at her computer, pushing Kira past her Friday deadline. Thank God Julie had been understanding.

After reviewing the captioned photos, Kira set them aside and began to read her manuscript, pleased with her work on the project and relieved that it was finally finished. The minutes slipped past, and she became so engrossed in the article that Frank startled her when he slipped into the booth.

Kira's head snapped up, and she looked across the table at Frank as she cleared her mind of the scenes in Africa that had transported her back in time. She set the manuscript down and smiled as she extended her hand. "Hello. Glad you were able to drive in."

"My pleasure," he replied, shaking her hand. "Sorry I'm a little late."

"No problem," Kira assured him, shoving her papers and photos out of the way to focus on Frank, who was dressed in tan khaki pants and a crisp pale blue shirt over which he was wearing a navy blue cable-knit sweater. Though more casually attired than he had been at the Meet the Candidates gathering, he still had an air of dignity that commanded Kira's respect. She glanced down at his hands clasped together on the table, admiring his thin gold watch, manicured fingernails, and the wide gold wedding band on his left hand, congratulating herself for having gotten to Frank Thompson so quickly. He knew quite a bit about the problems facing Monroeville, about its citizens, and especially about Ralph Roper. She was anxious to get to know this man, who struck her as an earnest, passionate citizen who had no trouble speaking the truth.

"I needed the extra time to go over this story that I have to get off to New York this afternoon," she told him.

"You certainly stay busy," Frank remarked, eyeing the stack of photos. "Do you mind?" he asked, inclining his head toward the colorful glossy scenes.

"No, not at all," Kira told him, watching as he picked up several of her photos. She leaned forward, craning her neck over the table to explain each scene to Frank. "And these," she said when he got to the shots taken in Pangi, "are from a village deep within Equatorial

Guinea. My driver had to cut through this area because the main road was washed out. We were not particularly welcome. Quite an experience."

"So I see," Frank solemnly agreed. He shuffled through the photographs, intensely studying each one. "Obviously, you were not expected, either."

"No, we weren't. And I still get nervous when I think about that night." She shuddered, throwing off the familiar chill that always came over her whenever she thought about that encounter. Pushing her memories aside, she went on to tell him what had happened. "Clearly, I was not supposed to photograph what was going on— the girls working in those shanties were very young. Maybe eight or ten years old."

"Must have been a scary situation," Frank murmured, handing the pictures back to Kira. "Sounds like your job can be pretty dangerous."

His assessment brought a quick laugh from Kira, who shook her head as she put her material away. "Not always. This particular assignment had its moments, but I assure you the industry trade shows and business conventions I usually cover are not that intriguing. My time in Africa turned out to be an eye-opening experience, to say the least."

"And what was your assignment? What were you after?" Frank wanted to know.

"My assignment was to document the remote factories and little-known sources of production in that part of the world, specifically related to the decline in North Carolina's reputation as a leader in textile manufacturing."

"The cheap labor that is undercutting most American manufactures?"

"Yes, and unfortunately a large portion of that labor is made up of very young workers. It's a huge problem, but the lower production costs keep prices down, and American manufacturers can produce their goods for so much less and make huge profits. It's not going to simply go away."

"I know exactly what you're talking about," Frank agreed, tightening his lips in thought. "I've lived in North Carolina all of my life, and though my family was never in textiles, I've seen many mills and factories fail because they couldn't compete with the imported products and materials that are flooding the market now. It's a crime that so many once-thriving plants are now shuttered—and Ralph Roper wants to close one more. A shame," he muttered, reaching for the menu that the waitress had come over to hand to him. "A damn shame, and I plan to do everything I can to stop him."

"That's precisely what I'd like to talk about. Flagg Valley Mill," said Kira as she looked over the menu.

"Fine. A topic I am passionate about," Frank said, squaring his shoulders as he opened his menu. "I drove past the place on my way out of town this afternoon. Roper's men were all over the grounds, using conveyor belts to unload boxes directly from big semi trucks into a wing of the mill. Hard to believe it belongs to Roper Fiber Technology now and is no longer Flagg Valley Mill."

"Seems Ralph took everyone by surprise, didn't he?" Kira asked, perusing the lunch specials, calculating how to best maneuver the conversation to personal information about Roper, a topic she was determined to explore with Thompson.

After ordering two plates of barbequed beef with potato salad and beans, Kira started the interview by asking about Frank's campaign goals. "What are the major differences between your strategy for winning and your opponent's?"

Kira turned on her tape recorder and listened closely as Frank outlined his plan to represent all of the people equally, beautify the city by focusing on neglected areas of Monroeville, and develop an employment task force to slow the rapid population drain that was occurring. She let him talk while she managed to get in a few bites of food.

"Do you plan to talk to Ralph, too? Have you ever interviewed him?" Frank suddenly asked.

Kira shook her head, pleased that Frank had introduced the subject of his opponent into the discussion. "No. I haven't approached him yet, though I hope to very soon." She gulped down a swallow of iced tea, not about to mention her personal interest in Ralph Roper, then cut into another piece of the tender beef smothered in Amy's famous smoky sauce while deciding on her next question for Frank.

"I understand," she began, "that if you win you would be the city's first African-American elected official."

"That's right," Frank agreed. "And it's about time. The population of Monroeville has shifted over the years, and blacks are now the majority. We have a substantial number of Native Americans in our town, too, and many of their concerns have not been addressed, either."

"So, you think it's time for a change?"

"Absolutely. The traditional white leadership of Monroeville is out of touch with the majority. We need to take issue with the lack of services and lack of interest in the problems that are affecting the working class."

"With your plans to focus on the north side of town?"

"Yes."

"Are you concerned that the white residents might accuse you of taking sides? Of dividing the city? As mayor you say you want to serve all of the people, both black and white, but it sounds as if your attention is on helping only the residents of color."

"To some extent that is true," Frank conceded. "However, bringing equity to these important factions can be unifying, not divisive."

"So what do you consider to be a unifying cause or issue that will serve you now—as a candidate?" she asked,

Frank placed his knife along the top of his plate and directed his comments toward the tape recorder that Kira had placed on the table. "To instill pride in each resident of Monroeville."

"Civic pride?"

"Exactly. Old-timers remember when our city was a vibrant, lovely place to live, full of activity and energy. I want to revitalize Monroeville, increase the quality of life, and give residents reason to feel proud to live there. Attracting new business and industry is key, but quality of life is dependent on more than having a good job and a nice house. I believe it is important for people to have a solid understanding of the history of the place they call home and to treat that historical legacy with respect. Ralph Roper doesn't understand that—or at least, chooses not to acknowledge it as important. All he cares about is making money and enticing a bunch of outsiders to come in and construct industrial complexes and computerized factories from which he will profit."

"So, you want to see a balance, a way to achieve necessary progress yet maintain the legacy of the past?" Kira said.

"Yes. A balance between the past and the present. Historical preservation and progress can go hand in hand, though Ralph Roper does not think so. He's only interested in the monetary gain that he—and perhaps his cronies in city government—would enjoy due to his ability to influence and control those in decision-making positions."

Kira nodded, then took another bite of barbeque. "Considering the demographics of Monroeville, doesn't Roper need quite a few African Americans to vote for him if he expects to be elected?"

"Most certainly."

"And from what I witnessed at the candidates' forum, I sensed the support for the candidates is somewhat divided along racial lines."

"To a large degree, yes," Frank acknowledged. "And can a candidate for mayor who is hell-bent on demolishing a structure that has a great deal of sentimental and historical value to the majority of its citizens win? I don't think so. Roper would win more of the black vote if he were seeking funds to restore Flagg Valley Mill instead of bragging about his plans to demolish it."

Kira took a sip of her iced tea, then decided to play the devil's advocate and see how Thompson would react. "But isn't it more economically feasible to tear the old mill down and sell the land to developers, Mr. Thompson? I've seen Flagg Valley Mill. It's in very bad shape, probably a dangerous place in which to work. Why shouldn't Ralph Roper demolish the building and build a safe, attractive plant?"

With a swipe of his paper napkin, Frank brushed his lips while giving Kira a clear look of annoyance. After calmly wiping the corners of his mouth, he ran it across his thin mustache then laid it beside his nearly clean plate.

"Young lady, I think you need a history lesson. In a small town like ours, understanding and respect for the past could do a lot to retain our population and attract new residents. If properly positioned in the tourism and cultural history market, Flagg Valley Mill could become a vehicle to increase revenue and stimulate the economy. All it takes is vision. What Roper didn't talk about on Tuesday, and what too many people don't know, is that Flagg Valley Mill sits on what used to be the largest and the only black-owned tobacco plantation in a three-county area."

"I didn't know that," Kira said, intrigued by this interesting bit of black history that had never made its way into the history books of her local school.

"You need to hear the story of Jeremy Flagg," Frank went on. "He was a free black man who was deeded that two-hundred-acre tract of land in 1850 when his white father, the owner, died. Jeremy encouraged slave owners from nearby plantations to let their slaves work his tobacco fields for a few pennies a day. Some of the liberal, sympathetic white farmers were happy to let their slaves work for wages, accepting tobacco in exchange for the use of their chattel. However, the pro-slavery planters considered Jeremy's farm to be a hotbed of sedition and abolitionist activity. As you can probably guess, Jeremy was not a popular man, and his farm soon became a target for race riots, hate crimes, and cruel attacks. During the years before and during the Civil War many blacks who worked there were lynched—strung up on trees that still stand on that property. But Jeremy and his plantation survived the war, and the land remained in the hands of Jeremy's descendants until Roper bought it from Perkins Roy, a descendent of a cousin of Jeremy Flagg."

"And when did the land change from a tobacco farm to a mill? When was Flagg Valley built?" Kira asked.

"When Perkins Roy's father took over the place in 1928. Old man Roy was a businessman, not a farmer, so he decided to build a textile processing mill where tobacco once grew and turned the original farmhouse into the main building."

"Quite a bit of history there," Kira admitted.

"Right," Frank replied. "The walls and foundation of that mill contain handmade bricks, and according to records in the county courthouse, each brick was shaped by the hands of the original slaves who were owned by Jeremy's white daddy. At one time, more blacks worked for wages for Jeremy Flagg than for any white man in a three-county area, and it was rumored that he was as wealthy as any white plantation owner in the state of North Carolina directly before the Civil War. Now mind you, all of this happened during the time that many white men, like Ralph Roper's great-granddaddy, were living in log cabins, scratching the ground to raise enough cotton to hold on to their tiny plots of land."

"Amazing," Kira remarked, keenly interested in what Frank had said. "I was born and raised in North Carolina and I've never heard that story."

"Why would you?" Frank tossed back, a smug expression on his face. "Nobody has ever bothered to pull the records of Flagg Valley Mill out of the dusty courthouse and write the story. I'd like to put that story out into the world, create a place where the young people of North Carolina can come and learn about what really happened here. It's valuable history, worth saving, but few seem to think so . . . except old folks like me, I guess."

Kira pushed a piece of meat around on her plate, thinking. "What you've told me, Mr. Thompson, is worthy of documentation, but how will it help Monroeville's economy? A cultural center run by a nonprofit agency might be nice, but don't you agree that a modern plant that would provide jobs for the citizens is what's needed?"

"Just takes a different mindset, that's all," Frank countered. "There's state money available for small towns like Monroeville to turn their historical sites into moneymaking ventures to attract tourists, which in turn create new enterprises. But we've got to get the ear of those in Raleigh, go after the funding, write proposals, submit grants, document our history. We need to restore, not tear down. Ralph Roper doesn't share my vision."

"Why do you think that is?" Kira prompted, swinging the focus of the conversation to his opponent.

"Because Roper is too obsessed with money. He's a greedy man. Only interested in increasing his own wealth, even though he has more money, property, and commercial interests than any man in the county. He doesn't have to use Flagg Valley Mill as a temporary warehouse. He could have rented storage space anyplace in the area. On the south side, too."

"So why is he over there?" Kira asked.

"To move his name into the black community and establish a presence. To prove to the black residents that he has the power to make things happen. And in my opinion, all he's doing is demonstrating his ability to control other people's lives. He's underhanded and will do anything—and I mean anything—to get what he wants."

"Have you known him a long time?"

"All of my life. His daddy and his momma, too. You see, I wasn't always a Deere tractor salesman. I grew up on a small farm in the rural parts of the north side of Monroeville—in the shadow of Flagg Valley Mill. But I left Union County when I was sixteen, after my daddy died. Took a job with a construction firm in Raleigh, doing carpentry labor. Eventually I worked my way up to a supervisory position with the company, so I stayed. When I got a letter from my mother, who was still living in Monroeville, telling me that Ralph Roper wanted to buy her home and put her off her own land so that he could cut a road from the highway to that new plant of his, I returned to Monroeville to see about it. I protested, but it was too late to do anything about it. My family's loss, Roper's gain."

"How could that have happened?"

"County folks said they had the right to grant Roper an easement to access the highway, and that easement included my father's land. I'm certain he got his cronies at the county to redraw the lines, but what could I do? Over the years, Roper has continued to buy up the best land in the county. Now it's got to stop."

"With your family land gone, why did you return to Monroeville to live?"

"Two reasons. First, my wife, Ava. She wanted me to come home, be near my mother . . . eighty years old and getting frail. Second, because the Deere tractor franchise here came through for me, so I decided to come home. And now that I'm back, I plan to stay—and make some changes, too."

His tone was laced with anger, but Kira also detected a strong sense of pride and self-respect for what he had decided to do with his life. Frank Thompson's story would make an interesting column, in which she could highlight the intriguing African-American history that lay hidden at the heart of Monroeville while detailing the challenge of revitalizing a city on the decline, a task facing many small and midsize cities across the South. She would focus on the economic impact that tourism could have on a small town, and how historical sites could be used to encourage tourism and thus stimulate the economy.

After fifteen more minutes of conversation, the waitress came to clear the table, and Kira, who felt she had enough to write her column, reached for the check. However, Frank moved quickly to take it from her.

"No, this is on me," he said. "My pleasure. I appreciate you giving me an opportunity to tell a different side of the story." After looking over the bill, he pulled out his American Express card and placed it in the leather folder, then went on. "Ralph Roper cannot be trusted. He will say whatever he thinks the people want to hear in order to further his own interests, then do as he pleases. I challenge you to check out my story, verify what happened to Jeremy Flagg's land, and write the truth. I believe that Roper only wants Flagg Valley Mill for the timber on that land, not in order to construct a brand-new factory. Wait and see what happens. Pretty soon there will be men with chain saws on that land."

"I most certainly will follow up on your theory," Kira replied, struck by the certainty in Frank's voice. "I want you to know, Mr. Thompson, that I don't plan to make this article a race-driven piece, but I do want to highlight the changing demographics of Monroeville and how they translate into an important election where the African-American vote is crucial. Your candidacy is news. Is there anything more you want to say?"

"Nothing. And you can quote me verbatim on everything I've told you."

"Good," Kira replied.

"When do you think the column on me will run?"

"Should be in next week's edition. *BPR* comes out every Thursday," Kira said, looking over at the cow-shaped clock on the wall above the bar. She frowned, lifting her shoulders. "Gotta run," she told Frank, gathering up her tape recorder, slipping the photos and the manuscript into the large FedEx envelope. After sealing it, she grabbed her bag, shook Frank's hand, and stood. "Thanks again. I'm sorry to rush off, but I have exactly six minutes to get to Federal Express and drop this package, then I have to make it over to the Doubletree Club Hotel on West Trade. Covering the Greater Charlotte Business Council meeting at two."

"Better hurry," Frank said with a laugh, waving her off. "I'll watch for the article."

"We'll be in touch," Kira promised, then she eased her way past a knot of people standing at the bar and headed out into the street.

CHAPTER 12

The quaint, European-style bistro in the hotel lobby was nearly empty, and as Kira walked past it on her way to her car, she thought about the crosstown traffic she was about to face and changed her mind about going home. Might as well relax for an hour and let it thin out, she decided, not anxious to sit in bumper-to-bumper gridlock for an hour.

Entering the bistro, Kira glanced around for a quiet place where she could sit and have a cool drink, feeling relieved that she had managed to make it to the Federal Express drop box before pickup time on her way to the hotel. Her manuscript was on its way to New York. With that behind her, she could concentrate on her profile of Frank Thompson.

The Business Council meeting had run thirty minutes over the scheduled time due to a lengthy discussion on the pros and cons of the wording on new signs that were to be erected on a stretch of freeway feeding directly into downtown. Of course, the businesses benefiting most from the signage were pleased with the new wording, which included references to popular, well-known eateries and nightspots, while those that were less well known protested the references to companies whose names were already synonymous with downtown attractions. She had thought the argument would never end, and had left the meeting while two angry retailers remained engaged in a heated conversation.

The hostess on duty greeted Kira and asked her preference for seating.

"One. Nonsmoking," she requested.

"Take your pick," the hostess told Kira, sweeping the near-empty room with her arm. "It's the lull before the evening rush," she added, picking up her menu to follow Kira to a round table facing the circular salad bar in the center of the restaurant.

After ordering a cup of coffee and a piece of cheesecake, Kira looked around, enjoying the soft music that was playing in the background and the scent of freshly baked bread, which added to the cozy, European atmosphere. At the windows, white lace curtains filtered the late afternoon sunlight into the room, creating a delicate pattern of scrolling leaves and roses on the opposite walls. In addition to Kira, there was only one other customer in the bistro, a young man who was sipping a cup of coffee and reading a newspaper.

Kira removed her tape recorder from her bag, intending to begin transcribing her notes on the Frank Thompson interview, but then she glanced up at the small television suspended in a corner, and froze. A photo of Ralph Roper had just popped into the screen, and Vernon Young, the local five o'clock anchorman on WSOC, was speaking. Jumping up, Kira immediately moved closer to the television, reached up, and increased the volume enough to hear what the anchorman was talking about.

"Monroeville businessman and candidate for mayor Ralph Roper made a surprise announcement today," Vernon Young began. "And his news has nothing to do with his current campaign, or even his highly successful textile empire. Here is our "Eye on the State" reporter, Tracy Hoten, with the story."

Kira inched closer, her eyes widening as film of Ralph and a woman she assumed to be Helen Roper began to roll. The couple was strolling down a walkway bordered with bushy green hedges, wearing huge grins on their faces as they each held one hand of a little girl who was walking between them. The threesome gave the appearance of an ordinary family out for an afternoon stroll, except that Kira knew the adults were hardly ordinary and the little girl was her niece.

"Vicky," Kira murmured, immediately recognizing her sister's child. She held her breath, every muscle in her body tensing as she took in the sight of Vicky dressed in a red and blue plaid jumper with a white blouse and a navy blue sweater, walking fast, as if trying to keep up with the Ropers, her dark curls bouncing as her fluffy ponytail swung back and forth.

"Right you are, Vernon," Tracy agreed. "This news has nothing to do with politics or spreadsheets. Ralph Roper, local businessman and candidate for mayor of nearby Monroeville, announced this afternoon that he and his wife, Helen, are well on their way to becoming parents for the first time. Roper says that their decision to adopt the little girl we see here with them was a direct result of the aggressive, statewide campaign by the Department of Health and Human Resources to inspire North Carolinians to open their hearts and homes to one or more of the many children in foster care across the state."

The sensation that shot through Kira was a mixture of joy at seeing Vicky after so many years and resentment that the Ropers were going to raise her niece. Seeing Vicky walking with the Ropers, as if she already were their child, took Kira aback. She bit her lip and focused on her niece, who had paused on the sidewalk with Helen while the reporter approached Ralph. Kira watched Vicky peer curiously at the microphone, her head craned forward, her sharp eyes intensely focused on the equipment in the reporter's hand.

"She must wonder what all the fuss is about," Kira murmured, not taking her eyes off the scene.

Tracy placed her microphone in front of Ralph Roper's face, then asked him how he thought being a dad was going to change things for him.

"Helen and I are very happy and proud to expand our family to include a daughter." He glanced down, placed his index finger beneath Vicky's chin, and lifted her face toward the camera. "Isn't she pretty?"

"Yes, she is," Tracy agreed. "Tell me how about . . . Vicky, isn't it?"

"Yes. She is a very special little girl who came to us through Sheltering Hearts. She has been through some extremely difficult times for someone so young. Her father abandoned her before she was even born, and when her mother died four years ago, Vicky was placed in foster care. Then, tragedy struck once again when her foster mother died. Sheltering Hearts put us together, as Helen and I have been interested in adopting an older child, and Sheltering Hearts is an agency that works with DHHS to find homes for hard-to-place children. We feel blessed to have found Vicky. This is the fulfillment of a long-delayed wish for us."

"So, why now?" the reporter asked, turning to Helen Roper. "What spurred you and your husband to make the commitment to adopt in the middle of his campaign?"

Helen stepped back from the microphone and began to vigorously shake her head, indicating that Tracy should address her questions to her husband. Kira's mouth dropped open to see the fright on Helen's face. "What's wrong with her?" Kira muttered, scrutinizing Helen's flustered expression, wondering why the woman, who was neatly dressed in a pair of black slacks, a red blouse, and a navy blazer with a pale blue scarf tied around her neck, seemed so nervous and edgy. The woman looked extremely fragile, too, and not as vibrant as Kira had expected her to be in light of Evan's description of her as an active volunteer who was very visible in the community. When the reporter turned back to Ralph, Helen moved to the side, completely out of camera range, taking Vicky with her.

Tracy addressed Ralph once again. "You are in the middle of a very important political campaign. What made you decide to take such an important step at this time?"

Roper puffed up his chest, flashed the woman a picture-perfect grin, and lifted one eyebrow, eager for the opportunity to speak. "There are too many children in foster care, and the state's recent campaign to move these children into permanent homes is what spurred Helen and me to think seriously about what we could do to help. Rhetoric is one thing; doing something is quite another. It's easy to talk about what ought to be done, but how many of us are willing to put our words into action?"

Tracy nodded.

"I am a man of my word, and as I have repeatedly stated during my campaign for mayor of Monroeville, I plan to do everything possible to make Monroeville the kind of city to be proud of, a good place to live and work and raise families. That includes my own. I want to demonstrate that we can draw closer as a community, learn to get along with each other, and not fall into the divisiveness that my opponent, Frank Thompson, encourages." He locked eyes with the camera lens, speaking to his invisible audience. "I urge everyone watching who has been thinking about adopting but has not done a thing about it, to stop thinking and call Children's Services today. Take the steps to make it a reality."

"Do you think interracial adoption is one way to help unify a community?" Tracy asked, clearly directing her question to Helen Roper, who had edged back into the range of the camera.

Instead of answering, Helen waved one hand, as if shooing the attention away. Shrugging, the reporter turned to Ralph. "What do you think?"

"The statewide goal of DHHS is to find a safe, permanent home for each child within a year, regardless of race and ethnicity. They see value in diversity, and believe that it can help create a strong family unit where everyone works together to meet the child's needs. No child should grow up without parents or a real home," Ralph stated. "We must look beyond racial issues if we want to strengthen our communities. If more people could focus on loving a child instead of hating his neighbor, just think how much progress we could make."

"For the first time in your city's history, an African American is running for office. With the election rapidly approaching, how do you feel about the outcome of the race, Mr. Roper?"

"Confident," he replied. "I *will* be the next mayor of Monroeville. My commitment to the success of the entire town, as well as to the business community, stands as my record, and I challenge my opponent to match it. What has he done for his community, other than stir people up? This is my home, and I plan to do everything possible to make it the most progressive city in North Carolina."

"Thank you, Mr. Roper," Tracy finished, facing the camera as she continued talking. "For those of you out there who would like more information about how you can adopt a foster child, contact the Department of Health and Human Resources at 704-555-6699 for details. Back to you, Vernon," she closed out the report.

Kira sank back in her chair and took a long, slow breath, digesting what she had just witnessed. Why didn't she feel good about the happy family scene? Wasn't this exactly what she had hoped for, for Vicky? Could Ralph Roper actually be a good choice for a parent? His closing remarks pricked her conscience: it was easy to talk about doing good deeds, but how many people took action? She had not had the courage to take Vicky when the child had needed her, but Ralph Roper was doing his part. But then resentment warmed her face as Frank Thompson's words echoed in her mind. Had this televised announcement simply been an opportunity for Roper to promote his candidacy for mayor? A ploy to get support from those who doubted his sincerity in regard to racial issues? And why hadn't Helen Roper said a word? She had shunned the spotlight and deferred to her husband as if she had been afraid to speak about the pending adoption.

Something isn't right, Kira thought. Helen's actions, as well as her demeanor, were more disturbing than Kira's gut feeling that Roper was using the transracial adoption for his own political gain. She was curious about Frank Thompson's reaction, certain that this piece of news would only deepen his distrust of his opponent and strengthen their deeply rooted rivalry. What would this announcement do to the campaign climate of a town like Monroeville? Would the African-American residents believe that Ralph Roper's decision to adopt was honestly based on his desire to love and raise a child of any race? Or would they feel, as Kira did now, that his motivation was more political than personal, and his objective was to win at all costs?

Too upset to eat her cheesecake or concentrate on anything other than the anger that rose in her throat, she took out her cell phone and called Sheltering Hearts, demanding to speak to Evan Conley.

"Did you see Ralph Roper on TV with my niece?" Kira snapped as soon as Evan said hello. Before waiting for him to answer, she rushed ahead. "I am shocked that the man had the nerve to mention the words 'adoption' and 'election' in the same breath. How obvious can he be? And I am sick to think that he is using my niece to further his political career."

"Hold on, Miss Forester," Evan quickly interrupted. "This was not politically motivated. I knew about this interview and agreed to it."

"You agreed?"

"Yes. This was very carefully supervised, Miss Forester, since Vicky was to be on camera. The Department of Health and Human Services, as well as Sheltering Hearts, encourages adoptive families to share their positive experiences."

"*Adoptive families?*" Kira repeated, underscoring Evan's words. "Did I miss something? When did Vicky's adoption become final?"

"True, it isn't yet, but a client as well-qualified and visible as Ralph Roper can do a lot to help our statewide campaign to move children out of foster care. His endorsement carries a great deal of weight."

"Endorsement?" said Kira incredulously. "You agreed to let him use Vicky to advertise for families for DHHS, knowing he would plug himself?" The idea that Evan had been involved in arranging the interview increased Kira's irritation. For the past two weeks, she had been struggling to accept Evan Conley's rationale regarding the upcoming adoption, determined to view the situation from his perspective. His job was difficult, black adoptive families were hard to find, and she wanted to be fair. But how could she support him now? This was unacceptable.

"The reporter brought up Mr. Roper's candidacy," Evan countered. "All he did was answer her questions. Really, Miss Forester, I think you are blowing this out of proportion."

"I don't think so," Kira shot back. "I'm very annoyed with what transpired today, and I can't wait to tell Mr. Roper so to his face. He and his wife may be wonderful people who do love Vicky, but I don't like the way they are going about this, and I plan to let them know. When will I be able to meet them, Mr. Conley?"

"I left two messages with their attorney, but I haven't heard back. I'll try to get through directly to Ralph on his private line and see if I can arrange a meeting with you as soon as possible." He stumbled over his words.

"Fine, I'll expect to hear from you very soon," Kira told him, fumbling in her purse for a five-dollar bill, which she distractedly handed to the waitress before hurrying from the café.

CHAPTER 13

Ralph Roper swiveled back and forth in his desk chair, alternately scrutinizing the gardener who was tending the hedges outside his office window and the dense rows of text that covered the screen of his computer monitor, too preoccupied to concentrate on the report he was reading. He enjoyed working in his ground-floor office on Saturdays, when the place was quiet and his secretary would not interrupt him every few minutes. An office on the ground floor made life a little easier, and saved Ralph time that would otherwise be wasted waiting for the elevator. Though during the week his proximity to everything going on outdoors could prove distracting, on Saturdays he could enjoy the sweeping view of his beautifully landscaped grounds and the solitude of being left alone. Though many executives preferred to locate their private offices on the top floor of their buildings, Ralph had insisted that his be placed on the first floor of the five-story Roper Fiber Technology headquarters building.

He stopped swinging his chair and remained staring out the window at the sweep of blooming dogwood trees in the distance. The first blossoms usually filled him with a deep sense of peace to know that winter was behind him and warm weather was here to stay. Today, however, the sight of the delicate white flowers barely registered in his mind, which remained crowded with bits and pieces of the conversation he had just had with Evan Conley. Ralph could feel his initial irritation turning into anger, an anger that he knew he had to control if he planned to finish reading the audit on the output of the Tokyo branch of his operation.

Vicky Jordan's long-absent aunt wanted to meet him and Helen, and Evan Conley was encouraging her to do so. *Why should I accommodate the woman?* Ralph silently fumed. Simply because she was blood kin to Vicky? Because she was black? Or, as Evan Conley had stated, because she was a vital link to Vicky's heritage?

"Hogwash," Ralph grumbled, clenching his jaw. Conley had described Kira Forester as a local journalist with a solid reputation and a sincere interest in getting to know her niece. *So what?* Ralph thought, wondering where Kira had been when Vicky's mother had died. And when her foster mother had passed away. *Well, I'm not about to give in to her demands, and I have enough pull to make sure she never gets near my daughter.*

A cold fury descended over Ralph as he considered Evan's request, which in his opinion was ludicrous. He knew nothing about this long-lost aunt, who was probably an opportunist who had just found out how wealthy Vicky's adoptive family was. She probably wanted to meet him to ask for money, to make it worthwhile for her to disappear. He knew her type: pushy, nosy, threatening to spoil things unless she benefited from the deal. Yes, he was a wealthy, visible businessman, and he'd been strong-armed by people like Kira Forester too many times to remember. But they never got the best of him.

Ralph exhaled, trying to ease the pressure of remembering the disturbing conversation with Conley. No way was he going to invite this woman into his and Helen's world. His wife didn't need the stress of having to be civil to someone who was probably as irresponsible and flighty as Vicky's natural mother had been.

After all, Ralph thought, recalling what he had told Evan Conley, *Vicky is only six years old. Her foster mother, the mother she truly bonded with, recently died, and Vicky is still adjusting to that loss, as well as her new home and parents. Bringing a stranger like Kira Forester into the picture would only create additional stress on the child.* He had mentally added to himself, *As well as on my wife, upsetting the delicate balance of her emotional well-being.*

With a grunt, Ralph swung to his phone, grabbed it and punched in a speed-dial code.

"Joe?" he blurted out in a rush. "Yes, Ralph here. You going to be in your office for the next fifteen minutes? Good. I'll be right over."

Ralph got up from behind his desk, grabbed his suit jacket off the hanger by the door, and pulled it on as he hurried from his office. The corridor on the executive wing of the first floor was quiet and empty, and he was glad no one else was around. He was not in the mood for small talk. He had to concentrate on how to handle this damnable situation.

During the short drive to Joe Hickman's office Ralph thought about Helen and what this news was going to do to her. When Helen's doctor had confirmed, after three miscarriages, that she would never bear children, Ralph had suffered along with his wife as her emotional health deteriorated. She had tumbled into a downward spiral of guilt and depression that lasted for two years. It wasn't until her involvement with International Relief Now that she had begun to improve. The short-term hosting of foreign children for the agency had helped lift her dark moods and pull her out of that awful chasm that had nearly driven them to divorce. Now he had his old Helen back, due to Vicky's presence in their life, and no pushy reporter with delusions of entitlement was going to ruin everything.

Ralph slung his Mercedes into the parking spot next to Joe Hickman's red Ford pickup and threw the gearshift into PARK. Slamming the car door, he hurried up the driveway that separated Joe's one-story redbrick ranch-style home from the white-frame office building he had constructed next door. An attorney who specialized in industrial and agricultural law, Joe had been Ralph's best friend since they shared a sandwich in the first grade thirty-five years ago. Joe's successful law practice had made him wealthy enough to afford office space in a modern downtown building, but he preferred to conduct business in the two-room cottage in Monroeville that kept him close to Teresa, his wife and secretary, who managed the business side of his practice.

Giving Teresa a quick wave and a forced nod, Ralph strode directly to Joe's office and, without knocking, walked in. He started talking as soon as he closed the door, filling Joe in on his conversation with Evan Conley.

"She wants to adopt her niece?" Joe asked in the slow, southern drawl that made his sentences seem to go on forever. He chewed on his unlit pipe and waited for Ralph's answer.

"I didn't get that impression from Conley," Ralph replied, finally slipping into a chair across from his lawyer and friend. Leaning forward, he clasped his hands between his knees, scowled, then went on. "From what I understand, she wants to *bond*. Do you believe the nerve? She wants to *bond* so she can erase her guilt for deserting the girl when she was two years old. And you know what will happen next. She'll get real cozy with Vicky, turn her against us, and drive a wedge between the girl and Helen." Ralph clenched his hands into fists, tense with irritation. "I will not let that happen, Joe. You know what that would do to Helen."

The way Joe shifted in his chair and inclined his head gave Ralph his answer, though little emotion showed on the attorney's full, ruddy face. He had an intense set to his small blue eyes. After a long silence, he spoke again. "What do you know about Kira Forester?"

"Not enough. She's a columnist and reporter for the *Business & Professional Recorder* out of Charlotte. I think I've read a column or two of hers. Nothing earth-shaking or memorable. She's single . . . no relatives . . . and that's why Conley thinks she wants to get close to her niece at this late date, but I don't buy it. I'll bet she wants something else."

"Money?"

"Yes. Or the opportunity to get close to it. I don't want that woman coming to my house, nosing around, insinuating her presence into my life."

"What else do you know about her?" Joe wanted to know. "Who does she hang out with? How does she spend her free time? What's she been doing for the past four years while her beloved niece was in foster care?"

Now Ralph perked up, his mind shifting with Joe's, realizing that what they needed was a plan. "I don't know. But I can find out."

"No . . . I'll do that, Ralph," Joe said, then he took a deep breath and leveled hard blue eyes on his client. "I understand that Helen is dead-set on adopting this girl, but I warned you how sticky a transracial adoption can be. Some judges are adamant about creating ways to link black children, especially, with their blood relatives in order to maintain cultural identity. I had hoped you and Helen wouldn't have to deal with this."

With a lift of his shoulder, Ralph agreed with his attorney, remembering the strong words of caution Joe had used with him and Helen when they had approached him to handle the adoption. Joe was a typical white southern man who had grown up in a place and time where the races had been routinely separated in all aspects of community and business life. Ralph knew and understood Joe's reservations. He, too, had never been close to black people while growing up, and though he did not consider himself a racist, he had never gone out of his way to get to know people who were not white. Over the years, Ralph's international travel as he'd expanded his business empire, coupled with Helen's work with IRN, had increased both his tolerance for difference and his ability to understand and interact with people who were different, making the prospect of adopting a child who was not white more acceptable. However, he had found it difficult at first to understand why Helen wanted to do this.

"Ralph," Joe went on, "the only way we're going to convince a judge to keep this woman away from her niece is prove to the court that she would be an unsuitable influence on the child. And our case must be based on facts, not feelings. When did you tell Evan Conley that you would meet with the girl's aunt?"

"I told him I'd call him back this afternoon."

"Okay," Joe mused. "That's good. Call him back and set it up for a week from yesterday. Next Friday. That will give me some time. I may not be able to get enough on Kira Forester to totally shut her out, but we can make her rethink her request about bonding with Vicky Jordan."

"What do you need me to do? Hire a private detective?" Ralph asked his attorney, sitting back as he scratched his chin.

Joe shook his head, pulling his lips into a thin pink line. "No, Ralph. You don't need to do a thing. Leave this with me. Kira Forester can't be a saint. There must be something out there we can use for leverage, I just need to get my hands on it."

With gratitude in his voice, Ralph spoke in a husky whisper. "Thanks, Joe. I knew you'd know how to handle this. And Helen can't know a thing about this, you hear? I don't want her upset . . . or thinking that someone is going to take that child away. It would really set her back."

"I understand," Joe replied.

"Good," Ralph said, shaking his friend's hand.

It was late Saturday afternoon when Kira returned from the gym, anxious for a hot shower and lunch. It had been unusually crowded at the gym, and she'd spent more time than usual on her workout. When she opened the door, the phone was ringing, and she raced to answer it, hoping it might be Evan calling to make arrangements for her visit with the Ropers. But when she snatched up the ringing phone before her voice mail took the call, Julie Ays was on the line, not Evan.

"I thought I was going to have to leave you a message," Julie said in a cheery tone.

"Just walked in the door," Kira replied, tossing her car keys on the kitchen counter.

"Kira," Julie began, "I don't have but a minute. I'm on my way to meet a friend for dinner, but I wanted to ask you something."

"Sure. What is it?"

"One of the photos didn't make it back."

Puzzled, Kira frowned. "Really? That's odd. I'm sure I put everything into the FedEx envelope. Are you sure?"

"Yes. I sent you twelve photos and there were only eleven in the packet you returned. Have any idea where it might be?"

"No," Kira drew out her response, thinking. "I remember looking them over while I was in a restaurant waiting for a client I was going to interview. I even showed them to him before I packed them up. God, I'm sorry, Julie, but you have the negatives, don't you?"

"Sure. It's no problem to print it again. Just thought I'd let you know. Maybe you stuck it between some papers you were carrying, or left it on the table at the restaurant."

"Must have," Kira agreed, trying to recall the details of that hectic afternoon that had ended with her clash with Evan.

CHAPTER 14

The headline of *Business Week Watch* brought a smile to Frank Thompson's face. The wording in the caption summed up his message precisely: "Thompson Plans to Preserve History While Making Progress." Though he had read Kira's column three times since picking up his copy of the paper today, he scanned it once more, relieved that she had correctly couched his opposition to the destruction of Flagg Valley Mill in terms of his desire to preserve important local black history and instill pride in the town's citizens. She had included an old file photo of Flagg Valley Mill as it had been in the1950s, when production had been at its highest and the place had been alive with activity. She had not shied away from presenting Frank's pointed criticism of Roper's demolition plan, either, and Frank hoped that after reading Kira's column, few if any self-respecting African Americans living in Monroeville would feel inclined to support Roper in the upcoming mayoral election.

Frank read through Kira's vivid description of the history of the city again, and found himself intrigued anew with Jeremy Flagg's proud struggle to hold on to his land and increase his wealth, putting his life in danger. He reread the quotes that Kira had chosen to use, smiling to see his remarks in print, especially, "In my opinion, Ralph Roper is a greedy, insincere man who purchased Flagg Valley Mill to demonstrate to the black community that he has the power to do as he pleases, regardless of what the residents want."

"She really came through for me," Frank murmured, setting the paper aside and walking from his modest office at the rear of his Deere showroom to the front of the building, where a large plate-glass window faced the street. Standing there with his final cup of coffee for the day in his hand, he watched the cars carrying the citizens of Monroeville home from work. As they zoomed past, he wondered how many of them had read the story and if it would make any difference in how they voted. Surely others had to feel as passionate as he did about preserving the heart and soul of their city.

He thought about the television interview he had seen with Ralph Roper and his wife, considering their announcement that they planned to adopt a black child—an outright insult. Frank shuddered in revulsion as he recalled the way Roper had talked about his political future while his wife and the little girl had remained in the background, watching, letting Ralph have all the attention he craved.

Blatant pandering cloaked as a noble gesture, Frank thought, furious that Roper would involve a matter as serious as transracial adoption in his campaign, knowing the man was desperate to win over the black voters who made up sixty-nine percent of Monroeville's population. Frank's stomach turned over in disgust.

Only a selfish man consumed with his own power would use a child to increase his visibility and political support, he thought as he turned off the showroom lights and double-checked the security system, preparing to go home. Now Frank was more determined than ever to force the real Ralph Roper to the forefront so the citizens of Monroeville could see who he really was.

And thanks to Kira Forester, I have exactly the weapon to do it, Frank mused, grateful to the reporter for initiating their meeting, which was turning out to be much more valuable than she would ever know.

Ralph Roper crumpled the newspaper into a ball, shoved it from the dining room table, and frowned into the dish of chocolate mousse that Helen had just placed in front of him. Too angry to think about eating dessert, he slid the footed crystal dish aside, slumped back on his spine, and began circling his thumbs, thinking.

Without a word, Helen stooped down and retrieved the paper from the carpet, folded it neatly, then returned to her seat at the other end of the formally set table and began to read the story that had so quickly plunged Ralph into a very foul mood.

"He's coming pretty damn close to slander," Ralph growled at her, clenching his jaw to control his temper, not wanting to take his anger out on Helen. Up to this point he had chosen to wage his campaign against Frank Thompson in public forums such as civic club speeches, community debates, and a few carefully scripted televised interviews, conducting himself with great restraint, especially after that heated exchange at the school board meeting. He had hoped to keep the campaign focused on issues of importance to the community and away from personal grudges. Clearly, Frank Thompson felt otherwise.

Ralph cringed to recall the words his opponent had used to describe him in the published story, quoted extensively by the reporter whose name he now recognized as Vicky's long-absent aunt. How dare Frank call him "greedy" and "insincere?" Ralph fumed, angry with himself for not having moved more aggressively against Frank earlier in the campaign. But it was not too late, Ralph knew, and he was not about to let this unethical, blatantly personal attack on his character stand without a vigorous response. The fact that the damaging article had been written by Kira Forester enraged him further and made him wonder just what kind of person she was. Certainly not one he wanted involved in his private family life.

"Frank Thompson ought to be ashamed," Helen finally said, sighing as she placed the newspaper to the side of her dessert plate and reached for her husband's empty coffee cup. At the buffet table at the side of the room, she filled both hers and her husband's cups, added two spoons of sugar in each, then handed Ralph's to him. "And you have never said an unkind word about that man. Not once since he announced his candidacy. He seems to overlook the fact that you are trying to do a lot for this town—for his people, too. He ought to remember that."

"Hmph," Ralph grumbled. "What did you expect from a whiner like Thompson? All he does is complain, blame others for his misery, and whip up people's emotions so they can't see how little substance he has. He thinks his reputation as a civil rights crusader brings respectability, and owning a Deere franchise makes him automatically an upstanding businessman in the eyes of the people. But I know who he is—he's nothing but a posturing meddler. And I'm not worried. He hasn't a chance in hell of being elected mayor of this town, and his snide remarks won't affect me personally or my candidacy at all. Mudslinging is part of political campaigning, and if he's ready to start throwing dirt around, I can too. After this is over, he'll be sorry he ever talked to that reporter. I'll deal with him."

Ralph glared at Helen, who lowered her eyes and sipped her coffee, saying nothing, giving him space to vent. He was glad that Helen had let Vicky eat dinner early and go upstairs to watch TV. This was not a conversation he wanted her to hear.

Ralph's irritation made his face burn and brought perspiration to his forehead. The unpleasant slant of the article bothered him greatly, but his anger had as much to do with who had written the story as the words it contained. But he couldn't tell that to Helen, who had no idea that Kira Forester was Vicky's long-lost aunt—a woman with no scruples who seemed hell-bent on causing them trouble. Tomorrow he would finally meet her, and when he did, he planned to tell her exactly what he thought about her, her politically slanted article, and her scheme to get close to him and Helen. Ralph had to keep Kira as far away from Helen as possible, at least until the adoption was final.

"I wish Frank had not turned this into a personal fight," Helen commented, twin folds of concern deepening her brow. She propped one elbow on the table, then placed her chin on her hand, focusing on her husband. "I always liked Frank . . . and his wife, Ava, too. I don't understand how a political race can make such a nice man say such ugly things about you."

Frank gave Helen a look of utter disbelief and groaned, shaking his head. "Helen. Politics is not about *nice*. It's about winning. Frank Thompson wants to win because he needs a real job. He's losing his ass over at that Deere franchise and he's got nothing to fall back on. And if he thinks he can turn the black people of Monroeville against me by getting stories like this in the paper, he'll soon find how wrong he is. It's going to backfire. I can offer the people jobs, financial security, a future. What does he want to give them? A run-down factory, for which he can't finance the renovation, to use as an historical site so the people can take pride in their heritage? Give me a break. Wait and see. On election day he'll regret every negative word he ever said about me, and he'll be glad that he has a Deere dealership to occupy his time and earn a living. He needs to leave politics alone."

The long table in the conference room on the fourth floor of Roper Fiber Technologies was a sleek oval disk of polished blond wood with black ebony inlays radiating from a bold, dark center.

The modern industrial lighting suspended above the table reflected its mirrored surface, adding to the sense of contemporary elegance in the spacious room. A wall of tinted glass provided a shimmering view of the lushly landscaped grounds behind the building, now cast in the early shadows of dusk. The decor reflected the company's reputation as a successful, worldwide operation, as well as Ralph Roper's personal wealth and power. No expense had been spared to create the luxurious setting with its soft leather chairs, modern art on the walls, and carpet so soft and thick that Kira felt as if she were walking on a Carolina beach of soft white sand when she entered the room.

Evan greeted her as soon as she appeared and quickly introduced her to Ralph Roper and his attorney, Joe Hickman. The two men walked over and shook her hand.

"Please have a seat," Ralph said in a formal tone, indicating that she was to sit at the end of the long table with Evan Conley, opposite him and his attorney. "I'm glad you could come, Miss Forester."

"Thank you for agreeing to the meeting," Kira responded, trying to sound sincere. After nearly two weeks of waiting she was finally face to face with the man who wanted to adopt her niece, and she was shaken by the encounter. The luxurious surroundings, Roper's commanding presence, along with his authoritarian manner of speech and striking attire, all screamed wealth and power. It was obvious that Ralph Roper was a man who had everything—everything except a child of his own, she reminded herself as she sank into the soft burgundy leather chair that Evan pulled out for her.

"Will Mrs. Roper be joining us?" she inquired, glancing around. Her only impression of Helen Roper was the one she had formed after seeing her on television, and the image of the camera-shy woman still haunted and confused Kira. If only she could meet the woman who was going to raise Vicky, talk to her, and get to know her, Kira felt her anxieties might lessen. She hoped that Helen Roper might represent the more congenial half of the prospective adoptive couple.

Lifting a brow, Evan cleared his throat and tilted his shoulder toward Ralph in an unspoken reiteration of Kira's inquiry.

Ralph waved his left hand, the diamonds in his wedding band glinting under the lights as he dismissed Kira's question. "Not necessary," he tossed back, pushing back a few strands of dark blond hair that had eased onto his forehead. "Helen doesn't need to be involved with this. I can speak for both of us."

His casual response struck Kira as odd and gave her an uneasy feeling. She gave Evan a puzzled glance, then sat back, holding her tongue, thinking it best not to say anything right then, wanting Roper to take the lead. But it was Evan who began.

"I believe we all know why we are here." He paused to glance at each person seated around the table. "Miss Forester, who has not seen her niece, Vicky Jordan, in four years, came to me and requested visitation. This is a matter of grave importance. Ralph, I've been working with you and your wife, Helen, for some time now, and I would like to know how you feel about this."

Ralph gave Evan a quick nod, then pulled back his shoulders. "I have to say that I am not very comfortable with the request," he said. "I don't know Miss Forester or what she really wants, so I need a great deal more information before we proceed."

"Understandable," Evan agreed. "Vicky Jordan's welfare and happiness is what we must keep uppermost in our minds, and I hope we can stay focused on that. The last thing we want to do is jeopardize the adoption or create a situation that has a negative impact on what is a very promising placement. Don't you agree?"

"Yes," Kira replied in a strong voice, her eyes on Ralph Roper.

"Most certainly," Ralph replied, holding Kira's gaze for a moment.

Evan quickly went into a detailed summary of the status of Vicky Jordan's adoption, ending with the announcement that the Roper's home study was nearly complete and when it was, he would petition the court for a date to finalize the adoption. Evan turned to Kira. "You have expressed concerns about this adoption, Miss Forester, and I want to assure you that Mr. and Mrs. Roper, who might be strangers to you, are very dear to Vicky. Your niece is adjusting well, and from all indications is looking forward to having a family of her own."

"And I am glad to know that," Kira replied, deciding to enter into the discussion at a very cautious pace. There were so many legal aspects of the case, and she had a lot to learn. It was best to ask questions, listen, and be patient as she worked her way into investigating the issues that were crowding her mind. "I admit," she began, "that I was very upset when I learned that it was a transracial adoption. I reacted badly, and I apologize for my behavior, Mr. Conley. You're right. Race should not be the determining factor in an adoption, but I can't deny that I still believe it's important for Vicky to have contact with those who share her heritage and culture. As I told you when we first met, what I want is to be able to visit my niece, be a part of her life, and let her know that her mother's sister loves her and is there for her."

"How touching, Miss Forester," Ralph threw out sarcastically.

Kira stiffened. Roper's voice was as clear and forceful as a blast of cold wind.

"You're Vicky's aunt. So what?" Ralph went on. "My wife and I were led to believe that she didn't have any relatives—at least none who were interested in her well-being."

The remark hit Kira like a dart, but she forced herself to ignore the sting of it, determined to keep her cool. "I am her only blood relative," Kira stated. "As far as I know, no one has seen or heard from her natural father since she was born. And, yes, I do care about her well-being; that's the reason I'm here."

Ralph grunted, clearly not impressed.

Evan opened his briefcase, which had been sitting on the table in front of him, took out a sheaf of papers, and addressed Roper. "Miss Forester's relationship to Vicky is documented in her case file. It is true that she has not been actively involved in her niece's life until now, but there was a standing request to inform her of changes in Vicky Jordan's status. That's the reason I contacted her to let her know about your interest in adopting Vicky."

"Why did it take so long for you to surface?" Roper wanted to know.

"I was in Africa on a long-term assignment when DHHS sent the letter informing me that Sheltering Hearts had custody of Vicky," Kira replied, not about to let Roper ramrod the meeting. "I'm a journalist—"

"I know," Roper cut her off. "I read your column on Frank Thompson and the upcoming election in yesterday's edition of *BPR*. Quite a *colorful* piece you did on my opponent, Frank Thompson."

The taunting way in which Roper pronounced the word "colorful" struck Kira as almost degrading, but she bit her lip and let the remark pass, desperate to keep their dialog from deteriorating into a tit-for-tat exchange. "Thank you," she forced herself to say. "I was fascinated with the story of how Flagg Valley Mill was founded, and I learned so much from Mr. Thompson. He's very knowledgeable about the city's history, and I enjoyed talking to him."

"He is quite a talker, I agree. But talking and doing are two different things. He's good at making promises he will never be able to keep, and—"

"If you don't mind," Evan interrupted, attempting to gain control of the conversation, "let's not get into a discussion about politics right now."

"Sure," said Ralph, folding his arms across his chest.

Kira noticed that Ralph's bright blue eyes immediately turned dark and cold when Evan cut him off, and she knew she had been right. He was a man used to having control, getting his own way, and he resented any interference.

"Fine," Evan said, going on. "Miss Forester has no interest in adopting her niece. She wants visitation, and I think it is best for us to try to work out a proposal that I can take to the court. Voluntary cooperation is the best scenario, though I know this issue could simply be placed before the judge. But do we want that? Can we work this out here?"

"I don't know . . ." Roper said slowly, letting the words drift off without closure, pulling everyone's attention to him. "I don't see why she should have access to a child she never bothered to contact in the past. Too upsetting for everyone involved."

Suddenly Kira felt small and vulnerable. She shifted her attention to Roper's attorney, whose serious expression seemed almost sinister. Swallowing hard, she let the reality of her situation sink in: Ralph Roper had the money and power to get his own way, and he could probably block her from ever seeing Vicky simply because of who he knew and who he was. Kira thought about Frank Thompson's assessment of Roper, realizing that he had been right on target when he had said that Roper enjoyed intimidating those over whom he wanted control.

Again, Evan spoke up and filled the prickly silence, hurrying to explain. "Mr. Roper, I arranged this meeting so that you would have an opportunity to become acquainted with Miss Forester." He turned to Kira. "What would you like to say?"

Gathering her courage, Kira plunged ahead. "I think it would be good for Vicky to know that she has an aunt." Kira made the statement with as much conviction as she could muster. She felt as tense as a tightly strung wire but was determined not to let Roper intimidate her. She had no intention of backing down. Inhaling to calm her nerves, she went on.

"It is true that I have not been visible up to this point, but th does not mean I don't care. I readily admit that I could have done more to stay in touch with my niece, but now I want to rectify that. Vicky needs someone in her life who can tell her about her mother, her grandparents, and help her feel grounded in her heritage. She must know where her family came from and who she is. Mr. Roper, there is a huge role for me to play in her life, and I sincerely wish you would consider letting me get to know Vicky. She is not an infant, and soon she'll start asking questions about her natural family, questions which only I may be able to answer."

"Don't place too much importance on that, Miss Forester," Roper interjected in a tight drawl. "I'm sure I can access any information needed to satisfy my daughter's curiosity. When the time arrives."

"It would not be the same as hearing it from her natural mother's sister. She deserves that, I believe," Kira boldly countered.

"I have to agree with Miss Forester," Evan finally said. "The success of a transracial adoption often depends on the level of support from all parties involved. A child growing up in a household with parents who are not of the same race often benefits from contact with blood relatives. And the more cooperation and harmony that exists between the adoptive family and blood relatives, the better. A tight kinship network increases the odds for a successful permanent placement. And that is what I believe brings us together this evening."

Ralph Roper shifted around in his chair so that he could make eye contact with his attorney. Joe, who had been sitting slightly back from the table, as if prepared to consult with his client when needed, leaned forward and whispered something into Ralph's ear.

Ralph refocused on Evan for a moment, a deadpan expression stilling his face, then centered his somber gaze on Kira. "Depends on the relatives, I'd say," he tossed back as he motioned for Joe to move forward. "I don't know anything about you, Miss Forester, except that you are single, don't have a stable relationship with anyone, and have never made an attempt to contact your niece. So tell me why I should allow you to be introduced to Vicky at all?"

Kira uncrossed her legs and pressed her feet to the floor, steadying herself against this unfair personal attack.

Tensing his jaw, Ralph pulled his shoulders back as if posturing for a challenge, assuming the stance of a company president at a board meeting determined to make sure everyone at the table paid attention. "Let's dispense with the platitudes, Miss Forester," he continued. "Let's get on with what we came here for, okay? You don't know me. Never seen me in your life, but now that I am about to bring your niece into my home as my adopted daughter you assume that I won't be able to give her what she needs? That is preposterous."

Unflinching, Kira stared down the long table at Roper, locking eyes with him. "First of all, this is *not* the first time I have seen you, Mr. Roper. I was in the audience at the Meet the Candidates forum two weeks ago. I watched you in action, and I must say that your tendency to dismiss other people's feelings was as much in evidence then as it is now . . . and as it was during your recent televised interview, which I found very upsetting."

"Oh? Upsetting? Sorry you felt that way," Roper coldly remarked, placing his folded elbows on the table in a move that made him seem even more in control of the discussion. "I don't care if you were upset. My wife and I have successfully completed every phase of the process required by the court. Vicky is adjusting, and our court date will soon come up. There is no need whatsoever for you to be involved in our lives." He passed a hand over his jaw and gave Kira a look that indicated how little her opinion meant to him.

Deciding to ignore Evan's request that they keep politics out of the discussion, Kira gritted her teeth. "I don't think your plan to adopt a black child will win you any votes, Mr. Roper. I'm sure your announcement caused quite a stir in Monroeville," she tested, hoping she might strike a vulnerable spot. "What has Frank Thompson had to say about you adopting Vicky?"

"I haven't bothered to check with him. I have more important things to do than seek my opponent's opinion on a very private matter." He gestured with one hand toward his lawyer. "Joe. Answer a question for me?"

"Sure," Joe replied, perking up, scooting closer to the table.

"What legal rights does Miss Forester have relative to Vicky Jordan?"

"None," Joe answered bluntly.

"Exactly," Ralph stated, turning back to Kira, a glint of satisfaction in his eyes. "Your consent, Miss Forester, is not required in order for me to adopt Vicky, and unless the court grants you visitation, which I doubt they would based on what I know about you, I can promise that you will never get close to your niece."

"What do you mean?" Evan asked, looking puzzled. "What are you referring to?"

Joe Hickman handed Ralph a folder.

"This," Ralph went on, opening it. "Miss Forester is not exactly who she makes herself out to be. Are you?" he directed at Kira.

Confused, yet chilled by his threatening tone, Kira froze, her heart pounding in her chest. Blinking, she tried to imagine what Roper might be referring to. She had never been arrested, or even been sued, and as far as she knew she had no enemies who would fabricate damaging information to hurt her. In fact, she thought she led a pretty dull life.

"What is that?" Evan asked, nodding at the folder.

Ralph smiled, then returned the folder to his attorney. "Joe, why don't you explain what we've got here?"

"Of course," Joe said, licking his lips, eager to join the discussion. "Miss Forester," he began. "Are you acquainted with a man named Brandon Melzona?"

The mention of her former boyfriend's name made Kira's heart beat even faster, though she did not know why. She had no feelings for him, and had not seen him since leaving for Africa months ago. What connection could he possibly have to this? "Yes, Brandon Melzona used to be a friend of mine. I haven't seen him in months. Why?"

"Isn't it true that you two were romantically involved and very intimate for a period of six months? Up until the time you left for Africa on your special assignment for *World Societies Today?*"

"Yes," she stated slowly, drawing out her response, trying to control the quiver in her voice. It unnerved her to realize that Ralph Roper had been snooping around in her business, digging for ammunition to use against her. She was beginning to understand just how powerful and dangerous he could be.

In a calm, courtroom tone, Joe continued his questioning. "You spent many days and nights at Melzona's condo on Matheson Avenue, and at one time he lived with you. Isn't that so?"

"He never *lived* with me. We dated for a few months and were romantically involved. So what? I'm single. He is, too. And it ended. What are you trying to imply?" Kira demanded, not about to let herself be pulled into some kind of a trap, now aware that Roper was not going to play fair. "And what does he have to do with this situation?"

"According to police files, three years ago Brandon Melzona

was arrested in Dallas, Texas, for possession and sale of several controlled substances—cocaine, marijuana, and ecstasy."

"I don't believe you," Kira snapped, shocked by the absurd accusation. A chill raised the hairs on her arms as she stared in shock at Joe. "Besides, I didn't know him three years ago. And I never saw him do drugs or participate in any activity that would support such an allegation."

"Here are the reports to prove it," Joe replied, shoving the open folder down the length of the table at Kira.

She gazed down at the official-looking papers but made no move to touch them, realizing that the dates of the charges on the papers were long before she had ever met Brandon. "This has absolutely nothing to do with me!"

"A judge might think otherwise," Ralph told her. "Mr. Conley, would the court be inclined to allow a person who has been known to consort with a felon and a drug user have visitation with a minor child, even a blood relative?"

Clearly shaken, Evan shifted the folder over to his side, squinted at the papers, then picked up them up and scanned them. "This is highly offensive, Mr. Roper. I didn't arrange this meeting in order to launch an attack on Miss Forester's reputation or her suitability to have access to a minor. If you had such strong opposition to her visiting her niece, you should have discussed it with me on the phone when I called, and I could have investigated this before we came here tonight. I thought you were willing to cooperate with me. My impression was that you felt bringing Miss Forester and her niece together would be beneficial. Obviously, you were neither truthful nor clear about your intentions."

Kira fought back tears as she studied her hands, which were tightly clasped in her lap. Looking up, she stated, in as cold a tone as she could manage, "Why are you doing this? All I asked for was an opportunity to meet and get to know Vicky. I never threatened you. I don't want to interfere with the adoption. I never intended to."

"Well, as far as I am concerned, Miss Forester," Ralph replied, "it would serve no purpose for you to meet Vicky. The girl needs stability, an environment that does not change, and that means no introduction of a long-lost relative who has never lifted a finger to be a part of her life. Neither Vicky nor my wife needs the stress or burden of your presence. For all we care, you can go back to Africa and stay there."

Evan gasped, his mouth wide open as he took in the implication of the insult.

"What did you just say?" Kira threw back, shocked at the racial slur.

Shaking his head in disappointment, Evan slammed the folder closed and leveled furious eyes on his client. "That was absolutely uncalled for, Mr. Roper," he said, pulling in a short, hard breath. "I see we are not going to be able to come to any agreement here, so it might be best to bring this meeting to an end."

Kira's face fell slack. Her heart was beating fast, and she could feel perspiration gathering between her breasts. This power-hungry man was a racist. She had known it! She was going to do everything in her power to get Vicky away from him. This meeting tonight had been just what she needed to reinforce her gut feeling that Ralph Roper was not the civic-minded, upstanding man that the people of Monroeville thought him to be. Again, she thought of Frank Thompson, knowing he had called it right during their interview. Now she better understood what Thompson had been trying to tell her, and she was not going to let Roper bully her into disappearing.

"I did not come here to discuss my past, Mr. Roper," Kira found her voice, though it was quivering with indignation. "How dare you threaten me with a police file on a man I casually dated? He meant nothing. I have never done drugs, and I was never aware of his record, and it means nothing now. Your attempt to scare me away won't work. Let the court decide. Now that I know what kind of man you are, I will do everything in my power to make sure my niece never becomes your daughter."

"Be careful," Evan warned Kira, placing his hand on her arm. "Calm down. Now is not the time to make threats."

Kira whirled on Evan, fury in her eyes. "This is a promise, Mr. Conley. And if you care about Vicky's welfare as much as you say you do, you will agree with me." Then she raised her arm and pointed a finger down the table at Roper. "You don't love Vicky! You are using her for your own selfish motives . . . for political gain, to pander to the black voters of Monroeville . . . maybe to please your wife, who may indeed care about my niece. I don't know. Where is she? Why didn't she care enough to show up tonight to meet me?"

Evan tugged on Kira's arm, trying to get her to stop. "I think it's best to stop now. We can cool off, meet again . . ."

But Kira snapped her head around and pulled her arm free.

"Why should we meet again? Let the court decide if I will be a suitable influence on Vicky. When I saw Mr. Roper and his retiring, nervous wife on television parading my poor niece around like a prize steer they had won at auction, it made me sick. Frank Thompson was right. He is a greedy, self-centered man who has stooped pretty low to get what he wants. If you think I am going to meet with him again, you are sadly mistaken." Kira stood up, looked each man at the table directly in the face, then left, racing toward the doors that led to the stairwell instead of waiting for the elevator.

Evan Conley tapped the sleek conference table with the tip of his silver pen, staring at it while waiting for the tension in the air to settle. After a long moment of silence, he looked up and was shocked by the smug, self-satisfied expression on Ralph Roper's face. Could he have totally misjudged the man? he worried, realizing the mess this meeting had made of his perfectly arranged placement. Now it would be up to a judge to sort it all out, unless Evan could calm the waters.

"Mr. Roper," Evan began, pausing to focus on exactly the right tone as he searched for a way to get his case back on solid footing. "You are correct in your desire and right to know as much about Miss Forester as possible, but the way in which you went about it was unorthodox and upsetting. Background checks, accusations . . . these are matters best left to the court."

"So they can drag their feet for months, maybe years, while overloaded caseworkers conduct a bunch of studies and do some silly investigations that I can get my hands on in less than twenty-four hours? No thanks. I do not have to go that route," was Roper's response.

"You may have to, now that you've not only offended, but also threatened Miss Forester. I am very concerned about what happened here . . . your behavior. I am shocked that you would make such an inappropriate remark to her."

"She needs to disappear," Ralph threw back. "Let her try to fight me on a legal level. I dare her. She's a paycheck-to-paycheck single woman with less than five thousand dollars in her savings account. She can't afford to fight me on this."

"How do you know how much money she has in the bank?" Evan asked, disturbed at the casual way Roper was tossing around private information about Kira.

"Because I sit on the board of Union Bank. That's why. She has nothing with which to fight me except words, and no judge is going to listen to her."

"You may be gravely mistaken," Evan replied, realizing there was no point in trying to salvage the meeting. He closed his brief-case shut with a snap, then stood. "We'll be in touch," was all he could say before heading out the door.

CHAPTER 15

All Evan could think of was Kira and how devastated she must be as he walked briskly down the same corridor she had walked a few minutes earlier. Never in his wildest imagination had he thought that the meeting would turn out so disastrously, though he had anticipated some blunt questioning from Ralph, who certainly deserved to know who Kira was. He had expected Ralph to inquire about Kira's home life, ask her about her work, and her expectations regarding a relationship with Vicky. And he would not have been surprised if Ralph had asked that Kira hold off on visiting her niece until after adoption was final so that he and Helen could become better acquainted with her first. But this aggressive attack on Kira's character had caught Evan completely by surprise.

When the elevator reached the lobby, Evan quickly scribbled his name in the visitors' logbook at the security desk, then headed into the adjoining parking garage, relieved to see Kira's black PT Cruiser parked near the stairwell on the first level. He increased his pace and went over to her car, then tapped on the passenger-side window to get her attention.

Kira lowered the tinted glass, one brow arched at him, indicating her disgust.

Evan could see that her lashes were wet and her mascara had created two dark smudges that rimmed her eyes, so he stepped back and gave her a moment to pull herself together, waiting while she dabbed at her nose and cheeks with a tissue. He felt embarrassed and ashamed of his client's behavior.

"What do you want?" Kira finally managed, her voice tight with indignation.

"First of all, to apologize for my client's behavior," Evan began, leaning down to peer into the dim interior of the car. The floral scent of Kira's perfume, mixed with the pungent smell of new leather, swept over him, and the sensation was intensely pleasing. He placed a hand along the edge of the open window and moved closer. "Mr. Roper's behavior was uncalled for, Kira, and I'm so sorry. I know he offended you with such an insensitive remark and I told him so before I left."

"I'm sure you did," Kira said sarcastically, dabbing at her nose again with the tissue.

"I had no idea he was going to react this way. When I spoke to him on the phone yesterday, he gave me no reason to believe that he didn't—"

"Mr. Conley," Kira stopped him, "I'm not going to sit here while you stand out there and mumble excuses for your client. However, I do plan on telling you what I'm going to do about what happened here tonight. Please just get in." Kira flipped the button to unlock the passenger-side door. "You and I need to talk."

"Sure, sure," Evan replied, opening the door and sliding inside. He placed his briefcase on the floor between his feet. Respecting Kira's anger, as well as her disappointment, he remained quiet, waiting for her to speak, studying her shadowed profile: the slight upward tilt of her nose, the fullness of her lips, and the fine mist of crinkly hair that touched her forehead and hugged her cheeks. Sitting so close to her, Evan could not help but notice with how slim and fit she was, nor miss the shapely curve of her leg when she stretched it out to adjust her seat and push it back a few inches from the dashboard. This was the same feisty young woman who had marched out of his office in a huff only a few weeks ago. He inhaled softly, preparing himself for a good dressing-down.

"I am furious. And don't like what I think just happened in there," Kira began.

"Neither do I," Evan agreed, jerking his attention away from her legs, and turning his thoughts to salvaging the evening. He swallowed hard, tasting the bitter aftermath of the unsettling encounter and the fury he still felt toward Ralph Roper for having created this awful confrontation. Evan was upset, but he still had to be cautious and not allow his emotions to guide the conversation. "What Mr.

Roper said about you, and to you, was highly disturbing. In all of my dealings with him, he has always been very professional . . . though a little impatient with the bureaucratic aspect of the proceedings. I never thought he was the kind of person who would deliberately set out to hurt anyone."

"Well, now you've seen another side to the man, and hopefully you'll do something about it."

Evan flinched, not surprised that Kira expected him to rectify the situation. He shifted in his seat and touched his jaw, unsure of how to reply. "Your niece's adoption was progressing so smoothly. No problems until—"

"Until I showed up and interfered?" Kira interrupted, her voice cracking with irritation.

"No," Evan whispered, a swell of sympathy crowding his throat. "I wasn't going to say that. I was going to say that things were fine until you showed up and managed to bring out a side of my client that I had never seen. I think you deserve a chance to prove that your presence in Vicky's life would be beneficial."

Kira faced him and spoke in a voice that riveted his attention. "Do you plan to help me get such a chance?"

"Yes, I do," he firmly replied, but added, "Unless there is some reason for me not to recommend you to the court as a suitable participant in this adoption."

"I did not know about Brandon Melzona's criminal past, if that's what you are referring to," Kira coldly stated. "Listen, I'm a journalist. I know how to dig up dirt, and I know that people are quick to manufacture dirt if there's the tiniest bit of information to build on. That's what Roper did. I'd be foolish to think I could step forward and try to gain access to a minor child if I had anything remotely connected to drugs in my past. I swear to you. I've never engaged in any activity that would preclude my participating in Vicky's life."

"I believe you," Evan assured her.

"Besides," Kira continued, "if I had a police record, no matter how minor, Roper surely would have tossed that on the table, too. Right?"

"Probably so."

"Exactly! I may not have the wealth or influence of a man like Ralph Roper, but I do have friends in the press," Kira continued. "And, trust me, I will call on them if I need to, to vouch for my character and vindicate my reputation if Ralph Roper persists with his unfounded, vile allegations. I know politicians are accustomed to using underhanded tactics to get what they want, but his calculated attack on me tonight was frightening. Obviously, he is not a person who cares much about other people's feelings, and I am not comfortable with his plan to adopt my niece. Not at all."

Evan nodded, thinking back to the numerous interviews, discussions, and interactions he'd had with Ralph and Helen Roper over the past two months. Certainly, he had never seen signs that they might be insensitive, calculating people. Such characteristics would have been impossible to ignore. Ralph's tongue-lashing of Kira had been motivated by fear, he decided, fear that she might take Vicky away. His remarks were disastrous, a blunder that would not sit well with a family court judge, but not grounds to toss out a petition for adoption. A judge might even see his reaction as an indication of how much he wanted to protect the child.

Evan's disappointment in Ralph was pulsing through his body, but he knew that Ralph Roper was not a racist. He was simply a man under pressure, desperate to protect his family, and that included Vicky Jordan. However, Kira's concerns were valid, and Evan had to put them into perspective, allow her to examine them from the practical—and legal—point of view. "Miss Forester," Evan started.

"I think you can call me by my first name," Kira managed, sounding exasperated and resigned. "After all, if you're going to help me get to know Vicky, as you promised, we might as well drop the formalities and get to work. Tell me, where does Vicky's case stand? What do I need to do?"

"What do you want to do, Kira? Do you want to adopt her?"

Kira's answer came quickly, though it was riddled with uncertainty. "I wish I could say yes, but I can't. I'm not in a position to take on raising a child. But Ralph Roper, in my opinion, is not a suitable parent. Can't you place her with another family? A black family?"

Groaning under his breath, Evan shook his head. "There is no other family available for her right now. Kira, let me explain how this might play out. Let's say I go before the judge and tell her that I don't think Ralph Roper is a suitable candidate to adopt Vicky Jordan because he took it on himself to check out a stranger who popped up out of nowhere asking for visitation rights to his prospective adopted daughter. What do you think the judge would do?"

Kira sighed. "Tell you that Roper was right to check me out?"

"Possibly," Evan replied. "He has not done anything criminal, and no more than any concerned adoptive parent might do. It's the way he went about it that is so troubling, but do you see how complex this is?"

"But what about his less than politically correct remark? Borders on racism, if you ask me."

"I know. An unfortunate choice of words made during a heated exchange." Evan turned to Kira and locked eyes with her, emphasizing his point. "I don't condone his remark. In fact, I am outraged. But let's be pragmatic here. If somehow the Ropers' petition were withdrawn, Vicky would immediately be placed in another foster home while we seek a new family. Is that what you want?"

"Oh no. I'd hate to see that happen. It would be very traumatic for her," Kira admitted.

"I agree," Evan said, a glimmer of hope rising. He had to move quickly to set Kira's mind at ease and give her a clear understanding of just how difficult it was to find families willing to adopt children like Vicky. Thinking it best to shift the conversation to a more personal level, he told her, "I was adopted when I was an infant."

"Really?"

"Yes. I never knew who my real parents were and never wanted to find out. I didn't choose my adoptive parents; they chose me, and it worked out fine . . . as it does for most placements if the agency handling the adoption does its job. My childhood was stable, filled with love and purpose. The Ropers are no different. They have chosen Vicky, and they love her. Try to understand."

"But you need to take a harder look at Ralph Roper," Kira pressed. "That man has a huge responsibility to do what is right. He throws his weight around, and his position in the community, as well as his supposed devotion to his wife, might be masking another side of his character."

Evan inclined his head in agreement, though hating to think that Kira might be right. "I will reexamine every aspect of the Roper's home study. I promise."

"And what is the deal with Mrs. Roper, anyway?" Kira asked, shifting her curiosity to the absent member of the couple. "Don't you think it is odd that she lets him do all the talking and stays in the background?"

Evan was quiet for a moment, a thoughtful scowl touching his features as he recalled his first meeting with Helen Roper. She had come to Sheltering Hearts with her husband, eager to talk about adopting a child after reading about the agency in a magazine article on placing special-needs children. The Ropers had been on a waiting list for a Caucasian child for nearly a year. After exploring the possibility of adopting Vicky, and asking quite a few questions about her background, they soon began the process to formally adopt her. Helen Roper had seemed fragile, a little nervous, though eager to move forward. And once the process was fully underway, Helen had stepped out of the picture, leaving Evan to communicate with Ralph, who made all of the decisions.

"Yes," he said, resuming his conversation with Kira. "I was surprised that Helen was not here tonight. She's the one who was so adamant about adopting Vicky Jordan. No other child would do for her and her husband. My contact with her has been limited lately, but I doubt very much that she had any idea of what Ralph was planning tonight. And I doubt that he would have made such an insulting comment to you if his wife had been in the room." Evan shook his head, wishing he could erase the sense of discomfort that stayed with him, then adjusted his tone to a less serious level. "I'll document what happened tonight and make it a part of the case file, but I can't predict how the court will react. What Ralph Roper said and did may have no effect on the judge's decision on the final adoption. The court wants to see your niece placed with the best possible family, and that very well may be Ralph and Helen Roper."

"I know, but you can slow things down, can't you?" Kira asked.

Evan placed a reassuring hand on her arm. "Absolutely. Try not to let this upset you too much. I do think Helen Roper is a fine woman who is doing a great job of mothering Vicky. Let's focus on getting you into the picture. I have a feeling that once you and Helen meet, a lot of your concerns will disappear. The first thing you need to do, Kira, is file a petition to request the court to grant you visitation while Sheltering Hearts continues with its home study. A caseworker will interview you and prepare your profile. Do you have an attorney?"

"I can get one," Kira replied.

"Good. Your attorney should accompany you when you go before the judge. You will be closely questioned, and it would be a good idea to have someone with you who understands the legal ramifications of your answers." Evan gave her a tentative smile, relaxing as her uncertainty began to fade.

"That's fine with me," Kira said, finally letting her body go slack as she sat back in her seat and slid her palms over the steering wheel, gazing through the windshield.

Evan watched her, wondering what she was thinking about, yet he was comfortable with the silence in the car. He saw how her long, full lashes shaded her hazel eyes, which had seemed lit from deep within when she'd looked at him. Her sophisticated beauty had touched him briefly when he'd first met her in his office, but he had pushed the attraction aside in order to focus on the business of Vicky Jordan. Now he deliberately lingered on her attractive profile, no longer feeling threatened by her unexpected appearance in his case. His first impression of her as a selfish, close-minded person who refused to look beyond the racial aspects of the case was quickly fading. She wasn't the inconsiderate, contentious person he had thought her to be, but rather an attractive, determined young woman who regretted her estrangement from her niece. She had made a mistake by disappearing from Vicky's life at a time when she might have been able to play an important role, and now she regretted it. Evan had to give Kira credit. She was honest, forthcoming, and remorseful . . . ready to turn over a new page and set things straight. As he studied Kira's profile, he wished the circumstances of their relationship were different, that their professional association did not prevent him from telling her how much he wanted to spend private time with her.

"How long do you think this period of intense scrutiny will take?" she asked, still gazing ahead.

"A few weeks—a month perhaps," he stated, speaking as much to himself as to her. "Long enough to give the court—and me—an opportunity to get to know you better."

Kira turned then, and, removing one hand from the steering wheel, she placed it on Evan's arm. "Thank you," she murmured, gratitude in her voice. "I don't feel quite so alone in this now."

Impulsively, Evan placed his fingers over hers and held on to them for a long moment before speaking. "You aren't alone, Kira. I'll be there with you, no matter how this situation turns out." When he felt her slender fingers curl around his, he gave them a squeeze, suddenly wishing he could feel them caressing the back of his neck.

CHAPTER 16

On Monday morning Kira called Kenneth Lane, an attorney and longtime friend who immediately agreed to assist her with the petition for visitation. Lane, a successful, well-respected family law attorney in Charlotte, met with Kira that evening, and together they inched their way into the maze of paperwork and procedural requirements related to her request.

On Tuesday afternoon, Kira received a surprise call from Ralph Roper, who profusely apologized for his behavior the previous Friday and begged her to understand.

"I am so sorry that I made such an insensitive remark to you, Miss Forester," Roper stated in a very sincere tone. "What I said to you about going back to Africa was not intended as a racial slur, and I regret it. My wife and I are totally dedicated to being good parents to Vicky, and the thought of you—a stranger—interfering with the adoption pushed me to say and do things that were not appropriate. I hope you can forgive me."

Listening, a warning bell sounded in Kira's mind. Though she appreciated his attempt to extend an olive branch, she was still angry with Ralph Roper. His overture of forgiveness had come too quickly, too easily, and most likely after a stern warning from Evan. Did Roper realize how brutish and invasive he'd been with her? Forgive him? Maybe. But forget? Never. She'd never let down her guard with that man again. He had blindsided her once with his private investigation and personal attack. She was not going to let him do it again. Listening to his apology, she felt pretty sure it was delivered under protest, and she grew determined not to let him off too easily. She'd go along with his strategy for now, see where he was headed, and maybe find out who he really was.

"I appreciate you calling to tell me this," Kira replied coolly, choosing her words very carefully. "I was very distraught to think that my niece might be living with a family that does not understand how hurtful such statements can be."

"I understand your concern," Roper hurried to reply. "I assure you, my wife and I want nothing but happiness for Vicky. I just spoke with Evan Conley and told him that I overreacted and spoke too hastily out of concern for the integrity of our adoption petition. He said he understood."

Though Roper's tone was contrite, Kira remained cautious. "I don't know much about you . . . or your wife, Mr. Roper," she said. "And though I accept your apology and thank you for calling, I have no plans to disappear. In fact, I think you are going to see quite a lot of me from now on."

"Then we'll have to find a way to get along, won't we, Miss Forester?"

"Yes, I guess we will."

In the days that followed, Kira became consumed with the petition, faxing information to Kenneth, e-mailing him late at night to ask a question, dashing to his office between assignments or meeting him on her lunch break so they could hone the information on the court papers into a clear presentation of who Kira Forester was and why she ought to be granted visitation with her niece.

During this time, Kira also found herself in close contact with Evan, upon whom she relied to clarify procedures and answer questions about the adoption process. She liked the way he used frank, honest language with her, not sugarcoating anything about the situation. He kept her informed, sent her books and videos about transracial adoption, and boosted her spirits with encouraging words. While talking to him on the phone, she found the memory of his touch, of his fingers entwined with hers, surfacing often in her mind, but she buried the recollections as quickly as possible, terrified of the emotions they created. A relationship with Evan Conley would be a big mistake, and she had made enough mistakes to last another lifetime. His professional allegiance remained with the Ropers, whom he had not ruled out as Vicky's adoptive parents. And involvement with Evan would work against her in court, diffusing the impact of her petition, ruining all of Kenneth's hard work. She could not take such a chance.

The next seven days passed in a blur as Kira channeled her energy into her work, leaving Kenneth to finalize the necessary paperwork to prove that she was worthy of the court's trust. When Kenneth called to inform her that the petition had been filed, a sense of peace finally came over Kira. However, her personal curiosity about Evan Conley and the memory of his body so close to hers inside the dark interior of her car would not go away.

"Take your time, Corey," Frank Thompson said, easing away from the man who was studying a shiny green rotary cutter with great interest. Frank walked over to his transaction counter at the side of the showroom, leaving his customer to ruminate about the information Frank had provided. The price, the features, and the warranty had all met Corey's specifications. Now it was just a matter of whether or not he'd buy the new equipment or the used one he'd looked at out back.

Frank shuffled some papers around on the countertop, trying to look busy, praying Corey would hitch up his overalls, scratch his head, and say yes, he'd take the brand-new cutter. Frank desperately needed this transaction to make up for a very slow week, and he knew Corey Sherman had the cash to provide a very good ending to a miserable day.

For this time of the year business had been extremely slow, and Frank was worried about how he was going to make his next payment on his franchise to the home office. His location used to be one of the most profitable in the region, but many of the local farmers who had been regular customers had moved away over the past five or six years. Now he hoped every day for a big spender to walk through the door and rescue his bank account, but so far this month it had not happened.

His campaign for mayor was rapidly eating away at his personal funds, but he refused to panic. He would win. He had to. And after he became mayor, he would no longer have to worry about courting stingy customers, meeting outlandish sales goals, or making huge franchise payments. He would finally be in control of his life and have the power to make decisions for himself. No more taking orders from a supervisor in a head office hundreds of miles away. No more anxiety attacks over how he was going to pay for his inventory. No one understood what he was up against now that Monroeville was no longer the farming center it used to be. Equipment sales would never return to the zenith they had reached only four or five years ago.

Frank sneaked a peek at Corey, who was busy examining the blades of the cutter. He rolled his eyes, then sat down on the high stool at the counter, determined to leave the man alone. He had done all he could. He reached under the oversized desk calendar on the counter and removed his copy of the *Monroeville Mirror* that he had stuck under the blotter when he'd arrived that morning. It was still folded in half, and when he opened it to spread it out, the story at the bottom of the front page made him jerk alert. Ralph and Helen Roper were facing him, smiling, holding hands with a little girl between them. The photo made Frank's blood boil, just as it had when he'd seen them parading their soon-to-be-adopted daughter on television a few weeks ago. He skimmed the story. Not much more information than what he'd heard Ralph tell the reporter during his interview on TV, he thought, disgust rising in his stomach.

There is more to this than Roper is telling, Frank decided, studying Helen's face. Her smile seemed genuine, and her eyes were lit with happiness, as if adopting this girl meant the world to her. But Ralph's wide grin appeared stiff and uncomfortable, as if he were simply posing for another campaign photo. *Why would he do this?* Frank wondered. Surely not because of the statewide DHHS campaign to increase adoption of foster children, as he had bragged into the camera. Was it to win over black voters? Appear more liberal? A plot to unify the community to shut Frank out? Well, Frank knew the African-American constituency of Monroeville well enough to suspect that they would not buy it, and the thought of a backlash against Roper brought a smirk to Frank's face. He let himself relax, thinking that the adoption just might work to his advantage.

If Ralph Roper thinks a transracial adoption will make him appear liberal in the eyes of the citizens of Monroeville, he's mistaken, Frank mused, now concentrating on the attractive little girl who was smiling up at the Ropers. *Who is she? Why did they pick her?* he wondered, setting the paper aside, thinking his wife might be able to help him answer those questions. In her work as a school counselor, Ava often interacted with a variety of state agencies and knew her way around the bureaucratic hierarchy of the Department of

Health and Human Services. Ava would get him the lowdown on the girl, he was sure of that.

When Corey Sherman headed toward him, Frank detected less confusion on the man's ebony face. His mouth was set in a tight pucker, and his work-gnarled hands were thrust deep into his pockets. Frank forced himself to perk up, though he was certain he already knew what the tightwad had decided to do.

Frank looked up at Corey and gave him his best salesman's smile. "Well, what did you decide to do?"

"Better write up the one you got out back," Corey said, hooking his thumbs into the straps of his overalls, his dark face turning solemn. "That's a beauty over there," he indicated the shiny new cutter with a jerk of his head, "but I gotta watch my budget. That refurbished one will do just fine."

"No problem," Frank said as cheerfully as he could manage. "Wanna take it with you? Or want me to bring it out later today?"

"I got my truck. I'll take it."

"Fine. Just take a minute to write it up," Frank said as he began to write up the sales slip.

Corey Sherman handed Frank his MasterCard, then reached over the counter and picked up Frank's copy of the *Monroeville Mirror* and began reading the story about Ralph Roper. "That's really somethin,' ain't it?" he said.

"What?" Frank raised his head up from the credit-card machine.

"Ralph and his wife adopting a black girl. Gotta give the man credit. Now, don't take this wrong. You know I want you to win, Frank, but Ralph's not so bad. He gives his word, and he sticks to it, I'll give him that. Most black folks wouldn't do what he's done."

"Most black folks got families of their own and don't have to take on someone else's child," Frank grumbled in reply.

Corey shrugged, continuing to examine the story in the paper. "You know, my son is working over at the Roper warehouse. Temporary. Frank kept him on when the mill closed down, and he's paying my boy a real decent salary to unload trucks. And now he's adopting a poor child that has no family. You gotta give the man credit for doing the right thing."

Frank's mouth dropped open in disgust. Why would Corey Sherman, a hardworking black man, buy into Ralph Roper's obvious attempt to win over the African-American voters of Monroeville? Was he blind? Didn't Corey see what was going on? Frank continued to process the purchase, his mind spinning. If Corey Sherman would say these things to his face, how many other black citizens were thinking the same things? Clenching his jaw, Frank made up his mind that he had to deal with Ralph and expose the man for who he really was.

"You want me to meet you at the Starbucks on Glenwood?" Kira repeated, realizing Evan was very close by. Easing onto the bar stool at her kitchen counter, she calculated that it would only take a few minutes for her to touch up her makeup, get dressed, and get over there—if she decided to meet him.

"Right. I've just finished my book-club discussion at the Barnes & Noble over here, and I . . . I realized you live in this area, don't you?"

"Not far," she cautiously replied, though pleased that he had called. "Is there something we need to discuss about the case?" she asked, groping for a better handle on his intentions.

Her petition for visitation had been filed yesterday, and Kira knew that Kenneth had sent a copy of it to Sheltering Hearts. If that was what Evan wanted to discuss tonight, she was going to pass. Her mind and her heart had been so crowded with worry over the upcoming hearing, that all she wanted to do now was push the issue far from her mind until the court made its decision. And if Evan wanted to give her an update on the Ropers, he could just as well tell her over the phone and save her the trouble of getting dressed and going out at eight thirty-five at night.

"No, I don't want to discuss the adoption," Evan told her, a slight stammer in his reply. "Really, I was wondering if you might like to have a cup of coffee. But if you're busy . . . if it's not a good time, I understand," he finished, his words dropping to a near whisper.

Don't answer too quickly, Kira silently cautioned herself, not wanting to make the wrong decision. Of course she'd love to meet Evan for coffee, but should she? That was the question. He sounded as nervous as she felt at that moment, and his shift in demeanor, from a man who had always seemed professional and self-assured to one whose voice was now touched with uncertainty, suddenly made Kira want to laugh. She placed her fingertips over her mouth to hold back a giggle, thinking that Evan sounded like a teenager who did not know quite what to say.

They had spoken to each other on the phone many times since the blowup at Ralph Roper's office, their conversations becoming less strained and formal each time they talked. However, meeting Evan at Starbuck's tonight would shift their relationship beyond established boundaries, and Kira wasn't sure she wanted to take such a risk.

"Do you think it's a good idea for us to spend time together socially?" she probed, curious to hear his rationale for moving their business relationship to a more personal level.

"Well, yes." Evan drew out his response, as if carefully considering what he ought to say next. "It's only a cup of coffee in a public place. I thought you might want to . . . oh, I don't know. Look, if you're busy—"

"I'm not," Kira softly interrupted, surprised by the tremor in her voice. He was right. What harm could there be in simply sharing conversation over a cup of coffee in a crowded shop? After all, Evan Conley was the custodial agent for her niece, and getting to know him outside of his role with the agency might be a very good move. She needed a better understanding of who he was and where his loyalties lay. "Okay," Kira agreed. "I can be there in about fifteen minutes." She held her breath and gazed at the tiles on the kitchen floor as she waited for his reaction.

"Great. I'll hold a table at the front and watch for you."

What am I getting into? she asked herself as she slid off the bar stool and hung up the phone. Kira raced into her bedroom, pulled on a pair of straight-leg jeans, her most comfortable low-heeled boots, and frantically searched her closet for her favorite black V-neck sweater. A few strokes of eyeliner and mascara, along with a pass of blush over her honey-tan cheeks, brought the makeup she had applied that morning back to life. Running her fingers through her hair to shake out the curls, she locked her door and hurried to her car, suddenly enjoying the spontaneity of the invitation. It had been a long time since she'd felt this relaxed, and she knew she needed to stop dwelling on her problems and get out more often. However, during the short drive to Starbuck's Kira reminded herself that this was not a date and she should not consider it anything other than an opportunity to learn more about the man who held Vicky's fate.

Kira took Evan's hand and held it briefly in hers when she met him just inside the entrance to the coffee shop. She was jolted by the same rush of warmth that had raced through her body when his fingers had curled around hers in the dark interior of her car. Kira's eyes widened in surprise, then she lowered her lashes and stepped in front of Evan as they headed toward the serving counter.

Standing slightly ahead of Evan, Kira could feel his eyes on the side of her face and sense the nearness of his body, only inches from hers. She inhaled the light male scent of his cologne and closed her eyes, tempted to turn around and reach out to him, and let him take her hand in his once more.

The server appeared, requesting her order in a cheery voice, breaking her mental wandering. Kira asked for a latte, and Evan requested a mocha. Coffee cups in hand, they slipped into chairs facing each other at the small square table Evan had snagged for them at the front of the coffee shop.

"Tell me about your book group. What kinds of books do you discuss?" Kira asked, breaking the lull that followed after they had settled at the table.

"All types," Evan replied, slowly moving the stirrer in circles in his coffee. "We discuss fiction and nonfiction—reference books, too. We've done travel books and even a few cookbooks."

"Interesting. Who chooses?"

"The one who volunteers to lead the discussion, and, believe, me some of our leaders can get quite creative. They bring in props, present slide shows, make crafts. Once we made those paper sculptures . . . what's it called? You know, the Japanese art."

"Origami?"

"Right." Evan chuckled, shaking his head. "I never did get the hang of that, but it was fun trying."

"And tonight who was the speaker?" Kira asked.

"Me, but I'm ashamed to admit that I didn't finish the book."

"So you had to wing it?"

"To a degree," Evan admitted, reaching for a small bag on the seat next to his. He pulled out a softcover book and handed it to Kira. "I know I promised not to talk about your niece's case tonight, and I won't, but I'd like you to have this book. It's autographed, too."

Kira studied the book's cover and title. *"Questions to Ask and Answers to Seek in Transracial Adoption,"* she murmured, then flipped through the pages, nodding. Glancing up again at Evan, she frowned. "Isn't this a rather narrow topic for a book discussion? I mean . . . how many members of your group are involved in transracial adoption?"

Evan laughed. "I was worried about the same thing at first, but as it turned out, a surprising number of people were extremely interested in the topic. We had a very stimulating discussion. Talking about race-related issues always generates a lot of emotion, but it also kind of forces people to open up and get into a topic they might not ever discuss. A woman from Peru told us about her own cultural heritage and what she is doing to pass it on to her children, who have never visited her homeland. A few touched on tolerance and acceptance, and how difficult it is to bridge the differences that separate us. Most of us are in close contact with people of different races and cultures, at work, at church, in our schools especially, but how well do we really know what is important to them?"

Kira nodded, thinking of Sharon, with whom she had worked for many years. Though they socialized occasionally and shared personal information, their relationship remained defined by their professional association.

"It's hard to get close to people whose culture and backgrounds are not similar," Kira agreed, then added, thinking of her own situation, "But we have to keep trying, don't we?"

"Exactly," Evan said. "That's one reason I chose this book for the club to read and why I thought you might find it helpful, too, as you get closer to Vicky. Which I hope will be very soon."

"Me too. Kenneth thinks we ought to hear something from the court next week." As Kira said those words, she silently chastised herself for delving into the topic she had vowed to avoid, but talking to Evan made it impossible for her to ignore the link that brought them together.

"The family court system moves at its own pace, so don't be discouraged if it takes longer than your attorney thinks." Easing back, Evan swept his fingers along the side of his cup and watched Kira take a sip from hers.

She captured his gaze over the rim of her cup, aware that his expression was definitely giving off signals that their discussion on professional matters was over.

"Now that I've told you all about my book club, tell me what you do when you're not interviewing business leaders for your column, or attending trade expos."

Kira set down her latte, bemused. "Or pounding my computer keyboard," she added. "Well, my days are fairly unpredictable, though I try to keep them free enough to respond to unexpected opportunities for a story. I have to deal with tons of phone calls, never-ending deadlines, lots of meetings, and then there is the writing. The writing never stops."

"And when you are not at the office?"

"I try to get to the gym a few times a week, which often seems more like self-imposed punishment than beneficial exercise. I travel when I can, though my last trip was not for pleasure, and I collect Indian art."

"American?" he asked.

"North American, South American. Western Hemisphere," Kira said, glad that Evan seemed interested. "Something about the colors and shapes intrigues me."

As they chatted, Kira found Evan to be an attentive listener who eased the conversation along. She told him a little about her childhood, revealing her resentment of Miranda for leading such a destructive lifestyle, and confessed her regrets over their estrangement. Kira decided to be as open and honest with Evan as possible, wanting him to know her as a person and to see that she deserved a chance to bond with Vicky. Kira appreciated the fact that he listened without comment and allowed her to express herself without feeling as if she were being grilled.

Kira told Evan about her job, her struggle to get along with her new boss, and how proud she was to have been chosen to write an article for *World Societies Today*. When she touched on her trip to Africa and the frightful shoot-out in the jungle, he was intrigued.

"You stay busy," Evan commented.

"Busy enough."

"But, busy alone?" Evan queried. "In all you've said, you haven't mentioned a significant other."

The one topic Kira had not planned on discussing tonight was suddenly in her face. She could duck the issue and inform Evan that her personal life was none of his business, or tell the truth: she had a disastrous track record with men.

"Well, you did get an earful about my love life from Ralph Roper," she stated, giving Evan a grim smile. "That relationship was an unfortunate lapse of judgment, to say the least. Dating Brandon Melzona was a huge mistake, and after untangling myself from that mess, I haven't been very eager to dive back into the dating scene."

"Oh, you shouldn't be so hard on yourself. Everyone has had at least one relationship that had to be chalked up to experience in order to move on," Evan advised.

"Easy to say . . . though it was an experience, all right," Kira said with a laugh, tossing back her head as she ran her fingers through her hair. "Certainly one I don't plan to repeat." She took a sip of coffee, then shook a finger at Evan. "And you. What was yours? What did you chalk up to experience in order to move on?" she teased.

Evan shrugged. "I admit that my work takes up most of my free time, and that my book-club discussion group, which meets once a month, is probably the extent of my current social life. I guess my failed marriage is what I had to chalk up to experience in order to move on."

"Any children?" Kira asked, glad that Evan felt comfortable enough to reveal this to her.

"I have a twelve-year-old daughter who lives with my ex-wife in California."

"Are you close?"

"I'd like to think so, though it's hard to stay involved with her when I'm thousands of miles away."

"What's her name?" Kira asked.

"Lora," Evan replied, his voice growing solemn and low.

Kira wrapped her arms around her body and watched Evan closely, detecting a glimmer of sadness in his eyes. She did not speak, giving him time to compose himself before going on.

Evan told Kira about his past and how he had started Sheltering Hearts seven years ago. He spoke about the joy of becoming a father when his daughter was born, and the painful sense of failure he had felt when his marriage fell apart. Kira understood how devastated he must have been when his ex-wife moved away and separated him from Lora, the most important person in his life.

"It's not what I wanted, or ever dreamed would happen to me, but it's the way things turned out," Evan finished.

Kira reached across the table, took his hand, and held it loosely in hers, watching his face closely. "Almost like what happened to me and Miranda. I wish things had been different between us, but they weren't. So now it's up to me to make the best of what I have, and being a good aunt to Vicky is what I want to do. Miranda would have wanted me to know her daughter, I'm sure. That's all that matters now, and if the Ropers are approved as her adoptive parents, I've made up my mind to accept them . . . in order to move on."

"Ralph called me and apologized. Said he was going to call you, too."

"He did," Kira replied. "It would be easy for me to hold a grudge and make a huge deal out of what he said and did, but for the sake of my visitation hearing, I've decided to let it go. I refuse to get myself in a situation that might make things more difficult. I'm not going to be run off."

Blinking thoughtfully, Evan continued. "I know. I refuse to let my ex-wife drive me away from Lora. I don't want my daughter to forget me, or think that I don't love her. It's terribly hard, losing a child, whether it's through death, divorce, or any kind of separation. I call Lora and send her little gifts all the time, not just on important occasions such as her birthday, and I know my efforts may not seem like a big deal to her right now, but I hope one day they will. I'm not with Lora enough to know if she resents me for divorcing her mother, but I do know that when she grows up and looks back over her childhood, she'll know she had a caring father, whether he lived with her or not. My hope is that she never feels abandoned or alone, that she knows she can come to me, call me, depend on me. It's tough, but, I wouldn't have it any other way."

"Really? There's nothing you'd change? Nothing else you want?" Kira said, easing her hand from his, struck by the odd tone of resignation in Evan's statement.

"No, nothing else. Well, that was true until I met you," Evan murmured, raising his chin slightly, as if daring Kira to object.

His remark sent a shiver through Kira. She ran her hands over her arms and waited for him to go on.

"Interesting that you can see how stuck in the past I've become, Kira. You're right. I ought to want more, but I haven't been brave enough or willing to take the risks to go out and find it. My work and my long-distance relationship with Lora are all that have mattered for years. I want her to feel secure and loved, the same thing I want for every child under my protection at Sheltering Hearts, but I do need more, Kira. You've made me realize that." Evan's features stilled, then he shrugged and gave Kira a half-smile. "Getting out into the dating scene is not easy. And I'm not a young man now."

"Go on," Kira interrupted, lightening the mood. "How old are you?"

"Forty-four," Evan said.

"That's young! And I know you've read my vital statistics in my case file, so you must know that I am only a few years younger than you. Forty-four is not old. Stop using that as an excuse to turn into a hermit."

"I'm not. Just making a point. I have a business to run, responsibilities to my staff, and children to place. The pressure never eases, and it often occupies my mind and my time twenty-four hours a day, seven days a week. It's easy to become isolated in my kind of work, and unless I make an effort to reach out, as I did tonight when I called you, I can become very content to let things drift." He reached over and touched the underside of Kira's chin, his fingers lingering just below her bottom lip as he spoke. "I'm very attracted to you, Kira."

She held her breath, mesmerized by the way he was looking into her eyes.

"You're a very special person," he said, shifting his touch momentarily to the soft hollow at the base of Kira's neck where his fingers brushed the edge of Kira's V-neck sweater. Removing his hand, he leaned back from the table. "Can I tell you that I want to see you socially?"

A sensation of lightness cascaded through Kira, making her pull in a short gasp of air. Her chin burned where he had touched it, and she could still feel the sweep of his fingers at the base of her neck.

"I'm serious, Kira. I'd like to get to know you outside of our professional relationship. Is that possible?"

Not trusting herself to speak, she let his question drift without answering, her lips slightly parted in a disarming smile. Finally, she nodded. "I think so," she whispered, observing an immediate softening of his features, noticing how nicely arched his brows were, how delicately they framed his eyes, how they created the perfect balance to his well-modeled nose, square jaw, and lips that were rounded and full.

"I'm glad," he replied huskily, leaning in closer to Kira, his face so near to hers that she could see the clarity of the white space surrounding his dark brown pupils and inhale the scent of mocha escaping through his parted lips. "I had hoped you might be willing to explore that possibility."

Kira shifted in her seat, bringing her shoulders forward and her face even closer to his. She clasped both of Evan's hands in hers and propped her elbows on the table. "I do enjoy being with you, Evan, and I would love to get to know you, too, but are we setting ourselves up for trouble? After all, we're involved in a family court case, aren't we?"

"True," he agreed, tightening his fingers around her hands. "But look at it this way: we have a common goal of seeking what's best for Vicky, don't we?"

"Right," Kira answered.

"And, I'm not your attorney, nor an officer of the court, though I do represent Vicky. Didn't you just tell me that if the Ropers are awarded final adoption of Vicky that you will support the adoption?"

"Yes," Kira replied, holding her breath as Evan lifted a knowing brow, then let his gaze linger on her lips. He eased his thumb along her wrist, still gripping her hands.

"Then it's settled. Don't worry," he said softly. "Trust me. I know what you want, and I will do everything in my power to make sure you get it."

CHAPTER 17

Frank pressed the VOLUME button on the remote control and zapped the television into silence as soon as Ava walked into the den, more interested in talking to her than watching the Cosby rerun that had been putting him to sleep.

"Find out anything from your friend at DHHS?" he asked, yawning as he turned his full attention on his wife.

Before answering, Ava took her time sitting down in the red recliner next to her husband's. She pulled the lever to prop up her feet. She swept a hand over her short, curly salt-and-pepper hair, then sank back with an audible sigh, releasing the tension of a very exhausting day. As one of two guidance counselors at Monroeville High School, her days were crammed with tense encounters with teachers, students, and parents. Because of her even-tempered manner as much as her position, she was often called upon to intercede with defiant students and administrators, as well as work with a variety of authorities ranging from the local police to the Department of Health and other statewide governing agencies. With the end of the school year fast approaching, it seemed to Ava that everyone, including herself, was marking off the days on the calendar until summer vacation.

After twenty-four years in public education, Ava was seriously considering retiring, especially if Frank became mayor of Monroeville. As the city's first lady, she'd have civic duties to perform and obligations that would take her beyond the endless meetings and conferences and training sessions required of her at the high school. Her time would be her own, and she would be able to pick and choose among the many activities and social events vying for her support. She and Frank would no longer have to worry about money, and they'd be the envy of everyone on the north side of town. Frank would finally get the respect he deserved.

Ava placed the copy of the *Monroeville Mirror* that Frank had given her the day before on her lap, and tapped the photo of the Ropers with their soon-to-be-adopted daughter.

"I sure did talk to Thelma," Ava finally replied. "It took most of the day, but I got through to her late this afternoon. She says her department lost four senior managers this month, but she took time out of her busy day to dig up what you wanted."

"And?" Frank said impatiently, eyebrows raised in anticipation.

"And it seems that Vicky Jordan is the niece of Kira Forester— that reporter who works for *BPR* out of Charlotte. The one who did that piece on you."

"Oh?" Frank became immediately more alert. He leaned over the arm of the recliner, eyes squinted in suspicion. "Are you sure about that? Who'd Thelma talk to?"

"No one. I told you, she's a case manager supervisor. She went directly to the file and found it. Thelma works with Sheltering Hearts a lot, and she was the one who assisted them when they brought the girl from Wilmington to Monroeville so the Ropers could see her. Thelma said she's a sweet child who deserves a family."

"I can't believe it," Frank murmured, slumping back in his recliner to stare blankly at the mute TV, too stunned to speak. This new, unexpected turn of events was baffling. First, Kira Forester pops up out of nowhere and seeks him out for an interview. Now her niece shows up as the soon-to-be-adopted daughter of his opponent. What was going on? he wondered, suddenly more interested in Kira Forester than Vicky Jordan.

"Does this Forester woman know that Ralph Roper is about to adopt her niece?" Frank asked his wife, not turning to look at her.

"Obviously she does, because Thelma said she recently filed a petition for visitation. Guess she's going along with Ralph and Helen on adopting the girl, but I can't imagine why."

"Me neither," Frank breathed, drumming his fingers on the arm of the chair, his mind whirling with possibilities. "She must have known about this when she approached me for an interview. Why didn't she say anything?"

"Maybe Roper asked her to keep quiet about it. You know the lengths that man will go to, to get what he, or that sickly wife of his, wants." Ava paused, then impulsively asked, "Is she married?"

Distracted by the revelation that Kira was clearly connected to Roper, Frank snapped back at his wife, "Who?"

"Kira Forester. Is she married?"

"How would I know? She didn't say and I didn't ask. What difference does it make?"

Lifting one hand, palm facing her husband, Ava shook her head. "If she's a single woman with no husband, odds are she's more interested in increasing the size of her bank account than the size of her family. Wouldn't surprise me a bit if Roper hasn't paid that child's aunt to stay out of his hair. Money talks, you know. And he loves to throw it around. She isn't interested in adopting her own niece, so why not let a rich white man do it? Makes her a part of a very wealthy family, in a roundabout way."

"Surely not," Frank managed. His breath caught in his lungs as a wave of disappointment washed over him. The idea that Kira would do such a thing made Frank's stomach lurch with disgust. She had seemed so sympathetic to his cause, genuinely interested in his efforts to preserve the most historical building in Monroeville, and he had thought she was supportive of his bid for office. Frank went limp. Had he misjudged her? He knew how to read people, not only from what they said but also from the way they reacted to what he said, and he was certain he had not read Kira Forester wrong. She was black. She was extremely interested in his efforts to preserve Flagg Valley Mill. And she was no fan of Ralph Roper's. So why is she letting this happen to a blood member of her family? He tensed his jaw in frustration.

The luminous green glow emanating from the face of Ava's radio alarm clock seemed to bathe the room in bright light, though Frank knew it was no more intense than usual. On most nights he paid no attention to the subtle shade of green that the radio alarm cast over the bedroom walls, but tonight it riveted his attention and kept him thinking about what he ought to do. He turned onto his side and cupped his hand beneath his cheek, wishing sleep would come and empty his mind of the knotted worries that filled it. The sly way in which Roper was courting voters who ought to be solidly in Frank's camp was a serious threat, and Frank knew he had to corral his runaway thoughts and come up with a plan to halt his opponent's momentum.

He lay in the dark next to Ava, whose breathing told him she was deep into sleep, and thought about Kira Forester. *What was she really after when she first approached me?* he wondered, suddenly suspicious of the reporter's motives. She had written a fair enough article and had treated his interest in the mill seriously, but now he had little respect for her. He had not spoken to her since the interview, though he had meant to call and thank her, as well as tell her that he had found one of her photos on the floor of the restaurant after she left, but he had not gotten around to calling. Now he wasn't so sure he wanted to talk to her at all.

I can't just lie here thinking about all of this, he decided in frustration, folding back the lightweight blanket from his side of the bed. Easing from beneath the sheet, he slipped on the pants and sweater he had tossed across the chair on his side of the bedroom and shoved his feet into his shoes, not bothering to put on socks. Gingerly, he removed his car keys and his wallet from the shallow bowl on the dresser, made his way through the darkened house to the kitchen, and turned on a small fluorescent light that was tucked beneath one of the kitchen cabinets. After opening the drawer beside the refrigerator, the one into which he tossed papers, carryout menus, tape, and rubber bands—anything that didn't have an assigned spot in the house—he rummaged through the pile until he came to the photo he had planned on returning to Kira. Frank moved closer to the light, then reached for the magnifying glass in the glass jar of pens and pencils on the countertop and studied the photograph closely.

"Interesting," Frank murmured, setting the magnifying glass on the counter as he tried to make sense of the images flashing through his mind.

Impulsively, he shoved the photo into his shirt pocket and opened the back door, easing it shut behind him as he moved in short, hurried steps across the wooden deck that wrapped around the back of his house.

Inside the garage, he removed his wide-beam flashlight from a hook and, taking it with him, got into his car and backed out into the driveway. Quietly, he got out of his car and slowly pulled the overhead garage door down by hand instead of using the automatic closer, which would have rattled and clanked as it brought the door down—though disturbing a sleeping Ava was nearly impossible. In thirty-two years of marriage, he had never known her to wake up without the assistance of an alarm clock, and he envied her ability to slumber through wicked thunderstorms, noisy parties in the neighborhood, and the dreaded boom-boom of the teenagers' car radios as they cruised down his street.

The drive to Flagg Valley Mill took less than ten minutes, and as soon as Frank pulled up to the rusty iron gates he knew that he had the answers to his questions. Leaving the car's headlights shining onto the property, he got out, not surprised to see several Roper Fiber Technology vans parked on the lot, gleaming pristine white in the darkness. Frank walked up to the unlocked gate and pushed it open. The squeaking hinges whined loudly into the night, and for an instant Frank's mind latched on to an image of a slave beneath a whip, screaming for mercy. The ghosts of slaves who had labored for their freedom on the soil beneath his feet called out to Frank, pulling him deeper onto the property, urging him to save the old mill from demolition. Shining his flashlight on the pitch-black asphalt, he cautiously made his way toward the overflowing Dumpsters, where he could hear the scurry of rats busy foraging for food.

When Ava's alarm clock went off at six o'clock the next morning, Frank did not hear it. When Ava gave him a hard shake to tell him that she was leaving for work, he opened one eye and sat up long enough to give his wife a quick good-bye peck on the cheek, then tumbled back into the covers.

"What's wrong with you, Frank? You staying home today?" Ava asked, checking her hair in the dresser mirror as she picked up her purse.

"No," Frank mumbled, turning back the blanket to look at his wife. "Just moving a little slow. Didn't sleep very well last night."

"Well, you'd better get moving for real, Frank. It's seven-ten, and I've got to go. There're biscuits and sausage in the toaster oven keeping warm."

"Fine," he mumbled, watching Ava as she hurried off to work. He remained in bed until he heard the sound of the automatic garage door sliding down, then got up and went into the bathroom. He turned on the shower and stepped in, jolting himself fully awake as he lathered soap over his face and finalized his plan. The first thing he had to do was call Kira Forester.

Frank watched the clock carefully as he dressed, made coffee, and then ate the biscuits and sausage Ava had left for him. At exactly eight-thirty, he opened his wallet and removed the business card Kira had given him. He dialed the number to her direct line at the paper. When she answered, he inhaled deeply, then spoke.

"Yes, Kira Forester? This is Frank Thompson. Do you have a few minutes to talk?"

"Of course, Frank. Glad you got to me early, before everything spins totally out of control around here. What can I do for you?"

"Did you see this week's *Monroeville Mirror* by any chance?"

"Can't say that I did. Why?"

"There was a story in it about my opponent, Ralph Roper. Seems he and his wife are about to adopt an African-American girl." Frank paused, allowing his news to sink in, wishing he could see Kira's face. "Were you aware of this when you interviewed me?"

Silence followed, then Frank heard Kira clear her throat.

"Yes. I was," she told him.

"Why didn't you say anything?" Frank asked in as even a tone as he could manage, determined to get as much information from Kira as possible before letting her know how much he knew. When she did not answer, he plunged ahead. "And I understand the girl is your niece? Why didn't you tell me?"

"I didn't think my personal connection to Mr. Roper was relevant to your story. And I still don't," she replied in a more testy voice than she had used when greeting him only seconds ago.

"You're wrong," Frank stated flatly. "And you can tell me it's none of my business if you want to, but I think it is. Other residents of Monroeville might also want to ask you the same question: why you would allow a man like Ralph Roper to raise your sister's child?"

"What do you mean, a man like Ralph Roper?" Kira shot back. "Is he a criminal? A child molester? An abusive husband? Let's get one thing straight, Frank. I know you don't like or trust Ralph Roper, but don't try to drag me into your political battle. My situation is private, as are my reasons for supporting the adoption of my niece."

"But that's not good enough, Kira. Don't you realize that he's using this transracial adoption issue to gain sympathy from black voters? To undercut my campaign? You ought to publicly condemn him. Make it known that you're not happy with what he's doing. Create a fuss, and help me turn Roper's underhanded ploy to my advantage."

"I can't do that," Kira stated. "I admit that I was very upset when I first learned that the Ropers were white. But now I see things differently, and I have to support the agency that's handling my niece's adoption. I trust Sheltering Hearts. The director knows what's best, and he's doing a good job."

"You ought to be ashamed," Frank coldly chastised her. "How can you turn your only blood relative over to white people who have never gone out of their way to do anything positive for the black community of Monroeville? Where is your pride? Your loyalty to your race? You ought to do everything in your power to halt this folly, instead of standing on the sidelines while the Ropers make a fool out of you! I am deeply disappointed. I thought you were on my side."

"I am not on anyone's side, Frank, except my niece's. She deserves a family and a stable home, and according to the agency that's handling the case, she'll get both with Ralph and Helen Roper. True, they may not be the parents I would have selected for Vicky, if it had been up to me, but it wasn't my call. I agree with you that Ralph Roper is an aggressive person, a shrewd businessman, and he sure can rub people the wrong way. I don't particularly like him, or the way he goes about proving a point, but that does not make him a monster or an unsuitable candidate to adopt. He seems devoted to his wife, and they want to make a home for my niece, so I have resigned myself to the situation. No one is perfect, Frank, and you should not use race to measure a person's worth."

"This is not entirely about race," Frank spoke each word distinctly and slowly, hoping to get Kira's attention.

"No?" she shot back. "Then why else would you interfere in a matter that does not concern you? Do you have hard evidence to prove that the Ropers are not decent people?"

"He can't be trusted," Frank stated in a hard voice.

"What proof do you have? Other than your personal vendetta against him because he supposedly stole your family's homestead. What do you have, Frank?"

"More than you can imagine," Frank quietly told Kira.

"Then tell me what you know."

"You'll find out soon enough. And when you do, you'll be very surprised. I think you'll thank me for interfering."

Frank softly placed the handset of his cordless phone back into its cradle. Smiling, he turned off the coffeemaker, picked up his car keys, and left, locking the back door securely.

Inside the garage, he opened the trunk of his car and leaned in, nodding, reassured that what he'd done last night was right on target.

"She'll wish she had listened to me," Frank said to himself as he backed his car out of the driveway.

Kira placed a hand to her jaw, stunned. Furious that Frank had hung up on her, she slammed down the phone. Frank's accusations rang painfully in her head. How dare he accuse her of turning her back on her responsibility to her race, or of allowing Ralph Roper to make a fool out of her? Didn't he understand that interfering with Vicky's adoption would be a very selfish, destructive thing for her to do? It would only work against her. Frank Thompson was totally out of line.

Kira grabbed the phone to call him back and curse him out, but then she halted, hand in midair, deciding she'd better keep her cool. Frank didn't strike her as a man who played fair, and the last thing she needed was a hassle from him. Julie's warning came immediately to mind: Small-town politics can get ugly, she'd said. Uglier than you think.

Kira picked up a black felt-tip pen and began to sketch random images on her desk calendar, forcing herself to calm down. Wasn't she under enough self-imposed pressure to do the right thing without Frank adding his two bits?

He's a kook, she told herself. A desperate kook who is afraid of losing the election to a white man, of losing face in his hometown. Kira stopped doodling on the calendar and focused on the date: April 12. Less than thirty days until the election. The ungrateful bastard, she thought. I featured him in my column, pumped up his candidacy, told the story about the history of Monroeville, and even quoted his opinion of Roper verbatim. And he never even thanked me for my effort. Kira felt weak, shaken by the encounter. Frank's final words, which had sounded more like a threat than a warning, haunted her for the rest of the day.

CHAPTER 18

Instead of heading home after work, Kira found herself driving toward Stallings, even though she did not know if Evan was in his office or would be able to see her. She had telephoned him earlier and left a message with the receptionist, requesting that he call her on her cell phone when he returned from his meeting.

What am I doing? she thought, threading her way around two cars that had collided in the intersection. *What can Evan do about Frank Thompson? Nothing. So why bother him?* But as she continued up the ramp leading to the freeway, she knew the real reason she was putting herself through this torturous rush-hour traffic was simply because she wanted to see Evan again. Two days had passed since she'd met him at the coffee shop. Two days of thinking, wondering, and hoping that Evan Conley might actually be the man with whom she could safely enter a relationship that might have a real future. Thinking of him brought back the same rush of emotion that had swept over her when he'd held her hand, when he'd placed his finger near her lips and looked into her eyes. She had never before experienced such an intense sense of anticipation when thinking about a man.

As soon as Kira pulled into the parking lot in front of the office building that housed Sheltering Hearts, her cell phone rang. Praying it was Evan, she hurried to answer.

"Yes," she said, grinning at the sound of his voice. "I called."

"Something wrong? My receptionist said you sounded upset."

"Nothing is wrong. But I'd like to see you. Today was a horror. I had a very upsetting phone call today."

"That so? From whom?" Evan asked.

"It's complicated. I'm in the parking lot at your office. Where are you?"

"On Sterling Road. Leaving the Nature Museum."

"The museum? Have you been playing hooky from work?" Kira teased.

"No, I've been attending a lecture on a program that encourages the use of plants and other aspects of nature as therapy to help calm children who have severe behavior problems. Many of our foster parents have had success with the program, and I wanted to check it out. So . . . where can we meet and talk? Are you hungry? Maybe we can meet for dinner?"

Kira, who had worked straight through lunch while munching on a Snickers bar, was starving. Dinner with Evan might be just what she needed.

"Yes, I'd love that," she admitted.

"Good. Do you know where Chaio's is? On Providence?"

"Sure," Kira said, impressed with his choice. Chaio's was an elegant, upscale Italian restaurant known for its fantastic pasta and its extensive wine list, though Kira was not much of an expert when it came to choosing wine. "That's fine. See you there in a few minutes."

The drive was a short one, and traffic was light. When Kira pulled up beside Evan's car, she turned off the engine and got out, but stayed by her car, waiting until Evan got out and looked over at her. He pulled on the jacket to his gray suit, shrugging it over his broad shoulders, then glanced again at Kira and smiled. Though his eyes were shaded by sunglasses that reflected the late afternoon sun back at her, Kira sensed how intensely focused they were on her. Kira's heart began to pound as Evan walked toward her.

"Well, hello," he said, stopping beside her.

"Hi. Our timing was right on," Kira laughed.

"Sure was." He glanced around the crowded parking lot, then frowned. "We may have to wait for a table. Hope you're not in a hurry to get home."

"Not at all," Kira said, linking her arm through his as they walked toward the entrance. She had been looking forward to seeing Evan, unsure about how or when it would happen, and now that they were together again, she was in no rush to be separated too soon.

Once inside the restaurant, Evan placed his name on the waiting list, then eased out of the crowded entry, guiding Kira to the far end of the noisy bar in an adjoining room. The place was crowded, with people sitting at the bar or standing around in small groups talking or watching CNN on the big-screen television in a corner while waiting for their tables. Evan spotted two empty bar stools and hurried to grab them, helping Kira up onto her seat.

"What would you like? A glass of wine? Champagne? " He removed his sunglasses to examine the menu, then looked into her eyes. "You do drink, don't you?"

"Of course," she replied. "A glass of wine would be fine, but I'm not very knowledgeable when it comes to choosing. I usually order the house white wine and pray it won't be too dry. I'm not keen on really dry wine, you know? So you decide, okay?"

"I'd be happy to," Evan said, reaching for the large trifold wine list. "I think we can do better than the house chardonnay." He took a few minutes to peruse the wine list, then glanced back at Kira. "I took a wine-tasting tour of Napa Valley a few years ago when I was on the West Coast visiting Lora. Thoroughly enjoyed it. Since then, I've attended a couple of local wine tastings, and I've discovered that there's no mystery about choosing a wine. Drink what you like and what you can afford. Those are my rules."

"Sounds good to me," Kira replied, sitting back to let Evan make a choice.

Soon they were sipping a fruity off-dry red wine while Kira told Evan about Frank Thompson's phone call.

"Don't pay any attention to him," Evan said. "That man sounds like a rabble-rousing politician who enjoys stirring things up. You don't owe him, or anyone in Monroeville, an explanation. He ought to be happy you interviewed him in the first place."

"Amen to that," Kira said, absently twirling her wineglass on the polished wooden bar. "And he never even thanked me."

Evan placed one hand on Kira's arm and leaned close. "See how ungrateful and selfish he is? Forget about him."

"I wish I could, but his attack this morning was such a shock. I wanted to reach through the phone and slap him. He's got a lot of nerve, charging me up like that. Evan, when he said he was going to prove me wrong, his tone made me very nervous. What do you think he's up to?"

"Nothing. He's blowing hot air," Evan said, pouring more wine into Kira's glass. "So what if Frank Thompson doesn't agree with your decision? There's nothing he can do about it."

"Maybe," Kira said slowly, accepting her refreshed drink. "It's almost as if he's trying to draw me into his political fight with Roper . . . use me to whip up sympathy for him among the residents of Monroeville. Evan, has everything checked out okay with the Ropers? There won't be any surprises, will there?"

"None. Everything is in order," he reassured Kira. "And I have a sense that Judge Burton will give your visitation hearing priority. It may come up in a few days, so it might be a good idea to distance yourself from Frank and the politics of Monroeville for a while."

"I have no interest in ever talking to the man again."

"Good, because you are in a uniquely sensitive position, Kira. As a journalist, your job is to investigate and write about matters of interest to the public, and I realize that your initial contact with Frank Thompson was on a professional level. But now he's coming at you on a personal issue and seems determined to complicate things for you. My advice is to keep a low profile right now. Avoid getting involved in the politics of Monroeville, and keep your professional endeavors separate from your personal life . . . as much as possible."

Evan's remarks struck at the heart of Kira's worries, yet she found them oddly incongruous. Here she was, sitting at a bar, drinking wine with the man who was key to her niece's case, yet he expected her to avoid contact with Roper and Thompson? Before taking a moment to think over his remarks, she quickly stated, "It's not as if I went to Monroeville looking for trouble, Evan. Thompson had an interesting story, and I covered it for the paper. My intention was to provide a profile of the first African-American candidate for political office in Monroeville and highlight the city's history. I never set out to endorse him as a candidate."

"But by including Thompson's negative remarks about Roper in your article, you gave him the impression that you were on his side."

"So now I am being victimized for quoting Thompson verbatim? I was trying to create an honest profile of the man. All I did was write about what I had been told. This is crazy."

Evan calmly drained the last of the wine in his glass, then set it down just as the waitress came to tell them that their table was ready. Taking Kira's hand to help her down from the bar stool, he said, "You're right. It's crazy, but it's also the way things are right now, and we certainly don't want them to become crazier."

Dinner was smoked crabmeat and artichoke pasta accompanied by another bottle of wine—a sparkling white this time, that Kira thoroughly enjoyed—and by the time they had finished eating and talking, it was nearly nine o'clock. Kira felt buzzed by the lively conversation, wonderful food, and the wine Evan had so liberally poured for her.

"This was fabulous, Evan," she said as he walked her to her car. "Thanks. I really needed to get out, and I enjoyed the evening."

"Me too," Evan said. "We'll have to do it again." He stepped closer, looking down at Kira.

"I'm sure we can," Kira replied, watching Evan's face, which was illuminated by the lamplight in the parking lot, yet partially shaded by the shadows from the trees that bordered the area. Kira could feel the effects of the wine rushing to her head, making her heart beat faster. When Evan placed his fingertips beneath her chin, she stifled a moan of pleasure and savored his touch, not pulling back. She allowed her body to sway closer to his, until her chest was only inches from his shirt.

"I never drink more than a glass or two of wine, and rarely go out like this in the middle of the week," she murmured, knowing she didn't want the evening to end.

"Same here," Evan confessed, splaying his fingers in a caress of her cheek. "But I've been thinking about you so much. Kira, I enjoyed this so much. It was nice, wasn't it?"

"Yes," she answered, every fiber of her body aching for his touch. "Very nice." Discarding her reservations about getting too close to Evan, she rose onto her tiptoes, eased one arm around Evan's neck, and gave him an invitation to lean down and kiss her.

His kiss was soft, but solid, with just enough intensity to let her know it would not be their last. His tongue danced gently over hers, exploring, but not demanding. And when his hands swept the length of her back, urging their bodies closer, Kira knew his touch was one with which she wanted to become familiar. She pressed her heart to his, opening herself to the desire ignited between them, and kissed him hard, drinking in his taste, his scent, his desire to be as close as possible to her.

When she finally pulled back and broke their kiss, she realized she was gasping for air. Placing her forehead against his, she rested for a moment, enjoying the delicious impact of their kiss. A shiver of wanting crept over Kira, and she held her body very still, waiting for her heartbeat to settle into a more regular pace. Stepping back, she tried to appear composed, though his nearness felt like an invisible link that was pulling her back into his arms.

"I'd better get going," she told Evan, opening her purse to take out her car keys, so overwhelmed that she was unable to say more. But Evan shattered the tightly strung silence by taking her keys from her hand and stating huskily, "Let me drive you home."

"It's not necessary," Kira replied, easing farther from their embrace. "I'll be fine. I was just joking about the wine. Really, I can drive."

Evan swung his hand away from her reach and held her keys up, shaking them as he insisted, "I'm sure you can drive, but I don't want you to. Let me take you home, please? Besides, I'm not ready to say good night."

"And your car?" she asked, smiling to see how serious he was about doing this.

"I'll take a cab back to get it. Okay?"

Convinced that he would not take no for an answer, she relented, secretly thrilled that he wanted to spend more time with her.

"All right. You win," Kira relented, shaking her head as she walked around the car to the passenger side, opened the door and slid in. Sneaking a peek at Evan's profile as he adjusted the mirror and fastened his seat belt, she thought about the last time they had been together in her car, when she had been in the driver's seat and he had been seated next to her. It was then that she had realized how attracted she was to him, and now she felt the attraction even more deeply. Evan Conley was perfect. He was easy to talk to, intelligent, and interesting. His straightforward, no-nonsense approach to solving problems made her feel safe and appreciated, yet he was never dull or predictable, as she had thought he might be. He treated her as if she was important, and this tender, caring attitude was something that Kira found powerfully alluring. Sighing, she settled back to enjoy the ride, deciding to trust him with her heart.

The following morning, Evan's prediction came true just as Kira was about to leave for work. When her phone rang, she grabbed it, thinking it might be him. He had driven her home, walked her to her door, and then bid her good night with an even more intense kiss than the one they had shared earlier in the parking lot. Kira had been tempted to invite him in, extending the evening even further, but had resisted the impulse, deciding to wait and see how their relationship progressed before she made such an overture. She had lain awake long into the night, too emotionally charged to sleep, and now, as she grabbed the phone, automatically checking the Caller ID, she sighed in disappointment to see that it was her attorney, not Evan, who was calling.

"Judge Burton has granted us a hearing," Kenneth Lane told her in a rushed, relieved tone.

"Already?"

"Yes. I just got word that she has an opening today and wants to see you as soon as possible. I suggest we take it, or it may be weeks before we can get rescheduled."

"What time?" Kira asked, sagging with relief to have reached this critical juncture in her mission so quickly.

"Two o'clock this afternoon. In the judge's chamber," Lane replied.

"What do I need to do?"

"Nothing more than show up prepared to explain who you are and why you should be granted visitation with your niece. It's up to you to make your case, but I'll be with you to clarify any legal jargon or offer advice if you need me. However, you will have to convince Judge Burton that your presence in this child's life is vital. I've been before this judge many times, and I'll tell you now, she doesn't want to debate the pros and cons of transracial adoption with you. She wants to know how you plan on supporting the family unit when the adoption is final. Sheltering Hearts has already forwarded a positive recommendation on your behalf to Judge Burton, including background information on you and the required security forms and clearances. She will have gone through everything with a critical eye, so you'll only have about fifteen minutes with her, enough to move the process forward and provide the judge an opportunity to question you."

"How long before we know what she decides."

"Hopefully, immediately after she's heard what you have to say."

"Oh, Ken, I'm so nervous," Kira admitted.

"Don't be. You're an asset, not a detriment to this case. So let's get over there so we can get moving on bringing you and Vicky together. Got it?"

"Got it," Kira said, hoping she'd feel stronger and more in control of her nerves by the time she got to court.

After hanging up the phone, Kira raced back into her bedroom and put on her most conservative navy blue suit, the one with a skirt that fell two inches below her knees.

Though it was difficult, Kira made it through the first half of her workday without discussing the upcoming court date with anyone, not even Sharon, with whom Kira usually shared her lunch hour as well as office gossip. In an effort to keep her personal business out of the office, she took her phone calls from Kenneth Lane and Evan on her cell phone, retrieved their messages on her personal time, then called them back in the privacy of her car or at home. Too many calls from her attorney or from Sheltering Hearts showing up on her phone log at the office would only have triggered her boss's interest in what she was doing and bring up questions she was not prepared to answer.

Today, she planned to go to lunch late, at about one-thirty, then call back into the office and inform Davison that she needed an hour or so to take care of a personal matter. She'd miss the afternoon staff meeting, but that was just too bad. Nothing was going to prevent her from keeping her appointment with Judge Burton.

Kira arrived at the courthouse at one-forty and miraculously found a parking spot in the crowded lot next door to the building. After nervously gulping down a banana and a few grapes while she sat in her car, she telephoned Davison and informed him that she would be late returning to the office. He sputtered a reluctant acceptance but urged her to return as soon as possible, not pleased about her mysterious, impromptu request.

At one forty-five Kira met Kenneth at the entrance to the Mecklenburg County Courthouse and gave him a tight, thin smile.

"Nervous?" he asked, stuffing his bulging leather briefcase under one arm in order to clasp both of Kira's hands in his.

"A little," Kira tossed back in a lighter voice than she had expected to hear from herself, giving Kenneth's hands a quick squeeze of welcome. At that moment she was so glad she had turned to him to represent her.

Kenneth Lane was a large man with sandy brown hair and a complexion so fair and liberally sprinkled with freckles that he was often mistaken for white. His round, boyish face and laid-back style made him appear years younger than he actually was, but Kira knew that he was thirty-seven, same as she. While they had been in college together at Wake Forest, she had dated Kenneth a few times during their sophomore year, but had never been attracted to him, mainly using him to pass away an empty Friday night now and then. And when he hooked up with her roommate, Linda Valine, in their senior year, Kira had been happy that Kenneth had found the perfect woman for him, and had even hosted a wedding shower for Linda a month after their graduation.

Now, Kira mentally rehearsed what she planned to say to the judge as Kenneth, who was busy greeting colleagues and county staffers as he passed through the crowded lobby, guided her by the elbow toward the elevators at the center of the hall. She could tell by the way Kenneth gently but firmly shouldered his way into the packed elevator, then eased Kira inside with him, that he knew the courthouse well and how to get around. He stabbed the number 4, remained at the front, and when the doors slid open, pulled Kira out and turned to the left, headed toward a polished wooden door that had a brass nameplate with Judge Carmen Burton's name etched on it in scrolled lettering.

The outer office of the judge's chamber was only large enough to hold the receptionist's desk, a side table where legal publications and pamphlets had been placed, and two peach and green floral wing chairs facing each other over a squat rattan table. Kenneth approached the receptionist, gave her Kira's name, and was immediately invited to follow the woman into the judge's inner chamber. Once inside, Kira was engulfed by a realization of the gravity of her request, which up to this point had been more of a wish than a legal matter to be settled by an officer of the court.

Only seconds after Kira and Kenneth had been seated in chairs in front of the judge's desk, a door to the side of a massive oak credenza opened, and Judge Burton swept in.

Kira sat up and pulled back her shoulders as Judge Burton, who was the tiniest woman Kira had ever seen, went to her desk, sat down, and pushed back the billowing sleeves of her black robe, which fell open to reveal a plain gray sheath dress. She had an oval face that was smooth and unlined, and her glossy black hair had been pulled back, twisted, then rolled into a loose knot at the back of her head. She wore small gold earrings set with tiny pearls and a single strand of matching pearls around her neck. After rummaging in her desk drawer for a pen, she placed the folder she had brought with her into the room in front of her and looked up, appraising her afternoon visitors.

"Good afternoon," Judge Burton said, glancing first at Kenneth, then at Kira, nodding curtly as she acknowledged their greetings in return, making it clear by her tone that she was a very busy person on a schedule she planned to stick to. "I have read through the petition and have a few questions, Miss Forester. I am hopeful we can work this out here in my chambers and not have to take this matter to another level. Understand?"

"Yes," Kira replied, not sure what the next level might be, but sensing that it would most likely be costly, time-consuming, and not beneficial to her case. "I would like it very much if we can settle this issue today."

"Good," Judge Burton replied. "I have consulted with the Ropers and Evan Conley at Sheltering Hearts, who strongly recommends that your visitation be granted. I have reviewed the home-study report on Mr. and Mrs. Roper as well, and think I have a good understanding of what is going on. So, Miss Forester, you want to get to know your niece, do you?"

"That's right," Kira said, nervously moistening her dry lips with a quick flick of her tongue.

"Tell me why you think it is important for her to know you," Judge Burton said in a less rushed manner, sitting back in her seat, crossing her arms, adopting a calm, expectant expression.

The change in the judge's businesslike demeanor to one of genuine interest made Kira relax. She reminded herself that the judge wasn't an ogre out to get her, but an officer of the court who was charged with doing what was best for Vicky. Realizing this was her best, if not only, chance to make her case, Kira launched into the story of how she and Vicky had become estranged, accepting full responsibility for her lapse of attention, admitting that she had not been prepared to make a commitment to take the child after her sister died. Judge Burton nodded her understanding and listened carefully, not interrupting while Kira went on to talk about her work, her personal situation, and how she hoped the Ropers would welcome her interest and not block her efforts to be a part of Vicky's life. When Kira touched on the subject of Ralph and Helen Roper, the judge gave Kira a curious look, uncrossed her arms, and finally spoke.

"I detect a tone of anger in your voice when you mention Vicky's prospective adoptive family. You are not happy that they want to adopt Vicky, are you?"

Kira exhaled, trying to decide how to phrase her response.

"And neither are you convinced that the Ropers are the best family for Vicky, are you?" Judge Burton went on.

Swallowing dryly, Kira glanced at Kenneth, who lifted a brow and inclined his head, as if urging her to speak from her heart.

"I'm not sure," Kira admitted, wishing she could say, one way or the other, how she felt. It would be easy for her to simply blurt out nasty, hurtful things that might reflect negatively on Ralph Roper, but Kira knew she had no basis to do so. He had hurt her feelings and invaded her privacy, but trying to get revenge on him by lambasting him in court would serve no purpose, she knew. "Judge, I admit that I am not totally comfortable with the idea of them becoming my niece's parents, but I am working hard to overcome my reservations."

"Are you uncomfortable because they are white?" Judge Burton asked.

"No," Kira said too quickly, then rethought her response, determined to answer as honestly as possible. "Well, yes and no," she amended, angry with herself for not being able to put the race issue into better perspective. "I have never met Mrs. Roper, and I would love to, because I sense that she is a very sensitive, caring woman. She will most likely be a good mother to Vicky, but I wonder if she understands how important it will be for Vicky to have contact with black people—her family especially. Mr. Roper is another matter. He went too far when he personally investigated my background instead of relying on Sheltering Hearts or the court to do that for him, and then he made an unsettling remark to me during—"

"I know about that," Judge Burton interrupted, flipping through the pages in the case file. "Mr. Conley spoke to me about it and included what was said in his written report."

"Then," Kira continued, "you must understand why I'm concerned. I thought it was very insensitive of Mr. Roper to disregard my feelings, and based on that encounter, I doubt that he realizes how damaging such insensitivity can be to a young, impressionable child. I don't think he is a racist. I do think he has a lot to learn and has had little interaction with African Americans on a personal level. I do think he wants to provide Vicky with a good life, and I have forgiven him for coming on so strong when I met him. He was acting out of fear. He and his wife have their hearts set on adopting Vicky, and he saw me as a threat. Who knows? I might have done the same thing if some stranger had popped up and threatened to take away a child I had come to love. I don't know. But I do know I want Vicky to have contact with me . . . and other people of her cultural and racial background. I'd like to be there for her and make sure she knows who her natural family is."

When Kira finished speaking, tears were brimming in her eyes. Judge Burton handed her a tissue from the box on the credenza behind her desk. Kira dabbed at her eyes and blinked back more tears, hoping Judge Burton had understood her interpretation of the complicated issues that were swirling around in her head, issues that would take time to settle.

"I have to inform you, Miss Forester," Judge Burton began in a tone that was once again official and cool. "As it stands now, there is no indication, from what I have read in the case file or discussed with Evan Conley, that Ralph and Helen Roper's petition to adopt Vicky Jordan is in jeopardy. That means, whether you like it or not, your niece may very well have parents who are not African American."

Nodding, Kira sat in silence, aware of a slow-moving wave of dread washing over her.

"And," the judge went on, "though you may have found the remarks Mr. Roper made to you during your meeting with him insulting and insensitive, they are not serious enough to interfere with a placement that Sheltering Hearts has taken quite a good amount of time to arrange. It is difficult to find homes and families willing to accept black children, especially older ones. Vicky Jordan is a very lucky girl. Do you understand what I mean?"

"Yes," Kira managed, her heart tight with worry over what the judge was going to say next.

"However, in light of my personal belief that cultural and familial connections play an important role in the success of transracial adoptions, coupled with what you have told me today, I will extend the home study of the Ropers for an additional thirty days and postpone finalization of their petition for adoption until I get the report from Sheltering Hearts. During this time you are granted court-supervised visitation with your niece. You may see her for no more than two consecutive hours a week on either Saturday or Sunday starting this coming weekend. Evan Conley of Sheltering Hearts will make the arrangements and supervise your contact with Vicky. Afterward, he will provide the court with weekly reports. Any questions?" Judge Burton asked as she scribbled notes on a page in the case file.

"No, Judge," Kira answered, hardly able to contain her joy,

reaching for Kenneth's hand. She squeezed it hard, smiling. "Thank you very much, Judge Burton."

"Have a good afternoon, Miss Forester. Mr. Lane." Judge Burton closed the case file, got up, straightened her robe, and left through the door at the side of the room.

CHAPTER 19

Kira bolted out of the elevator and hurried down the hallway, checking her watch as she made her way to her desk. She jammed her purse into the bottom drawer and slammed it shut, ready to get to work. Her meeting with Judge Burton had lasted less than fifteen minutes, but the paperwork required by the court to implement her court-ordered visitation had taken nearly two hours to complete. The slow-moving clerks, the long lines, the waiting in the corridors to be called to the window and present one more piece of identification or information had been horrendous. Thank God Kenneth had insisted on remaining with her. Without his expertise, and his patient reassurance that her ordeal was quite routine, she might have given up in frustration and gone home. *No wonder people get lost in the bureaucracy of the legal system*, she had thought, blindly following Kenneth's directions.

Now Kira looked over at Sharon, who jerked her chin toward Davison's office, her bright freckles wrinkling across the ridge of her nose. "He was more than a little irritated that you missed the staff meeting, and he was out here a few minutes ago, asking me if I'd heard from you."

"What did he want?" Kira asked.

"He didn't say, but I told him you'd called and told me you had car trouble but were on your way in."

"Thanks for covering for me, Sharon. I thought I'd be back sooner, but . . . well, it's complicated, girl. I was at the courthouse taking care of some personal business, and you know how crazy that place can be. Glad I don't cover the judicial beat. I'd go insane hanging around those people."

"The courthouse?" Sharon repeated, sounding worried. "Kira, what's going on? Are you in trouble? You sure look frazzled. Is something, like, really wrong?"

Kira lifted a shoulder but did not reply. The only person other than Evan Conley with whom she had discussed her niece's pending adoption had been Julie Ays, who was too far away to share the joy and relief Kira was feeling now. With the first major hurdle behind her, perhaps confiding in Sharon might be a good idea. Sharon was practical, plainspoken, and was raising a daughter by herself. And she was white. Her blunt take on the situation might help Kira make the most of her two hours a week with Vicky. Kira had no idea what a six-year-old girl would want to talk about, and she wanted her time with Vicky to be special

Kira flexed the fingers of her right hand, then tapped her computer keyboard, checking her e-mail. As she clicked through the prompts, she weighed the pros and cons of bringing her coworker, who was well known for her ability to spread other people's business around the office, in on what was going on. The last thing Kira wanted was to have the entire office asking for progress reports on her bonding sessions. Sharon would have to swear not to discuss Kira's attempt to reunite with her niece with anyone, at least for now.

Sharon pushed back from her desk and reached for a folder from her IN box, one eye still on Kira. "You don't have to tell me unless you want to. But I've had the feeling for weeks that you're under a lot of pressure and it has nothing to do with this place. Am I right?"

Kira exhaled slowly, swiveled around in her chair, and came face to face with Sharon. It had been a long time since she and Sharon had gone out for Chinese and really talked to each other about the kinds of things that women are able to share. Since Kira's return from Africa, all they seemed to talk about were their assignments, office politics, and their frustrations with their new boss. She liked Sharon, trusted her, and needed her friendship now more than ever.

"I can't talk about it now, Sharon, but I do want tell you," she told her friend.

"Finally," Sharon said, almost in a hiss. "I hoped you'd trust me, Kira. Whatever it is, if I can help, you know I will."

Warmed by the sincerity of Sharon's offer, Kira was relieved to have someone with whom she could talk about the complicated situation she was in. "Let's go out for Chinese. The Jade Moon? After work?" she proposed.

"You got it," Sharon tossed back. "I'll call Ellen and ask her to take Rachel out for pizza tonight—on me. Then I won't have to rush home to cook."

"You sure that's okay?"

"Hey, girl. My sister never turns down a free meal. Besides, she really loves spending time with Rachel."

Immediately after work, Kira and Sharon met at the Jade Moon, ordered dim sum, moo-goo gai pan, kung pao shrimp, and ate their meal with chopsticks while Kira told Sharon everything, starting with the letter she had received from DHHS on her return to the States and ending with her court date with Judge Burton.

"And now it's finally arranged," Kira finished. "The judge was fair—not too warm, but fair."

"I'm happy for you, Kira. It's going to be hard work, getting on the good side of a six-year-old who doesn't know you, but it'll be fine. And I think you ought to cut the Ropers some slack," Sharon said, reaching for the spicy mustard. She spooned a large dollop on top of her egg roll, then added a generous splash of sweet-and-sour sauce. "If that's what you gotta do to make it work, then you gotta do it."

"I know," Kira admitted, less than enthusiastically. "There's no way I can avoid contact with them, and we're going to be practically related . . . legally at least. So I've decided to work on my attitude. For Vicky's sake."

"Good. Now, tell me *all* about Evan Conley. He sounds like a keeper. You met him for coffee, then for dinner? What's up with that? More than a professional interest, perhaps?"

Kira laughed, then went on to tell Sharon the details of their impromptu date and what she knew about Evan.

"You said he's *divorced?*" Sharon repeated, underscoring the important word.

"Right."

"Newly divorced or a veteran?" Sharon wanted to know, rounding her shoulders over the table, her features animated with interest as she munched on her egg roll.

"Why do you ask?" Kira noticed that the lighting in the dining room had turned the other woman's bright red hair into a deep burgundy color, emphasizing the paleness of her fair skin.

Sharon held her chopsticks in midair, shaking them as she

clucked her tongue in admonishment at Kira. "Because it makes a huge difference in how you proceed," she stated with authority. "You don't want to get caught up in some messy rebound scenario, or have to deal with a jealous ex-wife who hasn't gone on with her life. However, neither do you want to beat your head against a stone wall trying to change a veteran bachelor who is set in his ways."

Grinning, Kira thought for a moment, then answered, "I'm sorry to say, but I guess Evan is a veteran. Been divorced for ten years."

"Hmm . . . not too bad. There's still time," her friend remarked with serious approval, making Kira laugh.

Kira knew she should not have been surprised. Sharon was a firm believer in marriage, though hers had failed after only three years, and believed that any woman over the age of thirty ought to at least be engaged, if not married and well on her way to raising a family.

"Now, tell me more," Sharon insisted. "Where's the ex-wife? Any kids?"

"Both in California," Kira said, setting aside her chopsticks to pick up a fork, tired of struggling with the little sticks. She had never gotten the hang of eating with chopsticks, though she faithfully started each Chinese meal with them, only to opt for convenience midway through. Continuing to eat, she told Sharon the little Evan had revealed to her about his family, including how he tried to remain in touch with his twelve-year-old daughter.

"Sounds like a real sensitive guy," Sharon murmured. "Not only is he dedicated to finding homes for children no one wants to adopt, he's a loving father, even though it's a long-distance relationship. He's attentive to your feelings and supports your effort to establish a relationship with Vicky. Sounds perfect to me, girlfriend."

"Perfect?" Kira sighed. "I doubt there's such a thing as a perfect man, but I have to admit he's got a lot going on. When I first met him, I admit I was impressed. You know, the usual stuff. He was polite, well groomed, professional, wearing a nice suit, great tie, overall attractive, but then he got to the part about placing Vicky with a white couple and I lost all interest. I really blasted him— hard."

"And now?" Sharon prompted. "Your opinion seems to have changed."

"All right, you got me. Now that I've gotten to know him, I

think he is a good guy. A sincerely nice man. Calm, intuitive. A real gentleman, too. I had too much wine with dinner at Chaio's and he insisted on driving me home. Took a cab back to get his car. Wasn't that sweet?"

"Sweet," Sharon agreed. "And after that messy hookup with Brandon, you could use a gentleman, for sure."

"I know that's right."

"So, you see what he has to deal with to run his agency," Sharon stated.

"I do," Kira admitted. "We're both concerned about the way Ralph Roper came off in that meeting, and Evan told me Roper did call him to apologize. Roper called me, too. It's confusing, Sharon. I know where Ralph Roper stands, even if I don't like it, and I think I could tolerate the guy. But his wife—that's another story. I can't help but think there's something odd going on with her. Why is she so far removed from the situation?"

"What does Evan think?"

"He tells me that she is a wonderful candidate to adopt and is very attentive to Vicky. So I guess she's for real, but I won't feel comfortable about her until I meet her."

"She sounds like a woman who has learned how to live with a man who insists on controlling everything," Sharon commented. "Maybe she wants him to handle everything for her, protect her, make her feel safe. But now that you've told me about this, I wonder what's the deal with the wife, too. Ralph Roper sure as hell wants to make sure his wife adopts your niece."

"So it seems," Kira mused, pondering Sharon's words while making a mental note to press Evan for details about Helen Roper's background.

It was nearly nine o'clock when Kira pulled out of the parking lot of the Jade Moon and headed home. She felt calm and reassured. She had made the right decision by confiding in her coworker. Talking to Sharon had allowed Kira to step back and look at the situation from a less subjective perspective, and that was exactly what she had needed tonight in order to untangle the mixed emotions that the judge's ruling had brought on.

The court saw her as a valuable asset in Vicky's life, and Evan's supportive statements had helped her win visitation. She was happy about the positive outcome of the hearing, yet apprehensive about meeting Vicky. What would the child think of her? Would Vicky resent her sudden appearance? Hate her for not having been around earlier? Or was she still young and accepting enough to allow Kira to prove herself worthy of her love? The cycle of worry continued until she got home.

After checking her messages, Kira telephoned Evan, eager to talk to him about her experience with the judge. By now he must have gotten word from Kenneth or the court that her petition had been granted and that he would be responsible for setting up her visitation schedule. She was glad that Evan would be present when she visited with Vicky. His calm, reassuring manner and experience with children would be exactly what she needed to help her make a good impression.

"I called earlier and no one answered," Evan said, not probing for an explanation, yet sounding disappointed.

"Why didn't you leave a message?"

"Just thought I'd try later. Were you working late?"

"No, I went out with a friend for Chinese."

"Oh? A friend? A date?" Evan blurted out.

"If you can call dim sum, kung pao chicken, and a heart-to-heart with a coworker named Sharon a date, then yes," Kira threw back.

"Oh, girl talk, huh?"

"Yes. And I had an important reason to celebrate. You know I was victorious in court today, don't you?" she bragged.

"Yes. I got the message from Judge Burton's clerk. Two hours a week on either Saturday or Sunday, beginning this weekend. How do you feel about that?"

"Absolutely relieved, though a little nervous."

"Understandable. But you've got to take your time getting to know Vicky. Focus on building a real relationship with her, even if it moves at a snail's pace, and don't rush. You will not be her best friend. It won't happen like that. You'll be lucky to get her to even talk to you, so take it easy. Your goal is to let her know that you are going to be around forever. That she can count on you. Not just on a Saturday afternoon for a few hours."

"That's exactly what I plan to do," Kira said.

"It might be difficult at first, but don't give up. That child has been through a lot, and as confident as I feel that she will respond in a positive way to you, she might not. Will you be able to handle that?"

Exhaling, Kira gripped the phone, turning Evan's warning around in her mind. He was the expert on foster children, while she was entering an arena where she knew little or nothing about what to expect. Evan was Vicky's best ally, and Kira wanted to follow his lead. "Yes, I can handle rejection, and I expect her to be reserved, maybe even hostile, but with your help I'll be fine. You *are* going to give me pointers along the way, aren't you?"

"Of course. I'll call you tomorrow evening with the details of your first visit. Right now, I've got to call the Ropers and consult with them. They'll have to set the time for your visit."

"Let's hope your conversation with them goes as smoothly as my appearance before the judge," Kira said, wondering how Ralph and Helen Roper had taken the news that she had been granted the right to visit their daughter.

"I don't understand how you could have kept this from me," Helen Roper told her husband as soon as he entered their bedroom. She sat up in the middle of their king-size bed, a legal-size sheet of paper in her hand. She watched him in stony silence for a few seconds, then impulsively crushed the paper and hurled it to the foot of the bed where it settled on the purple silk bedspread. Frowning, she shoved a plum-colored, fringed pillow behind her shoulders and leaned back onto the tufted headboard, slumping wearily. Her eyes were red-rimmed and puffy from crying, her face blotched and sullen.

"Don't lie to me, Ralph." Helen bit down sharply after each word, her voice cracking with resentment. "Tell me the truth. You've known about this woman Kira Forester for some time, haven't you?"

The pain in Helen's voice hurt Ralph, who had known this confrontation was on its way. Helen was usually calm and soft-spoken, but tonight her disappointment had broken through her facade of composure. Ralph moved past her, holding his silence, and went to the mirrored folding doors of his walk-in closet. He pulled them open and sucked in a calming breath, preparing himself for the confession he had put off as long as he could. Helen had to know, sooner or later, that Vicky had an aunt who wanted visitation. He had wanted to be the one to tell Helen about the sudden appearance of Vicky's only relative, but he'd kept putting it off, not wanting to upset her. Today, when Evan had called him with Judge Burton's decision, Ralph had been in the middle of a executive staff meeting and had pushed the upsetting news to the back of his mind in order to concentrate on the sales figures and production projections he had been discussing. On his way home he had rehearsed his confession, but clearly Sheltering Hearts, or Joe Hickman, had gotten to her first.

He loosened his tie, yanking the expensive gray and red silk from around his neck, dreading the discussion he had to have with Helen. It had been a hectic day filled with production problems at his local factory, a luncheon appearance at the Monroeville Citizens Community Forum, and the staff meeting that had run an hour over schedule. Tonight was not a good one for dealing with the unpleasant issue of Kira Forester or his wife's obvious anxiety, but it had to be done.

"Yes," he finally admitted without looking over at Helen. "I've known about Kira Forester for some time."

"I wish you had told me," Helen whispered, her voice small.

"I was going to . . . at the right time," Ralph mumbled, kicking off his shoes. He shoved them to one side of the closet and slipped on his well-worn, brown leather house shoes.

"Evan Conley called me and told me what had happened," Helen continued. "He was surprised to learn that I knew nothing about Vicky's aunt. He assumed you had discussed all of this with me, as you apparently promised him you would. I asked him to fax me a copy of the judge's ruling"—she kicked at the ball of paper at the foot of the bed, pushing it to the floor—"a fax . . . informing me that the court has granted a total stranger visitation with my child. I can't believe it. How do you think this makes me feel, Ralph? What is going on? I tried to get you at the office, but you were in conference, so I called Joe. Even he knew about her and what she's after! How could you do this, Ralph? I am so upset—" she broke off, shuddering with anger.

Ralph removed his suit jacket and tossed it over the valet stand just inside the entrance to his closet, then calmly turned around and picked up the crumpled fax. He read it quickly, and facing Helen, stared at her with no emotion on his face. "There is nothing to worry about, Helen," he finally said, his blue eyes steady and wide. "Just because the court has granted this woman visitation rights does not mean we won't be able to adopt Vicky."

"How do you know?" Helen tossed back, her voice now sharp with fear. "She's a blood relative, and she obviously has rights. You know how it is. Just because she's black, the court has favored her, granted privileges she does not deserve. Now I have to hand Vicky over to her? Let my daughter go off and spend two hours with a woman she does not know? I can't do it, Ralph. I won't!"

Ralph sighed aloud, feeling his wife's anxiety, and even her pain, wishing he had been able to derail Kira Forester's mission and avoid this upsetting scene. Though the court may have ruled in Kira's favor, he was not worried. She had won nothing. "I understand how you feel, honey, but don't worry. This will blow over. For heaven's sake, just do as the court has ordered for now. With the election still ahead of me, I don't want any trouble with the law or a reason to be going in and out of court. I can't afford an incident that might reflect negatively on me—or you. Stay strong, Helen. After the election, we will fight this and make that woman sorry she ever got involved."

"But why did Vicky's aunt show up at all?" Helen wanted to know. "Evan Conley mentioned her during one of our sessions, but he did not indicate that she was going to be involved. You know she'll take Vicky away from us, don't you?"

"No, she won't," Ralph countered, approaching the side of the bed. He gazed solemnly down at Helen, worried about the effect that this news was having on her. She had a distracted look about her, as if she was unable to come to terms with this news. It would be difficult to get through to Helen now, but he had to try. "Evan Conley has assured me that Kira does not want to adopt her niece. She even told me so herself. Try to remain calm, Helen," he soothed, reaching out to brush a damp lock of hair from his wife's forehead.

Instead of calming down, as Ralph had hoped, Helen's agitation increased. She jerked back from his intended touch, as if shocked, her eyes bright with apprehension. "Then what does she want?" Helen snapped, shrinking farther into her covers. "Money? How much? If that's what she wants, pay her, Ralph. Give her whatever she wants to get her out of our lives."

"It's not about money," Ralph admitted, easing down on the bed next to Helen. Ignoring her look of distrust, he took her limp hand in his and rubbed it, calmed by the soft feel of her skin. "She wants to rid herself of the guilt that's been eating at her ever since she abandoned her sister's child. I had Joe check her out. Did Evan Conley tell you that?"

Helen shook her head. "No."

"Well, I found out plenty. Enough to know that she better not try to take Vicky. Even Conley knows what it is, and he's assured me that we are very much on target with the adoption. The judge had to grant visitation, so we'll deal with it. In my opinion, Kira

Forester is a flighty, self-centered woman who, after a few visits, will get tired of playing auntie and disappear. And when that happens, the court will see her for who she really is and permanently ban her from access to our daughter. Maybe it's best that we go through this now, so we'll be done with the woman forever."

"I want to meet her," Helen blurted out, dabbing at her eyes with the edge of her lavender sheet. "I want to talk to her, see her, learn everything about her."

"I don't think that's a good idea. Not right now. According to the court order, I can take Vicky to Sheltering Hearts and remain in the next room while she visits with her aunt. Evan Conley will be there, and despite his firm belief that Kira deserves to see her niece, I have to trust him to handle our situation in a professional manner. After the visit, I'll bring Vicky home. Don't worry," Ralph comforted his wife.

"I don't like it," Helen said, sniffling. "Two hours? That's too long. Don't you see how destructive these visits are going to be for Vicky? Her aunt will use that time to undermine me . . . to wipe out my efforts to make Vicky feel secure and safe with us. In time Vicky will turn against me; you know she will!" Helen bit down on her lower lip, struggling to hold back more tears, her chest rising and falling as she drew in long breaths.

"I won't let that happen, " Ralph promised. "I'll talk to Conley . . . see if he can get the aunt to agree to a shorter visit . . . maybe one hour for the first few times at least."

"Oh, would you?" Helen wailed. "If this woman upsets Vicky, I will never forgive her. Or you! Or Evan Conley, either." Helen slid down in the bed, turned her face into her pillow and began to sob, her cries muffled among the layers of lavender cloth that she crushed to her cheek.

"Nothing will go wrong. Trust me, Helen. I told you when we decided to go through with this that you would have the child you wanted, and you will, " Ralph promised, stroking Helen's hair, infuriated to see her so distraught. He was not about to sit by and watch her slowly deteriorate into a state of hopelessness. Her infertility had initiated the depression that had almost taken her away from him, but Vicky had pulled her out of it. Ralph continued to caress Helen's hair, thinking of how to proceed. He had a campaign to run, an opponent to crush, a company to manage, and little time to deal with the likes of Kira Forester, though he knew he would do whatever he needed to do to keep Helen happy.

"Kira's not going to become a threat to you," Ralph comforted his wife, lightly brushing a few wisps of hair from her cheek. She was the most important thing in his life: more important than the worldwide business he had built, more important than a political career, and more valuable than any treasure he owned. She provided him with a sense of permanence that he needed in order to face each day with a positive attitude. His life would mean nothing without Helen in it. "You've got to be strong, Helen. You must believe that Vicky loves you, depends on you, and trusts you. Kira Forester doesn't want the child. Can you please go along with the court order and make Vicky believe that you are friends with her aunt? Pretend that you're happy about the woman's sudden appearance, and encourage Vicky to be polite. That's all you need to do. Let me work out the rest. You are Vicky's mother, I guarantee you that."

CHAPTER 20

Kira removed the gold and pearl earrings from the oval, velvet-lined drawer inside her jewelry box and clipped them on her ears, though they were really too elegant to be worn with the simply cut maroon gabardine slacks and jacket she had decided to wear for her first visit with Vicky. The shimmer of the lustrous pearls peeking out from beneath her crinkly hair created an immediate connection to Miranda, and Kira wondered if it would be inappropriate to tell Vicky that the earrings had belonged to her mother. Kira stood back from her dresser mirror and nervously checked her appearance, anxious to make a good impression.

What would they do for an hour? she worried, thankful that Evan had encouraged her to go along with the Ropers' request to reduce this first visit to one hour, though the court had specified two. Kira had readily agreed, thinking it would be best to ease her way into her niece's life rather than overwhelm the child, and Kira was determined to demonstrate to the Ropers and the court that she could be polite, flexible, and accommodating in order to serve Vicky's best interest.

Should she give Vicky a hug? Kira wondered. Touch her? Or keep a reserved distance? *Evan will guide me,* she decided, reaching for the photo of Miranda and her infant daughter, Vicky, that had been taken in Miranda's trailer. Kira slid the photograph into her purse. When the appropriate time came, she'd show it to Vicky. But not today, she told herself, grabbing her car keys and heading out the door.

During the next twenty-five minutes, Kira made her way down US-74 toward Stallings, her worries about meeting Vicky slowly evolving into thoughts about the Ropers. What had they told Vicky about her, and how had they reacted to this court-ordered visitation? Would the extended home study turn up anything about them that might affect the adoption? Evan had informed her that Ralph was going to bring Vicky to his office at noon and she was to visit with Vicky in an area at Sheltering Hearts especially designed for such visitations. The arrangements suited Kira, yet she was disappointed that there would be no opportunity for her to meet Helen, whose reluctance to surface was beginning to alarm her. Kira had assumed that, as a prospective adoptive parent, Helen would want to meet and get to know her child's aunt. Apparently, she was wrong.

At Sheltering Hearts, the receptionist immediately ushered Kira into Evan's office. He was at his desk, on the phone, but he looked up and smiled at her, then motioned for her to come in. Kira returned his smile and entered but did not sit down, deciding to wait on the far side of the room where she pretended to examine the model ship on the bookcase shelf while Evan discussed the agenda of an upcoming conference where he was going to be the speaker. From the corner of her eye, Kira watched Evan, her eyes moving over his profile, his shoulders, down his arms to his hands. She was impressed with how self-assured and professional he sounded as spoke on the phone, and she was glad he was handling Vicky's case.

Evan Conley was steady and mature, yet not uptight or old-fashioned. He was knowledgeable about the complicated procedures and policies related to the adoption process. It was obvious that he loved his work, and Kira could tell from the way he spoke about his agency that he was proud of the job that he and his small staff were doing. He was not like any man she had ever known; his unique mix of energy, commitment, and tenderness was very attractive to Kira. At that moment, all she could think about was being alone with Evan again, of kissing him, of holding him close as their bodies and lips came together.

Evan glanced up and caught her looking at him. His gaze initiated a warm flood of pleasure in Kira. Breaking the unexpected connection that had suddenly linked them together, Evan hung up the phone and swept her with an appreciative glance. "It's great to see you, Kira. You look wonderful."

"Thanks," Kira murmured, thinking, *And so do you.* She gave the front of her jacket a tug and approached the chair in front of Evan's desk. Before sitting, she said, "I wasn't sure what to wear. Do you think Vicky will feel comfortable with me?"

"I'm certain she will. You look fine—no, better than fine. You look fabulous."

Kira laughed and sat down.

"Vicky is a pretty easygoing child," Evan said. "I've spent a lot of time with her, and I've always been impressed with the way she handles herself. Never cranky or moody. Surprisingly outgoing for a girl of six. Still, I think your agreeing to a shorter period of visitation today was a good idea."

"Yes," Kira said. "Takes off some of the pressure."

"Are you nervous?" Evan asked.

"A little," Kira admitted.

"Don't be," he assured her. "It will be fine." He stood up and walked from behind his desk to stand next to Kira, looking down at her. "As much as I enjoy staying here and talking with you, I think we'd better go. I certainly don't want to cut into your time together."

"Is Vicky already here?" Kira wanted to know.

"Yes," Evan replied, motioning toward the door that opened into the hallway. "She's in our Visiting Room with Sue, one of my caseworkers. Ralph Roper is here, too, but he'll wait in another area."

"Why didn't Helen Roper come?" Kira asked. "Don't you think it's odd that she's not here?"

Evan's expression betrayed his concern, but his response was what she had expected. "She needs time to get used to the idea that Vicky has someone else who cares about her. I was the one who broke the news to her about you—and about the court-ordered visitation. She was very upset. I know she's not happy about sharing Vicky with you."

"Do you mean to say that Ralph never told his wife about me? About our meeting at his office?"

"Apparently not," Evan said. "I think he was waiting to see how the judge would rule before he said anything to Helen. But I got to her before he did, and I admit it was a surprise to me, too, that she was not informed."

"Evan, I don't have a good feeling about Helen. Ralph . . . well, he is who he is, and at least I know where he's coming from and what to expect. But Helen? Why the mystery act?"

"Oh, don't make too much of it, Kira. She'll come around. Let's give her time to adjust to you being in the picture. I predict that eventually you two might become good friends."

Kira rolled her eyes. "How can you say that?"

"Because I've seen it happen more times than I can count. Blood relatives and adoptive parents who love the same child . . . there is nothing more powerful over which to forge a friendship."

"Maybe," Kira reluctantly agreed. "If I ever meet her. How long does she think she can avoid me? Sooner or later, I am going to meet that woman, and when I do, I have a lot of questions to ask."

The receptionist tapped on Evan's door, then stuck her head into his office.

"Yes?" he asked.

"It's twelve-fifteen. You know . . . I'm leaving now. Sue is in the Visiting Room with Vicky. Mr. Roper is in the staff lounge. Okay?"

"Fine," Evan told her.

"Good, then everything is set and I'm off. See you Monday."

As soon as the receptionist left, Evan motioned for Kira to follow him into the corridor. "The Visiting Room is an area set aside at Sheltering Hearts especially for visits like this," he told her. "It's a comfortable place where prospective adoptive parents can spend time with a child they are considering adopting. It's set up to look like a typical family room, with a big-screen television, lots of books, a sofa, a recliner, tables where the children can paint, color, or play games. It's a safe place where children and adults can interact in a setting that helps take their minds off the formality of the situation. I hope you'll feel comfortable there, too."

As soon as Evan pushed open the door to the Visiting Room Kira understood what he meant. The soft yellow walls, beige carpet, and cozy groupings of upholstered furniture created an atmosphere of welcome and comfort, making Kira feel immediately at ease. The high windows that surrounded the room were free of coverings, allowing bright sunlight to stream down into the area, emphasizing its sense of openness and freedom. One wall was covered with bookshelves on which had been placed a wide assortment of reading material for both children and adults. A computer stood on a metal table in one corner, next to a large aquarium that was filled with a variety of colorful fish. A sofa and two chairs faced the television, and a nature program that Kira recognized as one from the Discovery Channel was playing.

Kira's attention swung to the child seated on the sofa, and she was immediately mesmerized by the girl's resemblance to Miranda.

The same dark curly hair and big brown eyes, even the same prominent cheekbones that had given Miranda the haughty look of a model. The miniature image of her sister struck Kira hard, arousing old fears and uncertainties.

Would Vicky ever forgive Kira's lack of attention and failure to prioritize her niece in her life? Was Kira foolish to hope that Vicky would welcome her attention now? The thought of failing at being a good aunt nearly brought tears to Kira's eyes.

Giving herself a mental shake, she focused on the woman accompanying Vicky, who was busy explaining what the black bear in the program on TV was doing. Kira hung back near the door, listening.

"I think he's looking for honey," was Vicky's reply to the woman's question.

"But I don't think he can climb that tree," the young lady replied.

"You don't?" said Vicky. "Why not?"

"Because he's too fat," the caseworker replied.

Vicky giggled and squeezed her eyes shut, shaking her head. "Oh no! He's going up there. I think he's going to fall!"

Evan motioned for Kira to follow him as he crossed the room toward Vicky and the caseworker who was keeping her company.

"I agree with you, Vicky," he said, smiling as he entered the conversation. "That bear will never get to that honey."

"I know," Vicky agreed, nodding, making her dark curls dance around her face as she kept her gaze fixed on the screen.

"Sue," Evan said, addressing the young woman sitting beside Vicky, "thanks for sitting with Vicky."

"No problem," Sue replied. Turning to Kira, she smiled a welcome. "You must be Vicky's aunt?"

"Yes," Kira said, extending her hand. "I'm Kira Forester."

"Sue Goodwin. Good to meet you," she replied, shaking Kira's hand. Turning back, she gave Vicky a quick hug. "I'll see you later, Vicky," she said. "You can tell me if the bear gets the honey or not. Okay?"

"Okay," said Vicky, still concentrating on the program.

Sue left, leaving Vicky, Kira, and Evan alone in the room. Evan muted the TV and sat down on the sofa next to Vicky, indicating that Kira should sit in the chair opposite them.

Hesitantly, Kira sat down, unable to take her eyes off her niece. She pressed her fingernails into the palms of her hands and tried to remain in control of her emotions. Vicky's dark curls were tied into two ponytails, held in place with twists of multicolored ribbons that swayed whenever she turned her head. She was much taller than she had appeared to be on television, and the impact of her childish beauty made Kira catch her breath. Vicky was dressed in a blue, long-sleeved T-shirt, jeans with bands of red and green paisley ribbon around the cuffs, and white sneakers. A swell of love came over Kira, and for a moment her thoughts turned back to her mother. If only she was still alive and could see how lovely her granddaughter was. The flicker of memories that came to Kira were filled with laughter, fun, and adventure, when her mother had taught her and Miranda how to make mud pies, sew dresses for their dolls, and roller-skate on the sidewalks of their neighborhood. The absence of family had created a hole in Kira's life that she was eager to fill, and Vicky was the only one who could do that.

"Vicky," Evan began, drawing her attention to him. "I understand that Helen told you about your Aunt Kira, didn't she?"

"Yes," Vicky whispered, narrowing her eyes to steal a glance at Kira.

"And," Evan continued, "did she tell you why you're here today?"

Vicky nodded at Evan, then widened her eyes and scrutinized Kira more intently, creating a wrinkle in her forehead that pulled her silky brows together. After a moment, she smiled, showing off her dimples and her small, even teeth; then, squaring her shoulders in a very grown-up gesture, she said, "Yes. Helen told me I'm here to meet my Aunt Kira. She's my real mother's sister."

"That's right," Evan said, in a congratulatory tone. "For a long time your Aunt Kira has lived far away, but now that she is closer, she wants to get to know you." Evan turned to Kira and gave her an encouraging smile. "Kira, this is Vicky."

"Hello," Kira said, her voice tight with emotion. She swallowed dryly, then plunged ahead. "I've waited a long time to meet you."

"Do you live in Monroeville now, too?" Vicky asked bluntly, clasping her tiny hands in her lap, her fingers laced together.

"No, I live in Charlotte."

"Is that far away?"

"Not very," Kira said.

"I didn't think you lived in Monroeville because I've never seen you."

"Do you like Monroeville?" Kira asked.

"Oh yes," Vicky quickly replied. "It's nice, but I miss Terry and Ron."

"Her former foster brothers," Evan clarified.

"Oh yes," Kira murmured, realizing how much change her niece had experienced in her young life. "I'm sure you miss them. Do you talk to them on the phone?"

"Only once since I came here," Vicky replied.

"So, what do you like most about Monroeville?" Kira asked, hoping she could keep the conversation going without showing her nervousness.

Without hesitation, Vicky answered, almost in a shout, "My piano lessons. I love playing the piano, and Helen lets me sit at the big shiny piano at home to practice."

Kira winked and smiled. "I took piano lessons when I was your age, too, but I didn't like it. It was hard for me, and I hated to practice."

"I think it's easy, and it's fun," Vicky told Kira, holding out her hands, wiggling her fingers. She began to hum, moving her fingers to the music, totally absorbed in showing Kira what she had learned so far.

"What can you play?"

"Only one song for now, but I'm going to learn more."

"I'm sure you will," Kira said, impressed by the candid, open way in which Vicky was accepting her. Evan had been right. Vicky was an amazingly lovable child, sweet and even-tempered—easy to love. Meeting her now was an astonishing awakening for Kira, and she felt a sting of regret for allowing so much time to pass before making a move to know her.

"Did my mother take piano lessons, too?" Vicky suddenly asked, still humming as she moved her tiny fingers, totally unaware of the effect she was having on Kira.

Kira gulped back a gasp of surprise at how innocently Vicky had introduced the subject that Kira had been hesitant to bring up. While she had been worrying about how to ease the topic of her sister into the conversation, Vicky, in her childish curiosity, had cut through layers of apprehension to get to the link that bound them together. Vicky was curious about her real mother, and Kira *was* the only person who would be able to satisfy that curiosity. Ralph and Helen Roper could never do that.

Vicky's question reverberated in Kira's mind like the chime of a distant bell, dissolving the worry and self-recrimination she had brought with her to the reunion. Vicky needed her. She needed Vicky. And they would become close whether the Ropers wanted it that way or not. Kira glanced at Evan, and immediately saw that he understood what she was thinking.

"I think I'll get a cup of coffee in the break room," he told Kira, standing. "Want something? We have a cold-drink machine."

"No thanks." Then, turning her attention to Vicky, Kira asked, "Do you want something to drink?"

"Do you have Sprite?" Vicky asked Evan.

"I think so. Want one?"

Vicky nodded.

Kira rethought her reply to Evan and added, "You know, I *am* a little thirsty. I think I'll have a Sprite, too."

"Good. Be right back," Evan said as he left.

Relieved that Vicky had been the one to bring up the subject of her natural mother, Kira said, "You wanted to know if your mother took piano lessons, too?"

"Yes. Did she? " Vicky asked.

"Yes. In fact, she played the piano very well," Kira answered, relaxing the muscles in her face. She remained silent, pondering where to begin. "Your mother took her piano lessons very seriously, and she was talented, too. She loved to practice and even used to make up little songs that she would play over and over. Like to drove your grandmother and me crazy, but once she got started, she wouldn't stop for hours."

"Really?" Vicky remarked, her brown eyes sparkling with interest. "Do you remember any of the songs?"

"At the time, I thought I'd never be able to get them out of my head, but now, I can't remember how they went. I do know they were loud and long." Kira chuckled softly, shaking her head. "It was a long time ago."

"I hope you remember them one day, and then maybe you can hum them to me, and I'll learn to play them, too."

The innocent remark forced Kira to blink back the pressure of approaching tears that had been building behind her eyes since the moment she saw Vicky. Who would have thought that such an obscure childhood memory would have such significance? Kira could still envision Miranda pounding on the keys of the old upright piano their father had purchased in a pawnshop for her to practice on. The piano had never been properly tuned, and the songs Miranda made up had been little more than excited bursts of energy, changing each time she placed her small fingers on the keys, many of which had lost their ivory casings long before Miranda got to them. That piano had been a wonderful outlet for her creative energy, drawing her into a world where she had been happy entertaining herself, and it had remained that way until she grew up and decided that boys were more interesting than music.

"I doubt I'll ever remember those songs, Vicky. But after you've taken a few more lessons, why don't you make up some songs of your own? Then one day you could play them for me. That would be nice, wouldn't it?"

Vicky rested her chin on the back of one hand, her brown, heavily lashed eyes fixed on Kira as she pondered the suggestion. Tilting her head to the side, as if still unsure about the idea, she asked Kira, "Do you have a piano at your house?"

"No, I don't," Kira replied.

"Then how would I play them for you? Would you come to my house?"

"Well, I'm not sure, but there is a piano here," Kira replied, motioning to the far side of the recreation room. "You could play for me here."

"But why can't you come to my house so I could play for you on my piano?" Vicky wanted to know.

Her blunt invitation, so innocently offered, brought a fresh lump to Kira's throat, but she gulped it back quickly, realizing Vicky had just verbalized her own vision of their relationship, one in which Ralph and Helen Roper would welcome Kira into their home to share the joy of Vicky's accomplishments and interests. But as things now stood, Kira knew it would be up to her to create an environment within her own home that allowed her and Vicky to be together, and if she'd have to buy a piano just for Vicky's use, Kira knew she would gladly do it.

Kira got up from the chair where she had been sitting and went to sit beside Vicky on the sofa, taking time to form her answer. As she settled down beside her niece, she pushed her hair from her face, brushing the pearl drop earrings with her fingers.

"Maybe one day I'll visit your house to hear you play. And one day maybe you will come to my house, too. But for now, we'll meet here."

Vicky looked over at Kira and grinned, but her inquisitive eyes quickly focused on the large pearls dangling from Kira's ears.

"Those are pretty," she remarked, pointing at the shimmering jewels.

"Thank you," Kira murmured, wanting very much to reach out and take Vicky in her arms, give her a hard hug, and tell her that the earrings once belonged to her mother, let her know that the jewels had touched her real mother's flesh and that they were the only things of value that Kira had managed to salvage from the home where Vicky had been born. But she held back, thinking it best not to talk too much about Miranda on this first visit. "I have lots of pretty earrings," Kira continued. "But these are my favorites."

"Why?" Vicky asked.

"Because they remind me of someone very special."

After giving the jewelry another close look, Vicky told Kira, "When I get big I'm going to have holes in my ears, too." Then she scooted back in her seat, crossed her feet at the ankles, and turned her attention once more to the muted television screen. "Can you turn it up now?" she asked, as if finished with her conversation with Kira.

"Sure," Kira said, pressing the remote to bring the program back to life, calmed by the easy way in which Vicky had interacted with her. Kira settled closer to her niece to watch the program, speaking only when Vicky asked her a question about the bear's actions or made a comment about what was going on. When Evan returned with the drinks, Kira looked over at him, nodding. He winked and handed her a cold can of soda.

"Thanks," Kira said, taking a sip, then setting hers on the table.

Evan popped the tab on the cold Sprite and handed it to Vicky, who indicated her thanks with a quick nod before returning her attention to the television, her elbow propped on the arm of the sofa, one cheek on her hand. She giggled when the black bear, who was now splashing in a stream, finally caught a fish.

A hint of a smile came to Kira's lips, and she locked eyes with Evan, who sat in the chair opposite her and Vicky. When he pointed to his watch she understood that it was time for her to go. The prospect of leaving was discomforting, not only because Ralph Roper would be the one to take Vicky home, but because she had not had nearly enough time with her niece. There was so much she wanted to say and show Vicky, but she'd have to pace herself. The last thing she wanted to do was overwhelm her. As long as the visits went well and the court allowed her to have access to Vicky, Kira knew she'd have plenty of opportunities to talk about Miranda, to show Vicky her family photos, and to learn more about Vicky's life with the Ropers. For now, Kira was simply grateful that Evan had made this connection possible so that, at last, Vicky knew who she was.

CHAPTER 21

Kira's brief introduction to Vicky left her edgy and exhausted, though elated to have satisfactorily completed a huge step in her mission to reclaim her niece. All of the stress and worry she had had about what to say or do during their reunion had been replaced by a persistent ache to see Vicky again. Upon leaving, she had gingerly touched Vicky on the shoulder and said good-bye, though she had wanted to gather the child into her arms and hold her tight against her chest, to feel the warmth of her sister's blood racing close to hers. The urge to hold her was still there when Kira entered her apartment and began to pace the floor.

With great precision, she mentally recalled every detail of the visit, savoring the sound of Vicky's voice, the sweet smell of her hair, the sight of her slender fingers wiggling up and down. Kira walked restlessly from room to room, thinking. The reunion had gone so much better than she had imagined, and now she realized how fulfilling it was going to be to share her life with a child. Kira wanted to give Vicky a part of herself, to encourage her, teach her, and expose her to wonderful new adventures. They would have fun at the park, go to the beach, enjoy shopping together, or sitting at the piano making up songs. Until today, Kira had had no idea what kind of a child Vicky was, or if her niece would reject her attention. But now that she had met her, Kira knew she loved her niece very much and would never allow her to slip away again. The child's innocent charm, obvious intelligence, beauty and inquisitiveness, not to mention her striking resemblance to Miranda, had all come together to strike a deep emotional chord with Kira, creating an instant bond.

But the euphoria left in the wake of this first visit was tempered by the reality that Miranda's daughter would be raised by strangers—white strangers who knew nothing about her family history and, most likely, little about her culture. Would it work for Vicky? Kira fretted. And what would happen if things turned sour and the Ropers wanted out? Could Vicky survive such a blow? Clearly, the child was content in her new home, and Kira could do nothing to stop the adoption from going through. All she could do was pray that this was best for now and be there for Vicky as her future played itself out.

Kira went into her bedroom to change her clothes, removing Miranda's pearl earrings first. Holding them in the palm of her hand, she let her imagination paint a scenario in which she was placing the jewelry on Vicky's ears on the night of her first date. She could imagine helping Vicky pick out a dress, giving her advice about how to conduct herself, then waiting up for her, watching the clock while listening for her key in the lock. That was what concerned mothers did, wasn't it?

Of course it would be that way if Vicky was living with me, Kira mused, realizing that Helen Roper would be the one sitting up, waiting for Vicky to come home, not Kira. For the first time, the idea of mothering Vicky, of having a daughter, settled into Kira's mind with a touch of plausibility that frightened her.

Shuddering, Kira quickly put the jewelry away and put the scenario out of her mind. Changing into a comfy pair of stone-washed jeans and a sweater, she went into the kitchen, sat down at the table, and began leafing idly through the Saturday paper, unable to concentrate on the advertisements, articles, or even the comics. Giving up, she shoved the newspaper into the wicker basket beside the patio door, ready for recycling, and wandered into the living room, where she zapped the remote to turn on the TV, then impulsively ordered a Steven Segal Pay-Per-View movie on cable, one she had seen three times.

As the action movie played out, Kira lolled on the sofa watching the actors engage in vicious fistfights, thunderous car chases through crowded urban streets, and deadly karate movements that made her flinch. But in reality she was paying little attention to what was going on, because her mind persistently drifted back to Vicky, whose tiny features, light voice, and childish mannerisms were ingrained in Kira's mind.

I wonder what Vicky thinks about me, her Aunt Kira? she mused, trying to gauge how well she had been accepted. Did Evan think the visit had gone well? And now that Vicky was most likely back at home, what was she telling her parents about her afternoon with her aunt? The questions swirled and shifted, moving through Kira's mind like the patterns in a kaleidoscope, like the colorful ribbons that had held Vicky's curls back from her face.

When the movie ended Kira forced herself off the sofa, pushed up the sleeves of her sweater, and loaded her favorite CDs into her CD player, then went into the kitchen, where she poured herself a glass of cranberry juice and surveyed the contents of her refrigerator. She wasn't really hungry, though she'd only had a cup of coffee and a Danish all day. Impulsively, she decided that all she could handle was some pasta and a salad, so she put a pot of water on to boil and pulled every fresh vegetable she could find from the refrigerator shelves. As she sipped her juice and listened to music, she washed and chopped and tore up the vegetables, forcing her mind from the extraordinary events of the afternoon.

The ring of her phone cut through the music, and Kira quickly wiped her hands on a towel and picked up the handset to her cordless.

"Hello," she said, moving toward the CD player to lower the volume.

"Hello, Kira. Evan here."

His voice sent a jolt of pleasure through her, and she smiled, glad to be distracted from her self-imposed pity party. "Well, hello," she replied as lightly as she could manage, turning to her pot of boiling water and tossing in a handful of penne pasta. Returning to her chopping board with the phone balanced between her shoulder and her ear, she picked up the knife and began slicing a green pepper.

"How are you doing?" Evan asked in a tone that indicated his concern.

Kira paused with her chef's knife raised, leaving the green pepper on the board half cut, then slowly lowered it and placed it in the sink.

"How am I doing?" she repeated, slumping down to prop her elbows on the kitchen counter.

"Yes."

"Terrible," she bluntly told him, glad to have someone to talk to about the roller-coaster emotions that were making her crazy. "It was wonderful to see Vicky . . . but I feel awful." She squeezed her eyes shut and waited for Evan to reply, but when he let the silence stand, she went on. "Is this normal? To be happy, yet feel terrible? It's as if everything around me is shifting, changing too fast, and I don't know how to make it settle down. Does that make sense?"

"Absolutely," Evan calmly consoled her. "I understand completely. When you left Sheltering Hearts this afternoon, I could tell by the expression on your face that you were having a difficult time. I was worried about you, Kira, and I still am. That's why I called."

The sincerity in his voice touched Kira, who exhaled in a whoosh of relief and gripped the edge of the green marble counter, anxious to talk to Evan. Kira needed him to guide her through this emotional canyon, which she knew could be damaging if she let it get her down.

"Evan, I'm not sure about how to deal with these feelings. I want to push forward—but how? I really need your help."

"Kira, you know I'll help any way I can."

"Can you help me get through this evening?" she blundered ahead. "I thought this was going to be easier to handle than it's turned out to be. All evening, my mind has been on Vicky. Nothing else. I can't concentrate on anything. Evan, she's so sweet. So smart. I understand why her foster mother adored her and why Ralph and Helen Roper want to adopt her. I hate myself for never getting to know her. I've been so selfish. Oh, Evan—" Kira broke off, embarrassed to realize she was about to cry, something she had struggled against all day. Swallowing the sob that choked off her words, she knew the emotional impact of the day was finally catching up with her. "When I was with Vicky, I was so happy to be with her, make a real connection, but now I'm absolutely miserable because I don't know what to do."

"Do about what?" Evan asked.

"The way I feel," Kira murmured, wiping her eyes. "Seeing her, talking with her . . . it was a lot more stressful than I had anticipated. I want her to be happy, and she seems to be. I want to be close to her, but I really can't adopt her. Oh, Evan, will the Ropers work out for her?" She pressed a hand over her lips for a few seconds to get control, fearful of breaking down in sobs. "She looks so much like Miranda. This is hard, Evan. How can I be expected to ignore my ache for her and hold my emotions in check until I get to see her again—and for only one or two hours a week? That's not normal or fair."

"Hopefully, it won't always be this way. Adjusting to a situation like yours takes time, patience, and cooperation between all parties involved. In time everything settles into a sense of normalcy. The Ropers may not be happy about your visitation rights, but they are not fighting it, either. Once the adoption is final, I'm sure things will smooth out. You're at the beginning now, and I know it's a tense, scary feeling, but it won't always be like this."

"For some reason, I don't feel so optimistic, Evan. The court ordered the Ropers to make Vicky available to me. I doubt they would have done so voluntarily."

"Maybe not. But once they realize that you are not a threat, and that Vicky is a happier child because she has knowledge of and a connection with her real mother, they will be much more accepting of you."

"I hope so," Kira said with a groan, thinking Evan had better be right, because she was never going to back away from Vicky again, so the Ropers might just as well get used to the idea that she was going to be around.

"Kira, I had a feeling this was going to be harder on you than you imagined. When you first came to my office weeks ago and told me all you wanted was visitation, I heard an underlying message that you really wanted more. It frightened me, because I've been interacting with Vicky for almost a year, and I know what a sweet child she is. I don't want to see her yanked around or caught up in a nasty fight. I've been through those before, and no one benefits from a fight. Now that I know you better and have seen you with Vicky, I give you credit for going about this in the proper way. Your presence in her life will only be a plus, and I'm not surprised that Vicky took to you so fast."

"Do you think she likes me?"

Evan chuckled lowly. "I'm certain. If she hadn't wanted to be with you or talk to you, she wouldn't have. I assure you of that. No one can force a child to be as pleasant and agreeable as Vicky was with you this afternoon. You've started off on a good note, you know?"

"I guess so," Kira whispered, knowing she would have sensed right away if Vicky had not wanted to be alone with her. "I thought it went well, too. It was comfortable, thanks to you."

"I'm glad the first meeting went so well, and since it was such a success, I was hoping we might plan to have the next meeting under less formal circumstances. Maybe at the zoo or a park? Weather permitting, of course. What do you think?"

"I think that would be great," Kira replied, already beginning to feel less anxious about the long journey that stretched ahead.

The sound of boiling water hitting the hot stove burner distracted Kira, who jumped around, then told Evan, "Hold on! My pasta is boiling over!" She slammed the phone onto the counter and hurried to the stove, rescuing the pot before it made a complete mess. Grabbing a paper towel, she began mopping up the starchy water, as she reached for the phone. "Sorry about that, but I got it in time." On an impulse, she asked, "Evan, what are you doing for dinner?"

"Uh . . . hadn't thought that far," he admitted.

"Well, I wish we could talk more about this. I really want to see you . . . plus I could use some company. I was just pulling together some pasta and a salad. Come over, please. We can put a couple of salmon steaks on the grill, too, if you'd like." She tensed when the line went silent.

They had not been alone socially since their dinner at Chaio's, when they had laughed and talked the evening away over seafood and wonderful white wine. And today their meeting had remained on a professional level, with neither making reference to the undercurrent of magnetism that was clearly pulling them closer. Kira had sensed that Evan was waiting for her to make the next move, and inviting him for dinner was a natural way to extend their conversation and provide an opportunity for them to explore their deepening attraction.

"I'd love to have dinner with you, but only on one condition," Evan told her.

"You name it."

"I get to bring the wine."

"That's a deal," Kira replied, grinning as a warm glow of anticipation spread throughout her body. "See you in about an hour?"

"Fine," Evan said.

Kira sighed and hung up the phone. At last she would be alone with Evan on her own turf, not in a public place. The evening stretched out in Kira's mind like a mysterious dark road waiting to be explored, and the prospect of entering it with Evan sent a ripple of excitement through her.

* * *

Evan stood with his back to the tall wooden fence that separated Kira's patio from her neighbor's and sipped his glass of wine. A breeze that still carried a touch of afternoon warmth ruffled the air of the mild April evening, though the sun had disappeared more than an hour ago, slipping behind the budding crepe myrtles that were planted throughout the apartment complex.

He glanced appreciatively at the softly illuminated setting that Kira had created outside, impressed by her transformation of what could have been an ordinary ten-by-ten concrete slab into a luscious minigarden. She had placed a mélange of candles of various shapes and colors throughout her pots of ferns and ivy, and had even hung a square, candle-lit lantern from the limb of one of the crepe myrtle trees. Its budding arm arched over her fence to create lacy shadows on a flowered chaise lounge. In one corner, a waist-high fountain in the shape of a girl sitting on a water lily pad made a gentle bubbling sound as its stream of water sluiced across the statue and blended with the smooth voice of Peabo Bryson coming through the partially open patio door.

Crossing to the wrought-iron round table set for two in the center of the patio, Evan placed his wineglass next to one of the tiny votive candles that was flickering in a blue glass holder, pleased that Kira felt comfortable enough to invite him into her home. The kiss they had shared after dinner at Chaio's blazed hotly in his memory, as it had all week, and he wanted desperately to taste her lips once more, feel her arms around his neck, her body pressed to his. He had hoped she would take the initiative to move their attraction to a more intimate place, wherever that might turn out to be, but he had never expected her to do so this evening. After Kira's emotional visit with Vicky, he had been reluctant to call, thinking she might want to be alone, that she might still resent him for having played a part in creating the situation he knew she was having a great deal of difficulty accepting. He bit his lip in concern as he watched her step through the door and come out onto the patio, a tray of salmon steaks in one hand, tongs in the other. Seeing her again stirred him in a way that was both unsettling and reassuring, and he struggled with his reaction, aware that his feelings for Kira were intensely real and growing stronger every day.

Tonight Kira was not wearing much makeup and looked even more attractive to Evan in her tight jeans and loose-fitting sweater than when she'd been all dressed up earlier in the day. Though she had greeted him with a big smile and a light hug, he had immediately detected an underlying sadness that she was trying hard to hide. She was struggling with a landslide of emotions today, and Evan knew that his role was simply to listen. Kira had to follow her heart. He couldn't tell her what to do, yet as much as he hated to admit it, and as much as she denied it, he had a gut feeling that Kira was the one who ought to be adopting Vicky Jordan, whether she knew it or not. But he had made up his mind when he agreed to come over that his mission tonight was to take Kira's mind off her worries, not complicate her situation.

"Anything I can do?" he asked, moving over to the hibachi where she was getting ready to place the fish. Heat from the red-hot coals drifted up and touched his face.

"Not a thing," she answered, sliding the fish onto the heated grill. A sizzle of smoke flared up as the salmon began to cook.

"Smells wonderful," Evan remarked, picking up Kira's wineglass and handing it to her, studying her as she took a sip. "You've really created a beautiful setting here." He walked to a potted fern and touched its delicate fronds. "I don't know much about plants, but these are lovely. Do you leave them out here all winter?"

"Oh no," Kira said with a laugh. "I bring them inside during the winter. My laundry room becomes my temporary hothouse. And since you were coming over tonight, I thought why not sit out here? At least while it's still warm enough to enjoy the evening. This is the first time I've used my patio since last summer. Is it too cool out here for you?"

"No, not at all. It's perfect," Evan said, sliding his hands along his arms, thinking he had been right to wear jeans and a sweater over his shirt. "You have a very nice place . . . I'm impressed with anyone who can pull things together as you have. My apartment is pretty boring compared to this."

"Boring? Surely not. You aren't the boring type."

Evan laughed. "Maybe a better term would be 'functional.' No plants, no exotic pottery, nothing fancy at all. I'm rarely there, anyway. Seems like my life is spent either at the agency or on the road at conferences."

"Nothing fancy? Well, maybe I can help you out . . . send you home with a pot of ivy or something. Most plants are easy to grow, just water them and put them in good light. Doesn't take a lot of time."

"I admit that I have tried to keep a few plants growing on the balcony of my apartment, but I stay so busy, I neglect them terribly. They usually die before midsummer. Then I just replace them every spring."

Kira's smile broadened in understanding. "On second thought, you might be better off with artificial plants. Some of them look quite real." Kira moved closer to where Evan was standing while he examined the fronds of a leafy fern. "You'd be surprised how difficult it is to tell the real ones from the fake."

Evan's blood raced when she approached, and, without hesitating, he took advantage of her closeness by gently slipping one arm around her waist. He tensed, waiting for her reaction, hoping she would not pull away.

Kira turned within his one-armed embrace and held her face up to his. Evan saw flickering points of candlelight in her eyes, a sparkling invitation that made him involuntarily draw in a sharp breath. His gaze traced her nose, lips, and down to the smooth line of her jaw. He became aware of a tightening sensation in the pit of his stomach and the lessening of tension in Kira's body. He increased the pressure of his hand on her back, drawing her still closer, aware of a thundering pulse in his groin and the uneven sound of his breathing, which matched the irregular beat of his heart. He sighed, a shiver of desire snaking its way through his veins.

The serene expression on Kira's face increased his desire to possess her completely, and he realized she was not pulling away, but neither was she assisting with his effort to more fully explore their attraction. *So, it's up to me,* Evan told himself, ever so gently massaging the small of Kira's back, urging her toward him until her breasts pressed softly against his chest. The warm breath that came from her slightly parted lips mingled with his, and finally, her jeans-clad thighs touched his.

Tenderly, Evan placed his lips to Kira's and kissed her fully, tasting her tongue, savoring her lips, letting her know how much he wanted her. Then he pulled back, breaking the moment, silently telling her that he would never push too far, too fast, giving her the opening to decide in what direction they should go.

Kira rested her head against Evan's chest and began to speak softly into the night air. "I'm so glad you're here, Evan. I was going crazy with no one to talk to about what happened this afternoon. I felt completely confused and absolutely alone. No one but you can possibly understand this."

Evan put his hands on either side of Kira's waist and eased her back just far enough for him to look into her face. "My being here tonight is a given, Kira, because I do understand what you're going through. I'm glad you trust me with your feelings. However, my feelings for you . . . I can't explain what they are, I just know they are real. Kissing you, holding you, it's like a dream for me, Kira. I can't describe how good you feel in my arms. Beyond that—"

"Shhh," she whispered, a finger to her lips. "You don't have to tell me. I know. I feel the same way, and I'm scared. I need you. I want you here, Evan. You know that."

"And I want to be with you . . . whenever . . . wherever. If that's what you want."

Reaching up, Kira cupped the back of Evan's neck with one hand and brought his lips back to hers, kissing him more deeply and urgently than before. "It is," she said firmly, lingering long enough for Evan to take her other hand in his and place it at the back of his neck.

"Good," he replied, settling into her arms. "That's all I need to know." He started to kiss her again, but she suddenly jerked away.

"The salmon!" Kira cried out, breaking away from him, hurrying to remove the steaks from the grill.

Evan followed, hoping the fish was not completely ruined, yet more concerned with satisfying an appetite that had nothing to do with food. He chuckled, shaking his head in relief when he saw that fish steaks were saved. Standing back, watching as Kira placed them on the blue and white plates, he felt a curl of desire winding tighter and tighter inside his gut. He let his gaze drift down Kira's back to her shapely hips encased in denim. He smiled to notice that her toenails, which peeked out of the low-heeled leather sandals she was wearing, were painted deep red. She was beautiful, as beautiful as she had been the first time he had seen her and as beautiful as she had been when he was with her this afternoon. He noticed that she was wearing the same exquisite pearl and gold earrings she had been wearing earlier and wondered if they had a special meaning.

When the salmon had been plated, Kira motioned for Evan to sit down, then went back into the house to change the music. When she returned, she had a basket of fresh bread in her hand.

"Are you hungry?" she asked, placing the bread on the table.

"Starving," he admitted in a voice barely above a whisper.

"Well, it's getting cold," Kira whispered back, allowing Evan to pull out her chair.

But instead of helping Kira sit down, he suddenly caught her by the arm and spun her around, his lips only inches from hers.

She tensed in surprise, then crushed her mouth to his, gripping his shoulders as he bent over her.

Without breaking their kiss, Evan guided Kira toward the leafy canopy of crepe myrtles near the small fountain that was bubbling in a corner. Gently separating Kira's mouth from his, he murmured, "The food can wait a few minutes longer, can't it?"

Kira hummed an unintelligible response and buried her face in his neck.

"Fine," Evan told her, speaking into her soft, crinkly hair, "because my appetite is focused on you right now, and I can't think about anything else."

Without waiting for Kira to reply, he covered her mouth hungrily with his, devouring her sweetness, shocked by his own intense response to the feel of her tongue against his. Her immediate and insistent response deepened his quest for intimacy; he wanted to explore every part of her. The attraction that had flared between them the first time they met caught fire, and any reservations he had had about pursuing Kira Forester became a distant memory.

Evan lifted Kira's sweater and stroked her back, urging her to come more fully against him, then moved toward the flowery cushioned chaise lounge that was shaded by the lacy limbs of the crepe myrtle tree. He set her down in that secluded spot. He could hear the fountain bubbling softly and the music drifting from inside Kira's apartment mingling with the gasps of surprise and pleasure coming from both Kira and himself.

Kira stretched out on the chaise, not resisting when he moved his hand from her back to gently caress the smooth skin of her stomach. He touched the soft silk of her bra and moved it aside to fondle her taut nipples. They moaned in unison, as if the warm touch of his fingers on her flesh had released a mutual spring of tension. Kira arched her body still closer, fusing her torso to his until together they filled the narrow space in the chaise from lips to thighs, their need for each other complete.

Evan rested the back of his head against the arm support of the chaise and pulled his lips away from Kira's long enough to take a deep breath. The spicy smell of scented candles, mixed with the aroma of the grilled salmon, suddenly filled his head, and when he lifted Kira's sweater again and sought out her rosy brown nipple, hard in his mouth, a hot ache tore though his body and blocked out the world.

Kira shifted slightly, allowing him room to more easily explore the wondrous sensation of his flesh against hers, and when he returned to take her lips in his once again, she placed a finger against his mouth and let out a long, low breath.

"Whew," she murmured, tracing her index finger along his jaw. "That was worth putting dinner on hold."

"Most certainly," he agreed, catching her hand in his, lacing his fingers through hers. He kissed each one softly, then rubbed her knuckles across his lips. "This is the kind of situation I never dreamed I'd find myself in. But now that I'm here, I don't plan to turn back."

"Me neither," Kira assured him, teasing him with a taunting half-smile.

"Are you sure?" he asked, pausing to give her room to bail out before they went too far.

"Very sure," she answered softly, lifting her free arm to reach around his neck, then pulling his head to her chest.

Evan let himself go weak, inhaling her perfume, shutting out all of the reasons he should not be in her arms, all of his reservations against entering into this relationship, and all of the obstacles he knew lay ahead for both of them on the path they were about to enter. Kira's hand on his belt buckle provided a jolt of reassurance that urged him to move forward. He wanted the night to play itself out in the natural unwinding of their unspoken desires, despite the high stakes involved.

We're grown, intelligent, and very aware of the risk we are taking, Evan mentally rationalized. *We can handle this.*

It did not take but a few minutes for both of them to shed their jeans and entwine their legs in the darkness beneath the spiky shadows from the trees. Evan stroked the sleek firmness of Kira's leg, moved his hand along her inner thigh, massaged her buttocks, and eased hot fingers across her stomach to the soft triangle that was hidden from view. He felt Kira's initial apprehension, then just as quickly she relaxed, and then opened herself completely to him, assuring him he was welcome.

Unable to suppress his reaction to her invitation, Evan moaned,

feeling as if he were on an exotic island being seduced by a beautiful native, and with little effort he drew her up against the hot ache
in his groin and plunged into the sweet darkness that pulled him to
new heights. As he smothered Kira with his love, encased in the
scented April night, she satisfied a hunger he had thought he might
never fulfill again.

CHAPTER 22

From her seat on a bench under the shade of a huge maple tree, Kira looked across the grassy lawn at a knot of children playing in the water fountain and thought about the remarks that had been made about Placid Park during the debate at the Meet the Candidates meeting. *She was right*, Kira thought, recalling one woman's protest about the less than equal amenities between this park and Inspiration Park on the north side of town. Kira studied the scene with interest. People were busy setting out plates on picnic tables while barbeque grills, loaded with sizzling hamburgers and golden brown chicken, poured billows of smoke into the air. It was the ideal setting for her second visit with Vicky, and nothing like the desolate patch of hard ground in Frank Thompson's neighborhood that had been severely neglected for too long. Despite her dislike of Frank, Kira had to give the man credit for bringing the disparity between the two parks to the public's attention.

Kira's gaze eventually drifted to the parking area, where a dark green sedan with shiny gold-colored trim was pulling into the crowded lot. She tensed to see the heavily tinted windows, certain that Ralph Roper was behind the wheel. A flurry of dust flew up around the car, then settled back into the crushed-gravel pavement as the driver brought the car to a stop in front of the low split-rail fencing that bordered the parking area.

The front and rear doors on the passenger side opened simultaneously, and two people emerged: Evan, and then Vicky, who immediately began scanning the park benches, holding one hand above her eyes to shade them from the brilliant afternoon sun.

Kira smiled to see her niece again, glad that Evan had arranged this second meeting at Placid Park instead of at Sheltering Hearts. Perhaps the visit would go even better than the last one in this relaxed, peaceful setting. But when the driver of the car got out, Kira's smile faded into a grimace of surprise: Helen Roper, not Ralph, was the one who had brought Vicky to meet her.

Kira watched Helen circle the car, give Vicky a quick hug, and then launch into an earnest conversation with Evan, her back to Kira. Keeping one hand on her hip, Helen used the other to gesture emphatically as she talked, clearly lecturing Evan on how she wanted the visit to proceed. She was as slim as a runway model, dressed in beige slacks and a cherry red sweater, and had placed her oversized, Jackie-O type sunglasses on the top of her head, which was bent close to Evan's as they conversed.

Kira knew that Helen was thirty-five years old, having been told by her attorney, Kenneth Lane. However, as Kira assessed the sheen of Helen's thick brown hair and the straight line of her back, she thought that the woman appeared much younger and more vibrant than she'd seemed to be on television. Today Helen's poised self-assurance contrasted sharply with the timidity of the woman who had shied away from the television camera, making Kira wonder if Helen adopted a different personality when her husband was around. Now, her stance alone sent a message of confidence that bordered on haughtiness, as if she was accustomed to ordering people around and getting whatever she wanted.

When it became obvious that Helen had no intention of making an effort to meet her, Kira scooted to the edge of the bench, her shoulders stiffly squared, and watched the two together, wondering what Helen was telling Evan.

When is this woman planning on acknowledging me? Kira fumed, resenting Helen's blatant dismissal. She took a peanut from the bag she had bought at the refreshment stand just inside the park, cracked the shell with a snap, and then ground the peanut into crumbs between her thumb and index finger as she studied Helen's profile.

Why should I tiptoe around this woman and allow her to act as if I don't exist? If Helen cares about Vicky as much as she professes, she ought to want to meet me, she thought, convinced that there was something about Helen Roper that did not ring true. *Well, I'll just have to introduce myself, whether she wants to meet me or not.* Shoving her bag of peanuts into her purse, Kira headed toward the parking lot.

"Aunt Kira!" Vicky called out and hurried across the lot toward Kira.

When Kira came up to Vicky, she leaned down and told her niece, "I'm so glad to see you again! I think we'll have fun in the park today." Straightening up, Kira glanced at Helen and Evan, who had stopped talking and were looking over at her. Evan nodded, as if pleased to see that Kira was making progress with Vicky, but Helen Roper frowned and pulled her sunglasses over her eyes.

"I'd love to meet your . . . mother," Kira told Vicky, not sure if she should use that word, remembering that Vicky had called Helen by her first name during their last visit. Kira completely understood the child's reluctance to refer to Helen as "mother" so soon after the loss of Alvia Elderton, the person who had mothered her for the past four years.

"Come on," Vicky said, extending her small hand to Kira.

The innocent gesture made Kira catch her breath, and she eagerly took Vicky's warm hand in hers and followed her toward the green sedan.

"Helen," Vicky said, tapping Helen on the arm. "This is my Aunt Kira." Vicky stood looking up at Helen as the woman turned to face Kira.

"Hello, Helen," Kira said. "I'm glad to finally meet you." She turned Vicky's hand loose and held her own out toward Helen, who hesitated, then briefly touched her fingers to Kira's in a weak, unenthusiastic greeting.

"Hello," Helen stated in a flat tone, then made no move to say more.

"Thank you for bringing Vicky to meet me today. I think we'll enjoy the park."

"I'm sure Vicky will," Helen replied sharply, then shifted her attention to Vicky. "Make sure you stay on the path with Mr. Conley, and I'll be back for you in an hour."

Evan, who had been standing to one side, came closer. "Glad you two are finally able to meet."

"Yes," Kira agreed. "And perhaps—at another time, of course—we could talk more. Get to know each other, Helen. I'd like that very much."

Helen simply stared at Kira, her face as unreadable as a blank sheet of paper, her eyes dim with disinterest.

"I agree," Evan interjected. "You could come over to Sheltering

Hearts one day this week. I can arrange a comfortable place for you two to chat and get acquainted. How about it?"

"That would be nice," Kira replied.

"What do you think?" Evan prompted Helen.

The disinterest in Helen's expression suddenly turned into fear, sending a chilling message of rejection as Helen drew her lips into a worried fold and frowned, deepening the crease on her pale brow. Kira waited, wondering why Evan's suggestion had initiated such an emotional reaction.

"I-I don't think so," Helen stammered, pushing her sunglasses higher on her nose as she backed away. "I have too much to do this week. Maybe some other time. I'll think about it."

"Sure," Evan said, glancing uneasily at Kira, who nodded her understanding.

"I'll be back in an hour to get you, Vicky," Helen called out as she opened the door to her car. "I've got a few errands to run."

"We'll be right here," Evan assured her, but his words were swallowed by the sound of the car's engine as Helen Roper started it, then roared off down the gravel drive toward the main road.

Kira shrugged in confusion and focused on Evan, noticing the uneasy expression on his face. He was squinting intensely into the trail of dust that Helen's car had kicked up, his jaw tight, as if torn by conflicting emotions.

"She wasn't very friendly, was she?" Kira commented, taking Vicky's hand, starting toward the nature path they were going to explore.

"No, she wasn't," Evan replied. "And I'm surprised. I've never seen her act like this."

Because you don't really know who she is, Kira thought, making up her mind to find a way to get to the woman who wanted to be Vicky's new mom.

"Well, forget about it," Evan whispered into Kira's ear. "Let's enjoy the afternoon." He handed Vicky a bottle of water that was small enough to fit in her tiny hand, then surveyed the park. "Where do we start?" he asked.

"Over there!" Vicky cried, racing ahead of them toward the first blue and white sign that indicated the entrance to the trail.

"Okay, hold up!" Evan laughed, moving closer to Kira, then whispering in her ear, "You look fabulous today."

"Thank you," Kira replied, swinging around to show off the tan linen slacks with matching shirt that she had chosen for the outing, stifling an impulse to put her arms around Evan and give him a quick kiss on the lips. She wanted so much to hold his hand, give him a hug, or simply touch his cheek, but knew better than to do anything like that, especially with Vicky nearby. Clearly, Helen Roper would welcome any chance to accuse Kira of inappropriate behavior, so she pushed her urge to be closer to Evan out of her mind and ran ahead to catch up with Vicky, who was waving at them to hurry up.

As they explored the twisted paths and trails, which were alive with toads, birds, butterflies, and other small forest creatures, Kira and Vicky chatted about school, her piano lessons, and the responsibilities involved in having a puppy, which Vicky told Kira she wanted very much. However, Helen did not want her to have a dog yet, and that disappointed Vicky very much.

"Maybe when you're older," Kira comforted.

"I hope so," Vicky said and sighed, shaking her head, making her dark curls bounce around her face.

They stopped to watch two squirrels playing tag among the branches of a tall pine, then decided to rescue a stranded frog from a tangle of weeds in the creek that meandered through the park. As the visit progressed, Kira could feel Vicky's trust and acceptance of her growing. She was thrilled that they were getting along so well, that they were able to relax and enjoy their short time together despite the forced conditions under which they were meeting.

While Vicky poked at the frog with a twig, Kira stole a glance at Evan, aware that his presence and subtle guidance were vital to this harmonious reunion with Vicky. Evan often gave Kira silent signals with his eyes or hands, letting her know when it was best to prompt a little more conversation or back off and let the silence stand. His interest helped ease the pressure Kira was feeling about saying or doing the right thing, and she loved him for helping her with this new experience. Indeed, she wondered how in the world she would have managed this without him.

Since their evening together at her apartment last Saturday, Kira had not stopped thinking of Evan, and meeting him today under fairly formal circumstances was unbearable. She wished she could slip an arm around his waist, touch his back, or place her head on his shoulder as they meandered through the park. She wanted to feel the heat from his body mingle with hers, taste his lips, and inhale once more his delicious scent. But that would have to wait—at least until she saw him later that evening. They were going to see a play at the Ensemble Playhouse, and afterward Kira had plans for them at her apartment. Anticipation rose inside her like a tightening thread.

When her short visit with Vicky had nearly drawn to an end, they headed back up the path toward the parking lot. While waiting for Helen to arrive and pick up Vicky, Kira thought about their earlier exchange.

Why would a grown woman be so frightened of getting to know the blood relative of her prospective adoptive child? *What is Helen Roper afraid of?* Kira wondered, more curious than ever to find out who Vicky's new mom really was.

CHAPTER 23

The mayoral campaign in Monroeville became even more polarized than it had been when Mattie Moore dropped out of the race due to health reasons. With less than two weeks until the election, her announcement that she was throwing her support behind Ralph Roper put the businessman in a solid position to become the next mayor and moved Frank Thompson into Mattie's former slot as the underdog of the race.

However, Thompson was a man with a mission, one who had no problem expressing his opinions, and with vehement passion, too. His opposition to the demolition of Flagg Valley Mill was unwavering. He told everyone who would listen to him that Roper's plan to turn the old mill into a brand-new processing plant was bull—that Roper was only interested in the timber on the land, and winning the election would mean he could use his mayoral power to increase his personal wealth.

Soon after Mattie's announcement, Frank and Ralph debated each other on a lively morning radio talk show, with Frank hurling insults at his opponent, who deflected them with ease. They appeared together for another heated round of topical discussion at a town hall meeting later that day. By midweek, every telephone pole in Monroeville held a campaign poster, and the lawns on the south side quickly filled with placards touting Roper's slogan, "Make Monroeville Marketable," while yard signs on the north side of town held Frank Thompson's "Build from the Past for the Future." As the week slid past, the intensity of the campaign increased, forcing residents to choose sides. A story appeared in the *Monroeville Mirror* analyzing the demographics within each camp:

apparently, Ralph Roper was quickly chipping away at the block of voters Thompson had once considered his. Frank's support among black voters was fast eroding due to Roper's promise of jobs at his new processing facility and the sympathy he was receiving from those who viewed his adoption of Vicky Jordan as a demonstration of his dedication to family values and racial tolerance.

A wave of respect and admiration had begun flowing toward Roper from the African-American community, heightening his image as a man who sincerely wanted to serve all residents of Monroeville. The article also stated that Roper's well-heeled supporters were donating liberally to his cause, threatening to swamp Frank Thompson's passionate but underfinanced campaign. Kira followed these developments with mixed emotions, glad that she did not live in Monroeville.

On the Monday following her third visit with Vicky, Kira arrived at her office early, her mind still swirling with pleasant memories of her quiet but satisfying weekend. Her third Saturday with Vicky had gone extremely well, though they had met at the Visiting Room at Sheltering Hearts instead of the park, with neither Ralph nor Helen Roper present. Kira and Vicky had conversed very easily, and Kira, with Evan's assurance that it was fine to do so, showed Vicky a photo of Miranda.

Vicky's first reaction had been surprise that her mother and Kira looked so much alike, and the family resemblance prompted many questions, with Vicky wanting to know all about Miranda. Kira chose her words carefully, avoiding the tragic aspects of Miranda's adult life, focusing on stories about her as a child—how she had loved music and dressing up, and how beautiful she had been. Kira had woven in information about her parents, too, providing Vicky with a glimpse of the family that made up her heritage. Even though Kira was Vicky's only living relative, Vicky needed to know that her grandparents would have loved her if they had lived to meet her.

Vicky had been solemn, yet keenly interested in everything Kira said, and had asked if she could keep the photo of Miranda. On Evan's advice, Kira had declined, thinking it best for the Ropers to give their approval first.

On Sunday Kira had invited Evan over for a quiet evening of popcorn and a rented movie, moving their relationship into a comfortable place where Kira felt safe, appreciated, and content. It was a feeling she wanted to hold on to forever.

Now Kira flipped over the weekend pages of her calendar and pressed the POWER button on her computer, ready to jump into her work. As she reached for the stack of mail in her IN box, she saw Bruce Davison coming toward her desk. She waited until he had stopped at her side, his presence casting a shadow over her computer screen.

Kira looked up, unable to predict what might be on his mind, though she was certain it was not good.

"Good morning, Bruce," she managed in a cheery voice, determined not to let him put a damper on her high spirits. Bruce Davison was a serious man, with not much of a sense of humor. On the rare occasions when he did find something amusing, his laughter was no more than a dry chuckle, often tinged, it seemed to Kira, with condescension.

"Good morning, Kira," Bruce replied in a cool voice. "I need to see you in my office."

"Sure," Kira said, pulling back from her desk, inhaling deeply, wondering what was going on now. She followed Bruce across the newsroom to the hallway leading to his office. Inside, she sat down in the chair facing his desk, as he indicated, and not at the small round table where they usually got together to discuss her weekly column.

Bruce unfolded a newspaper and handed it to Kira without saying a word. His eyes were hooded as he watched for her response.

Curious, Kira took the paper from him, recognizing it as a copy of the *Charlotte Observer*, and calmly glanced over the page, thinking he must want her to do a follow-up piece on something he had found of interest. However, as soon as she saw the photo at the top of the story, she knew she was in trouble.

"What is this?" she asked, slowly running her eyes over the page.

"You tell me," Bruce answered in a detached manner, sitting back in his chair, arms folded across his chest.

Confused, Kira studied the two photos in the paper. "One of these is a photo that I took in Africa," she replied slowly, recognizing it as the one Julie had told her had been missing from the packet she had FedExed to New York. "The other photo is of Flagg Valley Mill. What's the connection?"

"Read it," Bruce told her.

Kira hurried to read the accompanying story:

Monroeville mayoral candidate Ralph Roper may have some explaining to do, and his problems have nothing to do with his current campaign. Reliable sources tell the *Observer* that Roper's company, Roper Fiber Technology, currently has contracts with brokers overseas who routinely use child labor to fulfill their obligations to the American company. The photo on the right, shot by *BPR* reporter Kira Forester at a child-labor camp in the village of Pangi in Equatorial Guinea, clearly shows packing crates that carry the logo of one of Roper Fiber Technology's overseas brokers who produces goods for export for several American companies. The photo on the left is of similar packing crates that were found near the Dumpsters at Roper's temporary warehouse, established at the old Flagg Valley Mill.

"Did you give that photo to the *Observer*?" Bruce asked as Kira continued to read. "Did you talk to that reporter?"

"Absolutely not. Of course not, " Kira snapped. Her heart was pounding, her mouth was dry, and she chewed her bottom lip as she quickly retraced each sentence. Skimming the lengthy article, she read on, realizing that it was really about the close race for mayor in the small town of Monroeville, where for the first time an African American had a good shot at becoming mayor. The writer, Wade White, had included information about Roper's connection to child labor to create a headline grabber. The article went into a detailed overview of each candidate's qualifications to hold office, referring to Thompson as an inspiration for his people and a savior for a dying city, while calling Ralph Roper a shrewd, calculating businessman who might seem to be the best candidate but who might also be headed for trouble. The writer stated that Roper might soon have to explain to his constituency, many of whom were involved in textile manufacturing, why he would enter into contracts with brokers that used children to save on production costs.

Kira gasped at the allegations, then read on:

Shipping crates from Roper's African broker, as seen in the enlarged photograph taken by Kira Forester of *BPR*, are stacked high on the porches of shanties in Pangi, where girls as young as eight years old are known to labor over sewing machines for pennies a day. Forester, whose weekly column, "Business Week Watch," focuses on business issues around the state, recently returned from an investigative tour of the area, tracking sources of cheap labor and documenting practices that currently affect the economic health of the textile industry here in North Carolina and throughout the nation.

"This is awful," Kira murmured, focusing on the enlarged print of her photograph. All of the details on the crates were now clear, clear enough to see that they did indeed contain some kind of logo, one that she had never seen before. It was not the familiar Roper company logo, but a design with a black shield with African markings in the center. The second photograph in the paper showed similar crates lying on the ground next to the Dumpsters at Roper's temporary warehouse in Monroeville.

"This is news, Kira," Bruce reprimanded. "The kind of news *BPR* should have jumped on. How could you have overlooked this obvious connection? What were you thinking? Here this is, right in our backyard, and we missed it." He shook his head in disgust.

"I wasn't working on a connection between Pangi and the old Flagg Valley Mill. Why should I have leaped to that conclusion? The logo on those crates meant nothing to me," Kira defended herself. Yet she was angry with herself for not breaking the story.

"But to someone else, it did," Bruce growled.

Still stunned, Kira pulled in a short breath, unable to believe what she was reading. This writer had pointed an accusing finger at Ralph Roper and had used her photo to drive home his point.

"Can you explain how this happened?" Bruce demanded, hands lifted in resignation.

"No, I can't. And I didn't give that photo to anyone. I lost it the same day I interviewed Frank Thompson for that piece I did on him and the history of Monroeville. He must have found it, figured out the connection, and decided to use it against Roper. Or me. I don't know."

"And how would he have known where it was taken? Did you tell him about your assignment and the conditions under which that photo was taken?"

"Yes, I did," Kira admitted, wishing now she had never met Frank Thompson, who was turning out to be a major problem.

Bruce tilted his chair back and scowled. "I think you gave the photo to Thompson. You want him to win the election. You did it, didn't you?"

"That's ridiculous—and an insult, Bruce. I'm a professional journalist, and I would never do anything underhanded like that."

"You persuaded Frank Thompson to plant this story," he went on, ignoring her protests, tapping the paper with authority. "And you provided him with the photo in order to hurt Ralph Roper. You know, Kira, I have not been impressed with your attitude or your production lately, and though I was willing to overlook your less than objective reporting on the Monroeville-history piece, I can't tolerate this kind of personal promotion of a private issue."

"Private issue? What are you talking about? I don't live in Monroeville. I can't vote for Frank Thompson or Ralph Roper, and I could care less who wins. I wanted a story when I went to see Frank, and he had one to tell. I interviewed him, and I thought the angle on Jeremy Flagg would make good copy. That was it. Now I see that Frank has used me for his own purposes, and I'm very angry."

"That's too bad, but you should have been more cautious. I've been on the phone for the past hour, tracking down the pieces to this puzzle, and it becomes more interesting with each conversation. Wade White, the author of that article, told me that Frank Thompson came to the paper and personally gave him that photo along with several discarded shipping crates which Frank had recovered from the Dumpster on the grounds at the old Flagg Valley Mill. Frank took Wade out there to see the evidence for himself. I called Frank Thompson. He told me that Ralph Roper is adopting your niece and using this transracial adoption as a ploy to gain sympathy votes from the black community. That's why you did this, isn't it? To help Thompson win. You both would love to see Roper embarrassed and entangled in a messy investigation."

"No!" Kira said in a voice that was nearly a shout. "I may not be particularly happy that Ralph Roper is adopting my niece, but I would never stoop to tactics like this to make a point. If Frank did what you just said, it is unforgivable, and I expect an apology from the *Observer*. And your accusations, Bruce, are totally unfounded."

Trembling, Kira gripped the arms of her chair and tried to put it all into perspective. In her fifteen years at *BPR* no one had ever questioned her credibility or her dedication to her profession. Now, Frank Thompson, a man she knew nothing about, was threatening to ruin her reputation and possibly end her career.

He wants to make me sorry for not interfering with Vicky's adoption, she thought. *But he's the one who is going to regret doing this to me.*

"Kira, I doubt the *Observer* will give you an apology. The photo is properly credited, though it should never have been published. I spoke to Julie Ays in New York, and, believe me, she is not happy, either. *World Societies Today* feels betrayed. They put out a lot of money for you to go on that assignment, and they trusted you to protect their interests. Their exclusive has been compromised, and they are upset."

"B-but," Kira stuttered, "I had nothing to do with this."

"You neglected to ensure the safety of material that was time-sensitive and under contract to another publication. Not wise, Kira. Not wise at all. I'm afraid this little piece in the *Charlotte Observer* may force *World* to drop your story."

"I don't think so," Kira breathed, unable to believe that Julie would do such a thing. Julie was her friend—a sister, too. She was going to get Kira a job at *World.* Surely she'd understand. "I'll call Julie and explain."

"I'm afraid that won't do any good. Kira, I had to tell Julie that I am releasing you. My reputation is on the line here, too. How can I keep a reporter on staff who allows herself to become so personally involved in her stories that her professional judgment clouds objectivity?"

"You're firing me?" Kira was shocked. "Over this?"

"Yes, Kira. Sorry."

She glared at him, speechless, knowing from the expression on his face that it would do no good to argue.

"You'll get a month's salary for severance, and since you have no vacation or sick leave left, there won't be a payment for unused time. However, I'll make sure you are eligible to draw unemployment."

"Great," Kira grumbled, slumping back in her chair, feeling as if her entire world had just collapsed. "That's real big of you, Bruce. Thanks a lot."

"What do you mean, you're going home?" Sharon repeated, interrupting her typing to concentrate on Kira. "Uh . . . why are you taking your ivy with you?"

Kira placed the potted plant that had been sitting on the corner of her desk for the past year into the cardboard box she had salvaged from the copy room, then bent down to pull open the center drawer of her desk. "Because Bruce just let me go," she answered, still in too much shock to reveal how devastated she was.

"He fired you?" Sharon hissed, eyes wide in amazement.

"Yep. After fifteen years with *BPR*, I'm out of here."

"Why? What happened?"

"Bruce said my attitude and my production have not been up to par, and he really doesn't want to keep me around. And there was a problem with a photo that somehow got into the *Observer*, credited to me," Kira replied, going on to tell Sharon about the piece by Wade White, Davison's reaction, and Frank Thompson's betrayal.

"Shit. That sneaky man," Sharon said. "And after you gave him so much play in your column. Why would he do such a thing?"

"Because I refused to interfere in Roper's plan to adopt my niece. Frank wanted me to make a fuss, create negative press that would damage Roper's high approval. I told him no way." Kira sat down in her chair and looked dejectedly at her coworker. "Bruce said *World* probably won't run my story. He spoke to Julie Ays this morning. She's upset . . . might cancel the Africa piece altogether."

"Oh, no," Sharon gasped. "That's going a bit far."

Shrugging, Kira blinked back tears and continued to remove personal items from her desk, tossing them haphazardly into the box.

"What a prick," Sharon grumbled, just as her phone rang. Before reaching to take the call, she told Kira, "Girl, I'm so sorry. Call me tonight. We'll talk. Okay?" Then she picked up the phone and began talking.

It did not take Kira long to finish cleaning out her desk, hoping to escape the office before more of her coworkers, who were eyeing her cautiously from across the room, came over to ask her what was going on.

They'll soon know what happened, she thought, aware of how quickly news, especially bad news, found its way into circulation. Right now, she couldn't bear to talk to anyone other than Sharon, and it would be too awkward for her to go around the newsroom and tell each of her coworkers good-bye. She'd miss them terribly, and *BPR* too, but she had to get out of there, fast.

Kira shouldered her purse, grabbed the cardboard box of personal items, and made a quick exit, heading for the elevator.

When the doors slid closed in her face, she slumped against the wall and let the impact of what had just happened wash over her, astonished that she had been able to hold it together until now. Her story for *World Societies Today*, the highlight of her journalistic career, would never make it into print, and there would be no job in New York for her. Ralph and Helen Roper, whom she had been trying damn hard to accept, must be furious with her, believing she had assisted Frank in planting this horrible story. Kira dropped the box to the floor with a disgusted gesture, covered her face with her hands, and cried, releasing her disappointment and anger in a flood of tears that melted her mascara and streaked the makeup she had so carefully applied that morning.

The elevator hit the lobby floor, and the doors slid open. Sniffling, Kira wiped her eyes, took a deep breath, and picked up the box. She stepped out and strode past the guard with her head held high. Less than an hour ago she had entered this same lobby in a lighthearted mood, brimming with joy after having spent a wonderful weekend with the two most important people in her life. Her progress with Vicky had been encouraging, and her optimism about her future with Evan had been strong. Now she was dejected—and worried. Would this incident affect her visitation rights? And what would Evan think of her, once he learned what had happened?

CHAPTER 24

Once inside her car, Kira called the *Observer*, ready to charge Wade White up.

"Mr. White is out of the office today," the receptionist told her in an overly sweet voice. "Would you like to leave a message?"

"Yes, I would," Kira snapped. "Connect me with his voice mail." When the message prompts on his service ended, she launched into her tirade. "This is Kira Forester. Who in the hell gave you permission to use my material? I don't know why you would think Frank Thompson has the right to hand over my photos but you'd better get ready for a lawsuit, buddy, because this is serious. I expect an explanation and an apology. Today. Call me as soon as you get this." She gave her home number, then she turned off her cell phone and stuffed it into the console, adding it to the jumble of CDs, tapes, and maps inside. He could reach her at home. Right now she needed to be out of touch with the world, totally inaccessible to anyone who might want to dump on her again. Besides, there would be no urgent calls from the office today reminding her about a deadline or an interview or a staff meeting.

Groaning, she pulled down the mirror over the passenger side seat, checked her reflection, and then groaned again. She *did* look as awful as she felt. Staring at the reflection of her streaked, puffy face, she silently reprimanded herself for letting this happen.

How had she so gravely underestimated Frank Thompson's threat to punish her for not doing as he'd wanted? Why hadn't she done more to track down that misplaced photo? Julie had called her in plenty of time to do something about it. She could have gone back to the restaurant to ask the waitress if she had found it, or called Frank and asked him about it. Who knows? He might have returned it to her immediately. But, no, she had not done a thing, and look at what it had cost her—her career, her reputation, maybe her right to visit Vicky. The seriousness of her situation was suddenly over-whelming, and a rush of tears sprang into her eyes, blurring her vision. Kira squeezed her eyes tightly shut and sucked back her anger, unwilling to let her emotions take over. She had too much to do.

Grabbing her purse, she removed her black satin makeup bag and immediately began to repair her face, determined not to let Frank Thompson see her like this. When she got in his face and told him about himself, there could be no trace of the emotional devas-tation he had caused.

It took a great deal of restraint for Kira to drive the speed limit, but she managed to hold back her impulse to speed and kept her eye on the speedometer until she arrived at the exit off US-74 that would take her to Monroeville. She passed Inspiration Park, with its tall weeds and broken swings, and the old Flagg Valley Mill, now sporting a new sign that read PROPERTY OF ROPER FIBER TECHNOLOGY: NO TRESPASSING. She noticed that there were no dis-carded packing crates heaped beside the Dumpsters now and no shiny white vans tooling around.

Once Kira entered the business district, where the streets were filled with cars and people were going in and out of the shops, she headed east toward the main intersection. It did not take long for her to find Thompson's place of business. When she pulled up, she saw that the sign on the front door said OPEN.

Kira parked in the space directly in front of the entrance, notic-ing that only one other car was in the lot.

"Good," she murmured, as she got out of her car. "I hope he's in there alone."

The jangle of an overhead bell announced Kira's arrival when she opened the door and stepped into the showroom, where an as-sortment of shiny green and yellow equipment sparkled in the sun-filled open space. The smell of new rubber and motor oil wafted to her as she strode confidently toward the counter where Frank Thompson was holding a copy of the *Charlotte Observer* while star-ing suspiciously at her. She pulled off her sunglasses and glared at him, and he jumped up from the stool where he had been sitting, dropping the newspaper to the floor.

"What do you want?" Frank snapped, clearly agitated.

Kira lifted a brow, assessing his confusion, sensing his uncertainty over what she might do. "I want to tell you to your face what I think of you," she replied, continuing to walk closer.

"You'd better go," Frank ordered.

"Oh no, Frank. I don't think so, you meanspirited, deceitful man. You had no right to give my photograph or information you gleaned from me in a private conversation to that reporter."

"You get out of here," Frank said again, nervously tugging on his tie. Licking his lips, he swallowed hard, then scowled at his unwanted visitor.

Kira, ignoring his order to leave, continued talking. "I trusted you, Frank. I showed you my photographs and told you about my assignment in Africa simply to share my experience with someone I *thought* would appreciate the story. You have a lot of nerve, turning around and using my words against me."

In a jerky movement, Frank pushed back from the counter, putting more distance between himself and Kira. "Okay. Yes, I admit that I found the photo and kept it. When you left the restaurant, it was on the table, so I took it. I was going to call you, give it back, but when I got home—"

"You forgot?" Kira sarcastically prompted.

"Well, yes. Then things kind of got out of control," he began, wiping one hand across his mouth, as if trying to think of how to proceed. "Really, Kira. I did not know that there was a connection between your experience in Africa and Roper until I saw some crates piled up beside the Dumpster and thought they looked familiar. I checked your photo, then went back to the mill and got a few boxes out of the Dumpster. Then I went to see White, who was curious. He's a friend of mine. I asked him to track down the connection, put it together. That's all. He said he'd do some nosing around and get back to me. That was the last I heard from him. Next thing I know, his story is in the paper. I had no idea Wade was going to write it or use your photo. Really, I didn't."

"You expect me to believe that? You deliberately set out to undermine me. It was my material. Why feed it to White? Why didn't you come to me?"

Now Frank snorted in a curt, dismissive way, his nervousness suddenly gone. "I would have—before you refused to help me. You weren't interested in helping me win, and, you know, now that the information is out about Roper, I'm glad. Let him deal with it. He needs the pressure, and he's going to have to do some fast talking to explain this one." Frank rested one arm along the top of the counter as he craned his neck toward Kira, who shook her head, but said nothing.

A mirthless grin came to Frank's lips. "You're afraid of Roper, aren't you? You've probably already had a run-in or two with him, haven't you?"

Tensing, Kira tried to keep her reaction from showing, but her mind flashed back to the awful confrontation she had had with Roper in his office only a few weeks ago.

"You want to stay on Roper's good side because he's adopting your niece, don't you? Well, that's crazy. You don't know him, or his wife, like the people of this town do. Seems to me you ought to be interested in getting to know people who share your heritage and not be so fast to suck up to the likes of Ralph and Helen Roper. Hmph! The Ropers. You don't know who they are, and I'm sorry for you."

"So, that's a reason to hurt me? Get me fired? And you think your behavior will win you votes?" Kira sadly shook her head.

"Oh? You got fired?" Frank repeated, the corners of his mouth now turning down.

"Yes. This morning. What did you expect?"

"Well, I didn't think it would come to that."

"Oh? Did you think my boss was going to give me a raise for allowing an unauthorized photo and material intended for use by our parent company to be used in a politically charged article in the *Charlotte Observer*? Get real. You're a businessman, Frank. You knew my credibility would be compromised once you handed my material over to Wade White." She stopped talking long enough to compose herself and gather her thoughts, hoping to get through to him. "Frank, when I met you, I was impressed with your passionate desire to win the election and become an advocate for the black community. Now I'm ashamed to say I ever helped promote your cause, and I hope you will not be elected mayor of this city."

Frank came around from behind the counter and stood in front of Kira, his eyes narrowed defensively. "You don't understand because you don't live here. You need to feel the anger that comes from watching men like Ralph Roper lord their money and connections over the little people in this town. We send our children to play in a park with no equipment, and they have to walk to that park on streets with little or no paving. They fight rats and mosquitoes that thrive in the weed-filled ditches, while across town men like Roper send their children to a beautifully landscaped nature park."

"There is nothing stopping anyone from going to Placid Park. I was there two weeks ago."

"But why should we have to get in our cars and drive across town when we have a park in our neighborhood? The black community of Monroeville desperately needs an advocate, and I stepped up to the plate."

"What makes you think that Roper will ignore the needs of the people on the north side? Hasn't he promised to focus on all areas that need attention? You're not going to win, Frank. Not like this."

"Oh, I *will* be mayor of this town. Wait and see."

"I wouldn't be too sure of that, Frank. And as for your and Wade White's collaboration—you'll both hear from my attorney very soon." Giving him a final look of disgust, Kira turned and left.

Driving down Main Street, Kira's blood raced and her chest rose and fell with each breath she struggled to pull in. Frank's smug attitude had infuriated her, and though she had threatened to take legal action, Kira worried that financing a lawsuit was not how she wanted to spend her energy or the little money she had saved. She had openly shared her photos and her story with Frank without setting any boundaries on her discussion, but she had never dreamed he'd use what she told him to hurt her. But the damage was done. She no longer had a job or the prospect of one in New York. Still . . . her reporter's instincts were intact. She had to get to Ralph and explain the situation immediately.

Kira made her way out of the business district and headed toward the south side of Monroeville, thinking she ought to call Kenneth and get his advice on how to proceed. However, she was not looking forward to an intense, stressful conversation about a legal matter. She'd call him later, after she got home. At this point she needed to do some damage control, and hoped that Ralph would listen.

The narrow two-lane road that paralleled the highway took Kira past the elementary school that Vicky attended, past Placid Park, which was deserted except for a few late-morning joggers, and on to Roper Fiber Technology, which sat on a slope facing the highway at the turnoff to Pine Arbor Road. At the gated entrance to the glass-and-steel complex, Kira pulled up to the security guard and told him that she wanted to see Ralph Roper and, no, she did not have an appointment.

"Please wait here," the guard told her, leaning back into his shelter to pick up the phone.

While waiting for the guard to reach Roper's office, Kira took in the carefully landscaped grounds, the perfectly tended shrubs, and the three-tiered water fountain at the base of the tall flagpole. Her eyes gravitated to the parking garage, where she and Evan had sat and talked at a time when she had vowed never to trust Ralph Roper—and now she was trying to get to him to convince him to trust her.

"Sorry, miss," the guard said, leaning down to speak to Kira through the open window. "Mr. Roper is not in his office. Is there anyone else who can help you?"

"No." Kira exhaled in disappointment.

"Would you like to leave your name? A message?" the guard politely inquired.

"No, thanks," Kira replied, putting her car in reverse. "I'll call him tomorrow." Then, pausing, she asked the guard, "How do I get to River Walk Road?"

Nodding, the guard stepped out of his shelter and pointed toward the south. "Go back to the highway and continue on it until you come to the second exit past the Texaco station. You'll see a sign that says River Walk Road. Can't miss it."

"Thanks," Kira said, backing out of the gated area. She swung back onto the highway and continued south, gathering her courage. She'd seen the Roper's home address many times on paperwork in Vicky's file, but had never dared scout out the house. Since she was in the area and had nothing but time, she'd satisfy her curiosity about where Vicky was living.

The security guard's directions were easy to follow, and within minutes Kira was driving down River Walk Road, gaping at the huge estates interspersed throughout the heavily wooded area. Many of the homes had wide verandas, soaring pillars, and tall, arched windows that overlooked massive stretches of soft green lawn. Imposing in their size and beauty, the homes stood as symbols of the residents' wealth and respectability.

At the end of the road, Kira came to a DEAD END sign, where a private drive branched off to the right. The name ROPER was printed on a brick mailbox the size of a small doghouse. Slowing down, she peered up the winding drive at the massive Tudor house nestled among the oaks and pines shading the property, unable to believe her eyes.

"My God," Kira murmured, stunned by the opulence that greeted her, amazed to think that Vicky, who had been born and raised in a trailer, now resided inside the sprawling mansion that seemed to take up the equivalent of a long city block.

The grounds were immaculate, with colorful beds of poppies, roses, gladiolas, and iris in full bloom. A beautiful magnolia tree with glossy green leaves and creamy white blossoms shaded the front of the house, rising nearly as high as the rooftop, its ancient limbs reaching far out over the driveway. The house was gray stone, with too many windows to count, and atop its steeply pitched roof was an American-eagle weathervane swinging slightly in the breeze.

Kira noticed that Helen's green sedan was parked in the circular drive, its gold-toned trim glittering in the sunshine.

"She's at home," Kira murmured, stopping her car, contemplating whether or not she ought to drive up the road, go to the front door, ring the bell, and force Helen to speak with her in a rational, adult manner. She wished she and Helen could be allies. For Vicky's sake, they ought to try. Cautiously, Kira proceeded, inching her way closer to the house until she had maneuvered her car up the driveway and was less than twenty yards from the front door. Stopping beneath the magnolia tree, she pressed the button to lower her window and looked around. Then, deciding it was time to approach Helen Roper, she opened the car door.

Suddenly, she heard a loud gasp, followed by a thin voice that she recognized as Helen's calling out her name. Swinging around, Kira watched as Helen Roper stepped out of a bed of yellow lilies behind the magnolia tree, a pair of garden shears in her hand, a wide straw hat on her head.

"Kira Forester! What do you want?" Helen called out, squinting at her from beneath the brim of her hat.

Kira waited, not about to respond, curious about what Helen was going to do, and feeling oddly prepared for the confrontation, if that was what Helen had in mind. After her go-round with Frank this morning, why not clear the air with everyone who seemed so anxious to lean on her last nerve.

Kira waited until Helen had stepped close enough for her to smell the lilies in the basket before speaking. "Hello, Helen. I was in the neighborhood, and I have to admit that I was simply curious. I wanted to see where Vicky lives." She did not add, however, *since you have not seen fit to invite me over.*

"Well, you've seen where she lives, so I suggest you go," Helen said, raising her chin in a challenge.

Gritting her teeth, Kira remained standing with the car door open between her and Helen, with no intention of leaving right away.

"Helen," she began, "I really wish we could talk. I'm not a threat. I'd like to—"

"Not a threat?" Helen snapped, cutting Kira off. "What else can I call a person who spends her time thinking up ways to hurt people? Planting those lies about Ralph in the paper!"

"I didn't do that. I never told anyone that your husband used child labor overseas, and I am livid that the story has been attributed to me. I stopped by his office a moment ago; I wanted to explain, but he wasn't in. This is all a big mistake."

"Ralph runs a worldwide operation and uses hundreds of brokers to move goods in and out of countries around the world. You can't hold him accountable for the fact that some desperate African supplier rounded up a few local girls to do his work for him."

"I'm not trying to," Kira tossed back defensively. She might not have planted the story, but that did not mean that it was false. Apparently Wade White had thought he had enough credible evidence to publish what he had discovered.

"You have no idea how much damage you've caused, Kira. Ralph is with his attorney right now, and you will hear from him very soon. Now, get off of my property and stay out of our lives."

Helen's words forced Kira to pull back sharply, and she gripped the edge of the open door to gain her balance, suddenly feeling vulnerable.

"Helen, I did not give that reporter the photo or any information to connect your husband to the labor camp in Pangi. I had no idea that Wade White was doing a story on the subject for the *Observer*. But Frank Thompson did. I just left him in town. He admitted everything to me."

"That is ridiculous. How would Frank Thompson know any-thing about this? Why involve him in your messy little scheme?"

"Because he is desperate to win the election. When I interviewed him, he assumed I was going to help him undermine your husband's efforts to make inroads into the black community. Frank wanted me to take a public stand against your adoption, but I refused. He became angry and accused me of shirking my responsibility to the African Americans in Monroeville. So, this was how he got back at me. I'm just as much a victim here as your husband. I lost my job today."

The frown on Helen's face eased, and her jaw slackened. Slowly, she removed her straw hat, shook out her hair, and combed it with her fingers. Kira waited, hoping she had gotten through to her, and that they might finally be able to communicate in a less hostile manner.

"You were fired?" Helen repeated.

"Yes. Because I was irresponsible with sensitive material. That much is true, I suppose, so I have to suffer the consequences."

"Ha!" Helen spat out, her expression hardening. "Consequences? You have no idea what consequences are, especially for a man like my husband. He could lose the support of his board of directors, lose his company because of your carelessness. Did you ever think of that? Or is that what you hoped? That Ralph's company would fail? That he would be forced to give up Vicky? It will never hap-pen."

"Please. Don't let your imagination run wild. I would never do a thing like that," Kira pressed. "If Roper Fiber Technology does not use children to process their materials then he has nothing to worry about. All of this will blow over and no harm will have been done."

Helen backed up a step. "I have nothing more to say to you, and I suggest you leave. Don't come back. I plan to speak to Evan Conley about revoking your visitation, and if I have to, I'll go di-rectly to the judge."

"I wouldn't do that, Helen. Vicky will hate you for it. I may have spent only three afternoons with my niece, but you and I know she really likes me. A lot. She also realizes that I am her only connection to her real family. I love her, and I'll never let her get away from me again. How do you think she would react if she knew you had dri-ven me out of her life? She'd never forgive you, and as she got older, she'd come looking for me. Vicky's short life has been filled with abandonment and loss. Do you really want to add to her pain, just to spite me?"

Kira could see that her words had struck home. Helen paused, clearly shaken by the prospect of Vicky turning away from her. She opened her mouth to reply, but then shut it, appearing confused, her expression changing from spiteful determination, to doubt, and then to fear. Kira could not help but wonder, again, why Helen had chosen Vicky Jordan to adopt out of all the available foster children at Sheltering Hearts. It was a mystery that Kira planned to solve.

CHAPTER 25

Disappointment crowded Evan's heart as he hung up the phone, not bothering to leave a message. He had already left two on Kira's cell-phone voice mail, two at her apartment, and though he rarely called her at work, he had done that also, only to be told by the switchboard operator that Kira Forester no longer worked at *BPR*. The news had startled Evan, but not surprised him: Kira had not been happy at *BPR* for some time and had often talked about leaving. But why now? he worried, wondering if a position at the parent company had come through for her in New York and she was planning on moving away.

He walked to his refrigerator, opened the door, and absently looked in, then took out a carton of leftover fried rice, put it back, and slammed the door, too preoccupied with Kira to think about eating. He had slipped out of his office early to come home and grab a bite to eat before returning for a six o'clock meeting with a couple who was ready to commit to one of his children. Now he had no appetite.

"Where is she? What happened today at *BPR*?" he muttered, pacing the floor, trying to piece together a rational explanation for Kira's involvement in the dreadful exposé in today's *Charlotte Observer*. The reporter's accusations against Roper Fiber Technology had been quite specific, supported by a photo attributed to Kira, as well as her documentation of alleged child-labor use in Pangi.

How could the writer have known such details if not for Kira's cooperation? Evan thought as he made his way into the living room, where he searched through the pages of the newspaper that he'd left scattered over his brown leather love seat. He picked up the section he wanted and shook it out. He stared hard at the photos again, a sinking sensation in his stomach. How could Kira have done this? Impulsively, he crushed the newspaper under his arm, picked up the phone, and punched in her home number again, desperate to find out what was going on. Once more, her voice mail greeted him.

"Kira," he started right in, his tone sharp and direct. "What in the world is going on, and why are you no longer at *BPR*? Why did you have to get involved in Ralph Roper's business? This is going to make things even more difficult for you. Don't you realize that your cooperation with that writer could negatively affect your right to see Vicky, as well as the Ropers' petition? The accusations are very serious. Call me. Please. And where have you been all day?"

He slammed down the phone in frustration, yanked the paper from under his arm, and glared solemnly at the headline. It disheartened him to think that Kira would put Vicky's prospective adoption in such jeopardy. Judge Burton would surely want to know if the recent revelations in Roper's business practices were going to affect his financial situation, his family stability. Often, when high-profile people got into financial trouble, it spilled over into their domestic situation. Judge Burton might request an evaluation of the problem before proceeding with the Ropers' petition, or at the least, postpone the hearing until she received a satisfactory explanation about the allegations.

Ralph Roper was a highly visible public person, a successful businessman whose reputation as a trustworthy, upstanding member of the textile industry had now been publicly questioned. What could Kira possibly say to defend herself? Evan wondered, hurt that she had done this without consulting him. *And I thought we were close . . . close enough to trust each other, at least where Vicky is involved,* he thought, slamming the paper back down onto the love seat.

Kira turned her key in the lock and entered her apartment, exhausted. She had left Helen Roper glaring after her, hands on hips, standing in the middle of her garden, and had driven to Placid Park. There she had spent the rest of the afternoon sitting in the sun on a park bench, thinking, worrying, and wishing she had never met Frank Thompson. Because of him, everything was a mess: She had no job, no references from *BPR*, and, though she had given Helen a good reason to think twice about trying to talk to the judge about her visitation rights, Kira knew she was not home free.

What if she had to leave Charlotte to find another job? Could she do that? Disappear just when she was getting to know Vicky? The thought of moving to a strange city and starting over, and not in New York as she had hoped, was too depressing to linger on.

She considered calling the *Observer* again, to charge Wade White up for infringing on her copyright to the photograph, but didn't have the energy for a fight. Anyway, what good would that do? The damage was already done. Instead of calling White, she telephoned Kenneth Lane to discuss Helen's threat about going directly to the judge to lodge a complaint against her, but Kenneth's secretary told Kira that he was in court and she did not expect to hear from him until tomorrow morning. The seriousness of the situation brought a deep ache to Kira's soul.

Since her graduation from college, Kira had never been unemployed, and the idea of losing her connection to the paper made her feel at loose ends. Though she didn't have to worry about meeting tomorrow's deadline, what tomorrow's schedule would be like, or what she would wear to work, she felt no relief, only shame to have let her boss, her colleagues, herself, and Julie Ays down. Losing the opportunity to see her work published in *World Societies Today* caused the most pain of all. It was difficult to accept the fact that her professional coup, which she had worked so hard to achieve, had vanished in an instant.

Tossing her keys on her rolltop desk, Kira picked up her phone and punched in the code to retrieve her messages. She was not surprised to find two from local reporters who wanted to talk to her about the article and one from Sharon, whose distraught voice urged Kira to call her back as soon as possible, no matter how late.

"I can't deal with Sharon, right now," Kira decided, not ready to rehash what had transpired in Davison's office, knowing her dismissal had been the topic of discussion at the office all day. She didn't want to think about *BPR*, let alone discuss her situation with her former coworker. Such a conversation would only drain Kira's energy and force her deeper into the dismal state of anxiety she was trying to keep at bay. "I've got to get some perspective on this before I speak to Sharon," she told herself, massaging her right temple, fearing a headache was on the way. She had not eaten all day. Her nerves were strung as taut as barbed wire on a country fence, and her body felt drained and limp. Kira punched in the voice-mail code again and played the final message: it was from Evan, blasting her for interfering in Roper's affairs and for putting Vicky's adoption in jeopardy.

Kira's heart constricted in shock and disbelief. He had the nerve to reprimand her! Accuse her without hearing her side? How could he believe that she would deliberately trash Ralph Roper when she had been trying so hard to be cooperative and accept the adoption? He sure was pretty damn quick to believe the worst!

"Go to hell, Evan," she spat out, slamming down the phone. She'd untangle herself from him, too, she decided, not about to continue in a relationship that apparently was not based on trust.

"Evan," she whispered, feeling desperately betrayed, "you were the only person I thought would be on my side, and now you've turned on me, too." Kira slid down onto the sofa, propped her feet up on the coffee table, and let her head fall back, staring at the ceiling. Should she call him? Make him believe her? Or did she even want to speak to a man who obviously had very little faith in her?

The memory of Evan's lips brushing her neck, of his hands firmly planted on her back, and of his body warm and firm against hers rushed in and brought tears to Kira's eyes. It had all happened so quickly between them, their attraction emerging from her disappointment and fear, culminating in a kind of respectful intimacy that Kira had never before experienced in a relationship. She enjoyed being with Evan, a man who was mature enough to respect her independence, yet spontaneous enough to create ways in which to show her how much he cared. Kira had envisioned a long-term relationship with him, and had thought he felt the same way. But now all she felt was shame.

Silently, Kira chastised herself for not having been more cautious and for giving her heart so freely to Evan. The love she felt for him was real, but it was a love that might not survive unless he trusted and respected her, neither of which he had done when he'd left that disturbing message.

Kira glanced at the clock on the bookshelf next to her desk and saw that it was ten minutes before six. She thought of calling back, of clearing the air, and getting him out of her life, but hesitated. He was most likely still at work, she realized, and she did not want to leave a nasty message of her own. She'd call him tonight, when she would have his full attention.

Absently, Kira picked up the television remote control and

pressed the POWER button, hoping the evening news might occupy her mind instead of her worries for a while. She surfed through several channels, dodging commercials and pausing to check out a movie or two, then stopped when she saw Ralph Roper on a local channel standing with another man on the helipad on the grounds of Roper Fiber Technology. He was holding a briefcase, and behind him the blades of his company helicopter were whirling in anticipation of takeoff. Kira yanked her feet off the coffee table and sat forward, intensely focused on the screen, then pumped up the volume to hear what Roper had to say.

"Of course I deny the allegations."

"How do you explain the fact that, clearly, the markings on the crates at your warehouse indicate a connection to the broker in Africa with whom you have a production contract. Your company must be involved."

Roper pulled back his shoulders and rolled his lips into a pale pink fold before answering. He appeared puffed up and cross, like a petulant child who had just been reprimanded, and his eyes were sharp glints of blue, his fair face ruddy and colored by the glowering anger he was obviously trying to hold in check. "I plan to investigate this matter personally," he stated, nearly spitting the words at the reporter. "If the brokers I contract with in that part of the world are indeed using underage workers to fulfill their obligations to my company, then I plan to stop doing business with them immediately."

"So, you're not denying that your company unknowingly might have used children to manufacture products from textiles provided by your agents?"

"The allegations about my company that were in today's *Observer* are an example of irresponsible reporting, and I find it very disturbing," Ralph tossed back.

"Are you going to sue the reporter? The paper? Do you know Kira Forester? Is it true that you are adopting her niece?" one of the reporters called out.

Annoyed at the series of rapid-fire questions, Ralph frowned his disapproval at the bombardment, then stated, "I have no comment. My attorney will handle all legal issues that may arise from this matter. My company specializes in the manufacture of products that are used in the preparation of textiles for sale to wholesalers. We are not primarily a company that manufactures retail goods, though a small number of specialty items are produced for me in foreign countries and generally sold overseas. I am on my way to Raleigh right now to meet with my board of directors to sort this matter out. That is all I have to say."

Roper turned away from the knot of reporters, preparing to leave, but a man in a black leather jacket stuck a microphone in Ralph's face.

"Do you plan to continue to campaign for mayor of Monroeville?" the reporter pressed. "The election is next week."

"Certainly. This unfortunate incident will have very little, if any, impact on my political ambitions. The people of Monroeville know who I am, and know that they can trust me."

The exchange between Roper and the reporters left Kira shaken, though extremely relieved that he had not brought up her name nor addressed the last barrage of questions. Roper was correct to investigate the matter before making unfounded assumptions— which was more than Evan had been willing to do. She silently applauded the way in which Roper had handled the press. It would have been easy for him to rant and rave and point an accusing finger at Kira, call her names and further embroil her in a messy situation that had victimized her as much as him. But, thank God, he had not done so, and she respected his restraint. At the least he had derailed any unnecessary speculation.

A tiny shred of hope flared inside of Kira. Perhaps one day she and Ralph Roper would be able to move past their initial distrust of each other and forge some kind of amicable alliance for Vicky's sake. And if she and Ralph ever did, maybe Helen would eventually come around, too.

"He seems to be trying," Kira murmured, wishing she felt as positive about Evan, whose irate message still rang in her mind. She pressed the POWER button and turned off the television, unable to concentrate on the rest of the news.

After changing out of her suit into a comfortable pair of jeans and a T-shirt, she heard the phone in her bedroom ring. Checking the Caller ID, she saw an unfamiliar number and hesitated, assuming it must belong to another nosy reporter. However, while staring at the digital display, she felt compelled to answer the call. It seemed the number was one she had seen before. Where, she could not recall.

Curious, she picked up the receiver and said, "Hello," then listened with interest when an unfamiliar woman's voice said, "May I please speak to Kira Forester?"

"This is she," Kira answered. "Who's calling?"

"This is Ava Thompson. Frank's wife. I'd like to talk to you."

"About what?" Kira demanded, her irritation with Frank perfectly clear in her voice. *What does this woman want*, she thought? *To apologize for her husband's sneaky attempt to undermine his opponent and trash my reputation? Ava Thompson can't repair the damage Frank has done, so why is she calling?*

"I'd like to talk to you about the story in today's *Observer*— about Ralph Roper," Ava went on.

"So, talk," Kira snapped, in no mood to pussyfoot around the seriousness of the incident.

"I'd prefer to speak to you in person, if at all possible, Miss Forester. I know you must be upset, and I have information, important information, that may answer some of your questions. I'd really like to see you. I can't discuss this on the phone."

"Fine," Kira told her, eager to hear what Frank's wife had to say, wondering if Frank knew she was calling.

While waiting for Ava to arrive, Kira went out onto her patio to tend to her plants, hoping the activity would distract her from the craziness of her day. As she pruned, watered, and fed her plants, the phone rang several times, but she did not bother to answer. If it was Evan, she couldn't bring herself to talk to him. Not yet, though she was anxious to let him know just how disappointed she was in him.

Later, she decided, glancing back at the ringing phone inside, continuing to pack down the earth around a transplanted pot of pansies. *When I'm calmer and less emotional. I need to focus on exactly what I want before I talk to Evan.* She was stripping off her garden gloves when the doorbell rang. Hurrying to the door, she wondered what would make Ava Thompson drive all the way from Monroeville just to see her.

Kira greeted Ava in a cool though polite tone, then invited her to sit outside on the patio where they could talk. Ava settled at the round wrought-iron table in the shade, looking distracted and nervous. Her salt-and-pepper bangs were matted on her damp forehead, which she dabbed at with a floral handkerchief.

"Would you like something to drink?" Kira offered. "It's really warm today."

"Sure is," Ava agreed, giving Kira a hesitant smile. "That would be nice."

"Iced tea?" Kira offered, pausing at the patio door, uncomfortable with the tension that Ava had brought along.

"That would be fine," Ava replied. She stuffed her handkerchief into her black leather purse, then clasped her hands atop the table and waited.

Within a few moments, Kira emerged from the kitchen with two glasses of tea wrapped in pink paper napkins. She handed one to Ava, then sat down at the table facing her visitor.

"Now," Kira started, "you have important information for me?"

Ava sipped her iced tea, then carefully placed the glass on the pink paper square and cleared her throat. "Yes. I thought long and hard before calling you. What I am about to tell you is private information that I should not share, but after what happened today, I feel I must."

"Are you referring to the article in the *Observer*?"

"Yes," Ava muttered.

"Then it's true? Your husband did this to me? To Ralph Roper?"

"Yes," Ava confirmed. "And I am appalled. Frank is not himself, and I'm worried sick. When he admitted to me that he had planted that story to hurt Ralph Roper, I was shocked. That is not my Frank. I don't understand what's going on in his mind—giving your photograph to that reporter—creating such a stir over Ralph Roper's business. Terrible. I told Frank that this is not the way to win votes, but he doesn't listen to me. When it comes to this election, Miss Forester, he's obsessed. Dead set on winning, above everything else, and says that nothing is going to get in his way. I know business has been real slow at his dealership for a while now, and he thinks becoming mayor would be a wonderful move—get him out from under the pressure to produce the big sales numbers that his headquarters expects. But, in my opinion, he'd be trading one kind of pressure for another, though I think he'd be a good mayor. I do, but I've got a bad feeling about what's happening to him. What he did to both you and Mr. Roper is awful. He's taking this campaign much too seriously. I don't particularly like the Ropers, but Ralph has run a clean campaign. He's never lashed out at Frank."

"I'm sorry about all of this, too, Mrs. Thompson. But the damage has been done."

A contrite grimace came to Ava's lips, and she appeared weighed down with worry. "People call Frank a rabble-rouser and a troublemaker, but he's not. He's fifty-five years old . . . a survivor of the civil rights era. When he was a young man, he marched in demonstrations and picketed for desegregation in front of stores and hospitals and restaurants all over the state. More than once he chained himself to the front door of a building or to a counter stool in a coffee shop, daring the police to harm him. When it comes to a cause that he believes in, there's no stopping Frank. But I'm afraid for him now. Times are different," she said in a voice brimming with concern. "I've never seen him so . . . driven. And it's scary. Stays up all hours of the night calling and faxing folks, asking for their votes. Disappears in the middle of the night and won't tell me where he's been. He used to be so easygoing and relaxed. Now he's edgy and tense. Spends every waking minute calculating how he can discredit Roper, whom, you know, he detests."

"Because of the proposed demolition of the mill?" Kira interjected, her sympathy for Ava growing.

"Oh, it's more than the old mill," Ava replied, sighing. "Frank has always believed that Roper stole his birthright when he bought up Frank's momma's land. I think Roper most likely had the right to buy the place, but Frank will never see it that way. However, I have to admit that Frank has a point about the need to save Flagg Valley Mill. It ought to be preserved. But sometimes we have to let go of the past. He goes out there all the time, snooping around. He told me that a demolition crew has started stripping the old place, getting ready to bring it down."

"Oh?" Kira remarked. "I thought Roper was using it as a warehouse."

"Not anymore. Apparently he's moved everything out. Frank knows people who work out there for Roper, and he's been asking questions. God, he's so consumed with all of this. If I had had any idea that this election would turn into a battle over that old mill, I never would have encouraged him to run for mayor."

"I'm sorry," Kira murmured. "I guess there's no easy way to deal with progress when it affects something you care deeply about. I'm surprised to hear that Roper is moving so fast to tear down the mill; but, Mrs. Thompson, what does this have to do with me? What did you come here to tell me?"

Ava did not answer right away but fingered the napkin under her drink, a frown of concern making deep ridges between her eyebrows.

Kira watched Ava closely, sensing her indecision, wondering

what was on her visitor's mind. "Mrs. Thompson?" she prompted, causing the other woman to look up and focus on her. "What do you have to tell me?"

Ava sucked in a long breath and raised her chin, hooking Kira with an expression that made her tense. "So, the Ropers are planning to adopt your niece," Ava finally managed.

Kira simply nodded, realizing that everyone in Monroeville probably knew about it by now.

"How well do you know Helen Roper?"

"Interesting that you should ask," Kira replied, letting herself relax. So Ava Thompson had not come to talk about the *Observer* article or her husband's campaign, but about the one person Kira most wanted to know more about: Helen Roper. "Unfortunately, I don't know her at all. I've met her twice, and on both occasions, she was rather unfriendly and cold."

"I'm not surprised," Ava stated. "I also understand that you are not against this adoption."

"I was at first," Kira confessed, "but I've accepted the fact that this is best for Vicky, and I want to make it work for her. I was granted visitation privileges by the court, so I'll get to know my niece, and hopefully develop a good relationship with her. My feeling is that in time the Ropers will accept me, but if they don't, that's their prerogative."

"Helen Roper will never accept you." Ava's voice was hard with conviction.

"How do you know that?" Kira demanded, going on to add, "If you have anything important to tell me, please do."

"I'm from a little town called Cedar Grove, up in Orange County. So is Helen Roper, and she's got a sister named Ruth who still lives there. She might be very willing to talk to you."

"About what?" Kira asked, now suspicious.

"About Helen wanting to adopt a black child."

"Why do you think Helen's sister would see me?"

"Because I was still living in Cedar Grove when Helen had some trouble. Ruth hired my mother to help out around her house, and my mother came into some information that she passed on to me in confidence. I promised never to reveal what I knew, and it didn't seem important at the time. But now that I know you are Vicky Jordan's aunt, I can't keep quiet. Go talk to Helen Roper's sister before you step back and let this adoption go through. There are things you ought to know."

"Like what?"

Ava shook her head. "I can't say. I'm a person who keeps her word, and to divulge what I know would not be right. Over the years I've learned that there are things that women, especially, ought to honor, no matter what. This is one of them. Few people do what they promise anymore, but that's not me. Know what I mean?"

"Yes, I do," Kira said, nodding.

Ava gave Kira a timid smile. "Good. Then you see why all I can do is point you in the right direction?"

"Yes, I understand. What is Helen's sister's name?"

"Ruth Downy."

"How do I contact her?"

"Go to Cedar Grove. She's in the book."

CHAPTER 26

L ess than thirty minutes after Ava went home, Kira had checked
Yahoo maps for driving directions to Cedar Grove, packed an
overnight bag, and was in her car, on her way to find Ruth Downy.
As the first street lamps blinked to life above the freeway and the
glimmer of the city began to fade behind her, Kira let herself go
limp, easing her tight grip on the wheel. It felt good to speed off
into the fast-approaching darkness and leave Charlotte behind, at
least for a few days. The break would provide the necessary space
for her to rethink her relationship with Evan, too, and give her
heated emotions time to cool. Kira knew he would be worried
when she did not return his calls, and though she ached to talk to
him, she refused to give in, determined to wait and see if he would
come to his senses and apologize. She had done no wrong, and
until he understood that, they had nothing to say to each other.

Kira had never made the drive from Charlotte to Orange
County and was not familiar with the route, but she bravely
headed northeast toward IH- 85, calculating that she ought to be in
Cedar Grove by ten o'clock. She would check into the first motel
she came to and get a good night's rest. In the morning she'd track
down Ruth Downy and, hopefully, find the answers to the questions that had plagued her for weeks: what was Helen Roper so
afraid of, and why did she think Kira was a threat?

At nine-thirty, Evan pulled up to the covered parking space in
front of Kira's apartment. It was empty, and he sat there, wondering where she could be. His meeting at the agency had run very
long, but he was certain that Teddy and Mona Jeffers were about to

have themselves a child at last. Memory of the evening's success brought a quick smile to Evan's lips, buoying him momentarily, but quickly his concern about Kira intruded again.

After his session with the prospective adoptive couple, Evan had gone to Denny's for a quick sandwich, hoping Kira might be home by the time he got to her apartment. He had been calling all evening, with no luck, and now he was worried that the stern message he had left earlier on her voice mail might have been too strong, upsetting her. Kira could not have cooperated with that writer, Evan was certain. Someone who had much to gain from discrediting Ralph Roper had to be the culprit, and Evan had a pretty good idea who that might be.

"God, what was I thinking?" he said under his breath, now searching the dark parking area. Her car was gone, there were no lights in her apartment windows or coming from the patio, and he had no idea where she might be. Placing his forehead on the steering wheel, Evan exhaled, then cursed aloud, wishing he had had better sense than to mix his professional and personal lives. Kira Forester was beautiful, smart, intriguing, and a woman he wished he had met under different circumstances. But he hadn't, and now he was trapped. He wanted to drive off and forget about her, return to the life he had been living before she walked in and took control of his emotions. Life before Kira had been simpler, easier to deal with, but it had not been particularly happy. Evan squeezed his eyes shut, remembering their most intimate moments spent on the patio that was now dark and cold. Though he had let down his guard when he should have been more vigilant, knowing it was improper to get involved with a client, he had no regrets.

Reluctantly, Evan started the car and put it into reverse, anxious to go home and decide what to do, knowing he was not prepared to walk out of Kira's life. Not now. He loved her too damn much.

For the first time in years, a light was burning in the guardhouse at the gates of the old mill and a man in a dark green uniform was sitting inside, his head bent over a paperback book, an unlit cigar stuck into the corner of his mouth. Beyond the dim glow that came from the guardhouse windows, the rest of the complex remained dark and still.

Frank crept closer, pushing aside a low-hanging tree branch to get a better look. The sight of the mill, now battered and stripped to a bare brick skeleton, brought a chill to his arms in spite of the muggy night air that was making him perspire. Yesterday he'd hidden in the same shadows, holding back his anger as he'd watched a demolition crew descend on the place with jackhammers, pickaxes, shovels, and crowbars to batter the interior crumbling walls, pry off doors, remove thick beams, and punch out most of the dirt-streaked windows to weaken the structure and enable the explosives to bring it down in a series of shuddering blasts.

The demolition date must be pretty close, he thought, concentrating on the lone guard who had been left behind to prevent anyone from entering the fractured facility.

Easing himself to the ground, Frank squatted on the grass and leaned against the weather-beaten wall of what had once been an old barn. The farmhouse that used to be on this property was long gone, but enough markers remained to jog his memory back to a time when the land had been covered with tall rows of corn, their silky tassels waving high above his head as he played hide-and-seek with his friends among the dark green stalks. He stared glumly across the road at the mill, a ghostly edifice that had been there, in his mind, forever. He knew every inch of this land, from the overgrown footpaths that crisscrossed the acreage, to the abandoned wells, cracked foundations, and piles of broken brick that lay hidden among vines and layers of sifted dirt. When he had been young, he had ridden his bicycle up and down this very road, waving at the men and women inside the gates of Flagg Valley Mill. Back then, everyone had known him, his mother, and his father, but now none of those people were willing to fight to save what had been their source of survival.

Frank gazed at the turrets at either end of the old mill's main building, bathed in white moonlight, their shattered windows staring down at him like the eyes of a wounded animal. The broken glass, splintered lumber, and twisted wires that littered the grounds were covered with a white haze of dust, the rubble glowing like a mound of silver in the moonlight.

With a shudder, Frank shifted his weight and got up on his knees, placing one hand against a shaggy sycamore tree to steady himself as he studied the scene, memorizing it. *A damn shame,* Frank thought, his hatred for Ralph Roper rising. *I will stop him,* he vowed, pleased that his tactic with Wade White had paid off. The reporter's story had put Roper on notice that he was vulnerable and had shown the residents of Monroeville that the man they thought was so damn perfect might not be so upstanding after all.

Frank knew that it would not take long for Roper to trace the story back to him: Kira Forester's boss had managed to get to him after only a few phone calls. But none of that mattered. He had managed to stir up a cloud of doubt that would have to be diffused, forcing Roper's attention to matters more pressing than his campaign, providing Frank with an excellent opportunity to maneuver himself a notch closer to the top of the ballot.

Frank's heart pounded with anticipation as his mind groped for the next step in his plan. He had to stall the demolition, at least until after the election. Then he'd have the power of his new position as mayor of Monroeville to back him up, to make sure that Ralph Roper never went through with his destructive, insensitive plan.

Once I'm elected, Frank mused, *I'll finally be important enough for those preservation snobs in Raleigh to take me seriously. They won't be so quick to ignore me, or so quick to let Roper bring down a building that should have their protection.*

Frank got up, dusted off the bits of twigs and crushed leaves that were clinging to his trousers, and started across the road to the guardhouse, deciding it was time to find out exactly what was going on.

"Who's there?" the guard called out when he heard Frank's footsteps crunching on the asphalt road. He stepped farther away from his tiny enclosure, shining his flashlight into the darkness to create a strip of bright illumination. "Who's there?"

Frank stepped quickly into the beam of light, waving one hand in a friendly gesture. "Frank Thompson," he called back. "I live just on the other side of the mill."

The guard walked toward Frank, meeting him in the middle of the deserted road, then directed the beam of light at Frank's face. "What are you doing out here?" he asked, standing with his legs slightly spread, planting himself firmly between Frank and the mill.

"Car trouble," Frank replied in an irritated tone that he hoped sounded convincing. "I had to leave my car a ways down the road."

"So, you need me to call a tow truck or someone to come get you?" the guard offered, unbuttoning the leather holder at his waist to take out his cell phone.

"Oh no," Frank said, dismissing the man's offer of assistance. "I can walk home. It's not far, and the exercise will do me good. I'll call Triple A to come out tomorrow and take care of the car."

"Suit yourself," the guard replied, replacing his phone in its holder. "Be careful. Not much traffic out here. Better stick to the side of the road."

"I will," Frank said, not making a move to leave. He craned his neck to see over the guard's shoulder, then asked in a neighborly voice, "So, pretty soon, I guess, the landscape around here is going to change."

"Yep," the guard said. "Come Saturday morning it's all coming down. Won't take but a few minutes to turn this place into dust, either. It's pretty shaky now."

"This Saturday?" Frank clarified, tensing. "I thought Roper might want to wait until after the election."

"Nope. First thing Saturday morning," the security guard told Frank, waving good night as he turned to go back into his tiny house.

Frank hurried down the road toward his car, which he had parked in a grove of trees more than a mile away. Now that he knew what Roper was planning, there was little time to waste.

CHAPTER 27

"I was wondering when you were going to call," Ruth Downy said, rising from her wicker chair to greet Kira. She moved quickly across her wide, shady porch toward Kira, who remained at the foot of the short flight of steps, observing Ruth Downy closely. Though clearly older than her sister Helen, Ruth had the same lean frame and fair skin, but her eyes were much more expressive and welcoming. She was wearing a pair of loose-fitting white linen slacks, a bright turquoise shirt embroidered with pink flowers, and a pair of sturdy walking shoes. Her tawny brown hair, mingled with gray, fell in a fluffy mass of loose waves to her shoulders, and the huge silver hoops in her ears were very similar to a pair that Kira had purchased in a marketplace in Africa. In short, Ruth Downy seemed to be a vibrant middle-aged woman who was glad to have some company.

"Oh?" Kira remarked as Ruth stepped down off the porch. "You expected me to call?"

"Absolutely," Ruth replied, looking Kira over. "Helen told me all about what's going on, and I *do* want to talk to you."

"That's a relief," Kira said with a sigh. She had arrived in Cedar Grove at ten-thirty last night to find a quaint, hilly town that was already fast asleep. Exhausted, she had felt frazzled from the fallout of the worst day of her life. In less than twenty-four hours she had lost her job, had a confrontation with Frank Thompson, experienced an upsetting argument with Helen Roper, and entertained Ava Thompson, her mysterious visitor who had steered her toward the one person who might have the answers she sought. After checking into the Roadside Suites last night, Kira had easily located

Ruth Downy's number in the phone book, then taken a hot shower and collapsed in the bed, certain she would fall asleep as soon as her head hit the pillow. But she had lain awake for nearly an hour, listening to the semitrailers pulling into and out of the gas station next door, worrying that Ruth Downy might not agree to see her. But when she called Ruth this morning and explained who she was, Kira had been startled by the woman's eager reception.

"Thank you for agreeing to see me," Kira said. "I hope you can answer some questions that are really bothering me."

"You like to walk?" Ruth suddenly asked.

Shrugging, Kira nodded. "Sure."

Ruth scrutinized the flat leather shoes Kira was wearing, then asked, "You have some better shoes than those?"

Kira thought for a minute, then replied, "Yes. My gym bag is in my car, including my workout shoes."

"Good," Ruth stated. "Put them on. This is my walking time . . . and I don't allow anyone to interfere with it. I walk four miles every day." Turning from Kira, she pointed to a ridge behind her one-story cottage where pine trees and sycamores and hickory trees were thick. "I walk two miles up to that ridge and two miles back every day. So if you want to talk to me, you've got to come along." Then Ruth clamped her lips tightly shut and waited while Kira changed her shoes. That done, Ruth set off at a fast pace, which Kira hurried to match.

The footpath that wound its way uphill from the rear of Ruth Downy's country cottage was cushioned with pine needles, damp leaves, and several seasons of decayed foliage, muting the intrusive sound of footsteps in the cool, quiet woods. Popping up randomly among the underbrush were bursts of color created by clumps of red and yellow butterfly weeds, shaggy sprays of white larkspur, and rosettes of purple coneflowers. Other colorful wildflowers dotted the sun-spotted forest, glittering like fragile jewels strewn among the low-growing wood ferns. Except for the occasional twitter of the birds that swooped from tree to tree and the humming of bumblebees flitting among the flowers, it was silent. After ten minutes of steady walking, Kira ventured a question.

"Have you lived out here long?" Kira asked, envious of anyone who was fortunate enough to have such a spectacular hiking trail just beyond her back door.

"Oh yes," Ruth replied. "My grandfather built the cottage with his own hands. This land has been in my family for years. Helen and I used to spend our summers here when we were growing up."

"And where did you live? Closer to town?" Kira asked, snapping a shiny leaf from a thorny bush, shredding it into tiny pieces as they continued walking.

"Yes, on the west side. But back then, coming out here to visit my grandparents seemed like going on a long trip. It was a great adventure for us." Ruth chuckled, then turned serious. "After my grandparents died, I took it upon myself to look after their home, and when I realized I had enough money to retire from the post office at fifty, I left. Came out here to live permanently. Been here twelve years, and it was the best decision I ever made."

"Are you and Helen close?" Kira asked in a strong voice, not breaking her stride as they rounded a bend in the trail.

"We've had our differences over the years, but we get along as well as most sisters, I guess," Ruth replied. "When we were younger, Helen used to tell me everything. Being so much older than she, I used to have to listen to some things I'd rather not have known."

Kira did not respond, hoping her silence would encourage Ruth to speak freely.

"When Helen told me she and Ralph were going to adopt a black child," Ruth went on, "I was stunned. Afraid, really. Helen is flirting with disaster by bringing that child into her home, and I wish she'd abandon the idea that she must be a mother in order to be whole. Ralph is a good man, and he'd still love Helen if they never had a child. It's an obsession she's carrying too damn far."

Again, Kira kept her peace, striding alongside Ruth until the energetic woman slowed her pace as they arrived at a forested plateau surrounded by dense brush, climbing vines, and trees so tall Kira could hardly see their tops. The clearing fanned out in a half-circle, providing room for them to stand and admire the panoramic view of the landscape below.

"Take a look down there," Ruth told Kira, sweeping her arm toward the edge of the ridge. "Isn't it beautiful? I never tire of coming up here—even in the winter when there's snow on the ground and icicles on the trees. Quite a scene, isn't it?"

From the edge of the clearing, Kira peered down at the spectacular view, feeling a sense of light-headedness and isolation that was exhilarating, reminding her of a trek through the African bush when she had felt pleasantly removed from the world, plunged into a strange, intoxicating new space. Looking out, Kira saw a band of fat gray clouds lingering at the far edges of the horizon, moving slowly to the west, pushing their fluffy white counterparts out of their way. Looking down, she saw Ruth's quaint cottage, which now resembled a tiny dollhouse. The twisting path they had traversed lay bent and curled like a dark brown ribbon snaking its way through the trees.

Ruth left Kira to admire the view and walked to a huge section of log that had been rolled to the side of the lookout spot. She sat down, then motioned for Kira to do the same.

"Come and sit," she said. "You came to talk about Helen, and I will, though she's going to hate me for doing this. However, my mind is set. Things have gone too far."

Kira sat at the far end of the log, positioning herself so that she could observe Ruth while they talked. Launching the discussion, she asked, "Why did you say you're afraid for Helen?"

The grimace that tugged at Ruth's lips gave evidence of her reluctance to answer, but she lifted her jaw determinedly and said, "I'm afraid that Helen will lose the best thing that ever came into her life if she adopts your niece," Ruth stated.

"And that is?" Kira prompted.

"Ralph, of course," she replied, tossing her brother-in-law's name at Kira. "He loves my sister too much—so much that he'll do anything she wants, but he ought to put his foot down and stop this adoption."

"That's interesting," Kira murmured, disturbed by Ruth's comment. "I thought Ralph was pushing for the adoption. He seems totally dedicated to seeing it through."

"Don't be fooled, my dear. Helen has waited a long time to get her hands on a child, and now that she has Vicky in her home and the paperwork to make Vicky legally hers is in the works, I'm afraid she'll risk everything to keep her there."

"Risk everything? You mean Ralph? Her marriage?"

The slight inclination of Ruth's head was her only reply.

"But I don't understand. How? What kind of risk?" Kira asked, annoyed that Ruth Downy was being so vague. She was not in the mood for playing guessing games. But then she reminded herself that she had plenty of time and was too close to getting the answers she needed to scare Ruth off with her impatience. "Do you think Helen is aware of the risk she is taking?"

"Oh yes," said Ruth, vigorously nodding her head. "She must be on the verge of a nervous breakdown." After a pause, she added in a more deliberate tone, "Well, maybe this will help," as she reached into the pocket of her turquoise shirt and removed a faded Polaroid photo. She offered it to Kira. "Look at this. Then tell me what you think."

Kira's irritation with Ruth dissolved the moment she looked at the picture, but what she saw left her trembling with surprise and more confused than ever. The photo was of a young couple standing in front of a fountain in a parklike setting. They had their arms entwined around each other's waists, and the girl facing the camera was clearly a younger version of Helen. She was wearing a halter top and shorts, her tanned, lean body pressed against a young man whose face had been captured in profile as he gazed lovingly at her. The young man was tall, even tanner than Helen, and the red T-shirt he was wearing had a fire-breathing green dragon splashed across the front. Kira studied the image, then looked at Ruth Downy, afraid to utter the words that crowded her mind. "I can see that the girl is Helen. But . . . who is this with her?"

"Andrew Jordan," Ruth replied, confirming Kira's initial suspicion.

Though Kira had never met Andrew, and possessed only one photograph of him, she had memorized his image over the years, wondering where he was, why he had deserted Miranda, and if he knew he had a daughter. She recognized his stance, his crooked half-smile, his hair, which was even longer than it had been when he had been involved with her sister, and the tattoo of a guitar on his right forearm. Everything about the picture confirmed Ruth's startling revelation. A barrage of questions rose in Kira, but she wasn't sure she wanted the answers.

"This is scaring me," Kira whispered, squinting intensely at the image, trying to make it fit with her memory of the few details Miranda had told her about Vicky's father. "Were they involved?"

"Absolutely. When that picture was taken, Helen was twenty-five years old and very much in love with Andrew Jordan," Ruth said in a soft voice, as if afraid someone might overhear her words. "She met him while she was living on the coast, working at a fancy resort on Nags Head. She used to arrange conventions, parties, and plan big fund-raisers. You know, promotional events and things like that. She was very good at it, and loved her job. Apparently she hired Andrew's band to play at a function at the resort and fell for him immediately. They had a short but intense affair, which ended badly." Ruth gazed off toward the horizon, her eyes seeming to draw memories from the fast-darkening clouds that had begun to settle in ominous colonies in the gritty gray sky. "She telephoned me almost every day during that time, drawing me into her bumpy relationship, and I suffered right along with Helen . . . moment by moment, until the end. She was desperately in love, but he was a party boy—a young musician. All he wanted was a good time. I tried to tell her that, but she wouldn't listen."

"When did this happen? How long ago?" Kira demanded, suddenly afraid to hear the answer.

"Ten years ago. He moved on . . . apparently to your sister, while Helen fell into the greatest despair of her life. You see, she was pregnant when Andrew left her. She went after him and begged him to marry her. He refused. She attempted suicide . . . took a bunch of pills that didn't do anything but put her to sleep. The doctor called me, so I flew out to Nags Head and yanked her out of there, brought her home with me. We sat right here, right where you and I are sitting now, and decided that the best thing for Helen to do was have an abortion. I drove Helen to the doctor, then took care of her afterward, with the help of a woman who moved in with us for a few months to give me a hand taking care of her. You see, I was afraid to leave her alone. After her mental and physical health had improved, we buried the whole affair in the dirt, where it belonged." Ruth kicked at the red Carolina soil with the toe of her walking shoe, sadness creeping into her eyes. "We never talked about it again. A year later, Helen met Ralph, married him, and went on with her life. He's the best thing that ever happened to her."

"And all of this happened ten years ago," Kira murmured, her mind whirling with calculations. "Helen never saw Andrew Jordan again?"

"Never."

Kira sighed, her entire body sagging heavily into itself. "That's a relief. For a minute I thought you were going to tell me that Vicky was Andrew and Helen's child."

"Oh no," Ruth threw back with a dismissive wave of her hands. "But she would have been, if Helen had had her way."

CHAPTER 28

For the first time in years, Evan pressed the OFF button on his radio alarm clock, turned over onto his stomach, and buried his face in his pillow, unable to face a day in the office. He'd spent a miserable night tossing around in bed, trying to come up with explanations for events that still confused him, and every muscle in his body seemed heavy with worry, a feeling he'd never experienced before.

As sunlight began to wash over the transparent shades in his bedroom, he lay still, his mind slipping back to yesterday and the horrible mishmash of surprises and disappointments it had brought. He had no desire to get up, jump into the shower, put on a suit, and go about his day as usual. There was nothing usual about what was going on, and he had to find out why. He'd call Sue and ask her to cancel his appointments, tell her he was not feeling well, which was not exactly a lie. He felt terrible. His nerves were shot, a tiny hammer was pounding inside his head, and he was sure that his mental capacity for dealing with clients today was definitely diminished.

Where had Kira run off to last night, and why was she refusing to return his calls? Even if she was angry with him for the message he'd left, she was not the type to back away from an honest confrontation. After leaving her apartment complex last night, he had come home, uncorked a bottle of wine, and sipped it alone, telephoning her two more times before giving up.

Moaning over the pounding in his head, he sat up. She'd contact him when she was ready, he knew, and until then, he had other pressing issues to occupy his time. He had to find out who had helped Wade White write that damaging article about Ralph Roper. Certainly it could not have been Kira, not after she'd gone to such lengths to win visitation with Vicky, and not after telling him she'd accepted the fact that the Ropers would be her niece's parents. No, something about all of this did not ring true, including Roper's refusal to come out publicly against Kira during his televised interview yesterday. Was he guilty as charged? And if so, would his less than morally acceptable business practices have a negative impact on his campaign? Evan gritted his teeth and pushed his forehead deeper into his hands, frustrated by the widening circle of questions that needed answers.

The groan that escaped Evan's lips came from deep within his belly when he finally reached for the phone. After calling his office to tell Sue he would not be in, he dialed the number to the *Charlotte Observer* and followed the prompts to be connected with Wade White's voice mail, knowing that was where he needed to start.

It was nine forty-five when Wade White stuck his head into the visitors' area where the *Observer* receptionist had asked Evan to wait until the reporter was available. When Wade smiled and motioned for Evan to come on back to his office, Evan quickly rose, shook the reporter's hand, and followed him into his cubicle.

Wade White was a slightly built, studious-looking man with wildly tousled dark brown hair and a matching droopy mustache that blended into an equally unruly beard. The man seemed to be covered in hair, and as they greeted each other, Evan made an effort not to stare at the man's lips, a narrow slit nestled among the wiry mass that concealed the better part of his face.

"Your message indicated that you have information related to the Roper Fiber Technology story?" Wade prompted, one bushy eyebrow cocked in a wary expression. Without giving Evan a chance to respond, he swiveled his chair to one side and reached for a yellow stenographer's pad. "What do you have?" he asked, pen poised to record whatever Evan was going to say.

The blunt way in which Wade zoomed directly to the point caught Evan by surprise, and he mentally groped for an appropriate way to tell the reporter that he had lied. He'd left the message to ensure that he'd get not only a callback but also an invitation to visit. And now here he was.

"I'm not sure if you'd call what I want to say 'important information,'" Evan started. "I wanted to meet you. Talk to you face-to-face about the story."

"Why?"

"Because Kira Forester is a . . . a client of mine."

"And what kind of work are you in?" Wade cautiously prompted.

"Private adoption. I'm doing some background checking on her in relation to a case."

"Oh? Well, I'm sorry you wasted your time coming down here, because I don't know Kira Forester personally, if it's a character reference you're after. We journalists have our own beats—rather territorial, you see. As far as I know, she's a good reporter, does her job, and plays fair. That's about it."

"Ah, yes," Evan said, approval in his tone. "But there is one question I think you could help me with."

"Shoot."

"Was she your 'reliable source' for the Roper story?" Evan let his question drift, holding his breath as he assessed Wade's reaction.

Wade chuckled under his breath, then exhaled in a whoosh of air. "You're the second person who's asked me that question in the past twenty-four hours."

"Gee, I'd love to know who the first person was."

"Bruce Davison. Over at *BPR*. And I told him, just like I'm telling you, that Frank Thompson brought me the story and the photo. I've known Frank for years, and he's often provided me with interesting stuff to work with. Never had any reason to doubt his word. So, after Frank took me out to the old mill and I was able to corroborate the allegations, my editor said to jump on it, and I did. With the interest in this election and all, I thought the story would make good copy. Stir things up a bit. But I gave Kira credit." Wade paused, thinking. "By the way, where is she, anyway? I called over to *BPR* and they said she's left. What is going on?"

"I wish I knew," Evan muttered, anxious to talk to Kira himself, relieved to know that Frank, not Kira, had initiated the story. "Tell me, do you think Thompson has a chance at winning the election?"

Now Wade reared back in his swivel chair, his bewhiskered chin touching his chest as he assessed Evan. "I don't know, but I'll tell you one thing: Frank Thompson is determined to be the next mayor of Monroeville, and my hunch is that he's going to do everything in his power to win. The demographics are on his side. It's going to be an interesting race."

On his way to his car, Evan walked quickly, propelled across the parking lot by the anger that boiled inside him. Frank Thompson was a real disappointment . . . a devious, destructive man who hoped to benefit from Ralph and Kira's pain. He had threatened to hurt Kira for not backing him, and now he had followed through. Kira had no job. Her reputation was on the line. And Roper's credibility was under fire. And at the heart of all of this mess, Evan thought, was Vicky, an innocent little girl who deserved to have a family. If it was the last thing he did, Evan was going to make Frank see the damage he had done and hold him accountable for his actions.

Evan slid behind the wheel of his car and started the engine, irritated as hell for having thought, even for a moment, that Kira could have been capable of such an underhanded maneuver. Swinging onto the freeway, he headed toward Monroeville.

The drive gave Evan's temper an opportunity to cool, but as soon as he walked into Thompson's showroom and saw the smug look of triumph on the man's face, he lost it. Without saying a word, he walked directly to Frank, reached across the counter, and grabbed him by the shirt. Yanking his face close to his, Evan delivered his message through tightly clenched teeth.

"You prick. I'm not in your face because of what you did to Kira Forester—or Ralph Roper. I'm here for Vicky Jordan, an innocent child who could lose everything because of your selfish, greedy actions. Obviously you don't care about anyone but yourself, and I am going to make sure that the people of Monroeville know what you did. I'll make sure that they see you for the insecure little man that you are. What do you think of that?"

The thunderstorm that had been building while Kira visited with Ruth atop the high pine ridge broke loose with a fury immediately after Kira bid Ruth good-bye and started back to Charlotte. Wind-driven sheets of warm gray rain slashed the air and pummeled the highway, forcing Kira to slow to a crawl, and convinced quite a few of the long-haul truckers to get off the road entirely.

As her windshield wipers whipped back and forth with a rhythmic clack, Kira inched her way home, barely sensing the miles slipping past as she doggedly focused on the road instead of the disturbing thoughts that hung in her mind. In a way, she was grateful for the inconvenience of the sudden spring storm, as well as the tedium of the drive. Without these restraints she might have pressed too hard on the accelerator, recklessly passed the slow-moving vehicles that were testing her patience, and been robbed of this opportunity to quietly dissect Ruth's stunning revelations.

Kira ran her tongue over her lips, tasting the remains of the sweet anise-flavored coffee cake that Ruth had set out for them on her rough pine table after their return from the ridge. Kira had sat across from Ruth, coffee cup in hand, a tall pair of ceramic rooster salt and pepper shakers between them, and listened as Ruth had rattled on about the history of her cottage, describing each pottery vase, folk-art painting, cookbook, and rooster-themed plate decorating her country kitchen walls. She loved her home, her independent lifestyle, and her family—which now consisted of only Helen and Ralph—and, as much as she wanted a niece to expand her small circle of relatives, she was worried for Helen.

The visit had ended on a pleasant, yet tense note, with Kira thanking Ruth for her hospitality while saying little about what she planned to do with this new piece of the puzzle that made up Helen Roper.

"Don't get me wrong," Ruth had earnestly told Kira, pushing the entire upper half of her body across the table to make sure Kira paid attention. "My opposition to this adoption has nothing to do with race. I want a niece. I'd love to see Helen and Ralph with a house full of adopted kids, if that is what they want to do. But not the child they have now. It's a reminder of a past that needs to be forgotten, a disaster in the making."

"What do you want me to do?" Kira had asked, jittery with anxiety about what Ruth expected.

"Convince Helen to give up this folly. Adopting Andrew Jordan's daughter will not ease her guilt or replace the child that she destroyed. As long as you were not in the picture, I tried to justify this in my mind, telling myself that Helen had a vague but legitimate connection to this poor abandoned child. But you're blood. You can raise her. Oh, I can't tell you how long I struggled with this, how worried I am for Helen."

"Ruth," Kira had stated slowly, frowning, "I never thought I'd say this, but I think Helen is the perfect candidate to raise Vicky. I cannot. And I will not advise her to abandon my niece."

And now that I know the source of Helen's fear, what should I do? Kira worried, as she turned up the fan to clear away a film of vapor that clouded her windshield. She cautioned herself to think everything through before taking any action.

Ruth had confirmed Kira's suspicions: Helen was afraid of Kira—terrified that the humiliating ordeal she had endured in the seclusion of her sister's home might find its way to the surface. Kira had no intention of telling Evan about Helen's youthful involvement with Andrew Jordan. Her attempted suicide and eventual abortion would not be taken lightly, and he'd be obligated to investigate the matter further, stirring up old ghosts that needed to stay buried. Surely he'd have to add a footnote of a history of mental instability to Helen Roper's case file, putting the adoption in jeopardy. And to what end? Kira shook her head, recalling Ava Thompson's remarks about how women needed to honor their word and keep private matters to themselves. Hadn't most women, if they'd lived long enough to find real love, had a disastrous affair that they had tucked away somewhere in their hearts? Didn't everyone have an incident or a period in their life that they wished had never happened? Kira had had one herself: Brandon Melzona, and thank God she'd had the good sense to get out of that relationship before he trashed her life. What happened to Helen could have happened to any woman, but some people would not understand. They would not sympathize with the desperation, the hopelessness Helen must have felt after the end of her one-sided love affair. They had never been immersed in the thick fog of depression that had blinded Helen to what was the right thing to do—especially with a biracial unborn child jumbled up in the mix. No, Kira would talk to Helen directly and convince her that there was nothing to fear—that her secret was safe.

CHAPTER 29

The house was dark except for a dull spot of yellow in a second-floor window and a glow of muted light coming from the rear of the house. A four-globe gas lamp at the end of the driveway lit the way for Kira, who started up the deserted path, driving slowly, her eyes on the tall magnolia tree shadowing the front of Helen's house. The tree's leafy branches seemed to be dancing in the wind, waving and shifting with each new gust, while its thick gnarled trunk remained stiffly resistant to the assault of the raw, cutting rain. The multipaned windows at the front of the huge Tudor peered down on Kira in silence, as if daring her to come closer.

No cars were parked in the circular drive, so Kira boldly pulled right up to the front door. When she opened her car door, a black wall of cool rain nearly forced her back inside, but she quickly jumped out and dashed for cover beneath the angled overhang that protected the entrance, surprised by the unexpected drop in temperature since she had left Cedar Grove. Shivering, Kira rubbed her arms, focused her thoughts on her mission, and stabbed at the doorbell, her heart pounding when she heard it chime softly inside the house. Immediately, the entry light came on, and through the Harlequin-patterned glass panels that flanked the heavy door, Kira saw a shadowy figure approaching.

A matronly woman with pure white hair, who was wearing a full apron, small gold rings in her ears, and a black and white polka dot-blouse that had a ruffled collar, opened the door. "Yes?" she said, widening her eyes to take Kira in. "May I help you?"

"I'd like to speak to Helen Roper," Kira replied, thinking how foolish she had been to assume that Helen would greet her. Of course anyone with a house this large would have servants to do such mundane things.

"And you are?" the woman prompted, raising one pale, penciled-in eyebrow.

"Kira Forester."

"Is Mrs. Roper expecting you?" the woman continued her interrogation.

"No," Kira replied, then quickly added, "But please tell her I have just returned from visiting her sister Ruth in Cedar Grove, and I have a message from her."

"Oh? Well, yes." The woman stepped back and opened the door wider. "Please come in and wait. I'll tell Mrs. Roper you're here."

While Kira waited in the dim foyer, hoping Helen would agree to see her, she realized again how fortunate Vicky was, how many advantages the Ropers would be able to give her, and how much she now wanted this to be Vicky's permanent home.

The smell of cinnamon and apples came to her, a cozy, welcoming scent. From the little Kira could see from where she stood, it was evident that Helen and Ralph had created a comfortable, child-friendly home. Hanging on the coat tree in the corner of the hall were a small red rain jacket and matching hat. *Vicky's*, Kira thought, her eyes traveling to the umbrella stand beneath the coat rack, where her niece's tiny red umbrella and boots had been placed neatly side by side. She glanced into the small room off the entrance, furnished in an unpretentious style, yet very different from Ruth's folksy cottage in the country. Two overstuffed love seats covered in bright floral upholstery faced a low, sturdy table. On it, Kira could see a coloring book and crayons, abandoned in midplay, a Barbie still undressed, and a picture book left open. She smiled, imagining Vicky playing there, thinking of the security she hoped her niece felt in this luxurious yet comfortable place.

When the woman came back alone with a frown on her face, Kira's spirits began to sag, but then she told Kira, "Please come with me." She smiled in relief and eagerly followed the servant down a wide hallway to a large room at the back of the house.

The vaulted ceiling was crisscrossed with heavy beams, and the floor was covered with blue and ivory oriental rugs, strategically placed to create traffic patterns and protect the gleaming hardwoods. Within the huge, open room, wallpaper in muted tones of gold and blue created an intimate atmosphere. A highly polished wet bar, fronted by four tall bar stools made from the same dark wood, curved along one wall. For an instant Kira imagined the room full of people—chatting, laughing, and enjoying themselves in what was clearly a room made for entertaining.

Helen was alone, and it appeared that she had been reading. Her eyes, uneasy and wary, watched Kira closely as she entered. Helen pushed aside a shallow bowl of magnolia blooms that was sitting on the leather-topped table next to her chair and set down the book she had been reading, giving Kira her full attention. It was clear from her expression that she was not happy to be interrupted and did not plan on being so for very long.

"Thanks, Betsy," she told the woman. "Make sure Vicky stays in her room. I don't want her coming down here."

"Yes ma'am," the woman replied politely, closing the door behind her when she left.

Now Helen zeroed in on Kira, exasperation coloring her face. "You have a lot of nerve coming here. What message could you possibly have for me from my sister? And why would you be talking to her?"

Kira cleared her throat, stalling. "Well, it's rather complicated."

"Do you have a message from Ruth or not?" Helen demanded.

"Not exactly," Kira confessed.

"I thought as much. How underhanded. Forcing your way into my home with a lie. I made it clear the last time you were here: I have nothing to say to you, and I do not want you coming around."

Venturing deeper into the richly paneled room, Kira walked to the natural-stone fireplace, where a bowl of simmering potpourri was giving off the heady scent of cinnamon and apples mixed with pine that had greeted her upon entering the house. On the mantel above the hearth, three large photographs in matching heavy rosewood frames had been arranged in a row: Helen and Ralph in a formal pose, Helen and Ruth showing sisterly smiles, and Helen and Vicky standing in front of the big magnolia tree at the edge of the flower bed. Inhaling, Kira cautioned herself to keep a civil tongue, to speak in low, even tones, and try to prevent Helen from overreacting before she'd said what was on her mind.

"I understand your irritation, Helen," she began. "But I have been to Cedar Grove, and I did speak to Ruth. I had to come here tonight."

Helen's face went blank, but she caught her bottom lip between her teeth while silently studying Kira, as if trying to figure out what was coming next. "Why?" she finally said. "Why can't you leave my family alone?"

Certain that this might be her only chance to speak to Helen in private, Kira jumped right in. "Why? I came here because, whether you like it or not, I am a part of your family now, and I refuse to let you shut me out."

"You're not family! You're a con artist. A hustler, out to get whatever you can. Don't try to con me." Helen moved quickly, rising from her wing-back chair to move behind it, placing both hands on the top of its curved upholstered back, creating a barrier between herself and her unwanted visitor. "You're a needy, jealous woman who apparently has no life. You want to get close to my husband and me because we have everything you will never have. A beautiful home. Wealth. Family. If you had a husband and children of your own, you might not be so obsessed with mine."

"Oh, I do have a life," Kira quickly countered, though stung by the remark. The pain of Helen's assessment surprised Kira and forced her to suck back her resentment before going on. "I don't need your money, and I certainly don't need your approval to be a member of Vicky's family. The court has already granted me that."

"The court?" Helen lifted her jaw and tossed out a curt, short laugh. "Ha! The court! If you'd acted responsibly when your sister died, you would not have needed the court to help you make your threats."

"Threats? When have I ever threatened you?" Kira stated in a firm, yet calm tone, determined not to shout. Escalating their conversation to a shouting match would serve no purpose at all. Tonight, she had to reach Helen, convince her that they could be allies instead of enemies, and that what she'd learned from Ruth would never come back to haunt her. Kira suspected that Ralph was not at home, or surely he would have been in the room with them, or would have met her at the door to block her access to his wife. But now that she was alone with Helen she had to finish what she had come to do, and quickly, before Ralph returned.

"Helen, there is only one way to convince you that you have nothing to fear from me, and that is by telling you what I now know," Kira began. "I have no intention of using your relationship with Andrew Jordan against you," she blurted out between claps of thunder. The room fell completely silent, so silent that Kira could hear the tick of the ornate cuckoo clock above the mantel over the explosive pounding of her heart.

The stunned expression that claimed Helen's features gave Kira pause, and she held her breath, almost afraid to move.

"Get out of here before my husband gets home," Helen finally said, gripping the padded wings of the high-backed chair, clearly frightened by Kira's statement.

Kira noticed how the diamond rings on Helen's fingers caught the light and twinkled at her, as if taunting her, forcing her to face up to the disparity between their lives. Helen had money, security, a husband, a home. Kira had no job, no prospects, and perhaps not even Evan. The memory of Evan's last phone call unexpectedly swept through her mind, bringing a lump to her throat. What did she have to offer a child like Vicky? Nothing but love, and that was not enough. Vicky deserved all that Helen and Ralph could offer, and she had to make Helen see that she was on her side.

"I won't leave until you listen to what I want to tell you," Kira managed, her throat tight as she dared to take a few steps toward Helen.

Fright shone in Helen's eyes. She suddenly moved around the chair and slumped down into it, her lanky, slender frame swamped by its tall back and wide wings. She pressed both hands to her face, as if she was weary of fighting and was ready to surrender.

Kira eased over to the sofa opposite Helen and sat down, bringing herself eye-level with Helen. "Please. Let's not argue," Kira said softly. "Hear me out, okay? That's all I ask. And after that, I promise to leave and not bother you again."

Helen's reply was a subtle shift in body language as she moved her hands away from her face to reveal a sinking expression of resignation that gave Kira the courage to go on. "Ruth told me everything. About your affair with Andrew, the abortion, that you once tried to commit suicide."

"Oh no, " Helen gasped, pressing the fingers of one hand to her mouth. "How could she?"

"Well, I don't agree with Ruth's objection to you adopting Andrew Jordan's child," Kira assured Helen. "I think you *should* be Vicky's mother, and I'll do everything I can to help you, Helen. Vicky is happy living with you and deserves to have you as her mother. I wasn't sure at first about you. I thought you might be ill, too emotionally fragile to deal with raising a child, but now I know that you are hardly fragile, just afraid. Helen, you have nothing to fear. Not from me."

Helen glanced toward the rain-splattered window, her pale, weary profile reflecting her misery. Without looking at Kira, she began to talk. "You want to help? Coming into my home like this is certainly no help." Jerking around, she focused on Kira. "Thank God Ralph is still out of town, but he'll be back tonight. What do you think a man like Ralph would do if he found out that his wife not only had sex with a black man, but also aborted his child and tried to kill herself because he had rejected her? Did Ruth tell you that the reason I can't give my husband a child is because of complications following the abortion? I almost died. And I nearly lost my mind." Helen threw back her head and uttered a short, pain-filled laugh. "What this would do to Ralph is too awful to even think about, not to mention how such information would impact his bid for mayor. In a small town like this, the gossip would never stop. He'd be so ashamed of me, so disappointed."

Getting up, she began to pace, walking to the fireplace, to the bar, to the string of windows along the rear of the house, then to the hearth again, where she stood with her back to the cold fireplace. Sighing, she shuddered and wrapped her arms around her body as if trying to hold her pain inside. "I assume you grew up in North Carolina?" she asked Kira.

"Yes, Wilmington."

"Then you know what this means, don't you?" Helen's eyes flitted closed for a moment, but when she opened them, they were burning with worry and boring into Kira's. "Answer me, Kira. You tell me that I shouldn't worry. Tell me how Ralph, a good old boy from North Carolina—my husband—would react if he learned that the real reason I am barren is because I aborted a black man's child!"

Kira swallowed her distress, aware of where Helen was headed, familiar with the racial hatred and division that would always remain just below the surface in small southern towns like Monroeville. Helen was right to be worried, and Kira felt her pain. "Your husband would hate you," Kira managed. "He might never want to touch you again. Might never want Vicky in his sight."

"Exactly!" Helen tossed back, her words sadly triumphant, tears running down her cheeks. She reached over and gripped the edge of the fireplace mantel, her eyes unwavering as they pierced Kira's soul.

"But he never has to know," Kira said, anxious to put Helen's mind at ease. "He won't hear it from me, and certainly not from Ruth. He *never* has to know."

"How can I be sure?" Helen said, the words slipping out on a fresh cascade of tears. Leaving the fireplace, she went to sit beside Kira and began massaging her temples, making small circles with her fingers. "Ava Thompson's mother was the woman who—"

"No," Kira interrupted, drawing out the word in a murmur as she shook her head. "She's dead. And Ava. . . . well, I can vouch for her. She refused to tell me. That's why I had to go to Ruth. No one is going to tell Ralph anything."

"Ralph loves me so much," Helen said through her tears. "I adore him. He wants me to have Vicky. He does. I know you don't like him . . . that you are trying to hurt his company . . ."

"That's not true," Kira countered. "Your husband may be overprotective and a tad aggressive, but he is an extremely intelligent and successful man. His verbal attack on me was a shock, and I was hurt. I wanted to lash out and hurt him back, but I didn't. Frank Thompson is the one you ought to worry about. He planted that story to get back at me for not trying to block your adoption. He feels very threatened by the inroads Ralph is making into the black community. There was a time when I would have fought against you and Ralph adopting Vicky, but not now. I think Vicky belongs with you."

"Do you mean that?"

"I do," Kira promised. "And if your husband investigates that dreadful story in the *Observer* half as aggressively as he investigated me, he already knows who his enemy is. Frank Thompson is a dangerous man. I'd be afraid of him, not me."

"Ralph is resourceful. He'll get to the truth, and I have complete faith in him. My only prayer is that I never give him reason to lose faith in me." Helen wiped away the tears wetting her face, then went on. "When we decided to adopt, of course I assumed we would adopt a white child. What else? Then, while Evan Conley was reviewing the data on a child under Sheltering Hearts care, he told us about Vicky's case. Her last name, along with the information about her parents, made me think that I might know who she was. Then I met Vicky . . . so adorable and alone in the world. Something about her reminded me of Andrew . . . I was convinced that she was his daughter the moment I saw her. My heart broke. I couldn't turn my back on her. For several weeks Ralph and I went 'round and 'round as I tried to convince him that Vicky was the child we ought to take. He finally gave in and agreed, after realizing how determined I was. Then I felt a kind of peace settle in, as if everything was finally right. That is, until you showed up and started poking around. I've been terrified of you and what you might bring up. Your sister knew Andrew . . . What if he had told Miranda about me? What if Miranda told you about the affair he'd had with a stupid white girl who came running after him, hunting him down?" Helen sobbed into her hands. "I didn't know what to expect. All I knew was that the circumstances surrounding my secret were getting too close for me to feel safe. I thought about bailing out of the adoption altogether. But how could I? Vicky's an innocent child crying out to be loved, and I had already bonded with her. Well, what else could I do but push you away?"

Kira did not reply, but shook her head in sympathy.

Helen's voice grew stronger as she went on. "I can't destroy my marriage and lose the man I love because of an unfortunate, stupid period of my life. I will have Vicky and Ralph, and a family of my own. I will! Do you understand?"

Kira felt the weight of Helen's dilemma, but knew that she could help her. "Don't worry," Kira murmured, shifting to the side in order to watch Helen's reaction. Impulsively, she reached out, took Helen's hand and squeezed it hard, and was relieved that Helen did not pull away. "You're not in this alone. Use me, Helen. Let me be the shield between you and the past, and a bridge to a future as a family. I *am* Vicky's family. I belong on your side."

Helen's lower lip trembled as she tried to regain her fragile composure.

"For some reason," Kira continued, "too many people think they have to tell everything to everyone . . . that keeping secrets is a sin. I hate it when, on those awful talk shows, adults reveal all of their mistakes to their children or their mothers or their husbands. I cringe. We tell too damn much. Nothing is sacred anymore. Secrets are a part of living, and we all have things that we'd prefer others didn't know about us. The test of maturity, I think, is how well we learn to live with them. Helen, let go of this worry and stop feeling guilty. You deserve some peace."

Helen stared down at her slender white fingers wrapped around Kira's honey brown palm, then glanced up quickly and smiled, as if startled to realize what had just transpired.

"Yes," Kira whispered. "You can count on me."

CHAPTER 30

It was past midnight when Ralph parked his car in his garage and wearily entered the house. The trip to Raleigh and the lengthy board meeting had drained him, and he was glad to be back, anxious for a good night's sleep. He had left Monroeville yesterday afternoon, sick with worry and boiling with anger over the accusations printed about his company in the *Observer*. In Raleigh, he and his board members had worked through the night, arguing, speculating, and carefully examining their overseas suppliers in order to sort things out. It had taken this near-crisis to bring them to the realization that Roper Fiber Technology had left itself vulnerable by not taking the time to investigate those who represented their interests overseas. The situation had not been easy to clean up, but the board members had persevered, making overseas calls, asking blunt questions, cutting no slack with employees or contract suppliers as they examined the internal structure of their company. Now Ralph was eager to talk to Helen and share the news that, in his opinion, the problem had been solved.

He hung his soggy umbrella on the big brass hook just inside the kitchen door, grabbed a small bottle of water from the refrigerator, then headed up the back staircase, stopping to peek into Vicky's room on his way to wake up Helen. Vicky was asleep, her profile illuminated by the blush of the rose-colored night-light that glowed at the side of her bed. Standing in the doorway, he let out a long sigh and shook his head, feeling his love for Vicky swell in his heart. He had never thought he would feel this way, especially for a child that was not his, but she was so much a part of his and Helen's life now that he could hardly imagine a future without her.

He never could have imagined that a stranger's child, let alone a child of color, would have been able to fill the empty spaces left by the loss of his and Helen's unborn children. But Helen had known, and she had created the situation that had allowed this little girl to bind them together as a family.

Smiling, Ralph pulled the door closed and headed down the hall toward his bedroom, counting his blessings as he thought about tomorrow and what he had to do.

Quietly, he opened the door and was startled, though pleased, to find Helen waiting up for him, sitting in the window seat at the large bay window of their darkened bedroom, the shadows created by the magnolia tree outside etching a pattern of lacy shadows on her face.

"You're still up," he whispered, entering, but remaining near the door.

Helen lifted her chin toward her husband and nodded. "Yes. I couldn't sleep."

Ralph placed his briefcase on the floor, set the bottle of water on the nearby dresser, and leaned back against the closed door, his head to one side. "I'm glad. Not that you couldn't sleep, but that you're still awake. I wanted to tell you what happened at the board meeting."

"Is it good news or bad news?" Helen softly inquired.

Ralph loosened his tie before answering. "I don't know if it's good or bad, but the board voted to do the best thing possible."

"And that is?"

Walking toward Helen, Ralph continued. "We spent Monday night and all day today examining every detail of our overseas operations. Because of the time differences, getting to everyone involved was slow-going and tedious, but we managed to achieve the results I was after."

"What was that?" Helen asked, shifting on the curved window seat to make room for Ralph to sit down beside her.

"The truth," he quietly told her. After pulling off his tie, Ralph tossed it onto the bed, then leaned down and began to untie his shoes. Suddenly, he raised his head and looked over at Helen, glad that she was there for him tonight. He needed to talk, to release the restless energy that was keeping him awake even though he had not slept in almost thirty-two hours. Struck by Helen's easy reception, as well as her still-youthful beauty, which he knew would never fade in his eyes, he silently thanked her for being such a thoughtful, intelligent wife. He loved Helen so much that it was hard to remember his life before she came into it, and he planned on growing old with her, loving her until there was no more time to love. He would do everything in his power to keep their love alive.

"It took some convincing," he continued. "A few of the board members wanted to go at the problem in the usual way: deny the allegations, stonewall the press, and initiate a slow-moving investigation, dragging everything out until people forgot about the story. But I insisted that we immediately contact every person even peripherally involved with our overseas suppliers and get to the truth." He absently fingered the sleeve of Helen's soft silk nightgown, drawing reassurance from the familiar feel of the delicate material in his hand. He had had it made especially for her in Hong Kong and had brought it back to the States in his briefcase, not trusting it to his checked luggage. The memory of the night they had spent making love after he'd given it to her made him blush in the darkness and put a smile on his lips.

"But is everything okay?" Helen asked in a worried tone. "Are you going to sue the paper? Kira Forester? Were you able to come up with proof that your company is innocent of the allegations?"

Ralph slipped one arm around Helen, eased her head onto his shoulder, and tilted his forehead to hers. "We are not going to sue anyone. You see, the reporter got it right. Our Africa broker has been using underage girls in his factory in Pangi. We just didn't know about it."

"So everything that reporter wrote about the company was true?"

Ralph stroked Helen's thick, soft hair and let out a sigh of resignation. "As much as I did not want to admit it, yes. And we have Kira Forester to thank. She documented the problem and created the proof that brought it to our attention, but Frank Thompson was the one who planted the story, not Kira. Now we have to deal with the problem and put it behind us right away."

"Frank," Helen repeated. "I'm not surprised. I heard that Frank is very upset over the fact that some of his neighbors are supporting you for mayor and not him."

"Yeah," Ralph said. "Coupled with the fact that the mill is coming down this Saturday."

"Really? So soon?" Helen replied.

Ralph shrugged. "It has to be done. That's the only time the demolition crew I've hired can do it. So, Frank's preservation cause will be a moot point come election day. That's the way it goes, Helen. Frank's underhanded tactics might just come around to slap him in the face next Tuesday."

"Ralph," Helen murmured against her husband's neck. "How are you going to set it all straight? The election is next week, and a lot of people around here probably think your company knew about the use of child labor all along. This mess might cost you votes."

"Maybe," Ralph agreed, shuddering lightly, stirred by the brush of Helen's breath on his neck. He was grateful that she took his troubles to heart and was concerned about the effects of these unexpected events on his campaign. When he and Helen had made the decision that he should run for mayor, they had not anticipated such strange complications would arise to threaten what they had thought would be a very easy race. He was balancing a delicate adoption issue, negative press related to his company, a complicated business situation, and an out-of-control opponent. Ralph would be glad when next Tuesday had come and gone.

"Perhaps I'll lose a few votes, but not many," Ralph concurred. "You see, the board voted to cancel the contract with our current Africa broker and make retroactive payments based on our standard American pay scale to the families of the young girls in Pangi. It'll cost us millions, Helen, and it's going to put a strain on the profit margin for a while, but we're doing what's right by those people. My hope is that this offensive move will counter some of the negative press. Keep my supporters with me."

Helen sat up, pushed her hair from her face, and placed her hand on Ralph's cheek. Silently, she scrutinized him, as if trying to read his thoughts, as if this revelation meant a great deal to her. She cupped his jaw in her hand, then said, "So you *do* trust Kira Forester, Ralph?" Her voice was low and husky. "Do you really trust her?"

"Yes, I do. And for everyone's sake, I wish you could, too. We have a family now, Helen. Maybe it's not the family I envisioned when I married you, but it's real, and I plan to make it a happy one . . . as best as I can. And if that means including Kira, so be it. That's the only way I see it."

When Helen leaned toward him, Ralph was prepared to give her a short good-night peck on the lips, as they had become accustomed to doing over the years. But her mouth covered his with an urgency that set his heart racing and her hand gripped his thigh with a squeeze that brought every nerve in his body alive. The press of her breasts against his chest, warm and firm through the sheer silk of her gown, connected with the core of his need for her, and he moaned, feeling his desire grow large and hard. He pulled Helen to him in a possessive embrace that fused them from lips to thighs. He felt frightened, yet liberated, as if he were moving into territory never before explored in his marriage, and the anticipation of going there with Helen thundered in his blood.

It took only a few seconds for Helen to unbutton his shirt and help him shed the remainder of his clothing. Still holding her tightly, he slid down onto the soft cushions of the window seat, bringing her easily along with him. Ralph swept one hand beneath the silky folds of Helen's gown, across the smooth skin of her long, lean legs, and over the mound of tawny brown hair nestled at the base of her stomach. He buried his face in the hollow beneath her chin, inhaling the lilac scent she always carried, and then gently eased over her and into the secret place that never failed to lift him to exquisite heights. Ralph smothered her face, her neck, and her warm lips with kisses, overcome with love—and gratitude that Helen had chosen him.

CHAPTER 31

K ira sat on the edge of her bed and stared at her ringing alarm clock, irritated that she had automatically set it to go off this morning, as she had done for years. Reaching over, she groped groggily for the RESET button, snapped it back into place, and then groaned, relieved when the insistent chiming finally stopped. She rubbed the back of her head and opened and shut her eyes a few times, as if attempting to clear away the muddle of half-dreams and fuzzy images that remained after her too-sudden rush into consciousness. Sitting there, she forced her mind back over the startling events of the past two days, culminating with her conversation with Helen Roper late yesterday evening: the only memory that produced a glimmer of hope. Everything else—the ugly scene in Davison's office that had resulted in her being fired, the cancellation of her story for *World*, and especially her bitter disappointment in Evan—created a hollow sensation in the pit of her stomach that grew wider and more painful as each second ticked past.

After arriving home last night, emotionally charged and mentally exhausted, she had listened to Evan's contrite plea for forgiveness on her voice mail, torn between hating him for believing the worst about her and wanting to be with him now. Tears had come into her eyes, and she had picked up the phone, ready to call him back and reassure him that her feelings had not changed. And though she wanted to move past this first rough patch in their relationship, she had not been able to complete the call, too hurt and wary to make the first move. Was their relationship worth saving? Did it have deep enough roots of trust to survive? And how long would it take her to forget that he had thought so little of her? Kira felt paralyzed with indecision.

Sooner or later we'll have to talk, but not now. Today I don't want to think about Evan Conley, she told herself. *There are other, more important things I need to focus on.*

Unable to stray too far from her regular routine, she zapped the remote control to turn on the TV and tuned into the morning news. A grid of the city's freeways came up, along with the familiar face of the reporter who presented the traffic report. Kira found herself concentrating on the announcements about freeway slowdowns, blinking stoplights and traffic jams as if she had a reason to get out into the fray. With a grimace, she fell back onto the bed and lay very still, staring at a strip of light that was inching its way across the ceiling, feeling desperate to make sense of the restless anxiety that gripped her.

According to the weatherman, who replaced the traffic reporter on the local newscast, the thunderstorms that had pounded the state yesterday had moved on and it was going to be a beautiful day. The sun was rapidly pushing away the darkness, and through her window Kira could hear her neighbor's car pulling out of the parking space next to hers, as it always did at exactly six-forty. But nothing else felt familiar about this day.

So much had happened since Monday that she barely recognized her life anymore. There was no structure to her days now, no routine to force her up and out into the world. How easy it would be to lie in bed and drift through the day, wallowing in pity, hiding from the world. But Kira knew that she would not let that happen: she was a survivor. She was determined to keep her spirits high, and somehow pull out of this downturn.

Sucking back her disappointment, she sat up, pulled on her robe, and shoved her feet into a pair of yellow flip-flops with daisies on the toes. Pushing herself off the bed, she went over to the cardboard box she had shoved into the corner of her bedroom two days ago and looked down at its contents in puzzlement, as if she had never seen the items before. Inside were the pot of ivy, in desperate need of water; her daily planner, sprouting dozens of yellow sticky notes; two *BPR* coffee mugs, one with her name on it; five steno pads, all partially filled; a dog-eared Key map of the city, and a half-full box of tissues. Picking up the cardboard box, Kira padded through her apartment to the kitchen, where she paused long enough to rescue the ivy and set it to soak in the sink. Next, she slid open the patio door and went directly to the garbage Dumpster that was tucked away from view within an enclosure behind her fence. After glancing around, she heaved the box into the bin with a grunt, then went inside and put on a pot of coffee, ready to face her day.

The first thing Kira did after showering and getting dressed was call Julie Ays in New York. Their conversation was brief and strained. Julie listened to Kira's explanation of what had happened and how the material slated for *World Societies Today* had managed to turn up in the *Observer*, assuring Kira that she could keep the advance and that the decision to cancel the story had come from Julie's boss, not from her. Kira grudgingly told Julie that she understood the reason for the decision, determined not to burn any bridges or destroy a valued friendship. Who knew when Kira and Julie's paths might cross again?

Next, Kira logged on to the Web site of the Employment Security Commission of North Carolina and followed the steps to register for unemployment, fighting a sense of despair as she keyed in the requested information. Most of her generous advance from *World* had been put into certificates of deposit, creating a nest egg that Kira was determined to protect. And though she calculated that she was not in danger of financial collapse or compelled to rush out and take the first job she could find, she was definitely not financially secure enough to let much time pass without bringing in a salary. She'd proceed cautiously in her job search, considering not only her needs, but also Vicky's, as she moved forward.

Thinking over the last fifteen years, Kira realized that she had fallen into a dangerous complacency that had left her vulnerable and unprepared to strike out into the tight job market. By sticking with *BPR* for so many years she had limited herself to one professional reference, and that had evaporated when Bruce fired her. She had worked for one of the most prestigious publishing companies in the world, but now her reference carried little weight. By focusing on a coveted spot in New York in her quest to become an international journalist, she had allowed herself to be blindsided, distracted from the larger picture. And look where she was now— at the beginning again, about to start all over. Suddenly Kira felt terribly alone. There was little reason to talk to Sharon anymore, and Evan might be lost to her, too.

Kira got up from her computer and walked to the front window of her apartment, raised the miniblind, and looked out across the parking lot, now nearly empty of cars. Most of her neighbors had gone off to work, or school, or someplace where they had coworkers, friends, and connections to a larger world, while she was alone at home, filing for unemployment and fighting the urge to pick up the phone and call Evan. If only she could bury her pride and make the move. If only she could press her face against Evan's chest, hold him tight, and tell him how much she needed him in her life.

In an attempt to keep her spirits up and depression at bay, Kira threw herself into cleaning her apartment, then turned to the potted plants on her patio to continue the distraction. The probability that a new job might take her to a new town was vivid in her mind, though she wanted to remain in Charlotte in order to be close to Vicky . . . and Evan, she had to admit to herself.

He telephoned twice during the day and she let the phone ring, forcing herself not to answer. When her doorbell rang later that evening, she looked through the peephole in her door and saw Evan standing there, his eyes soft with longing, his jaw hard with worry. She couldn't turn him away.

"Hello," she said, fully opening the door, but then folded her arms across her waist, not inviting him in.

"You're back," he stated flatly, as if he hadn't expected her to answer the door.

"Yes," she replied. "I got back late last night."

"I guess I shouldn't ask where you went, should I?" he remarked, drawing in a ragged breath.

Kira could tell that he was uncomfortable, standing outside, trying to gauge her mood. So she relented and stepped back, telling him, "No, you shouldn't ask, but come in. We need to talk."

Evan came in but did not sit down, remaining just inside the entry while Kira walked to her cream-colored sofa and sat down in the center of it. She motioned for Evan to join her.

He shook his head. "No, I can't stay. I just wanted to tell you in person that I'm sorry. I know now that Frank Thompson was behind that mess, and I had no right to speak so harshly to you. I was stupid to think that you'd go to such lengths to attack Ralph Roper, and I apologize for the message I left on your machine." He shrugged, as if resigning himself to a well-deserved tongue-lashing. "You told me you wanted to get along with the Ropers, and I should have believed you. I was a jerk about this. Forgive me."

The sincerity in his voice cut through Kira's earlier vow not to forgive him too quickly, to make him feel as awful as he'd made her feel, to let him squirm long enough to worry that he'd lost her. But the tongue-lashing she had rehearsed all day wedged in her throat, leaving her staring wordlessly across the room.

"I know you got fired," he continued.

Kira nodded.

"And I know you went to see Helen Roper last night."

Now Kira pulled in a breath of surprise. "You spoke to her?"

"No, to Ralph. All he said was that Helen told him you had come by and that she had finally spoken to you. She no longer feels threatened by your visitation. Both he and Helen are in favor of you spending time with Vicky."

"I'm glad," Kira murmured.

"Me too. Easing the tension over your visits will make the adoption petition move through more quickly. Thank you for pursuing Helen, Kira. I knew she was simply a little afraid that you might try to undermine Vicky's affection for her."

"I'd never do that," Kira replied, in a tone much stronger than she'd anticipated.

"I know you wouldn't," Evan agreed, turning to the door. "Well, that's all I came to say, so I'll go."

Kira stood, unable to bring herself to let him leave but still unable to ask him to stay.

"What about this weekend's visit?" she asked. "Will it be Saturday or Sunday?"

"Sunday," he answered quickly. "The demolition of the old mill is set for Saturday morning, and Ralph told me that he has promised Vicky that she can come and watch. From a safe distance, of course. Ralph told me that he's hiring quite a security force to keep things under control."

"Of course," Kira agreed, finding this piece of news oddly disturbing. Flagg Valley Mill was coming down after all, and there was nothing Frank Thompson could do to stop it. What Ralph Roper did with his private property was his business, and what Frank Thompson thought about it was not her concern. "Will we meet at Sheltering Hearts or . . ." Her voice lost its strength in mid-sentence. Her eyes locked with Evan's, and she coolly appraised him, trying to read his reaction.

Evan clenched and unclenched one hand several times, making a fist as he nervously watched Kira. "I'll have Sue call you this afternoon with the details," he told her. "And I'll arrange for her to supervise the visit, too."

"Then you won't be with us?" Kira ventured, with a sinking sensation. Why was he deliberately being cold and distant, so impossible to read? But, then, what did she expect? That he'd beg her to come back? He'd said he was sorry, what else could he do? The next move, she knew, had to be hers.

"Do you want me to be there?" Evan asked softly, putting the question to Kira in a voice rippling with hope. "If you do, I need to hear you say so, Kira. And if you don't, I understand."

Kira was barely able to control the tremor in her voice as she swallowed her pride and said, "Yes. I want you to be there." Rising from the sofa, she went toward Evan and stood very close to him, so close that she could see the tiny worry lines at the corner of his eyes, the slight tremble of his lower lip. Reaching out, she touched his mouth, then ran her forefinger along the outline of his jaw. "Yes," she repeated. "I do want you with us, Evan. And I want you with me always. So much, that I can hardly stand it."

Evan opened his arms and Kira sank against his shoulder, knowing they had a lot to cover before reconciling.

"These last few days have been pure hell," she whispered, leaning back to look at him. "You don't know what I've been through . . . personally and at work. It's been very hard to make sense of what's happened lately, and I didn't need your criticism on top of everything else. Your message hurt me, Evan. What I needed from you was support, not a lecture, and I had to step back. Maybe we're moving too quickly. I don't know . . ." Lowering her head, she leaned back toward him, then murmured, "I love you, Evan. I need you. I don't want to go through this alone." When he tightened his grasp, all of her resolve melted into longing, and she slipped her arms around him.

"Neither do I," he breathed.

When he lifted her chin and forced her gaze to his, she made the first move and kissed him, pressing her hand into the small of his back to deepen the kiss and guide him into her bedroom, where she drew him down beside her on the blue and white quilt.

Within moments their clothing was on the floor and their bodies had become a sleek tangle of warm flesh, fused in mutual craving. Kira gave herself over to the numerous kisses that Evan rained upon her, kisses that, at first, felt like gentle caresses on every part of her body, then evolved into white-hot streaks of pleasure. Her soul ached for him, and she was startled by her hunger to make love to Evan. Digging her fingernails into his shoulders, she let him smother her with his presence, allowing his kisses to skim every part of her naked body, thrilling to his touch, which moved between gentle caresses and fierce groping that left her gasping with desire. There were maddening moments when he held back, teasing her with a feathery stroke, hesitating just long enough to increase her need to have him.

Evan's sensuous playfulness moved Kira to places she had never been before, and as she sank deeper into the pleasure of being with him again, Kira knew she never wanted to miss a moment of the incredible journey that lay ahead for her and Evan.

When she first met him, she had sensed this magnetic sexual pull beneath his smooth, professional facade, but never in her wildest dreams had she thought that he'd so completely fulfill her need to be loved. When they joined, their bodies slick with passion, an ache that had been in her heart far too long exploded and dissolved, forcing Kira to inhale sharply, then cry out, her voice mingling with Evan's as they held on to each other and rode the wave of desire. As Kira listened to the throbbing of her own heartbeat, she settled into the rhythm of making love to Evan, wishing it never had to stop.

Fueled by a restless search that pushed them both to exhaustion, Kira and Evan fell into a tumble of breathlessness and laughter, surrendering completely to each other. Their need to be one ebbed and flowed during the hours that followed, with Kira awakening several times during the night to simply watch Evan slumbering at her side. And though she dozed off and on as the night moved toward dawn, she never moved out of his arms.

CHAPTER 32

It appeared to Kira that the entire town of Monroeville had turned out to witness the much debated implosion of Flagg Valley Mill. When Evan pulled off the highway, headed to the road leading to the fragile building, a policeman waved them down and stepped up to the driver's side window.

"Sorry. You can't get any closer than this," he told Evan. "If you want to watch the implosion, you'll have to park in that field over there and stay behind the barriers."

"Okay," Evan agreed, quickly guiding his car toward a field that was already covered with cars, trucks, motorcycles, and bicycles.

"I can't believe this crowd," Kira said to Evan, turning around in her seat to look back at the road where streams of people, many carrying lawn chairs, protest placards, binoculars, and video cameras, were hurrying toward the designated observation area that the police had created at a safe distance from the mill.

"This is history," Evan commented as he put the car in PARK and removed his binoculars from the console.

"Or the destruction of it," Kira replied. "Depending on which side you're on." She slid across the front seat and got out with Evan, taking his hand in hers as they started up the road. They had been inseparable for the past three days, with Evan spending the nights at Kira's apartment and Kira meeting him for lunch. And when they were not together, Evan called every chance he got, sometimes simply to tell her that he was thinking about her, missed her, and could hardly wait for his day to end. When he did arrive, they'd eat a quiet dinner, sometimes on the patio, listen to music, talk, and make love. Kira knew that they were caught up in a romantic interlude that could not last forever, but for now it suited her just fine. Today's outing to witness the implosion of the mill was the first time they had ventured out together since their reconciliation, and Kira liked the feeling of being a couple, of holding on to the arm of the man she loved.

"Look," Kira said, pointing at a knot of very vocal citizens who were shouting their opposition to the scheduled destruction. Frank Thompson was leading the angry protest group, waving his arms as he paced back and forth and whipped the crowd into a frenzy. "I should have known he'd be here doing something like that." Kira noticed that Ava was not with him, and wondered if his wife had even bothered to come.

"Let's try for a spot over there," Evan suggested with a jerk of his head toward a far corner of the field that was much less congested because it faced the side of the mill instead of the front, where the majority of the onlookers had gathered. Evan began weaving his way through the crowd, pulling Kira along by the hand.

The atmosphere was charged with excitement, and the noisy gathering reminded Kira of a country fair, with the locals eagerly talking and laughing and shouting back and forth in neighborly greeting, remarking on the fact that the landmark that had once been the economic heart and soul of their town was now approaching extinction. Even a camera crew from WSOC-TV in Charlotte had come out, ready to capture the implosion on film. Kira was not surprised to see Ralph Roper talking to a reporter, gesturing with both hands as he described what was going to happen. She noticed that neither Helen nor Vicky were with him.

From behind the long yellow ropes that were holding back the crowd, Kira studied the skeletal structure across the road where a few men in hard hats were walking around, speaking to one another via walkie-talkies as they finalized the preparations. A few uniformed men were also nearby, ready to keep the agitators in line.

Kira glanced down at her watch. It was only nine-fifteen, yet the sun warming her face felt as if it were noon. She reached into her purse, took out her sunglasses, and slipped them over her eyes, cutting the glare coming from the piles of ashy white rubble that filled the area around the mill. Inching closer to Evan, she stepped in front of him, then leaned back, comforted by the press of his chest to her shoulders.

"Can you see okay?" she asked, turning her profile to him.

"Fine," he replied, giving her a quick kiss and wrapping both arms around her waist.

After a few minutes, the men in hard hats pulled back, and one of them motioned to Ralph Roper, who left the reporter and hurried to consult with him. Kira watched Ralph intently, wondering where Vicky was, looking forward to seeing her tomorrow.

The restless crowd calmed down when Ralph nodded to the man, then turned around and gave a grinning thumbs-up to the television camera crew from WSOC, as well as to those who were standing behind the yellow ropes with camcorders ready to capture the event.

Kira tensed, not knowing what to expect. The crowd was antsy, excited, and ready for the show. The protestors, who were now being led by a tall young man who had replaced Frank as the leader, was encouraging the chanting of "Save our history! Save our town!"

Kira stepped out of Evan's arms when she felt a sharp tug on her arm. Jerking around, she came face to face with Helen Roper, who appeared flushed and distracted.

"Have you seen Vicky?" Helen demanded in a breathless, frantic voice.

Evan let go of Kira and focused on Helen, his eyes narrowed in concern. "No," he answered. "What's wrong?"

"She was with me, right beside me a moment ago. I turned around to speak to her piano teacher, and when I looked back she was gone."

Kira gripped Helen's arm, drew in a short gasp of breath, and quickly scanned the crowd, which had nearly doubled in size since her arrival. "Where were you standing?" Kira shouted above the excited clamor of the people who were now shouting for the implosion to begin.

"Over there. Near that big tree. Ralph told us to stay there while he took care of everything." Helen swiveled her head from side to side, sweeping the field, tears staining her cheeks. "She has to be here. She would never wander off. Oh, God. Oh, God. Where is she?"

"Calm down. We'll find her. Don't worry. She's around," Evan shouted, scanning the area. "Helen, go back to the tree and wait," he ordered, indicating the tree with a jab of his finger. "Stay put. If Vicky wandered off, she might already have come back, looking for you. Go back, and don't move!" He swung around and faced Kira, one hand to his ear to hear himself speak, the other lifted in the direction of the line of security guards standing at the front of the crowd. "Get to a policeman and tell him a child is lost. Describe Vicky. Hurry."

"Right," Kira said, watching as Evan struck out toward the rear. She plunged into the crowd, pushing her way through grumbling onlookers who began shouting for her to get out of their way. She paid no attention, moving intently toward the front, not stopping until the taut yellow rope was pressing against her waist. She looked up and down the length of the barrier, frantically searching for Vicky's dark, bouncing curls, usually tied with a brightly colored ribbon, wishing she had had the presence of mind to ask Helen what Vicky was wearing today. A small six-year-old child was virtually invisible in a situation like this.

Kira grabbed hold of the rope and inched her way toward Ralph, jostling angry people out of her way. She tried to explain that a child was missing, that she had to get through to alert the police, but no one paid any attention to her, thinking she was just a pushy onlooker determined to get a better position from which to view the collapse of the mill. When she realized that no one was going to hear her, she ducked under the rope, raced across the road, and headed toward the heart of the demolition operation.

"What the hell do you think you're doing, lady?" a startled policeman who had been guarding the side entry to the mill shouted. He ran toward her, holding his bullhorn with both hands. "You get back behind the barrier! This area is off limits!" He caught Kira by the arm and shoved her back toward the crowd, pushing her with such force that she fell to the ground and hit her head.

"You don't understand!" she shouted, taking in his furious expression. Looking up at him, Kira struggled to catch her breath, then noticed a glimmer of bright light just beyond his shoulder, coming from one of the tall, fractured turrets in the mill. Kira gasped, then shook a trembling finger in the direction of a gaping hole that once had been a window. "Look! Look!" She pointed upward toward the turret. "Someone's there! Inside!"

As if in slow motion the policeman turned around to see what she was referring to, and Kira, whose eyes had never left the window gasped again when two figures emerged. There was Frank Thompson, clutching a jagged piece of glass in one hand and holding Vicky by the arm with the other. Again, sunlight struck the broken glass and reflected back at Kira. She flinched, then cried out when the policeman placed his heavy bullhorn to his mouth and yelled at the foreman down the road, "Halt all activity! Do not proceed!"

Kira stumbled to her feet, terrified at the sight of Vicky being forced to step out onto the ancient window ledge, trying to resist Frank's tight grasp on her arm. Kira could see Vicky's lips moving but could not hear a thing over the din at ground level.

"Stop the demolition!" the policeman screamed again, his order blending into the demands of the protestors who were pounding the air with the very same message.

Realizing that no one was paying attention to his command, Kira jumped up, broke into a run, and raced down the middle of the road, her lone figure drawing the attention she had hoped. The crowd screamed in horror, thinking she must be hurtling herself into the pending implosion. Their cries forced Ralph Roper to spin around and stare down the road at her, squinting as if he could not make out what was happening. The crew foreman cursed the interruption of his carefully planned event.

"What the hell is going on?" Ralph demanded, scowling when Kira caught up with him.

"Up there," she managed through ragged gasps, struggling to get her breath. She pointed at the turret. "Up there. Frank . . . Vicky. Please, stop everything."

At the same time that Ralph and his foreman focused on the horrible scene, the people who were watching also realized what was going on. Quiet suddenly descended over the crowd, allowing the policeman's voice to boom from his bullhorn and reverberate like the toll of a huge, heavy bell.

"Stay calm," the officer shouted up to Vicky. "Stay where you are."

The foreman of the demolition crew threw a hard look at Kira. "Do you know that man?"

Kira nodded. "Yes, it's Frank Thompson. He's the leader of the protest."

"And my mayoral opponent," Ralph added, his mouth dropping open in shock. "That's my daughter. You've got to get her down. Do something, dammit! Get her out of there!"

The policeman put the bullhorn to his mouth again. "Frank! Step away from the girl, but stay in sight."

Frank didn't move.

"Step away from the girl, and let go of her arm," the policeman ordered again.

When Frank still made no sign that he was willing to comply, Ralph grabbed the bullhorn from the policeman and aimed it at the turret. "Vicky! Don't worry. I'll get you down. Don't cry. Please! Don't cry."

Kira watched in horror as Vicky cast a searching look over the crowd, her gaze sliding from Ralph, to Kira, then off in the distance. "Mommy!" she shouted.

Kira turned to see Helen a few paces behind her, a hand to her mouth, her eyes blazing with fright.

"Mommy, I'm scared,"Vicky cried.

"Don't be scared. I'm right here, Vicky. We will get you down," Helen called back, her voice bristling with strain. "Stay calm, honey. Do what the man says. We'll get you down." Helen shifted closer to Kira, who reached out and took her hand. Together, the two women stared silently at the figures in the window, too enraged and frightened to speak.

"I told you I'd stop this," Frank's taunt boomed over the crowd as he spat his words at the people below. "This mill is not coming down. Not today." He stepped out beside Vicky and pushed her closer to the edge. "You didn't think I could stop this, did you, Ralph? Well, I have, haven't I? You underestimated me. All of my life, people have pushed me around, made me do what they wanted instead of respecting and listening to what I have to say. Now, I have everyone's attention, Ralph, even yours, so shut up and listen. Jeremy Flagg demanded respect and refused to let white folks control his life. He built this mill with his own hands and the sweat of men like him. Flagg Valley represents Jeremy's conviction that black men ought to be free, beyond the control of white men like you. This is more than a building, Ralph—it's a symbol of freedom, and from this day on whenever anyone mentions Flagg Valley Mill, they will have to mention my name, too, because I am a part of it now. I refuse to stand by and watch you tear it down. Today I'll become as immortal as Jeremy Flagg. No one will ever forget me. What do you think of me now?"

Ralph snatched the bullhorn that the policeman offered and directed it at Frank. "I think you're insane, Frank. Give up this crazy stunt, and let my daughter come down. Don't be stupid. End this mess before someone gets hurt."

Shaking a fist at Ralph, Frank shouted, "You dare call me stupid?" He snorted in amusement. "I'm smart enough to know about the tunnels under this mill that reach far across those fields." He swept his arm outward in a gesture of defiance. "Did you know that one of them leads right up and into this tower where I am standing? Did you know that slaves used to crawl on their naked bellies through those, and hundreds escaped without anyone knowing how they got away! And you . . . you say you care so much for this little black girl, yet you have no interest in preserving the legacy of freedom that this place represents. This mill belongs to her people. Her real people. Not you. And I refuse to let you take it away."

The flicker of defeat that briefly passed over Ralph's features incensed Kira. How dare Frank play the race card at a time like this to make his desperate antics seem acceptable? He was unstable, dangerous, and obsessed, a deadly combination involving the life of a child.

"Give it up, Frank," Kira screamed at him. "You have no right to hurt that child."

"Don't worry, I'm not going to hurt the girl. I have food, water, everything I need to stay up here as long as it will take to make you"—he pointed at Ralph—"give up this plan and remove the explosives."

Frank's triumphant laugh sent a chill through Kira. She was close enough to see the bristly shadow of his beard, the rumpled white shirt that was streaked with mud, and the grass stains on the knees of his plants. He was thin, haggard, and had a crazed look in his eyes. This was not the same man who had impressed her with his dignified manner and intelligent speech, who had easily drawn her to his cause when she'd met him only weeks ago. This was a stranger, a man who had allowed his obsessive need to be heard and respected to push him out of control. The situation was extremely dangerous, yet he didn't seem afraid, or even anxious to end his vigil. From high above, he calmly surveyed the scene below, as if daring anyone to make a move.

Ralph turned to the foreman, his jaw tight. "Do something, Bill. Go in there and get my daughter."

"It's too dangerous, Ralph. The structure is too weak. If I send a rescue team inside, the floors and stairs will collapse at the slightest disturbance and the entire place will blow."

Helen let go of Kira's hand and ran to join her husband, sobbing into her palms as she leaned against him. Quickly, the police and other members of the demolition crew gathered around Ralph.

"Well, what in hell *can* you do?" Ralph raged at Bill, hugging Helen to his side.

"We'll have to attempt a rescue from outside." Bill directed his attention to one of his crew. "Ray, get that boom lift over there, and drive it in as close to the building as you can get it. I'm going up."

"But, what about Vicky? When Frank sees you coming toward him in that cage, he'll surely do something awful to Vicky," Helen moaned, turning her tear-streaked face to the man.

The policeman with the bullhorn joined the worried circle. "I don't think that he wants to harm the girl. He wants attention . . . to stop the demolition. He's done that. Bill, you're right. If we can provide a safe way for the child to get out of there, Frank will most likely let her go. We have to try. The longer this goes on, the more unstable he will become."

Sensing that she could do nothing now, Kira backed away, heading to the edge of the crowd where Evan was waiting for her. She rushed into his arms, still shaking from the awful experience, which was not close to being over.

"What are they going to do?" Evan asked, rubbing Kira's shoulders.

"Attempt to get Vicky down by using that high-lift contraption over there." She pointed to the cherry picker, already being driven into position.

"Let's hope Frank will let her go," Evan replied.

"For some reason, I think he will," Kira said, almost to herself, as she watched Bill climb into the basket and fasten the safety strap around his waist.

Frank's taunting stopped when he saw the heavy piece of machinery come to a halt below the window. When the motorized lift began to inch its way upward, with Bill inside the basketlike cage, Frank slipped out of view, taking Vicky with him into the shadowy interior. A groan of worry escaped in unison from the mouths of the nervous onlookers. Within minutes, the basket had been cranked high enough to come to a halt outside the now-empty window, but there was no movement from within the turret.

"Send the girl out!" the policeman bellowed.

No response.

"You said you didn't want to hurt her, so send her out, Frank," Bill yelled again.

After several long seconds of unbearable silence, Vicky appeared, both hands over her mouth as she cast a wary look at the man in the basket. Kira could see that Bill was talking quietly to her, but could not hear what he was saying. Vicky, her brown eyes wide with fear, moved farther out on the ledge as Bill continued to talk to her. Bill nodded his head, then reached out and leaned over, grabbing her with a swift movement that landed her safely in the cage next to him. Quickly, he signaled to the man driving the heavy-reach machine to bring them down.

Loud applause and shouts of joy erupted from the crowd as Bill and Vicky began their descent. Kira went weak with relief, then started to run forward to be there when Vicky arrived safely on the ground, but Evan held her back.

"Stay here," he calmly advised.

At first Kira glared at Evan and tried to pull away, but then she stopped and nodded, knowing he was right. The reunion belonged to Vicky and her parents, and she had no right to intrude. The fact that Vicky had cried out and called Helen "Mommy" had not been lost on Kira, who could see how much her niece loved and needed Helen. Stepping back beside Evan, she allowed herself to embrace the sense of completion that began to rise in her heart. Things were as they should be for Vicky now.

All eyes were on the little girl whose face barely peeked over the edge of the basket as the cherry picker slowly brought her down. When Bill finally handed Vicky over the safety railing and into Ralph's open arms, the crowd surged forward, breaking the yellow ropes, forming a clamoring circle of curious well-wishers around the worried family.

No one paid any attention to Frank, who had reappeared in the window the moment Vicky was safely on the ground. No one saw him quietly looking down, his head bent as if in prayer. And no one heard him murmur the name "Jeremy Flagg" before he spread his arms and jumped.

EPILOGUE

Three months later.

"How's it coming?" Evan asked, poking his head into the room while remaining in the hallway. He kept his hands clasped behind his back as if afraid to touch anything.

"Fine," Kira said, turning her head to peer down at Evan from atop the ladder, interrupting the next swipe of her extended paint roller to adjust her bright red bandana so that it more fully covered her hair. "I thought Vicky and I might go check out the pool when we finish here." She finished off the spot she had been working on. "Like it?"

"Looks like a professional job," Evan replied, giving Kira and Vicky a big thumbs-up.

"We're almost finished. I love this color, and it makes the room look so much larger, doesn't it, Vicky?"

"Yes, I think so, too," Vicky agreed, dipping her brush into the metal bucket of lavender paint that was sitting on the newspaper-covered floor. "Can I have pink curtains?" she asked, making a wide arch with her arm as she slid the paintbrush over the wall, stood back to admire it, and then repeated the process.

"Of course, if that's what you want," Kira agreed, her heart swelling with love.

After the incident at the mill, Vicky had become withdrawn and quiet, terrified of being kidnapped again, though she understood that the man who had tried to harm her was dead and would not come back to get her. She had cried for weeks and shunned going outside with anyone other than Helen, Ralph, or Kira. When she slipped into a sullen personality that had alarmed everyone who loved her, Helen and Ralph had arranged for Vicky to see a top child psychologist, who had performed miracles with his intensive therapy. Now the old mill was gone, soon to be replaced by the Roper Textile Training Center, and Vicky was back to her usual, outgoing self.

When Kira and Evan married the previous month, Vicky had been included as the flower girl, wearing a long pink dress, flowers in her hair, and the first genuine smile they had seen in some time. And when Kira and Evan had gone house-hunting, a room for Vicky had been uppermost in their minds, as well as enough space for them to enlarge their family one day.

The house was a lovely, though dated, multilevel suburban ranch in great need of refurbishing, but Kira and Evan and Vicky were enjoying doing most of the work themselves.

"My room is going to be very pretty," Vicky told Evan, concentrating on executing another stroke.

"The most beautiful room in the house, I'm sure," Evan agreed, smiling to see Vicky so happily engrossed in her chore.

"And when the house is totally redecorated, we're going to have a party and invite your mother and father," Kira told Vicky. "I don't think I've ever thrown a party for a mayor before."

"He'd like that," Vicky assured Kira, biting her lower lip as she carefully traced the tip of her paintbrush along the edge of the closet door.

"And when you finish here, young lady," Evan interjected, "perhaps you could come over to my office building and help me redo your Aunt Kira's new office. It's going to need a lot of fixing up before she starts her new job." Looking up, he winked at Kira.

"Yes, it will," Kira said lightly. "As the new business manager for Sheltering Hearts, I insist on an office that reflects my good taste, as well as a glass nameplate on my desk with my new name: Kira Forester Conley." She grinned at Evan, returning his wink.

"And you shall have both," he teasingly agreed. Turning serious, he asked, "Can you break away for a minute? I need your opinion on something."

"Sure," Kira told him, finishing a long stroke with her extended roller before placing it into the paint pan. Starting down the ladder, she told Vicky, "I'll be right back. Then we'll stop and have lunch."

"Good," Vicky replied. "I'm hungry."

"Me too." Kira paused to refill Vicky's bucket before leaving the room to meet Evan in the hallway of their new home.

"There's something I want to show you," Evan said, using his thumb to wipe away a few dots of lavender paint from Kira's cheek. He kissed her on the tip of the nose, then put his arm around her waist.

"What is it?" Kira asked, dabbing at her forehead with a piece of cloth as she walked with Evan through their spacious but still-empty house.

"It's about this area," he replied in a serious tone, pulling Kira into an arched alcove off the living room. "What did you have in mind for this?"

Puzzled, Kira frowned, wondering why Evan was suddenly so concerned about a small space that she had not even thought about. When they began working on the house, they had decided to tackle the bedrooms, the bathrooms, and the kitchen first, then get to the other rooms as they had time. "Well, I guess I hadn't thought of it at all. Why?"

"Just wondering," Evan said, taking Kira by the hand to lead her to the front door. When he opened it, two men were standing there, as if waiting for instructions.

"What's going on?" Kira peered past the two men to the huge red and white van parked in front of the house.

"They want to know where to put the piano," said Evan, barely able to suppress his delight at her surprise.

"A piano?" Kira's jaw dropped in astonishment. "Really?"

"Yes," Evan assured her. "I thought we'd put it in the alcove off the living room."

"You bought Vicky a piano!" she shouted, grinning as she gave Evan a playful punch on the arm. "Of course, let's put it in the alcove off the dining room. That's a perfect spot."

"Good," said Evan, signaling to the men to bring the piano in. "Because once it's put in place, please don't ask me to move it."

"Never," Kira murmured, reaching up to bring Evan's lips to hers.

RELATIVE INTEREST

ANITA BUNKLEY

ABOUT THIS GUIDE

The suggested questions are intended to enhance
your group's reading of RELATIVE INTEREST by Anita Bunkley.

DISCUSSION QUESTIONS

1. How would you describe Kira's reaction to the news that her niece, Vicky, was about to be adopted by a white couple? Do you think this was a valid reaction? Why?

2. What characteristics possessed by both Kira and Evan made them so compatible?

3. Do you think Ralph Roper was racially tolerant? Was Helen? Why or why not?

4. Why do you think Miranda and Kira's lives took such different paths?

5. How do you think the political campaign in Monroeville brought out the best in the candidates? The worst?

6. Frank Thompson became obsessed with holding on to the past. Is this always harmful? Why? Why not?

7. Kira's relationship with Brandon Melzona came back to haunt her. Has such a thing ever happened to you?

8. What are your feelings about transracial adoption? How important do you think racial and ethnic heritage is in adoption situations?

9. Do you think Helen Roper was right to fear Kira? Why? Why not?

10. Do you think that women, generally speaking, can be trusted to keep secrets?